Kate Charles and her husband live in a large Victorian house with their two dogs – one white, one black. Her previous novels include *Unruly Passions* and *Strange Children*.

CRUEL HABITATIONS

KATE CHARLES

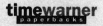

A *Time Warner* Paperback

First published in Great Britain in 2000
by Little, Brown and Company

This edition published by Warner Books in 2001

Reprinted 2001, 2004

Copyright © 2000 Kate Charles

The moral right of the author has been asserted.

A CIP catalogue record for this book
is available from the British Library.

ISBN 0 7515 2533 2

Typeset by Palimpsest Book Production Limited,
Polmont, Stirlingshire
Printed and bound in Great Britain by
Mackays of Chatham plc, Chatham, Kent

Time Warner Paperbacks
An imprint of
Time Warner Book Group UK
Brettenham House
Lancaster Place
London WC2E 7EN

www.twbg.co.uk

For Canon Bill Ritson: supporter, enabler, friend.

Author's Note

Alert readers may perceive certain similarities between Westmead and various cathedral cities. Westmead is in no way intended to depict any actual cathedral city, just as none of the characters are meant to correspond to their counterparts in any cathedral.

Acknowledgements

As always, I am indebted to a number of diverse people for their assistance and encouragement. This book could not have been written without the warm welcome and generous help of everyone at St Albans Abbey, most especially Canon Bill Ritson; I would like particularly to thank the Dean and Chapter; Andrew Lucas, the Master of the Music; and Paul Underhill, Head Verger. Among those who welcomed me at Winchester Cathedral, I must mention the Reverend Dr Brian Rees; Susan Rees; and David Hill, the Cathedral Organist. The Reverend Peter Moger, Precentor of Ely Cathedral, has also been most helpful.

Assistance of various kinds has been willingly given by Commander Philip Gormley and DI Claire Stevens of Thames Valley Police, Dr Andrew Gray, HM Coroner Dr William Dolman, Adrian Hutton, Robert and Nicola Marson, the Reverend Nicholas Biddle, the Reverend John Pedlar, and Canon John Tibbs.

Thanks also to Marcia Talley, Deborah Crombie, Cynthia Harrod-Eagles, Ann Hinrichs, Suzanne Clackson and Lucy Walker for editorial advice, and of course to my excellent agent, Carol Heaton, and my superb editor, Hilary Hale.

And very special thanks are owed to the Reverend Jacquie Birdseye for her generous hospitality, her friendship, and her wisdom.

Look upon the covenant: for all the earth is full of darkness and cruel habitations.

Psalm 74:21

Chapter 1

When Sophie Lilburn first laid eyes on Quire Close, she thought it was the most beautiful place she'd ever seen. At first glance it seemed perfectly symmetrical: two rows of stone mediaeval terraced houses, stretching into the distance and soaring into the sky, facing each other across tiny front gardens and a narrow stretch of cobblestones. After a moment, though, her photographer's eye registered the asymmetries, and those enchanted her even more. Here and there existed a touch of originality, a gothic stone-mullioned window or a fantastically zigzagged chimney, even taller than its neighbours. An occasional Georgian door or a Victorian flourish were perhaps incongruous, but those incongruities added to the beauty of the whole. She could, Sophie thought, spend the rest of her life photographing this place, and not tire of it.

It wasn't London, but perhaps it *was* time to leave the city. For the first time since Chris had suggested moving to Westmead, Sophie's heart lifted.

To live in a place like Quire Close would be an enormous privilege, a joy – that's what Chris kept saying. It had been built, Chris told her, back in the 1300s, to house the men of the choir of Westmead Cathedral, and had fulfilled that purpose to this very day. With the teaching job at the Cathedral School and the coveted position of Lay Clerk in the cathedral choir would come the tenancy of a house in Quire Close, rent-free.

Too good to be true: that's what Chris had said, when he first learned of the opportunity. His dark eyes had shone with enthusiasm – an enthusiasm that had been there in the early days of their marriage, the early days of his career, but which had gradually died out with the grind of teaching in a London comprehensive school.

The only thing that had kept Chris sane during those London years, apart from his naturally sanguine temperament, was the music. He was possessed of a fine tenor voice, and loved using it, so he had done a fair amount of singing as a deputy for various church choirs within the London area. There was no shortage of opportunities to do this, but his long-held secret ambition – as he now confessed – was to sing in a cathedral choir.

He'd heard about this job from one of his singing colleagues, who knew the person who was leaving. Tenor Lay Clerk and history teacher: the perfect combination. It would be well paid, he told Sophie, and with it would come the house.

From the eagerness in his voice, the look on his face, she could tell that he wanted this more than he'd ever wanted anything in his life. Laid-back Chris, who usually took what life had dealt to him without complaint. Who was she to stand in his way? And if – when – they had a baby, Westmead would be a healthier environment than London.

'It *is* lovely,' Sophie said now, poised at the entrance of Quire Close.

Chris took her hand, eager as a young lover, and drew her into the close. It was like stepping into another world, one which was self-contained and bore only passing similarity to the one outside. One way in, one way out: under the arch through which they'd come. At its foot, the close narrowed in a mediaeval trick of perspective, ending in a pair of larger and more substantial houses.

The mellow West Country stone of the buildings glowed in the sunshine. Spring was in the air, adding its intoxicating perfume to the magic of the close. Tulips bloomed, buds swelled with new life.

And behind them loomed the cathedral.

They had arrived in Westmead early, with plenty of time to explore Quire Close and the cathedral before the interviews were to begin. Chris was uncharacteristically nervous about the interviews; so much was at stake. First he was to talk to the Headmaster of the school, then he would have an interview and an audition with the Director of Music and the Precentor of the cathedral. Sophie would join them for lunch in the refectory.

'Good luck,' she said to Chris as he left her for the first of the interviews. 'It will be fine.'

She went into the cathedral. The enormity of it awed her, even intimidated her. Sophie was not easily intimidated, but she found that the sheer scale of the place unnerved her. The soaring stone vaults, the vast windows, the massive pillars with their improbably delicate carved capitals: none of it seemed to have any relation to the world as she knew it. She realised that she ought to be looking at it as a photographer, enjoying the play of light on stone, the texture of the carving. But it was too alien; she doubted that she would ever feel at home in that building.

Berating herself for her cowardice, she escaped through the great west doors and spent an hour in the town of Westmead itself. Officially it was a city, by virtue of the cathedral at its heart, but it had the feel of a rather sleepy West Country market town. Nothing, thought Sophie, like London. Its charms were soon exhausted, and she returned across the broad cathedral green in time to meet the men for lunch.

She had arranged to meet them in the cathedral refectory, tucked against the south side of the building in a converted bit of the old cloister. It wasn't difficult to find.

The men were already seated, but stood when she arrived: Chris, a nervous smile still plastered on his face, and across from him a tall, lean man in an impeccably cut suit. Chris made the introductions as she took the chair beside him. 'My wife, Sophie. Jeremy Hammond, the Director of Music.'

Sophie took the languid hand which was extended to her across the table. 'Nice to meet you, Mr Hammond.'

'My pleasure. Please, call me Jeremy.' He looked across at her under half-lowered lids and smiled, revealing perfect teeth. Sophie returned his gaze levelly, observing a good-looking man who was fully aware of his own charms. The charm was general, not focused specifically on her. She knew the type: London was full of them.

Sophie didn't consider herself a portrait photographer, but she was interested in faces, and she studied Jeremy Hammond's as he resumed his seat. It was a mobile, expressive face, blessed with sculptured cheekbones and wide blue eyes under beautifully shaped wings of eyebrows. Rich auburn hair fell from a centre parting and framed his face, just long enough to touch the collar of his shirt.

'We're waiting for the Precentor,' Chris explained. 'He was meant to be joining us earlier, but had a meeting he couldn't get out of.'

Jeremy Hammond shook his head. 'Oh, these clergy,' he said, raising his eyebrows. 'So very busy, always. Or so they would have us lesser mortals believe. But here,' he added, 'he is now.'

A shorter man in a black cassock joined them, moving to the seat across the table from Sophie. Jeremy introduced him. 'Canon Peter Swan,' he said. 'The Canon Precentor.'

Nothing at all like the elegant Jeremy Hammond – he might, thought Sophie, be described as ugly. Middle-aged and middle-sized. Unsmiling, even as he shook hands with them. Humourless and charmless.

'We have to get our own food,' Jeremy explained; he led them in the direction of the queue. 'Have whatever you like. It's on the cathedral.'

The food looked appetising and freshly prepared. Sophie chose quiche and salad and returned with her tray to the table.

Jeremy engaged Chris in an animated conversation about some particular piece of music, leaving Sophie to eat her quiche and look across the table at Canon Peter Swan. He clearly felt no need to talk to her, applying himself with concentration to his food, so she took the opportunity to study him. He had an interesting face, she decided, displaying a characterful sort of ugliness, rather like one of the gargoyles which perched along the roof of the cathedral.

Gravity was not his friend, Sophie observed. His skin and the underlying flesh seemed but lightly attached to his skull; gravity dragged his face, with its loose folds of flesh, downwards, making him look perhaps ten years older than he was.

His meal finished, Canon Swan laid his cutlery on his plate; the time for small talk had arrived. 'You're a Londoner, Mrs Lilburn?'

'We've lived there for a number of years – since we were married.'

'Your husband has done a lot of singing in London, then?'

Sophie nodded. 'Depping, mostly. Different churches, all over town. You'd have to ask him about it.' She gave an apologetic shrug. 'I'm afraid I'm not at all churchy.'

'Very wise of you.' And then, for some reason, he smiled across at her. The transformation was so astonishing that she caught her breath. His sagging jowls disappeared; the planes of his face moved upwards, rearranging themselves into those of a much younger man. Ten years, twenty years, younger. A different face altogether. He still wasn't handsome, but Sophie could now glimpse at least the potential for a hint of charm. How fascinating it would be, she thought, to photograph this face.

Breaking away from his conversation with Jeremy, Chris addressed the Precentor. 'I've sung at All Saints' Margaret Street, at Bourne Street, at St Alban's, Holborn. A few times at the Abbey. All over the place, really.'

'He comes very well recommended,' Jeremy said. 'And it must be said that he passed the audition with flying colours. That bit of Haydn was beautifully sung.'

'And Mrs Lilburn?' the canon asked, looking across at her.

Chris answered for her. 'Sophie is a photographer,' he said with pride. 'She's quite well known in her field.'

Still the canon looked at Sophie. 'How would you feel about moving from London? Would that be a problem for you?'

'I can take pictures wherever I am,' she evaded, dropping her eyes. She *mustn't* ruin things for Chris, she told herself. This meant so much to him.

Canon Swan, having missed out on the formal interview, seemed to feel that he had to get through a list of questions. 'How about family? Do you have children?'

'No,' said Sophie. 'No. Not yet.' She didn't dare to look at Chris, though she could feel his eyes on her.

Not yet. That was the problem. And it certainly wasn't for want of trying, at least not in the past year.

Chris had always wanted children, from the very first. He would have been delighted if they'd had a baby straight away, followed by several more. He came from a large family himself, and that was the natural state of things as far as he was concerned. Some men aspire to fathering an entire football team; Chris would have been happy with a respectable-sized chamber choir.

But he'd never nagged her about it, Sophie acknowledged to herself. He'd made it clear how he felt, but he had respected her decision to wait, to establish herself in her career before tying herself down with babies.

'Give me two years,' she'd said at first. Two years had turned into five in no time; now they had been married for nine years, and still there was no baby.

Sophie was thirty years old. A year before, on the eve of that birthday, as spring crept up on the frozen world, her biological clock had kicked into operation. Suddenly it seemed the most important thing in the world to her that she should have a baby. Now. Before it was too late.

Chris, of course, had been delighted. Delighted at her decision, and at the suddenly increased frequency of their lovemaking. For a few months it was bliss, and both of them glowed with new joy in each other.

But nothing had happened. Making love day and night, and not a sign of success.

After those first months, the joy of it had begun to pall. Going to bed became a chore, a duty, robbed of tenderness and tinged with a sort of desperation. *Would* this be the time it would happen? The potential of failure hung over their bed.

Sophie had begun reading up on conception. She'd begun taking her temperature, and insisted on even more frequent lovemaking – if it could even be called that any longer – when the time was right. She had even visited her GP, seeking referral to an infertility specialist. 'Give it a year,' the GP had said. 'Then we'll start thinking about that sort of thing.'

It had now been a year, and still there was no sign of a baby.

Jeremy Hammond invited them to have coffee at his house. 'I certainly wouldn't inflict the swill that passes for coffee in the refectory on you,' he said with a shudder. 'Come and have some decent coffee with me.'

Canon Swan declined, citing another pressing meeting, so it was just the three of them who went back to Quire

Close. 'Do you have one of those big houses at the end?' Sophie asked as they came through the arch.

'Not I. I'm merely the humble Director of Music.' Jeremy had a gliding sort of walk, and this, coupled with his long legs, meant they had to hurry over the cobblestones to keep up with him. 'Here we are.' He turned into an immaculate front garden and unlocked his door. 'You'll find that all the houses in the close are a bit different inside. Mine *is* one of the nicer ones, I think.'

The entrance hall was extremely narrow. 'Come upstairs,' Jeremy beckoned, leading them up a long straight staircase, back along a landing, and into the room at the front of the house. 'My sitting room,' he announced. 'A bit too small to be called a drawing room, but it will do.'

It was, Sophie saw, a lovely room. Jeremy was fortunate to be on the south-facing side of the close, so the room was light and sunny. Everything in it was in the best possible taste: a mellow oriental rug, a few nice pictures on the warm terracotta walls, some fine pieces of antique furniture. There were books in the alcoves, along with a well-disguised sound system, and a beautiful clavichord in one corner. 'Not enough room in here for my piano,' Jeremy explained, 'and they never would have got it up those stairs anyway, so I had this made to fit in here.'

Their host disappeared for a few minutes back downstairs to make the coffee, so Sophie wandered about and inspected the pictures while Chris sank into a comfortable armchair, clasping his hands nervously in his lap.

'How has it gone so far?' Sophie asked him.

Chris nodded. 'Quite well, I think. They seem to like me.'

'And do you like *them*?'

'You know me,' he grinned. 'I like everyone.'

It was true, Sophie acknowledged. Her husband was one of those uncritical people who saw the best in everyone. She wasn't like that.

Neither, it would appear, was Jeremy Hammond.

'Those clergy,' he said as he glided into the room bearing a tray. 'They think they're *so* important. Rushing about here, there, and everywhere. I mean, they think they actually run the cathedral. Can you imagine?'

Sophie, with her limited knowledge of cathedrals, was confused. 'I thought the Bishop ran the cathedral. And he's clergy, isn't he?'

'Oh, my dear! You have so much to learn!' Jeremy put the tray down on an exquisite mahogany side table and turned to her with delight. 'In the first place, the Bishop has absolutely nothing to do with the cathedral.'

'But isn't that his chair in there? The big one, near the pulpit? That's what someone said.' She hated to display her ignorance of this alien world.

Jeremy didn't seem to mind; in fact he clearly revelled in the opportunity to explain. 'The Bishop's chair – the cathedra, to use your actual Latin – is what makes it a cathedral. But the Bishop's job is to run the diocese, not the cathedral. That's what the Dean is supposed to be for. The Dean and Chapter. You'll note,' he added with a wicked grin, 'that I said *supposed*. This Dean, in particular, is completely useless. People let him pretend that he's in charge, but everyone knows he's not.'

Another word had baffled her. 'You said the Dean and Chapter. What's the Chapter?'

Jeremy handed her a tiny bone-china cup of fragrant

black coffee. 'That's the corporate name for all of the canons. The residentiary canons, that is – the ones who "live in", as it were. Most cathedrals have three or four of them. We're lucky in that we only have three – that's fewer of them to get in the way.'

Sophie accepted a dollop of cream in her coffee and took an appreciative sip. She loved good coffee; the fact that Jeremy Hammond shared that passion seemed to her a good sign. 'Canon Swan is one of them?'

'That's right. He's the Precentor. The one who sings the services,' he explained. 'He's the one who is generally concerned with the music, and the running of the services – or at least I let him think so. That's why he was in on the interview today.'

'He sings?'

Jeremy, in the act of offering Chris the cream, turned his head to look at her, raising his eyebrows. 'Oh, yes. Not too badly, either – for a man of his age,' he admitted.

'Has he been here for a long time, then?' Chris put in.

'Not long.' Jeremy stirred cream into his own coffee and took a sip, then smiled his approval of his own efforts. 'About two years, give or take. He got the appointment because he was an old friend of the Dean. That's the way things work around here – it's who you know that's important.'

It was the human element that interested Sophie. 'Is he married?'

Jeremy laughed. 'No.' With one elegant hand he made an expressive gesture. 'He *is* a bit of an old sourpuss. Who would have him? Let's be honest – he doesn't exactly spread sweetness and light about the place.'

To Sophie's disappointment, Chris shifted the subject. 'Tell me about the Dean,' he requested.

'The Dean,' pronounced Jeremy, 'is irrelevant. You don't really need to know anything about him other than that. Useless, as I said before. He breeds Burmese cats and grows old-fashioned roses and only leaves the Deanery when absolutely necessary. You'll see him now and then, sitting in his Decani stall in the choir for services, and sometimes he even stirs himself to read a lesson, but I promise you that he'll never impinge on your life in any way.'

He was speaking, Sophie realised, as though their future involvement at Westmead Cathedral was a foregone conclusion. 'Then who *does* run the cathedral?' she asked.

Jeremy put down his coffee cup and moved to the window. 'Come here, my dear,' he commanded.

Sophie obeyed, draining the last of her coffee and going to his side.

'Quire Close,' said Jeremy, 'is the seat of power. Not the Deanery.' Looking out of the window, he swept his hand dramatically from one end to the other. 'There are two people who matter in this place. One of them lives at the entrance, just through the arch.' He pointed up the close. 'Leslie Clunch, he's called.'

Her gaze followed his finger, though there was no one in sight. 'And who is Leslie Clunch?'

'Retired verger,' said Jeremy. '*Head* Verger, as he'd be the first to tell you.'

The word meant nothing to her; she looked towards Chris for enlightenment.

'The vergers are the ones who walk in front of the clergy and choir when they come in for services,' Chris supplied. 'And when they go out, or go up to the pulpit to preach or read. They wear black gowns and carry silver wands. It's sort of a ceremonial thing.'

'The wands are called "verges",' added Jeremy. 'Hence the name. But the vergers do far more than go walkabout with the clergy. They're the ones who really run the place on a day-to-day basis.'

'I saw some men wearing black gowns when I was in the cathedral earlier,' Sophie recalled. 'They seemed to be keeping an eye on the place.'

Jeremy nodded. 'Exactly. They keep an eagle eye on tourists, so they don't do anything naughty or walk off with the silver, and they make themselves indispensable to everyone else. They would be the first to tell you that the clergy couldn't manage without them.'

'So this Leslie Clunch . . . ?' Sophie prompted.

'Was Head Verger for donkey's years. The better part of thirty years, I reckon,' said Jeremy. 'He retired about two years ago, and in recognition of his long service to Westmead Cathedral, he was given a grace-and-favour residence in Quire Close.'

'Why do you say he's powerful? I mean, if he's retired . . .'

Jeremy's mouth curved in an arch smile. 'My dear, he knows where all of the bodies are buried, so to speak. There's nothing that's happened in this cathedral for thirty years that he doesn't know about. He has a very long memory,' he added. 'It's more than anyone's job is worth to cross him.'

Sophie was baffled: Jeremy was talking as if this were a den of iniquity, not a house of God. She thought that cathedrals were meant to be holy places, full of holy people who never did anything of which they might be ashamed. Before she could put this into words, though, Jeremy went on. 'And nothing happens in this close without Leslie Clunch knowing about it. Nothing.' His voice was light, but Sophie sensed that it contained a hint of warning.

'Does he live on his own?' Chris asked.

'Oh, no. There is a Mrs Clunch – Olive.' Jeremy grinned. 'The long-suffering Olive. She's an invalid now. Very poorly. Never goes out. Leslie looks after her night and day, as he'd be the first to tell you.'

Chris joined them at the window. 'Then how does he have time to know the business of everyone in the close?'

Jeremy shook his head and smiled, lifting his shoulders in an elegant shrug. After a significant pause he said, 'You'll find out soon enough what I'm talking about.'

Again that assumption that their future lay in Westmead. Sophie fought against a bubble of panic that welled up inside her; perhaps it was irrational, but all she wanted to do at that moment was walk down the stairs, out of Quire Close, and flee home to London. Instead she forced herself to speak normally. 'You said that there are *two* people who matter,' she recalled. 'Who is the other one, then?'

'Ah,' said Jeremy. 'Now *that* is a long story. Shall we have some more coffee, perhaps?'

He went off and prepared a fresh supply, then settled down in a wing-backed chair, crossing his long legs in front of him. 'Elspeth Verey,' he said, as if tasting the name in his mouth. 'Elspeth Verey.'

Sophie waited, understanding that this was Jeremy's way of creating a bit of drama.

'Elspeth Verey lives at the far end of the close,' Jeremy began. 'In Priory House, one of the larger houses.'

He took his time telling the story, relishing it. Elspeth Verey, he explained, had been in Westmead even longer than Leslie Clunch: more than forty years. She'd been a young girl in her teens when her father had been appointed Dean of Westmead Cathedral, and had spent those formative years living at the Deanery.

The Very Reverend Arthur Worthington, her father, had been a dean of the old school: Oxford-educated, well connected, with private means. Westmead Cathedral had become his kingdom, one he ruled as a benevolent despot. In those days, no one had ever been in any doubt about who was in charge, or where the power lay. Arthur Worthington was as near to an absolute monarch as was possible in the Church of England, yet in spite of that he had been much beloved.

And his daughter, growing up at the heart of so much power, had developed a taste for it. Indeed, she had even come to regard it as her birthright.

In the days when Elspeth Verey was growing up, there was only one way for a woman to achieve status in the Church of England: she had to marry it. Elspeth Worthington, as she then was, grasped this fact quickly, and set about putting her plans into effect in a calculated manner. Carefully she sized up each eligible clergyman who crossed her path – and in a cathedral city, there was an abundance of them to choose from. Even discounting those who were already married, she was spoilt for choice: canons, archdeacons, vicars, rectors, curates.

The curates were too young and untried; most of the vicars and rectors lacked the necessary ambition, the fire in the belly that Elspeth was looking for. The search proved more difficult than she'd anticipated. But when she was twenty-one, she met Richard Verey. He was thirty-eight, and had just been appointed as Archdeacon of Westmead. It was rare to find an archdeacon under forty;

the fact that he had already achieved that office indicated that he was on his way to higher things.

They were married within the year, and in another year she had given birth to a son and heir, upon whom she bestowed the honour of the family name: Worthington Verey. His godfather was, in fact, the Archbishop of Canterbury, and from him he took his middle names.

Worthington Michael Ramsey Verey was clearly born for great things. He was an only child, and on him his mother lavished her love, even as she inculcated him with her ambition.

Her choice of husband was proved to be a good one when he succeeded her father as Dean of Westmead. Elspeth Verey moved back into the Deanery in triumph, sure that it was her rightful place. In the Deanery her will reigned supreme, and through her husband she ruled the cathedral.

Everything had gone according to plan. Young Worthington grew in wisdom and stature, achieving fine results in his A levels and securing a place at his father's Oxford college.

Then came the great shock, the seismic upheaval. Worthington went off to Oxford, and a few months later, Elspeth discovered that she was being compensated for the loss in a most unexpected way: she was pregnant again, at the age of forty-one.

The new baby was another boy, and they called him Dominic.

But Dominic was not destined to grow to manhood in the Deanery. The Very Reverend Richard Verey proved to be a weaker vessel than his formidable and long-lived father-in-law; at the age of sixty he suffered a mild heart attack, and his doctors urged him to consider early retirement, at sixty-two. Reluctantly he agreed, and plans were under way for him to stand down as Dean when, a year later, another heart attack proved fatal.

Elspeth Verey was left a widow at the age of forty-seven.

Priory House, at the end of Quire Close, was in the process of being renovated as Dean Verey's retirement home. No one questioned Elspeth Verey's right to move into it with her young son, and there she had remained.

She was, Jeremy told them, the undoubted Queen of Westmead. Now fifty-eight, her ambitions were vested in her sons. Dominic was still at school, but Worthington was well on the way to fulfilling his destiny: he would, his mother was sure, be Dean of Westmead one day in the not-too-distant future. The present dean had been appointed through her string-pulling: an ineffectual man who would not do much harm until it was time for Worthington to take over.

Of course, Elspeth Verey was the social arbiter of Westmead. Those upon whom she smiled would flourish; those upon whom she frowned would be consigned to the status of non-person.

'Does she like *you*?' Sophie blurted; even as she said it she realised that the question was perhaps not as tactful or discreet as it should be.

But Jeremy didn't seem to mind. He grinned, uncrossing his legs and recrossing them the other way. 'Oh, yes. Our Elspeth likes me. She finds me . . . amusing.' He raised an eyebrow and lowered his voice. 'But I'll tell you who she *doesn't* like.'

'Who?'

'The Subdean's wife. Elspeth can't bear her.'

'Why?'

'Because,' Jeremy said, his mouth curving maliciously, 'the Subdean was one of those young curates whom Elspeth rejected all those years ago.'

Sophie processed the information. 'The Subdean? But if the Dean—'

Her question was interrupted by the ringing of the telephone. Jeremy went into another room to take the call, and when he returned he was beaming.

'That was the Headmaster,' he said to Chris. 'He's spoken to Canon Swan. We've all agreed. If you want the job, it's yours.'

Chris looked at Sophie, and she at him. His cheerful round face glowed with excitement; the smile on her face felt frozen.

Chapter 2

April 1989

No one would have taken the two girls for sisters. They were very different: Jacquie, the elder by a year, was dark and lean, while Alison was fair, with a tendency towards plumpness. Of the two, Alison was the prettier, though it might be argued that Jacquie, with her stronger bone structure, would stand the test of time better.

They were going on holiday together – a fortnight in Greece. Alison couldn't believe it. Their parents were actually allowing them to do it.

This would be their first trip abroad, the first time either of them had been out of England. Their parents had never been very big on holidays, considering such things to be a frivolous waste of money and time. When the girls were small, there had been the occasional foray to the north Norfolk coast, to Wells-Next-the-Sea or Cromer, for a day or sometimes even a weekend of sitting on the beach at the edge of the chilly sea, the parents keeping a vigilant eye on their daughters.

This was going to be different, Jacquie assured her sister

with enthusiasm. The sea would be warm – warm enough to swim in. The sky would be a perpetual blue, the air balmy. Most importantly, their parents would not be there. And there would be men.

If Joan and Frank Barnett had known anything at all about package holidays abroad, they would never have dreamed of allowing their daughters to embark upon one. But their sphere of existence was narrow, confined by their own world view. They didn't own a television, as a matter of choice; in their opinion, television was a waste of time, and worse – the Devil's invention, bringing filth and depravity into the home. Nor did they read newspapers, which were little better than television when it came to promulgating things about which it was better not to know.

Joan and Frank Barnett's main reading material was the Bible, and their knowledge about the world outside of Sutton Fen – a small market town near the Cambridge-shire–Norfolk border – was provided in the main by the fiery sermons delivered by the Reverend Mr Raymond Prew, the pastor of the Free Baptist Fellowship. The world was a wicked place, best avoided. That was how they lived, and how they had brought up their daughters, sheltering them as best they could from worldliness and evil. Joan and Frank were elderly parents; their girls had been a late gift to their marriage, and thus were doubly precious, doubly guarded from the perils of the wicked world.

Still, when Jacquie had suggested that she and her sister might go on holiday to Greece, Joan and Frank had eventually agreed. Greece was, after all, mentioned in the Bible. St Paul himself had been there. It wouldn't have been their choice, but surely the girls would be safe in the Bible Lands.

They were both earning their own money now, and had been saving up for the holiday. Alison, at twenty, had a good job as a secretary for Mr Prew. And Jacquie had been working, since she'd left school, at the Mini Mart.

She wouldn't be working there for much longer, though, and that was the real impetus behind the trip. In July, Jacquie was to marry Darren Darke, and she had begged her parents to allow her just one trip abroad with her sister before she settled down to domestic life.

Joan and Frank approved of Darren Darke. He was one of them – a member of the Free Baptist Fellowship. A sober young man, he had good prospects; his father owned a car dealership and garage in Sutton Fen, and Darren was already the manager of the dealership side of the business. He even had his own house, in the new housing estate on the outskirts of Sutton Fen. Darren would look after Jacquie and provide for her; there would be no need for her to carry on with her job. She could stay at home and do those things that a woman was divinely ordained to do: look after the house, look after her husband, and in the fullness of time look after their children. Those were the teachings of the Free Baptist Fellowship; they'd been good enough for Joan and Frank, and would be good enough for their daughter.

Jacquie loved Darren – or at least she told herself that she did. At any rate, she was looking forward to the wedding. Being Mrs Darren Darke would give her status in Sutton Fen; it would get her away from the stifling atmosphere of the family home.

But just once, before she settled down, she wanted to experience all of the joys of a foreign holiday.

Unlike her parents, and even her more innocent sister,

Jacquie knew exactly what those joys consisted of. During slow times at the Mini Mart she often read the glossy magazines intended for young women – magazines which would have curled her parents' hair with their explicitness. And most of her friends from school, as well as her friend Nicola from the Mini Mart, had been on package holidays abroad; they'd told her of the ready availability of men.

Sex. That was what it was all about, really. Plentiful, mindless sex with as many men as possible.

Before she settled down to become Mrs Darren Darke, before the walls closed round her for ever. Surely, thought Jacquie, it wasn't too much to ask.

Though her sister – and certainly their parents – didn't know it, Jacquie was not a virgin. She'd been having sex with Darren since their engagement; if it had been up to Jacquie, they would have started even before that, but Darren was an upright and devout young man, and it had taken some doing to get him into bed. Once there, though, he had found that he liked it, and it had become a regular feature of their time together.

It was a convenient thing, Darren having his own house, and as its future mistress Jacquie could legitimately visit it. This she did often, under the guise of overseeing its redecoration. Her parents would have died of shame if they had even suspected what really went on during those visits.

Alison, too, would have been shocked. Her knowledge of such things was limited, and coloured by her own romantic nature.

But when Jacquie told her that there would be men aplenty in Greece, Alison was not displeased. There were few eligible men of her acquaintance, or those her parents would have considered suitable, in Sutton Fen; so far she had not found any who attracted or interested her.

And Alison was ready to fall in love.

The hotel room was spare but adequate; there were two double beds, a chest of drawers, a wardrobe, and a chair. The room was clean, as was the adjoining *en-suite* facility, and best of all it had a window overlooking the sea.

Alison leaned on the window-sill and breathed deeply of the sea air. 'It's beautiful,' she sighed. 'I never dreamed there could be anywhere this beautiful in the whole world.' The colours were so bright, so vivid: the bright blue of the sky, the deep blue of the sea. Nothing could have been more different from the flat grey fens in which she'd lived all of her life.

'Two whole weeks,' said Jacquie, flopping down on one of the beds with a groan of happiness. 'It's too good to be true.'

'We won't want to go home,' predicted Alison. 'We're going to have a good time, aren't we?'

'Oh, yes.' Jacquie sat up and nodded. 'A wonderful time. I promise.' The thought seemed to galvanise her, after the exhaustion of the journey. She got up from the bed, which just a few seconds before she'd found so irresistible, and heaved her case on to it. 'And there's no time like the present to begin,' she announced. 'Let's go down to the beach.'

This was a suggestion that, even a few months ago, would have met with an ambivalent response from Alison, who was always self-conscious about her weight. But she had been scrupulously following a strict diet since they'd been planning the trip, and was now proud of her slimmed-down figure. She had a new bathing costume and could hardly wait to show it off. 'Great idea,' she agreed, following her sister's lead and retrieving her case from the floor where she'd dropped it.

Alison's bathing costume, though new, was conservatively cut, high in the front and low on the thighs; it had been bought with the reluctant approval of her mother, who didn't really believe that bathing costumes were decent. With modesty she turned her back on her sister and struggled into it, then spun round to show it off. 'What do you—'

The words died on her lips; she gasped at the spectacle in front of her. Jacquie was arrayed in the skimpiest of two-piece costumes, scarcely more than tiny triangles of fabric held together with string.

'Tah dah!' Jacquie posed, her arms outstretched.

'You can't wear that!'

'Oh, no? Just watch me!' She twirled around, showing that there was even less to the back than there was to the front.

'But where did you *get* it?' demanded Alison. 'Mum would never let you buy anything like that!'

Jacquie's grin was defiant. 'I bought it out of a mail-order catalogue that Nicola brought to work. It fits perfectly, don't you think?'

Alison just shook her head, her pleasure in her own new costume evaporating. Next to her sister, she now felt dowdy and old-fashioned. Disconsolately she trailed behind her to the beach.

It turned out that Jacquie had obtained a whole new wardrobe from the mail-order catalogue. She dressed for dinner that night in a low-cut, skimpy black dress, and looked scornfully at her sister's best Laura Ashley frock, Alison's idea of proper attire for a foreign holiday. 'We'll have to get you some new clothes,' she decided. 'I'm sure there are shops here that sell something with a bit more going for it than *that*.'

She led the way to the hotel dining room where they were to take their meals, revelling in the stares of admiration that followed her as they had done on the beach.

Now, Jacquie decided, it was time to get down to serious business. As soon as they were settled at their table, she surveyed the other diners. 'Not bad,' she said about one young man, but he proved to have a girl in tow. A crowd of rowdy British boys, still in their teens, she judged to be unworthy of her, though they leered openly and waved at her from their table across the room.

But their waiter – now he was a different story. Melting black eyes and a shock of black hair, teeth white and perfect against swarthy skin. Beautiful, thought Jacquie, and turned her most charming smile upon him. Her friends had told her about the waiters – what skilled lovers they were, and how passionate yet considerate. 'What are you called?' she asked him as he handed her a menu.

'Dimitrios.'

'I'm Jacquie. And this,' she added as an afterthought, 'is my sister Alison.'

His smile was breathtaking. 'I haven't seen you two charming ladies before. This is your first night here?'

'Yes. But not our last.' Her eyes held his for a long moment, until he turned away.

'Jacquie!' said Alison in a scandalised whisper. 'You were *flirting* with him!'

Her voice was smug. 'Yes.'

'But what about Darren?' she demanded.

'What about him?' Jacquie smoothed her dark hair down and licked her lips.

'You're going to marry him!' Alison reminded her. 'In July! So you don't have any business flirting with anyone else!'

Jacquie sighed and rolled her eyes. 'You sound just like Mum.'

'But, Jacquie—'

'Oh, Ally, you're so naïve.' She gave her sister a patronising look. 'Why do you think I've come on this holiday? It's not just to get a nice tan for the wedding, I can promise you.'

'Then *what*?' Alison was genuinely baffled.

Her sister sighed again. 'Do I have to spell it out for you? I'm going to be married to Darren for the rest of my life, and I don't want to have to say when I die that he's the only man I've ever slept with.'

Comprehension dawned slowly, incredulously. 'Do you mean that you're planning to . . .' She couldn't bring herself to finish the sentence.

Jacquie was blunt. 'I'm planning to sleep with that lovely Dimitrios tonight, if that's what you're trying to say. And with as many men as I possibly can, over the next fortnight. I'm going to make this holiday something to remember for the rest of my life.'

Shaken and appalled, Alison dropped her eyes. She couldn't bear to look at the triumphant huntress that her sister had so suddenly become; she didn't know how to cope with the revelations that had just been tossed so casually in her direction. Her eyes scanned the menu without seeing it. 'So, what are you going to order?' she stammered.

* * *

The subject was not referred to again that evening between the sisters, though Jacquie continued to flirt outrageously with the waiter as the meal progressed, and by the end of it, she had arranged to meet him after he finished his shift at the restaurant.

Their meal completed, the girls had a stroll round the village, then stopped at the hotel bar for a drink. Alison, who had never tasted a drop of alcohol in her life, asked for orange juice. Jacquie, though, had occasionally shared an illicit bottle of wine with her friends; she horrified her sister by ordering a glass of retsina.

'Come on – taste it,' she urged Alison. Of course, her sister refused, so she downed her drink in several brave gulps, admitting to herself – if not to Alison – that it tasted foul. Its astringent, resiny taste was nothing like the sweet wine she had drunk in the past, but it was the local drink, and it *did* add a dash of recklessness to her determination that the evening should go according to her plan.

So far the only hitch was Alison's evident disapproval. The girl was turning out to be a real wet blanket, little better than their mother; Jacquie hoped that she wouldn't manage to ruin the holiday. The only thing to do, she told herself with alcoholic bravado, was to ignore her sister and make the most of the opportunities that presented them-selves to her. In a day or two, seeing what fun she was having, Ally might even begin to loosen up a bit.

They returned to their room and Jacquie refreshed her make-up. 'Don't wait up for me,' she announced gaily as she departed. 'I have my key.'

'I won't.' Slowly, as if in a dream, Alison got ready for bed. She turned out the lights in the room, then leaned on the window-sill and looked out of the open window into the balmy night.

There was something unreal about it. The sky was so black, and beneath it the sea rolled like some glistening dark animal. A sliver of a moon hung surrounded by more stars than she had ever seen. And the air wasn't just warm – it was redolent with rich and complex smells, scents of sea and passionate life, nothing at all like the chill earthiness of the fens. This was Alison's first glimpse of a life outside of the narrow confines of her world, and it both frightened and intrigued her.

It wasn't until she crawled into bed that she allowed herself to think about her sister. She hadn't meant to think about Jacquie, but sleep eluded her, and her sister's triumphant face grinned at her even as she screwed her eyes shut to blot out the image.

She'd thought that she knew Jacquie. They'd grown up together, as close as two sisters could be. But suddenly her sister was a stranger – a wine-drinking, bikini-wearing, flirtatious stranger.

And the things that Jacquie had said, about sleeping with as many men as possible . . . At this moment, even, she was probably locked in the arms of the dark-eyed waiter. In his bed.

Here Alison's imagination failed her; she couldn't imagine what it was that they were doing. She knew the facts of life, but her information ended with the bare facts. She wasn't a farm girl; she'd never been allowed to watch television or go to the cinema.

What Jacquie was doing was wrong, of that much Alison was sure. It went against everything that they'd ever been taught about the sanctity of marriage and the importance of a girl keeping herself pure until her wedding night. It was a betrayal of Darren, of their parents, of God. And with a man she wasn't even in love with.

It was disgusting. Unthinkable.

Behind her closed eyelids, Alison could see them kissing – Jacquie pressing her lips against those of the waiter. And he was touching her: brown hands on white breasts.

Under the covers, in spite of herself, Alison's body grew hot.

It wasn't until the early hours of the morning that Jacquie returned, grinning in triumph. She kicked off her shoes and threw herself on her bed. 'It was wonderful,' she announced. 'He was brilliant.'

'I don't want to hear about it.' Alison, bleary from too little sleep, covered her ears with her hands and turned her face into her pillow to blot out her sister's face.

'All right then.' Not bothering to undress, she crawled under the covers. After a moment she said, dreamily, 'Darren could certainly learn a thing or two from him.'

Alison sat up, shocked out of her lethargy. 'Do you mean that you and Darren have . . . done it?'

'Oh, Ally.' Jacquie laughed, a throaty, knowing chuckle that her sister found even more upsetting than her words. 'You're such an innocent. It's sweet, really.'

'Before you're married?'

Her sister gave her a condescending smile. 'Lots of times. As often as we can.'

'But what would Mum say? Or Dad? Or Reverend Prew?'

'I can just imagine what they'd say. Reverend Prew would probably have a heart attack.' Jacquie narrowed her eyes. 'But you're not going to tell them, are you?'

Alison heard the threat behind her sister's words, and the fear. It gave her an odd sort of reassurance: Jacquie wasn't completely corrupt, then, or she wouldn't care. 'No,' she whispered. 'No, I won't tell them. But Jacquie . . .'

'What?'

'I just wish you wouldn't.'

Jacquie laughed. 'Too late for that.'

Chapter 3

The freshness of early spring had given way to the tired vegetation of August by the time that Sophie and Chris Lilburn moved into Quire Close. It had been a long, hot summer, with a hosepipe ban in effect, and with few exceptions the little gardens in front of the houses of the close were parched, unattractive. Number 22, into which the Lilburns were to be installed, was one of the worst, featuring a few wilted marigolds and some unidentifiable dead plants.

'My predecessor must not have been a gardener,' Chris observed. 'You'll have to have a go, Soph.'

Sophie had no interest in gardening; she couldn't imagine why Chris should think that she had. 'Maybe *you* could do it,' she countered, trying not to sound sharp.

'You know, I think I'd like that.' Chris beamed at her. 'Getting my hands dirty will make me feel like a real country gent.'

Sophie concentrated not on the garden, but on the front of the house. Number 22 was on the west side of Quire Close, nearer the far end than the entrance; in appearance it was much like its neighbours on either side, with the subtle difference of a blue door adorned with an elegant dolphin-shaped brass knocker, and an old-fashioned bell-pull.

This was the first glimpse they'd had of their new home; the previous occupant had only just vacated the day before, and the Lilburns were no more than an hour in advance of the removal van carrying their worldly goods. 'Let's go inside,' Sophie urged.

Chris had the key, an oversized iron one which looked as though it ought to fit the lock to some mediaeval gaol cell. With ceremony he slid it into the keyhole and turned. 'Behold, Mrs Lilburn,' he announced portentously as the door swung open. 'Your new home!'

Sophie's first thought was that the outside of the house was deceptive; it appeared to be double-fronted, but in fact the stone façade didn't match up with the interior. Over the centuries there had been much chopping and changing within, and their new house was much smaller than it appeared. The stone-flagged entrance hall was cramped; the rooms were low-ceilinged and of mediaeval proportions.

To the right of the entrance hall was the sitting room, dominated by an enormous stone fireplace, original to the house. The size of the fireplace in proportion to the room, the darkness of the wallpaper, and the low ceiling all combined to make the room seem even smaller than it was. If one were being charitable, that quality could be transformed into the virtue of cosiness, but at first glance, Sophie found 'claustrophobic' to be a more apt description. The only other room on the ground floor was the kitchen, narrow and antiquated; it didn't seem to have had anything done to it since the war. To the side of the kitchen was an eating alcove, just large enough to hold a table and chairs; there was no dining room.

Sophie, used to the modern kitchen of their London flat, sighed. 'How am I supposed to cook in here?'

Chris patted the grease-encrusted top of the ancient cooker. 'I'm sure this works just fine. And if not,' he added grandly, 'we'll buy a new one.'

Sophie turned away, depressed by the vision of spending time in that poky hole. 'Let's have a look upstairs,' she said abruptly.

The room over the sitting room, its window looking out into the close, was clearly the main bedroom. 'This will be splendid,' Chris enthused, going to the window. 'A lovely view. And if you stand here at the corner of the window, you can just see the cathedral.'

Sophie, though, was measuring up the room mentally; it seemed smaller than the sitting room below, as the fire-place was blocked up, and she wondered whether their furniture would fit. 'Do you think the bed will go along this wall?' she queried doubtfully.

'Oh, I'm sure it will,' Chris stated. 'No problem.'

Next they explored the bathroom, behind the bedroom. Sophie was delighted to see that it, at least, had been modernised: no claw-footed bath or chipped basin or tall pull-chain loo, as by now she had been expecting, but an up-to-date suite. There was even a power shower installed above the bath. 'Something for each of us,' Chris observed; Sophie liked showers, while he enjoyed spending hours in the bath.

Cheered, they moved on to the smaller back bedroom. 'This,' Chris pointed out with triumph, 'will make a perfect darkroom for you, Soph. Look – the windows even have shutters.' He demonstrated by pulling them closed, plunging the room into darkness.

That was a definite plus; she'd been wondering how she would manage to create a darkroom in the house when every room had windows. 'A bit small. But I suppose it will do.'

Chris was still playing with the shutters as Sophie went up the small staircase to explore the top floor. There was one room up there. Its door was shut; she pushed it open and found herself looking into a nursery.

The walls were colour-washed a sunny shade of yellow, and halfway up marched a frieze of teddy bears, on the way to their picnic. A nursery, without a doubt.

Sophie caught her breath sharply, hanging on to the door knob for support. Chris came up behind her. 'Oh, look,' he enthused as he draped an arm round her. 'A room for the baby! Perfect, eh, Soph? We won't even have to redecorate.'

She suppressed an urge to shake off his arm as her mind zoomed back a week in time.

The doctor's office – their preliminary visit to their GP, before he at last referred them on to the fertility specialist. Sophie had sat on the edge of her chair, waiting for him to deliver his verdict.

'Well,' he'd said cheerfully, grinning at them across his desk, 'at least we've eliminated Chris as the source of the problem. You understand, of course,' he added, 'why we check him out first, before we send you on any further – much less complicated a mechanism at work there, and much easier to test.'

Not Chris's fault. The doctor's voice droned on,

explaining what the next steps would be when their appointment came through to see Mr York, but Sophie was unable to take it all in. Her eyes roamed round the room, over the plethora of framed diplomas and certificates on the walls, avoiding the doctor's smiling face. Not Chris's fault.

Her fault, then. One way or another, it was *her* fault. There was something wrong with her, something deep inside. All of those years she'd assumed that she was normal, that her body functioned like that of other women, that when she wanted a baby, all she would have to do was go off the Pill and let nature take its course.

Chris was fine: his sperm count was on the high side of the normal range, the sperm healthy and mobile.

It was her fault.

A few hours later the furniture had all been moved in and slotted into place; the house looked remarkably settled, as if they had been there for ever. Of course there were still boxes to be unpacked, and Sophie's darkroom would need sorting out, but the worst was over. Sophie travelled lightly through life; she was not one for collecting possessions as she went along, and though Chris might have been an accumulator if he'd been left to his own devices, she had ruthlessly stamped out any such tendencies. He had his books and his music scores and his clothes, and that was about it. No collections, no clutter.

Avoiding the nursery, which remained empty of furniture, Sophie concentrated on the bedroom, while Chris was downstairs unpacking the kitchen gear. She hung her clothes in the wardrobe, then opened a box of bedding and made up the bed with sheets and pillows and duvet. That done, she moved to the window and looked out into the close, leaning her forehead against the cool glass. The glass was old and ripply; it distorted the view just a tiny bit.

'I've found the cutlery and the dishes,' Chris announced as he came up the stairs. 'So we're all set. And I've put the kettle on – I could murder a cup of tea about now.'

Sophie made a noncommittal noise, her head still against the glass.

'See, I told you that the bed would fit!' Chris came up behind her and wrapped his arms round her waist, nuzzling the back of her neck in a way that she'd always found arousing.

'Mmm,' murmured Chris after a moment. 'Let's forget about the tea, Soph. I think we should try out the bed. Christen it in its new home, so to speak.'

She felt her stomach clench, but tried to keep her voice light. 'Not now, Chris,' she said brightly, detaching his hands and moving away from him. 'I'd really like that cup of tea.'

Not Chris's fault. *Her* fault.

That evening they had a simple meal of bread and cheese. The weather was too hot for cooking, and their labours had made them more thirsty than hungry. Chris had popped a bottle of white wine in the freezer to chill it; they sipped it along with their supper fare.

Chris's eyes shone with enthusiasm. 'I have a good feeling about this house, Soph,' he said. 'We're going to be happy here. Really happy. And it will be a great place to bring up kids. I know that the back garden isn't huge, but there's plenty of room for a swing, and maybe even a climbing frame.'

'Maybe,' said Sophie carefully, not meeting his eyes, 'there won't be any kids.'

'Don't be silly.' He gave an affectionate laugh. 'You heard what the doctor said. It's early days yet. Lots more possibilities, so many different techniques that are available now. Mr York will sort it out. You'll see, Soph. By this time next year, there will be a baby in that nursery upstairs.'

She wanted to shout at him, to point out that it was easy for him to say: it wasn't his fault, after all. *He* was fine. She was the one who would now be poked and prodded by Mr York, her flawed body yet to yield up the secrets of its imperfection. Instead of shouting, though, she poured herself another glass of wine, clenching her jaw till it hurt.

They were having their meal in the cramped dining alcove, and though the window was open, suddenly the room seemed stifling to her. Pushing her plate away, Sophie picked up her glass and the half-empty bottle. 'I'm going outside,' she announced.

'What a good idea.' Chris followed her into the unkempt back garden and, with great ceremony, opened and arranged the two deck-chairs that they'd used on the balcony of their London flat. Seemingly unaware of Sophie's mood, he began to talk with some enthusiasm about the garden, pointing out possible areas for improvement and suggesting what plants might go in.

She let him chatter on, not listening but nodding occasionally. It was quiet in the garden, with its high walls separating it on either side from its neighbours, and as dusk descended it seemed a peaceful place. The sky darkened; the birds began to fall silent. Sophie closed her eyes and leaned back in her chair.

The silence was abruptly shattered by the high-pitched, frantic wail of a baby, coming from not far away. It wasn't the house next door, but it might have been the one next to that, or just beyond. The sound continued, the cries increasing in volume.

'I can't bear it,' said Sophie abruptly, getting up and going back into the house. She didn't even turn to see whether Chris was coming as well.

As she entered the hallway, though, the old-fashioned doorbell chimed. She went to the door to find Jeremy Hammond waiting outside.

'I was just about to give up on you,' he said.

'We were in the garden,' explained Sophie. 'Come in.'

With an elegant movement, Jeremy bent over and picked up an envelope which had come through the letter-box and now rested just inside the door. He presented it to Sophie with an ironic little bow, then stepped into the hall.

'Would you like a drink?' Sophie offered. 'There's a bottle of wine open.'

'Or I could find the gin,' added Chris from behind her. 'Though I'm not sure we have any tonic.'

'Drink,' said Jeremy, raising an eyebrow. 'Funny you should mention drink. Actually, I've come to invite you to join us at the pub. A few of the chaps from the choir are there already, and it would be a good chance for you to meet them.'

'What an excellent idea,' Chris said straight away. 'How about it, Soph?'

Sophie wasn't really in the mood for meeting strangers in a pub, but she could see that Chris was keen on the idea. 'All right, then,' she agreed with an attempt at enthusiasm.

Jeremy paused. 'You're welcome, of course,' he said carefully. 'But the wives don't usually come.'

She could take a hint, and was secretly relieved. 'Oh, that's all right. Chris, you go. I'll stay here and make a start at sorting a few things in my darkroom.' Sophie waved her hands as if to shoo him out of the door. 'Go on.'

'You're sure?' Chris hesitated.

'Of course.'

'I won't be late,' he promised. 'Just a quick one, I think.'

Sophie stood at the door and watched the two men disappear into the twilight, heading towards the arch at the end of the close: Jeremy tall and graceful, with his gliding walk, and Chris a bit shorter, bouncing along beside him. When they were out of sight she closed the door, then realised that she was still holding the envelope that Jeremy had handed her.

She examined it curiously. 'By hand,' it stated in the upper corner, and her own name was written in the precise centre. The envelope was thick and cream-coloured, with an expensive feel to it.

With a finger Sophie loosened the flap and eased out the envelope's contents. It was a stiff card of the same colour as the envelope, printed at the top: 'Mrs Elspeth Verey, Priory House, Quire Close, Westmead'. The message, written in the same elegant yet strong hand as the envelope, was brief and to the point. 'Would you care to join me for tea tomorrow at four? I look forward to meeting you.'

It was nothing less than a summons.

Sophie, who in the course of her work was used to mingling with rather important people, was nonetheless slightly nervous at the prospect of meeting the formidable Mrs Verey. She tried to construe from the invitation whether Chris were invited as well, hoping for the purposes of moral support that he was, but concluded with some regret that the summons was for her alone.

Before that meeting, though, another occurred. It happened in the morning, while she was in the bedroom unpacking one of the boxes, and Chris had gone to the school for a meeting with the Headmaster.

The doorbell chimed. Sophie dropped what she was doing and checked herself in the mirror. It was a hot day, and in her shorts and tank top she wasn't exactly dressed for visitors, but at least her hair was combed and she wasn't covered in moving grime. Perhaps it was only the postman in any case, she told herself, and went to the door.

A man stood on the doorstep, smiling at her as he looked her up and down; the smile revealed crooked teeth, unpleasantly yellow – disconcerting in one who could otherwise be described as dapper. 'Good morning,' he said in a dry, slightly raspy voice. 'I'm Leslie Clunch.'

Leslie Clunch. She remembered that Jeremy had told them about this man, the retired verger, and warned them of his importance in the close. 'Good morning,' she echoed. 'I'm Sophie Lilburn.' Conscious of her bare legs and bare feet, she hesitated for just a moment. 'Won't you come in?'

'Thank you.' Ceremoniously he crossed the threshold.

He was a rather small man, spare in build, but upright and dignified with a dignity which came of so many years in a job that depended upon that quality. His eyes were dark, swivelling round to take in everything, and what hair he had was grey, thin and plastered carefully to his skull.

'Would you like some coffee?' Sophie offered. 'I was about to have some myself.'

'That would be very nice.' He followed her into the sitting room, again giving her the feeling that he was missing nothing as he looked about.

She invited him to sit, then excused herself to make the coffee.

When it came to coffee, Sophie – like Jeremy Hammond – was particular. She loathed the instant variety, and ground the beans herself in a small electric grinder for maximum freshness, before brewing it in a cafetière. So it took her a few minutes to prepare it to her satisfaction, and to lay a tray with the jug of milk and a plate of biscuits.

Leslie Clunch hadn't moved from his chair, but Sophie had the feeling that he had absorbed the contents of the room and had passed judgement on the new residents accordingly. She could imagine what the room looked like to him: the incongruity of the sleek light furniture against the dark greeny-blue of the William Morris Willow Minor wallpaper. 'I'm afraid,' said Sophie, with apology in her voice, 'that the furniture doesn't go very well in here. Our flat in London was quite modern, but for this house we need something a bit more traditional.'

He didn't disagree. 'Perhaps some loose covers would help,' he suggested. 'There's a shop in the High Street that does them quite reasonably. And if you mentioned my name, they would give you a good price.'

The pompous tone of his voice, added to his air of self-importance, made him seem slightly ridiculous to Sophie, but she remembered what Jeremy had told them and was careful not to let her thoughts show on her face or in her voice. 'Thank you,' she said as she set the tray down on the glass-topped coffee table.

'I'm always glad to be able to help.'

Sophie pushed down the plunger of the cafetière and poured the coffee. 'I'm sorry that Chris – my husband – isn't here to meet you,' she said. 'He's gone over to the school this morning.'

'I know.' Leslie Clunch sat forward in the chair and reached for the cup. 'I saw him going.'

Sophie remembered that his house stood at the entrance to the close; he really didn't miss anything, she said to herself with the faintest stirring of unease.

'You don't have children, Mrs Lilburn.' It was a statement rather than a question; he'd been checking up on them, then.

She dropped her eyes, unable to bear his inquisitive stare. 'Not yet,' she said with a mixture of sharpness and defensiveness.

'Mrs Clunch and I had a daughter. A little girl. Just the one, after we'd been married for ten years and had just about given up hope. A real gift, she was, our Charmian.' His voice was soft, almost sentimental. 'Blonde hair, like you. And she would have been about your age, I suppose. She would have given us grandchildren by now. But she . . . died.'

'Oh!' Instantly Sophie felt guilty for her uncharitable thoughts. How sad, how tragic to wait so long for a child, only to lose her. She wanted to know more, wanted to know how the girl had died, and how long ago, but couldn't think what to say without sounding nosy and causing him more pain. 'Oh, I *am* sorry,' she said, raising her eyes to look at him.

His eyes, though they were swimming with tears, were focused firmly on her legs.

Sophie dressed carefully for her afternoon appointment, exchanging her shorts for a simple sun-dress and twisting her thick blonde hair up, securing it with a clip at the back of her head. She was unsure whether she ought to take some sort of offering to Mrs Verey – almost, she thought, like a propitiation to some ancient pagan goddess. Mentally she debated back and forth, in the end leaving it so late that the best she could do was to scour the overgrown back garden for a few flowers and arrange them into a modest if somewhat ragged bouquet. She didn't want to be late.

The flowers were probably a mistake, she realised as she reached the house. Its front garden was anything but overgrown; rather it was beautifully tended by someone who clearly enjoyed the task. Even after a long hot summer it seemed a green oasis, filled with fragrant climbing roses which scaled the mellow red brick of the house and encircled its stone-mullioned windows.

'Flowers,' said Elspeth Verey. 'How very kind.'

After what Jeremy had told her about Elspeth Verey, Sophie had built up a mental picture of her; the reality was quite different. There was nothing of the faded dowager about her: she was, after all, not yet sixty, and was still an attractive woman. Sophie registered this fact with some surprise as she came face to face with her at last. Elspeth Verey was above average height, and had retained a slender, if somewhat imposing, figure. Her skin was unlined, with something of the dewiness of youth yet about it, and her hair, though iron-grey and straight, was cut in a wedged bob that on anyone else of her age might have looked incongruous but somehow seemed just right, emphasising her strong, well-chiselled features. Her clothing, too, was a far cry from the twin-set-and-pearls look which Sophie had envisioned: she wore a loose white linen tunic, crisply pressed, over a pair of linen trousers striped in shades of blue and grey which perfectly complemented the grey of her hair and the ice blue of her eyes. Elspeth Verey had her own style, and was confident enough to carry it off with enormous success.

Priory House was dark with wood panelling, cool even in the heat of the day, and fragrant with flowers. Sophie noticed, as she followed her hostess through to the drawing room, that there were flowers everywhere. A bowl of deep pink roses, just on the verge of being overblown, filled the entrance hall with their pungent scent, and the drawing room contained several vases of mixed garden flowers, contributing a complex perfume. The arrangements were skilfully done: at first glance they seemed artless, as though the flowers had just been shoved into the vases, but Sophie could see that each bloom had been placed with care and with an eye for beauty, far surpassing the usual stiff and formal floral displays.

The drawing room was wonderful, Sophie perceived, taking in its details as her hostess went off to get a vase for her flowers. Gracious in proportion, it ran across the back of the house, yet its low ceilings and ancient linen-fold oak panelling contrived to give it a cosy feel. The sofa and chairs were oversized and soft, covered in a large-scale floral chintz in mellow shades of gold and yellow, and the heavy gold curtains, pulled back from the leaded windows, swept the floor. There was a sumptuous old oriental carpet, also in shades of gold, a set of french doors into the garden, a number of English watercolours on the walls, and a large fireplace, filled on this hot day with yet another vase of fresh flowers.

The surfaces of the dark oak furniture that were not covered with flowers contained photos in silver frames. With her professional interest in such things, Sophie couldn't resist looking at them. They included a mixture of formal portraits and informal snapshots, spanning what appeared to be a number of years. She tried to remember what Jeremy had told her about the Verey family: two sons, he'd said. Quite a large age gap between them. The photos seemed to bear that out, though the boys were quite alike at similar ages, both with a look of their mother.

Sophie started guiltily as Elspeth Verey re-entered the room, carrying the flowers. But Elspeth merely smiled. 'I see that you're looking at my family.'

'Yes. The photos are very . . . interesting,' said Sophie.

Elspeth shifted a vase on the mantelpiece to make room for the newcomers, indicating as she did so the large oil portrait which hung above the fireplace. 'My father,' she said, her voice reflecting satisfaction and pride. 'The Very Reverend Arthur Worthington. Painted when he was Dean of Westmead. It's a copy,' she added, 'of the portrait in the Deanery.'

Arthur Worthington, strong-featured and stern, dressed in his full canonical garb, stared down at Sophie. She wasn't sure what her response was meant to be. 'Very nice,' she said.

'My son is very like him,' Elspeth stated, handing Sophie a photo which seemed to have been taken when the boy was at school. There *was* a real likeness, even at that young age, Sophie acknowledged, though the boy had a delicacy about him that his grandfather lacked.

'His namesake,' Elspeth added. 'Worthington.' She searched among the photos and gave Sophie one that was clearly more recent: the boy was now grown to manhood, surrounded by a family of his own.

It was a formal portrait, taken in this room; Sophie could identify the linenfold panelling behind the family. Worthington Verey had matured into the resemblance to his grandfather, she could see on close examination of the photo: his face was harder than it had been in his youth, set and self-assured, verging on the pompous. Heavy horn-rimmed spectacles provided a certain gravitas, and he wore his clerical shirt with a dark suit that had obviously not come off the peg.

Sophie examined the photo with real interest, holding it far longer than mere politeness dictated, so after a moment Elspeth amplified. 'His wife, Heather. And their children – my grandchildren – Camilla, Chloe, and Richard. Named for his grandfather, my late husband.'

Heather looked as if she would have fitted in well with a certain set of women with whom Sophie had been familiar in London, well-heeled and complacent. Her clothes were expensive and her hair was fair, long and straight, held back from her face with a wide black velvet band. And her children were little carbon copies of her, varying only in their sizes. A perfect, beautiful, blond family.

'Camilla is nine,' Elspeth continued. 'Chloe is seven. And little Richard is five.'

Well spaced, Sophie thought, and the thought must have shown itself on her face; Elspeth went on with a wry laugh, 'Better spaced than my children – there's nearly twenty years between my two boys.'

There wasn't much to say to that which didn't verge on rudeness, so Sophie pretended that she hadn't already heard about it from Jeremy. 'You have another son, then?'

'Dominic.' Elspeth plucked another photo from the display and handed it to Sophie. 'This is his school photo from last year. He's sixteen now.'

He was a well-favoured boy, clear-skinned and clear-eyed, sporting the floppy hair so beloved of public school boys. Sophie recognised the school uniform – she had seen it on boys in the cathedral precincts during their earlier visit in the spring. 'He's at school here, then?'

'Yes, at Westmead Cathedral School.' Elspeth made a little deprecating face. 'He should have gone to Eton, of course. Like Worthington. But after his father died, he was all that I had left. I just couldn't bear to send him away.' As if feeling that she had revealed too much, she hurried on. 'He's done very well at Westmead. He got his GCSE results last week – thirteen As.'

'How splendid,' Sophie said heartily. A bright young man, then, with a brain as well as good looks.

A few minutes later she had an opportunity to meet him in the flesh. They were in the midst of tea – cucumber sandwiches, scones and cakes on a stand, and tea in delicate bone-china cups – when he popped his head in the door of the drawing room. 'Mummy,' he began, then stopped short. 'Oh, sorry. I didn't realise that you had company.'

'This is my son Dominic,' Elspeth said. 'Dominic, Mrs Lilburn. Her husband is the new history master and lay clerk.'

'How do you do?' the young man said politely, coming into the room. He was wearing tennis whites and carrying a racquet.

'How was your game, then?' his mother asked.

'We didn't play, actually. It was too hot.' He dropped the racquet on a chair near the door, crossed to his mother and gave her a peck on the cheek. Then he helped himself to a cucumber sandwich, eating it in one bite.

Elspeth frowned. 'Dominic! Manners!'

'Sorry, Mummy.' Chagrined, he took a plate and filled it with sandwiches while his mother poured him a cup of tea. 'I'm ravenous,' he confessed.

His mother's voice was tart. 'I can see that.' She added to Sophie, 'You'd think I never fed him. But he had a proper lunch, I can assure you.'

'That was *hours* ago.' Dominic sat down on the sofa, stretched his long legs in front of him, and gave Sophie an engaging, almost conspiratorial grin. 'And you know what they say about growing boys.'

'I'm sure that your brother never ate as much as you do,' Elspeth said, almost under her breath.

Sophie felt, rather than heard, the boy sigh.

'Your mother tells me that you got thirteen As in your GCSEs,' Sophie said. 'Well done.'

'And one B,' added Dominic. 'In biology.'

Elspeth looked pained. 'You just didn't work hard enough at it.'

'But I hate biology.'

Sophie sympathised with him. 'I hated it as well,' she confessed. 'And I didn't do nearly as well as a B. I just didn't get on with the sciences.'

The boy shot her a grateful look.

'It's a question of being well rounded,' stated Elspeth, directing her words at her son rather than at Sophie. 'And of working hard, no matter how much you dislike something.'

Sophie, her voice consciously bright, tried to deflect the subject. 'Will you be starting your A levels next term, then?'

'Yes, I—'

'English, history, religious studies and Latin,' his mother pronounced firmly.

'I want to do fine arts,' said Dominic.

Elspeth ignored him and addressed Sophie. 'Dominic is going to be a priest, like his brother. Like his father and his grandfathers and all of the generations of Worthingtons and Vereys stretching back through the centuries. He'll read theology at Oxford.'

'But I don't—'

'He's going to be a priest,' Elspeth repeated. With a graceful hand she lifted the Georgian silver teapot. 'Would you like more tea, Mrs Lilburn?'

'She was perfectly amiable,' Sophie said to Chris later, over supper. 'Very hospitable. But Jeremy was right about one thing – I certainly wouldn't want to cross her.' She described the conversation with Dominic.

'Sounds to me like the poor chap doesn't want to be a priest,' Chris analysed.

'I'm sure he doesn't. But I don't think he has much choice.' Thoughtfully Sophie speared some salad on her fork. 'I wonder,' she mused a moment later, after she'd eaten a bite, 'what would have happened if there'd been such a thing as women priests when Elspeth Verey was growing up.'

Chris grinned. 'She would probably be a bishop by now. If not the Archbishop of Canterbury.'

'But *would* she?' Sophie pursued the question seriously. 'Or is she the sort of woman who only finds meaning through the accomplishments of the men in her life?'

She was still thinking about Elspeth Verey a few hours later, lying in bed. Chris had again been persuaded – without much difficulty – to accompany Jeremy to the pub, so she'd taken a cool shower and crawled between the sheets, allowing her mind to reflect on the events and personalities of the day. Elspeth Verey, so very sure of herself, and the appealing young man who was her son. What *did* Dominic Verey want to do with his life? she wondered. And what were the odds of his doing anything other than becoming a priest, in view of his mother's strong feelings on the matter? Sophie found herself hoping that somehow he would get what he wanted, whatever it was.

Sleep eluded Sophie; she was still awake when Chris crept into the room, clearly trying not to wake her. The combination of alcohol and the still-unfamiliar arrangement of furniture meant that he was not very successful in keeping quiet as he blundered his way to the bed, but Sophie remained still, pretending to be asleep.

He peeled off his clothes and slipped into bed beside her. 'Soph?' he whispered with a blast of beery breath, stroking her shoulder.

She didn't move; her back was turned to him. After a moment she felt him relax, then heard his snores.

Still she couldn't sleep; Chris was throwing off heat,

and the room seemed unbearably hot and close, though the window was open.

And then the baby, two houses away, began to cry, rending the warm night air with its screams, as loud and distinct as if it were in the room with them. Sophie buried her head in the pillow and tried to ignore it, without much success. But when, some time later, weariness overcame her and she slept, her last thought was not of the crying baby, nor of Elspeth Verey, serenely presiding over the close, but of Leslie Clunch, baring yellow teeth as he looked at her legs.

Chapter 4

April 1989

The delectable waiter Dimitrios lasted for three nights. After that there was a succession of men, for one or two nights each, men Jacquie had met on the beach or in the hotel or at a taverna; she enjoyed them all, but was conscious of the time passing, of the necessity to experience as many different men as possible while she could. Alison was determinedly on the sidelines throughout these adventures, though she could easily have had men as well if she'd been so inclined; Jacquie's conquests often had a friend, several of whom tried it on with Alison, but to no effect.

The harder they tried, the more she clammed up and withdrew. This holiday was not turning out as she had expected, and she was miserable. The beach was fine; the scenery was beautiful. But the rest was a nightmare. There was no romance, only predatory men on the lookout for just one thing.

To Alison's further chagrin, Jacquie produced a camera – an inexpensive point-and-shoot – and insisted that her sister take snapshots of her with her various men, just so she'd have something to remember them by. 'But what if Darren ever saw them?' she agonised.

'He won't,' Jacquie said confidently. 'I'll make sure of that.'

Towards the middle of the second week, the sisters were sitting in the bar of the hotel before dinner, Alison sipping her orange juice while Jacquie knocked back the foul-tasting local wine. As always, Jacquie's eyes scanned the crowd for any new talent; she was promised that night to Anders, a delectable Swede with whom the lack of a common language had not proved much of a drawback, but Anders was returning home on the following day, and Jacquie was thinking ahead.

'English,' said Jacquie as a pair of young men came in. 'And they're new. Not bad,' she added appraisingly. 'Definitely not bad.'

With the radar that seemed to operate in these situations, it wasn't long before the men came to the girls' table. 'Hello,' said Jacquie, smiling up at them. 'Would you like to join us?'

'Delighted,' said one of the young men, and took the empty seat next to Jacquie. 'I'm Steve,' he added. 'And this is my friend Mike.' His accent was middle-class, educated – certainly a cut above the yobbish sort of British men whom they'd encountered before.

'Jacquie. And my sister Alison.'

Steve stated the obvious – something they'd heard often over the past days. 'You don't look like sisters.'

Jacquie simpered, as though this were the first time the observation had been made. 'No, I don't suppose we do.'

The conversation continued to follow the usual pattern. 'Can we buy you a drink?'

'That would be lovely,' said Jacquie.

After that, though, things improved. Steve turned out to have a well-developed sense of humour, or at any rate Jacquie seemed to find him screamingly funny. She laughed more than she had done in ages, and after a few minutes they were behaving like old friends.

Alison, as usual, felt like an observer, an outsider; by now she was used to watching Jacquie in action, while she fended off the unwelcome attentions of the chosen one's friend.

Except that in this case there weren't any attentions to fend off. Steve's friend Mike didn't say much; he seemed shy, as wary as Alison herself, content to let his friend have the limelight.

They were both good-looking, Alison observed, in an English sort of way. Steve perhaps had the edge, with his beautifully chiselled profile, but she found that she preferred Mike's shy smile. He had a slight gap between his front teeth which was rather endearing. And his eyes were a breathtaking shade of blue, behind metal-framed glasses. The glasses would have put Jacquie off, but Alison didn't mind; they gave him an air of trustworthiness which she found reassuring.

'May we join you for dinner?' Steve suggested, and Jacquie agreed with alacrity. They found a corner table in the dining room and spent the rest of the evening together, Jacquie laughing while Steve told funny stories.

After dinner they strolled round the village, the four-some breaking into two pairs as Jacquie took Steve's arm. At first Alison felt awkward about that, but Mike didn't try to touch her or seem to expect her to make scintillating conversation, and they walked side by side quite happily, saying little. She liked him, she discovered: she liked his gentleness, his diffidence. He was so different from the other men she'd met on this holiday, aggressive men who seemed to think that a smile was an invitation to much more.

'Your sister is very . . . outgoing,' said Mike.

'So is your friend.' They smiled at each other spontaneously, discovering a sudden bond.

'It was Steve's idea to come here,' Mike confided. 'Easter hols, you know. And it's our last year, so he thought we ought to get away and do something fun.'

'You're at university, then.'

'Yes.' He didn't elaborate.

'Jacquie wanted to come here as well. Or at least she wanted to go somewhere hot,' explained Alison. 'Mum and Dad weren't very keen, but they decided that Greece must be all right because it's in the Bible.'

Mike seemed to find this very funny. 'I think that my parents must have thought the same,' he said, grinning. 'They wouldn't normally encourage me to go abroad during the hols. And they don't really approve of Steve,' he added. 'But Greece . . . well.'

They discovered, then, that they'd lost the other two; somewhere along the way they'd melted into the shadows. 'We'd better go back to the hotel,' said Alison uneasily.

Other men might have taken advantage of the circumstances, but Mike remained courteous. 'Yes, if you like.'

He walked her all the way to the door of her room, and waited as she got out her key and opened the door. 'Thanks,' said Alison.

Mike smiled at her. 'Perhaps I'll see you tomorrow.'

'Probably.'

Still he lingered. 'I hope that I will.' Suddenly he took her hand and gave it a quick squeeze, then walked away.

She hoped so too, Alison discovered with astonishment as she shut the door behind him. She sat on her bed and looked at her hand; it still tingled from his touch.

Mike. She didn't even know his last name, or anything about him. But she knew that he was a gentleman, that she could trust him.

He wasn't like anyone she'd ever met before, in Sutton Fen or here in Greece.

He was the kind of man she'd always dreamed of, the kind of man with whom she could fall in love.

When Jacquie let herself into the room a bit later, Alison was still sitting on the bed, smiling to herself.

'Oh, you're here, then,' said Jacquie. 'I have to hurry – Anders will be wondering what's happened to me.'

'What *did* happen to you?'

Jacquie giggled. 'We found a quiet corner for a snog. Steve was quite disappointed when I told him that was all he was getting – for tonight, anyway.'

'He's nice,' said Alison dreamily.

'Steve? He's great. I haven't laughed so much in years.' She ran a comb through her hair and reapplied her lipstick, pursing her lips at herself in the mirror. 'And a brilliant kisser,' she added.

'His friend,' said Alison. 'Mike. I liked him.'

Jacquie turned from the mirror and looked at her sister with surprise. 'You did? He was a bit quiet for my taste. And a bit too studious-looking. Those glasses.'

'He's nice,' Alison repeated.

'Well, then, go for it!' Jacquie grinned. 'You could have him if you wanted him, you know.'

Alison averted her eyes. 'It's not like that.' Her voice was quiet but intense. 'You just don't understand, Jacquie. You don't understand at all.'

They didn't see Mike and Steve at breakfast the next morning. Alison found that she was watching the dining-room door, and sighing with disappointment when each new arrival turned out to be someone else.

This didn't escape Jacquie, who was also on the lookout for her latest conquest. 'You *do* fancy him!' she said triumphantly. 'You can't deny it, Ally.'

Alison admitted nothing. But that afternoon, on the beach, she scanned the crowds from behind the protection of her sunglasses, and together she and Jacquie selected a position from which they could see and be seen.

'There they are!' announced her sister eventually. 'And they're coming this way.'

The men made straight for them. 'We've been looking for you,' said Steve.

Jacquie patted the towel on which she was sitting and scooted over a few inches. 'And I was just wishing for some help with my suntan lotion.'

'My speciality!' He threw himself down on the fragment of towel, very close to Jacquie, his eyes alight with appreciation as he took the bottle from her and stroked the lotion on to her shoulders and back.

Embarrassed, Alison looked away. Mike was still standing in front of her, but she didn't dare to raise her eyes to him. 'May I sit down?' he asked courteously.

'Oh, yes. Of course.' How gauche she must appear to him, she thought. How unsophisticated. Nothing at all like the girls he must know at university. Alison bit her lip in frustration.

Mike spread his own towel out beside her and sat down. 'It's nice to see you again,' he said with seeming sincerity. Alison felt herself blushing.

'How is the sea today?' Steve asked.

Jacquie grinned at him. 'We haven't been in yet.'

'Then there's only one way to find out.' With no warning, he stood, picked her up, carried her down to the sea, and threw her in. Jacquie shrieked, and as she emerged she splashed water at him and pulled him in after her.

'Steve loves to swim,' said Mike. 'He's a very good swimmer. It's one reason he wanted to come here – for the beach.'

'And you?' asked Alison, eyes downcast.

'I don't swim,' he admitted. 'Or at least I don't swim very well. I can't say that I enjoy it. I'd much rather go and look at the ruins, to be honest.'

She looked up eagerly, forgetting to be shy. 'So would I!'

'Well, then.' He smiled at her. 'How about tomorrow? We could get an early start, after breakfast. Hire some bicycles, and go out to the ruins. Do you cycle?'

'Oh, yes!'

'That's what we'll do, then.' He gave her a mischievous look. 'Without the other two, perhaps?'

Alison, delighted with the suggestion, tried to be tactful. 'I don't think that Jacquie is very interested in ruins.'

He laughed. 'No, I don't suppose she is. And Steve knows that he ought to be, but he's more interested in Jacquie.'

*   *   *

It was a perfect afternoon, and by the time the girls were dressing for dinner, Alison knew that it was going to be a perfect evening as well.

She had, by then, abandoned her Laura Ashley frock; it was far too hot, for one thing, and looked completely out of place outside of its natural environs of the English countryside. Jacquie, true to her word, had taken her sister shopping for a more suitable dress, and though she hadn't been successful in talking her into something provocative and brief, they had chosen an attractive strappy sun-dress that showed off Alison's new tan and her blonde prettiness.

That was the dress she chose to put on before joining the men for dinner. 'Let me help you with some make-up,' Jacquie offered.

Alison didn't usually wear make-up; their mother didn't approve of face-painting, and with her fresh, fair complexion she didn't really need it. But the tan seemed to require a touch of compensatory colour, so for once she agreed. Jacquie used a light hand to apply a touch of blusher to her cheeks and a subtle but shiny shade of lipstick.

She knew she'd made the right decision when she saw the look of admiration in Mike's eyes. 'Nice dress,' he said.

It was, in many ways, a repeat of the previous evening: Steve was on good form, joking and chatting, and Jacquie responded in kind. Mike and Alison were once again quiet. But there was a different quality to their stillness that night, an awareness of each other that had not been there before. They didn't touch; they scarcely looked at each other. Yet both of them knew that there was something there between them in the silence.

When they'd finished eating, and drunk their coffee, Jacquie and Steve disappeared. 'Have fun, kiddies,' Jacquie said coyly as she took Steve's hand and led him away.

After a moment of embarrassment, Alison looked up to find Mike smiling at her. 'Well,' he said. 'I suppose you're stuck with me. Do you mind?'

'Of course not.'

They agreed to take a walk, as they had the previous evening. Again, though, something was different. The air seemed balmier, the stars brighter. They walked for a long time, making several circuits of the village, and after a while Mike took her hand.

There was no question of resisting, of snatching her hand away. There was something inevitable about the gesture, and something very natural.

'Shall we stop and have a drink?' he said eventually.

Alison could have walked for ever, but by this point she would have agreed to almost any suggestion Mike made. 'Yes, all right.'

They found a little taverna, dark and intimate, and sat down at a table illuminated by a flickering candle. 'Wine, I think,' said Mike. 'A nice bottle of wine is just what we need.' He picked up the wine list and scanned it with an expert eye, missing the momentary panic on Alison's face.

Wine! Whatever would Reverend Prew say? They used Ribena for communion at the Free Baptist Fellowship to avoid being polluted by the Devil's drink.

'My father has a good cellar, so he's taught me a thing or two about wine,' Mike said modestly. 'Most of the stuff on this wine list is rubbish, of course, but there's one claret that should at least be drinkable. What do you think?'

'Yes, that's fine,' she heard herself saying.

He ordered the wine, and while they waited for it to arrive, Mike fiddled with a paper napkin. 'Listen, Alison,' he said. 'I want to make sure to get your address in England, while I'm thinking about it. Would you write it down for me? If you don't think that's being too cheeky,' he added, with an uncertain smile that made her catch her breath.

'Of course.' After a moment's search she found a pen in her handbag, then printed the address on her own napkin in her neat, small hand and passed it across to him.

'Thanks.' He folded it up and tucked it into his wallet.

The bottle of wine came, and Mike went through the ceremony of tasting it. 'Yes, that will do,' he said, then filled Alison's glass.

She was committed; it was too late now to refuse it.

Mike filled his own glass and clinked it against hers. 'To . . . well, to us, I suppose.' His eyes met hers across the table, and she didn't look away.

Alison lifted the glass to her lips and took a sip, no longer thinking of Mr Prew or the Free Baptist Fellowship. The taste of the wine wasn't what she'd expected: it didn't have the sickly sweetness of Ribena, and it tingled on her tongue in a pleasant way. It was delicious; when she swallowed, it warmed her all the way down her throat. 'Mm,' she said. 'Lovely.'

'I'm glad you like it.'

After the first glass, Alison found herself telling him about her life in Sutton Fen. She talked about her parents, about Mr Prew and the Free Baptist Fellowship, about her job and her leisure time. As he gazed across the table into her eyes, looking at her as though she were the most fascinating creature imaginable, she talked on and on without self-consciousness.

He held her hand across the table; before long the bottle of wine was empty. 'We'll have another,' Mike decided.

Alison didn't mind. The wine was delicious, and she didn't want the evening to end.

Sometime during the second bottle of wine, time ceased to have any meaning. It might have been minutes, it might have been hours. They talked a great deal, but said very little. As the taverna cleared out and the waiters began extinguishing the candles on the empty tables in preparation for shutting up for the night, Mike said that perhaps they ought to get back to the hotel.

Alison stood up. She felt disassociated from her body, as though she were somewhere outside herself, watching what was happening yet not really there.

He took her arm and guided her into the street. The strange creature who was-but-wasn't-Alison leaned against him, feeling the warmth of his body, allowing him to lead her along.

'I have a confession to make,' she heard herself saying. 'I've never had wine before. Reverend Prew doesn't approve of wine – he calls it the Devil's drink.'

Mike laughed. 'I don't know how he figures that. Didn't Our Lord Himself drink wine? Didn't he turn water into wine at the wedding feast in Cana?'

Alison didn't have an answer for that, even if she'd been feeling able to deliver one. The idea that Reverend Prew might be mistaken about something in the Bible was a new one, scarcely to be considered.

Somehow they were back at the hotel; she wasn't sure how they'd got there. 'I'll see you to your room,' Mike said.

Alison fumbled in her handbag for her key, then found

that the lock was eluding her. Every time she stabbed the key in its direction, it seemed to shift position. Mike took the key from her hand and opened the door for her.

The room was empty: no sign of Jacquie.

Mike stepped inside with her, shutting the door behind them. Alison leaned back against the door; she needed its solidity to anchor her back to earth.

He moved close to her, so close that she could feel his warm breath on her cheek, and looked deeply into her eyes. 'Listen, Alison,' he said. 'I think I'm falling in love with you.'

It was like a dream, like a fairy-tale come true. He was the man she'd been looking for all of her life. 'I love you,' she whispered.

He leaned closer and their lips met. Alison felt a curious liquifying sensation in her lower body, unexpected and irresistible, as if she were melting like a candle in a hot flame.

When Alison woke, the room was flooded with morning sun. The waking was gradual, as though she were deep under water, struggling upwards towards the light and the air. At first she didn't even know where she was. All she knew was that her head hurt with an indescribable pain: blinding, throbbing, pounding.

Mike, she thought, the name flashing through her agony like a shaft of light, and with the name came a sudden remembrance, like a dream recalled at first waking.

What *had* happened last night? She pressed her eyes shut and tried to remember. Fragmentary images of strange and delicious sensations eluded her. Hands, mouths, flesh against flesh. Could it all have been a dream?

No, those things were beyond her experience, and thus beyond her imaginings. It must have happened. *Really* happened.

Fighting the pain in her head, Alison opened her eyes. She was alone in the bed, though there was a definite imprint of a head on the other pillow. Then she realised that she wasn't wearing her nightgown, and her clothes were strewn about the room rather than folded neatly on the chair.

The other bed was occupied; lifting her head a fraction – and regretting it instantly – Alison could just see her sister's dark head on the pillow. She groaned with the effort and closed her eyes again.

But the groan was enough to wake Jacquie, who sat up in bed with a grin. 'What happened *here* last night, then?' she demanded, looking significantly at the discarded clothing.

Alison buried her head in her pillow. 'My head hurts,' she moaned.

'You had it off with him, didn't you?' She couldn't resist adding, with satisfaction and a touch of malice, 'Little Miss Goody-goody is no better than she should be, after all.'

Alison mustered her defences. 'It's not like that,' she stated. 'We love each other. Mike loves me.'

'Yeah, yeah.' Jacquie giggled. 'That's what they always say, when they're trying to get your knickers off.'

How could her sister make it sound so crude? There had been nothing crude about it. It had been romantic, beautiful. Still, even in her distress, Alison retained her characteristic modesty, and pulled the sheet round her bare shoulders. 'My nightgown. Could you get it for me?'

Jacquie slid out of bed and found Alison's nightgown,

folded in a drawer. She was delighted. To give Ally her due, she wasn't the sort of younger sister who went tattling or carrying tales to their parents, but she *did* have a tender conscience, and she knew far too much about what Jacquie had been up to on this holiday. It was the one flaw in Jacquie's plans, and it had worried her. Who knew when her sister might blurt something out to their parents, to Reverend Prew, or even to Darren? But now she wouldn't dare; now Jacquie had just as much on Alison as Ally had on her. Now it was a level playing field, and they *both* had to keep their mouths shut to protect one another. Perfect.

She tossed the nightgown in the direction of her sister's bed and glanced at the alarm clock. 'We're going to miss breakfast if we don't go down soon.'

Breakfast. Alison's stomach lurched; she gulped, fighting back nausea. 'I can't,' she said faintly. 'I . . . can't.'

Her sister stood over her, grinning. 'You've been drinking as well? Oh, Ally! You really *have* fallen from grace.'

Alison turned her face into her pillow. She wanted to die.

The rest of the morning passed in a haze of pain. Jacquie forced her sister to take some paracetamol, which helped, but the thing that made the real difference to Alison was the recollection of the plans that had been made for the day. She and Mike were going to go out to the ruins – he had said so yesterday, in the distant past, before so many other things had happened. But they *would* do it. She had to pull herself together. Otherwise she would miss out on the ruins, miss out on seeing Mike. And he would know that she was a hopeless wimp, a sad case who let a few glasses of wine get to her like this.

Jacquie had been an angel of mercy; she'd given her the paracetamol, had bathed her face with a damp cloth, had sat with her and held her hand, not passing judgement or allowing her triumph to show. She was still there when Alison decided that it was time to get up.

'Mike,' Alison said, struggling to a sitting position. 'Has he been looking for me? We're supposed to cycle out to the ruins today.'

'No. He hasn't been here.'

'Did you see him at breakfast? With Steve?'

Jacquie giggled. 'No. In fact, I was trying to avoid them.'

'But Steve . . . I thought . . .'

'Steve was a big disappointment,' Jacquie admitted. 'Not exactly a disaster, but he didn't really have a clue, once we got past the snogging.'

'But Mike *must* be wondering where I am,' said Alison. 'We had an arrangement. Are you *sure* he hasn't been looking for me?'

Jacquie forbore from saying what anyone less naïve than her sister might have suspected: that, having got what he wanted from her, Mike wouldn't be seen again.

'Maybe he's left a note at the desk, or something,' Alison insisted. 'Maybe *he's* not feeling well either.'

'I'll check, shall I?' her sister offered.

A few minutes later, Jacquie returned to their room proffering a sealed envelope. 'You were right,' she said. 'This was left for you at the desk.'

Some rare impulse of delicacy prompted her to turn away, to allow her sister some privacy while she read what

Jacquie was sure would be a brush-off note: thanks for the memories and all that, but . . .

Alison gave a low cry; the note fluttered from her hand. 'He's gone,' she moaned, flopping back on to the bed and burying her face in her pillow.

Jacquie retrieved the note and scanned the few lines rapidly. 'My dear Alison,' it said. 'I write this in haste, as I have a plane to catch. I've just received word that my father has been taken gravely ill, and I must return home to Westmead at once. There is no time to see you, to tell you what last night meant to me. But I have your address, and will be in touch. We shall meet again. With all my love, Mike.'

'Well,' said Jacquie with a wry grin. 'It's an original brush-off note. I'll give him that.'

Chapter 5

Chris soon settled into his new jobs of teaching and singing in the cathedral choir. He enjoyed both enormously, and though there was always marking and lesson preparation to be done, he also fell into the pattern of going to the pub with the other lay clerks after Evensong on most evenings.

Usually Chris asked Sophie whether she minded, and sometimes issued a lukewarm invitation to join them. One evening, early on, Sophie decided to accept his invitation, and see what it was all about.

The pub where they gathered was a high-class establishment, she realised immediately – no spit-and-sawdust-type hostelry this. Located near the cathedral, the Tower of London – for so it was called – seemed to have absorbed something of its ambiance. Although the noise level wasn't particularly low, it was the sound of people having a good time rather than the artificial blare of piped-in muzak or the high-pitched clangour of computerised arcade games. And the clientele were of a genteel sort, merry rather than raucous with drink.

Sophie had scarcely met the other lay clerks; she had no interest in going to Evensong, and the opportunities for socialising seemed limited to these pub visits. They accepted her presence among them that evening with civility, if not warmth, and as they stood about chatting she found their conversation incomprehensible: they spoke their own language, wrapped up in things about which the average person knew nothing and cared even less. After a few moments, she took her drink to an empty table and simply observed them.

To her amazement, Chris seemed to be totally integrated into the group, accepted by them and privy to all of the in-jokes and arcane terminology. 'Can't you count?' he said with a grin to a tall, spotty youth who had been introduced to Sophie as a counter-tenor. 'Or maybe you had a different edition. I could have sworn that my copy had three crotchets instead of two.'

The youth laughed immoderately, shaking his head. 'A different edition. That's my excuse, and I'm sticking to it.'

Jeremy Hammond slid into the seat across from Sophie. 'This must be a bit boring for you,' he said with an apologetic shrug.

She smiled brightly without making eye contact. 'Not at all.'

'Liar.'

Startled, she looked at him: his lips were pursed, and his eyebrows quirked. Sophie laughed. 'All right, then,' she admitted. 'I'm a bit out of my depth.'

'Music, music, music,' he whispered melodramatically. 'That's all they're interested in. And as the person who is responsible for getting good music out of them,' he added, 'I really mustn't complain. But personally speaking, I find *people* more interesting than music.'

She gave him a grateful smile. 'Faces,' said Sophie. 'I like to look at faces.' That reminded her of a face that she hadn't seen since they'd moved to Westmead. 'Canon Swan,' she said. 'Doesn't he come to the pub?'

If he thought her question odd or irrelevant, Jeremy didn't reveal it. 'Only rarely. As I said to you before, he's a bit of an old sourpuss. Keeps himself to himself, mostly. And as a matter of fact, he's away on holiday at the moment. A damned awkward time for it, at the beginning of term, but he said he was going away and that was that.'

Sophie tried to imagine Canon Swan sitting on some tropical beach, sipping pina coladas or margaritas, but she couldn't quite manage it. A genteel English seaside resort was far more likely, or perhaps a solitary perambulation round the churches of Florence or Siena, or even a pilgrimage to Compostela.

Jeremy seemed to read her thoughts; he grinned at her across the table. 'White-water rafting, perhaps?' he speculated. 'Pony-trekking in the Himalayas? I think not.'

'How about the Australian outback?' Sophie went on. 'Or the Great Wall of China?'

'The Bolivian rain forest,' Jeremy suggested. 'Deep-sea diving? Whale spotting? Hunting for big game?'

Sophie giggled. 'How about something sporty? Parasailing or bungee jumping or hang-gliding? Or at the other end of the spectrum, drinking tea in Scarborough or Southwold or even Skegness?'

'That sounds far more likely. Though perhaps not Skegness.' He lifted a fastidious eyebrow and drained his pint.

She appreciated his efforts at putting her at ease; a

moment later he looked across at her empty glass. 'Another of the same?'

'White wine. Thanks.' Perhaps, thought Sophie, it was just an excuse to escape from her, and he would find a convenient distraction to prevent him from coming back. But a moment later he returned to the table, balancing her wine and his beer.

'How are you settling in, then?' he asked, with a shrewd glance at her over the top of his glass. 'Is Westmead what you'd expected?'

'It's not London,' she said frankly, without thinking.

'Obviously not.' Jeremy put his glass back down on the table in a deliberate way. 'But do give it a chance, Sophie.' It was the first time he had called her by her Christian name, and she was unexpectedly moved by that. She wished that she could tell him everything.

She wanted to tell him that she hadn't even begun to sort herself out professionally, that she'd scarcely had her camera out of its bag. She wanted to tell him of the strangeness of living in a place like Westmead, like Quire Close: the quiet, the closed-in-ness of it all, the feeling that life was being lived at half-speed, that somehow things had shifted into slow motion, like wading through treacle. And there was the all-pervasiveness of the cathedral, which dominated the lives and thoughts of the people here as its bulk dominated the landscape. The cathedral was like the sun in its own little universe, with everyone and everything orbiting round it; no matter how far they were from its centre, they were subject to its gravitational pull, and governed by it in so many subtle ways. There was no escaping the cathedral: it lurked in the background of every conversation, always visible just out of the corner of one's eye.

Sophie had started out feeling indifference towards the cathedral, tinged with unease.

Now she hated it. But she couldn't very well say so to Jeremy Hammond, or to anyone else.

The invitation to tea at Priory House had not been repeated. It was as if, Sophie told herself, she had been summoned to be vetted, and had been rejected as unsuitable. She didn't fit into the cosy community of Quire Close, and Elspeth Verey had known that immediately, had seen it as clearly as Sophie herself did.

Sophie didn't care, or so she told herself. Being accepted into the highest echelons of Westmead society was not her priority, was in fact a matter of supreme indifference to her.

But she had not, it seemed, been found wanting by Leslie Clunch. He called upon her regularly, every day or two, dropping in just as she was putting the kettle on for a morning cup of coffee or an afternoon cup of tea. And whenever she left the close, going into the town to do some shopping or run some errand – which she did often in those first weeks – she always looked up towards the first-floor window of Number 1, where the retired verger kept vigil over the close. Always he raised a solemn hand to her, in acknowledgement. When she returned he would do the same, and often within a few minutes he would be at her door. Just checking to make sure that she was all right, he would say, and Sophie would feel compelled to invite him in for a cup of something and a chat.

He never refused.

Never again did he speak about his dead daughter; his conversation revolved mostly round the cathedral. But the main fodder for his discourse was not, as Jeremy Hammond's was, larded with bits of juicy gossip or interesting things about people, known to Sophie or not. That she might have tolerated. Instead Leslie Clunch seemed to enjoy living on his own past glories, telling her about his job as Head Verger, recounting little incidents that either amused him or pointed up his own importance in the scheme of things. Sophie became adept at seeming to listen while her thoughts were elsewhere, far away from the precincts of Westmead Cathedral.

'I don't care!' she wanted to shout at him. 'I'm not interested!' Instead she learned to smile and nod, to offer another cup of tea.

It wasn't like her, she sometimes told herself, to suffer fools gladly. Why didn't she just tell him to shove off? Or why couldn't she just refuse to answer the door when he rang the bell? Somehow she couldn't bring herself to do either.

She did wonder about his wife – the long-suffering Mrs Clunch, as Sophie had come to think of her. He spoke about her sometimes, always in the context of his own martyrdom to her needs. Completely housebound she was, and he looked after her with devotion. What sort of woman was she? Married to a pompous bore, her only child dead . . .

Unexpectedly, Sophie was given the opportunity to find out. 'Mrs Clunch would like to meet you,' he told her solemnly one day. 'She wondered whether you might come and have a cup of tea with her. With *us*.'

Sophie agreed, and a date was fixed within the week.

Before that date arrived, though, something else possessed Sophie's thoughts to the exclusion of all else.

She thought that she might be pregnant.

* * *

Always conscious – especially in the past year – of her monthly cycles, Sophie one day realised that her expected period had not begun. No pain, no cramps, none of the heaviness or the ache in her lower back that inevitably heralded the dreaded day. Did she feel different? she asked herself. She'd always believed that when it happened – when she became pregnant – she would *know*, that by some mysterious process she would be instantly aware of the tiny cluster of cells which had become implanted in her womb and which would, by a miraculous process, grow into a baby.

There was none of that certainty, but neither was there any sign of her period. One day went by, then two more. She said nothing to Chris, who was in any case much absorbed with his job and didn't seem to notice her distraction or her growing excitement.

On the fourth day, the day she was to have tea with the Clunches, she received a letter in the morning post: it heralded her long-awaited appointment with Mr York, the fertility specialist. She was to present herself at his London surgery in a fortnight, for the beginning of the process of tests and diagnosis. 'If for any reason you cannot keep this appointment . . .'

Sophie read the letter with a smile, her hand curved protectively over her flat abdomen. Perhaps she would not *need* to keep the appointment; perhaps she could ring the office and cancel it, announcing proudly that she was pregnant, with no help from them. Her body had after all done what it was meant to do. She was *not* useless, barren.

She felt energetic, alive. In the morning she strode through the close into the town, almost unaware of the vast bulk of the cathedral as she passed it. It faded into the background of her consciousness, dwarfed by the enormity of what might – what *must* – be happening inside of her. A baby!

She would buy a pregnancy testing kit. But at the entrance to Boots, she was distracted from her single-minded impetus by an obstruction, a woman wrestling the door open while trying to manoeuvre a pushchair.

Ordinarily such a thing would have annoyed her, but Sophie was feeling magnanimous. 'Let me help,' she offered, holding the door.

'Thanks.' The woman smiled her gratitude, then did a double take as she looked at Sophie more closely. 'Don't you live in Quire Close?'

'That's right. Number 22.'

'We're neighbours, then. I'm on the other side, and down a bit – Number 17.' Belatedly she introduced herself. 'I'm Trish Evans. My husband sings in the choir. And this,' she added, 'is Katie.'

Sophie leaned over the pushchair and smiled at Katie, a scowling toddler who regarded her with suspicion. 'I'm Sophie Lilburn,' she said.

'I thought that you must be,' admitted Trish. 'Brian – my husband – does occasionally fill me in on the choir gossip, and he's mentioned Chris Lilburn, the new tenor.'

Sophie had a vague recollection of having heard of Brian Evans from Chris – a bass, she thought, though she hadn't made much effort to sort out the lay clerks in her mind. She tried to remember whether she'd met him at the pub, but drew a blank.

'I should have called round to see you when you moved in,' Trish went on guiltily. 'We choir wives – or choir widows, as I sometimes think of us – need to stick together. But I was too sick to think of anything else all summer. And I was hardly out of the house. It's better now,' she added. 'I'm over the worst of it.' She patted her stomach, and Sophie realised that she was perhaps four months pregnant.

'Oh – you're having another baby.'

'In the new year,' Trish confirmed with a proud grin. 'A brother for Katie.'

'I don't want a brother,' the toddler announced belligerently.

Her mother ignored her. 'You don't have children, do you?'

'Not yet.'

'Oh, you've plenty of time,' said the woman, secure in the blithe confidence of one who conceived without difficulty.

She was, Sophie observed, very young: at least several years younger than she herself, perhaps not yet twenty-five. There was something not quite grown-up about her face, with its soft, rounded contours and its open – almost naïve – smile.

They were blocking the entrance to Boots. An elderly woman, bent almost double over a Zimmer frame, lifted her head to glare at them.

'Oh, excuse us!' Trish steered the pushchair to the side and Sophie followed; she might have escaped at that point, but she was sufficiently intrigued by her neighbour to want to know more about her. Already she had a feeling that Trish was perhaps not on her wavelength; it was too soon, though, to make those sorts of judgements, and Trish was, after all, the first woman she'd met in

Westmead who was, even remotely, of her own genera-
tion.

'Let's have a coffee,' Trish suggested impulsively.
'There's that nice new coffee bar just round the corner.
Do you know it?'

'No, I've not been there.' Sophie allowed herself to be
led out of Boots and into what seemed, in Westmead, like
something that had been plopped down from another
planet: a sleek American-style coffee bar, serving latte and
mocha and espresso, every conceivable variation on a
theme. Such places had already become commonplace in
London, but Sophie had not expected one of them to have
reached the outpost of civilisation that was Westmead. She
was delighted, and ordered a large caffe latte in celebration.

Her companion was less confident. 'I'll just have an
ordinary coffee, I think. Or . . . wait a minute. Maybe a
cappuccino.'

'A bun!' The child in the pushchair had spotted the up-
market Danish pastries in the display case. 'I want a bun!'

'Not now, darling. When we get home you can have
something.'

'But I want a bun!' Katie scrunched her face up and
prepared to bellow her disapproval at being thwarted.

Recognising the signs, her mother capitulated and
ordered a pastry.

Sophie found a table and they sat down, though that
was not a simple procedure, as Katie insisted on getting
out of her pushchair and clambering on to a chair.

'I hate currants,' she announced with a baleful look at
her mother, and proceeded to pick the currants off the
top of her pastry and strew them on the table.

'You'll have to come to one of our get-togethers,' Trish said to Sophie. 'There's a little group of us who meet up on Friday mornings. Choir wives, mostly, and a few other women who are somehow attached to the cathedral through their husbands. We take turns having it.'

'That would be very . . . pleasant,' said Sophie, not at all sure that it would be. But Westmead was her home now, and for better or for worse, these people were her potential friends; she could scarcely afford to scorn their company.

Trish sipped her cappuccino. 'This is good. But it will probably give me heartburn,' she added, making a little face. 'Coffee does that to me, at the moment.' She patted the slight bulge of her abdomen with a complacent smile.

Katie had by now made a complete mess on her side of the table; the pastry had not proved to be as sweet as it looked, and she signalled her disapproval by dismembering it and turning it into crumbs. 'I need to go to the loo,' she announced. 'Mummy, I need to go.'

'Can't you wait just a minute till Mummy's finished with her coffee?'

'I need to go *now*. Now, Mummy.'

Trish sighed and rolled her eyes in Sophie's direction. 'She's almost trained,' she explained. 'It's been a long struggle, but we're nearly there. So I'd better take her.'

Even this temporary delay was proving vexatious. '*Now!*' the child bellowed.

'Excuse me,' apologised Trish. 'We'll be back in a minute.'

Sipping her latte, Sophie contemplated the sticky wreck of the Danish pastry. *Her* child, she was determined, would not behave like that. She would be the perfect mother, and Chris would be a marvellous father. Together they would raise a child who was well-mannered and secure. One child, or two, or as many as Chris wanted. Sophie smiled to herself, a secret sort of smile as she looked forward into the future. Perhaps Westmead wasn't so bad after all, she told herself. There would be babies. There would be companionship, of a sort – possibly friendship, with Trish Evans or some of the other choir wives. And she could even get a decent caffe latte.

Sophie didn't realise until she was home that she hadn't after all bought the pregnancy testing kit. Should she go back into town for it? she debated. But to her surprise, her high energy level had dissipated and she now felt tired, unable to summon up the energy to go out again.

She never took naps during the day; it just wasn't part of her lifestyle or her make-up. For a few minutes Sophie fought the urge to lie down, then gave in to it and went upstairs to stretch out on the bed. All part of being pregnant, she told herself – it was natural to feel exhausted, and she mustn't try to fight it.

When she woke, disorientated, several hours had passed. She reached for the clock, and realised that she was due at the Clunches' in just ten minutes.

'Oh, Lord,' she moaned. No time for a shower, then, or even to change her clothes. Sophie dragged herself into the bathroom, splashed some cold water on her face at the basin, and ran a comb through her hair. That would have to do; instinctively she knew that it would not be a good idea to be late.

Leslie Clunch answered the door seconds after she'd rung the bell. He'd been watching for her, then, Sophie said to herself. 'Come in, come in,' he urged, stepping aside to allow her into the hallway.

This house was, she saw, by far the smallest she'd been into in the close, smaller than Jeremy Hammond's or even her own. The ceilings were lower, and the entrance hall was scarcely big enough to accommodate two people.

'My wife is through here,' Clunch said as he led Sophie into the front room.

She had presumed that it would be a sitting room, and once it might have been. But now, Sophie saw, it had been converted into an invalid's bedroom. A hospital bed dominated the tiny room; round it crowded an impossible amount of furniture: chairs, a wardrobe, a dressing table, a bedside table strewn with bottles of medicines and the other accoutrements of chronic illness.

Mrs Clunch was sitting in one of the chairs, but made no attempt to get up as Sophie entered with Leslie Clunch.

Sophie wasn't sure what she had expected Leslie Clunch's wife to be like. Someone a bit wispy and frail, perhaps, and small of stature like he was. Olive Clunch – for so her husband introduced her – was neither wispy nor frail. She was enormously fat, her face like a steamed suet pudding with currants for eyes, her legs like the pillars of a Romanesque cathedral. Those legs were stretched out on a footstool in front of her, swollen and discoloured, and were evidently at least a partial source of her disability.

Olive Clunch must have noticed Sophie looking at her legs. 'Gout,' she stated. 'Among other things. Dropsy, varicose veins. Bad knees.'

Sophie didn't know what to say. 'I'm sorry,' she murmured.

'There's nothing for *you* to be sorry about,' Mrs Clunch

said matter-of-factly. 'Can't be helped. You'd just better hope that you never have to live with anything like this. You, with your nice long slim legs.'

It was said without envy, yet Sophie couldn't help feeling guilty. Awkwardly she sat down in the chair which Mrs Clunch indicated with a gesture. The chair was soft and low; Sophie could tell that it would be difficult to get out of with any degree of dignity.

'We'll have some tea now.' The words were addressed not to Sophie but to her husband.

'Yes, dear. It won't be a moment.' He left the room.

Mrs Clunch scrutinised Sophie, her fat lips pursed. 'I've heard so much about you from Leslie,' she said. 'I wanted to see you for myself.'

Unsure how to respond, Sophie dipped her head in acknowledgement.

'He said that you were like our Charmian.'

'And am I?'

In place of a verbal reply, Mrs Clunch reached for a framed photo on the table next to her and stretched her arm out towards Sophie, who then had to struggle halfway out of the chair to reach it.

The girl in the photo was in her teens – probably no more than sixteen, Sophie guessed. She wasn't a particularly beautiful girl, but certainly she was more attractive than one might have expected, with two such unprepossessing parents: she had a nice smile, and natural blonde hair, of a colour just slightly lighter than Sophie's. Charmian Clunch had been, Sophie saw, just a bit overweight, and that fact more than anything else made her heart go out to the girl.

She, too, had fought her weight as a teenager. She'd

endured the taunts of her schoolmates, had tried to slim down but found that she lacked the will-power to give up the foods she enjoyed. No boyfriends, and a cycle of despair, disgust, self-hatred and overeating that was self-perpetuating.

Then, at university, she'd met Chris. He had seen past the excess weight, had loved her for herself. And paradoxically that had given her the necessary will-power to lose those pounds, the confidence in herself and her own attractiveness to keep them off. She had never looked back.

But poor Charmian Clunch, she thought, studying the photo. She wasn't sure what she was expected to say. More than anything, she wanted to ask the girl's mother about what had happened to her. When had she died? How old had she been? Was it a natural death – a disease, perhaps – or had she died violently, the victim of some horrible accident? But Sophie didn't dare to frame the question; if Olive Clunch wanted to tell her, she surely would.

'Her dad's little girl,' said Mrs Clunch in a reflective voice. 'The light of our lives. You *are* a bit like her, I think. He was right about that.' She narrowed her eyes and scrutinised Sophie even more closely. 'How old are you?'

Embarrassed, Sophie replied, 'Thirty-one.'

Mrs Clunch nodded. 'Charmian would have been thirty this year. Just imagine that.'

Still Sophie didn't dare to ask the question that hung between them.

'We might have had grandchildren.'

That was a topic that Sophie didn't want to embark upon. Hurriedly she put the photo down on the nearest table and changed the subject to the first thing that came into her head. 'How long have you been in Westmead, Mrs Clunch?'

'Oh, years. Of course we've only been in this house for two years, since Leslie retired. Before that we were in the Head Verger's house, the other side of the cathedral.'

Sophie tried to think of something nice to say about the house, but nothing suggested itself to her, so she said the next-best thing, in a self-consciously bright voice. 'Quire Close is lovely, isn't it?'

Olive Clunch narrowed her eyes. 'I hate it.'

Startled, Sophie blurted, 'You *do*?'

'It's like a prison. A maximum-security prison. No escape, not even for good behaviour.' Her voice was bitter.

At that point Leslie Clunch re-entered the room, carrying a laden tray, and his wife quickly rearranged her face in a smile. 'Oh, that's lovely.'

The next few minutes were taken up with the business of pouring tea. Leslie Clunch offered Sophie a plate of little cakes, iced in improbable colours of pink and yellow, and she took one for the sake of politeness, putting it on the flowered bone-china plate he'd given her and wondering how she might get rid of it without either of the Clunches noticing.

They'd clearly gone all out for her, with the best dishes and the little cakes. Sophie was touched by that, and slightly unsettled.

'I think I'd like some bread-and-butter,' said Mrs Clunch.

Her husband turned to her, surprised. 'Bread-and-butter? But you said . . .'

'I'd like some bread-and-butter.' Her tone brooked no argument. 'Thin slices, mind.'

He sighed. 'Yes, dear.' Deliberately he put his cup back in its saucer and set it on the table, then rose and left the room.

Mrs Clunch leaned towards Sophie and continued where she'd left off. 'A prison,' she repeated. 'And I hate this house. I'd give anything to leave here.'

'Where would you like to go, then?' Sophie asked.

'The sea.' Olive Clunch turned her face towards the front window; miles away, far to the west, was the sea. 'I've always wanted to live by the sea. And when Leslie retired, I thought . . .' Her voice trailed away, then rallied. 'But he wouldn't hear of it. Wouldn't leave Westmead, he said. Not in a hundred years.'

Sophie tried again. 'But this is a nice house.' It sounded forced, false, even to her own ears.

'It's a horrible house. Poky and dark. No light, no air.' Still Mrs Clunch looked away from Sophie. 'Something terrible happened to me in this house,' she went on in a matter-of-fact tone. 'Last year. In broad daylight, while Leslie was out. Someone broke in – broke the front door lock and came right in.'

'But that's awful!'

'I was in bed,' Olive Clunch continued. 'Napping. I woke to find him going through my things. Through my drawers! He was holding my grandmother's watch, and I saw him put it in his pocket.'

'What did you do?' breathed Sophie.

Mrs Clunch turned towards her at last. 'I screamed. I screamed the house down. But the cheeky devil didn't run off – not at first. He could see that I couldn't do a thing, couldn't even get out of bed. So he just took his time, all the while I was screaming. Picked out the best things from my jewellery case, right in front of me. My grandmother's watch, my mother's best pearl earrings. Charmian's bracelet.' Her voice caught on a sob. 'Then he left. When he'd taken everything he wanted, and put it in his pocket. He laughed at me and left.'

Sophie didn't know what to say. 'That's awful,' she repeated, knowing how inadequate it sounded.

'And even after that, Leslie won't hear a word about moving. Leaving Westmead once and for all. Getting out of this hateful house.' Olive Clunch's fat face quivered with emotion; her eyes pooled. 'I'll die in this house. And all I ask is to be able to die by the sea.'

Was Olive Clunch dying? Sophie wondered. What exactly was wrong with her? No one had ever said, and she couldn't very well ask. She made a sympathetic noise, neither too dismissive nor too patronising. There was a pain in her own stomach which she tried to ignore.

'And there was that girl,' Mrs Clunch said in a different sort of voice, once again looking away and towards the close.

'Girl?'

'The dead girl.'

For a moment Sophie thought that she must be talking about Charmian, but decided that she probably wouldn't refer to her own daughter in that impersonal way. 'What do you mean? Which dead girl?'

'The girl in the close. Surely Leslie has told you about it,' stated Olive Clunch.

'No . . .' If he had, thought Sophie, she didn't remember. The only dead girl he'd mentioned, in her recollection, was Charmian.

'Ten years ago it was, maybe even more. Let me see.'

The woman touched her fingers, seemingly counting from some point of reference. 'It must have been the summer of 1989. That makes it over eleven years ago now.'

The pain in Sophie's stomach grew, gnawing at her; still she ignored it. 'But who was she?'

'That's the thing.' Mrs Clunch turned her eyes back towards Sophie. 'No one ever knew. She was never identified. Just some poor dead girl. In the family way. And murdered.'

'Murdered?' The word leapt out; involuntarily Sophie rubbed her own abdomen. Pregnant, and murdered.

'We have the newspaper cuttings somewhere. We'll have to show them to you. It was in all the papers,' Olive Clunch added, almost with pride. 'It put Westmead on the map. For a few weeks anyway. Until the next thing came along. Some bomb. Or maybe it was an airline crash. Or a child gone missing.'

'But who killed her?' demanded Sophie.

'Oh, they never found out.' Mrs Clunch's eyes were enormous, fixed on Sophie's. 'Never found out. The crime was never solved.'

For a moment Sophie stared into the woman's eyes, taking in the implications of her words. A dead girl, a crime unsolved. Perhaps, then, a murderer still on the loose. The pain in her stomach could no longer be ignored. 'Excuse me,' she said faintly, blundering to her feet. 'Could I . . .?'

Olive Clunch seemed to know what she needed. 'The lav is at the top of the stairs.'

Hoping that she wouldn't meet Leslie Clunch coming back from the kitchen, wouldn't have to make any further explanations, Sophie hurried through the tiny entrance hall and up the stairs.

The bathroom was as small and cramped as the rest of the house, the basin and toilet and bath crammed together in close proximity. Sophie turned on the water in the basin, feeling that she needed to splash a bit of cold water on her face. She stared at herself in the mirror; for the first time in years, she realised with a jolt, what she saw there surprised her. Not a fat girl, then, but the sleek, attractive woman she had become. There had been a time, early on in her marriage, when every glimpse of herself in the mirror had been a shock, when – newly thin – she had expected to see a fat person instead. That feeling of disassociation hadn't happened for a very long time.

The cold water felt good, but still there was the pain in her stomach. She needed the loo.

Then came another shock, though one that had a sort of inevitability about it. Fresh blood, meaning only one thing.

Sophie leaned her forehead against the cool porcelain of the basin and wept.

Chapter 6

Alison leaned over the toilet bowl, on her knees. After a moment the retching subsided, though she knew from experience that it could start again at any time. Wearily she rested her head against the cool porcelain, wishing that she could just die and get it over with.

There was a rap on the bathroom door. 'Are you going to be in there all day?' came her sister's voice, sharp and anxious.

'Just a minute,' Alison called out.

The Barnetts' house had only one bathroom, and today was Jacquie's wedding day: a sunny, hot July morning.

'What are you doing in there, anyway?' Jacquie demanded. 'You ought to be getting dressed by now!'

'Just a minute.' Alison used the toilet bowl as a prop to help her to her feet, flushed it, then turned to the basin to wash her face. She contemplated herself in the mirror: huge eyes in a very pale face. Not what a maid of honour should look like, she told herself ruefully.

'Come *on*, Ally!' Jacquie rapped again, even more impatiently.

Alison bathed her face in cool water and fixed a smile on it, then opened the door.

Fortunately her sister was too wound up to look at her very carefully as Alison slipped past her to her bedroom. Now, she thought, for the challenge of getting into the dress.

It was a lovely dress, made by one of the women at the Free Baptist Fellowship, a widow who was a professional seamstress. Rose-pink satin, snug in the bodice and full in the skirt, festooned round the neck with fabric roses. At the back, below the waist, was a large bow.

They'd had the final fitting for the dresses – Jacquie, Alison, and the two little bridesmaids – the previous week, and Alison's dress had had to be let out, while Jacquie's had been taken in. The seamstress wasn't fazed: all part of the usual way of things, she'd said. Brides often lost weight before their weddings, running on nerves and frantically busy. And everyone at the Free Baptist Fellowship knew about Alison's battle with her weight. She'd slimmed down in the spring, before the holiday, and now she'd put a few pounds back on. Probably jealous of her sister's wedding, and overeating in compensation, the seamstress concluded, though she kept that thought to herself.

A week ago the dress had fitted, Alison told herself as she slipped it over her head.

Reaching the zip was difficult, but she managed to get it up almost to her waist. There it stopped.

Alison stood for a moment, wondering what to do. She didn't want to go to her mother for help. And certainly not to Jacquie. Her father, perhaps?

She was in luck: her mother was occupied elsewhere, and her father was alone in their bedroom, struggling with the buttons on his starched best shirt. Alison helped him with the buttons, then turned round and presented him with the recalcitrant zip. She took a deep breath and held it while he eased the zip up her back.

'There,' said Frank Barnett. 'All done.'

Alison turned to face him and smiled, still not daring to breathe. 'Thanks, Daddy.'

'You look beautiful,' he said. His smile was fond; Alison had always been his favourite child, and had he been left to his own devices, he would have been inclined to spoil her, indulge her a bit. But her mother had always been hard on Alison for some reason, never giving her the benefit of the doubt.

Frank Barnett had been in his forties when his children were born; he'd never expected to have them, and treasured his little girls like the gifts from heaven that he believed them to be. Jacquie first, small and dark, and then his beautiful little Alison, blonde and plump as a tiny cherub. How he'd doted on her.

He'd been small and dark himself once. Now he was smaller and grey, shrivelled by the passing years. But his daughter had grown even prettier in those years, and she'd never looked more beautiful to him than she did on this day, wearing that becoming shade of pink. That little bit of extra weight suited her, he told himself. Joan, his wife, was inclined to nag Alison about her weight, and the girl had become positively thin a few months back. *Too* thin, to his way of thinking; he liked to see a woman with a bit of meat on her bones. Alison looked just perfect to him today.

The pink of the dress *did* compensate somewhat for the paleness, Alison told herself as, back in her room, she stood in front of the mirror. Just as well; even today, for such a special occasion, her mother would not relax her standards and allow the girls to wear make-up. Face paint, she called it: a tool of the Devil.

But there was no denying that the dress was tight. With her father's help it had spanned her waist – just – as long as she didn't take a deep breath. And across the bust it was even tighter, the shiny fabric straining at the seams and compressing her breasts uncomfortably. Would Jacquie notice? Alison hoped not. Not today. As long as she could get through today . . .

Jacquie made a beautiful bride, radiant in a froth of white. She'd managed, by judicious exposure to the sun, to retain much of the tan acquired on the Greek holiday, so the lack of make-up was not so evident, and the contrast with the white dress was a becoming one.

She arrived at the church in style, riding with her father in the back of a ribbon-bedecked white Daimler. The limousine had been provided, of course, by Darren's father's garage, and her future father-in-law had even supplied a driver dressed as a chauffeur. It was an appropriate start to what Jacquie was sure would be a storybook wedding, the crowning moment of her life, something to remember for ever.

If only the premises of the Free Baptist Fellowship weren't quite so ugly, she allowed herself to think as she stepped out of the car in front of the church, smiling for the photographer. As a backdrop for her perfect day the building was inadequate, with its grimy yellow brick exterior and its plain, unadorned interior, bereft of even a hint of stained glass. The parish church, a resplendent

mediaeval structure boasting a fine angel roof, would have
been so much more appropriate. One of Jacquie's friends
had been married in the parish church earlier in the year,
and in the photos it had looked wonderful.

Alison and the two little bridesmaids – the grand-
daughters of her mother's sister – had come ahead in
Darren's father's second-best limousine, and were waiting
for her in the vestibule at the back of the church. The
church, Jacquie noted with satisfaction, was full: relatives,
friends, and regular members of the Free Baptist
Fellowship crowded together in the pitch-pine pews, tense
– it seemed to her – with anticipation.

Her sister helped her to arrange the train of her dress
and the folds of her long veil. How glad she was, thought
Jacquie, that she had insisted on a new dress, one of her
own choosing, rather than wear her mother's old gown,
as her parents had wanted. Wedding dresses had changed
so much since her mother's day, moving through phases
of fashion and influenced by royal weddings, from the slim
outline of Princess Anne's gown of the early seventies to
the Princess of Wales's meringue-like confection of the
early eighties. Jacquie's own dress bore the influence of
the Duchess of York's gown, with a form-fitting satin
bodice and a full skirt, overlaid with an even fuller sheer
train and trimmed with bows, ribbons and pearls. It had
cost a packet. And worth every penny, thought Jacquie
complacently as the reedy portable organ struck up the
Wedding March and she launched herself down the aisle
on her father's arm.

Down the aisle towards Darren, who was staring at her
in undisguised admiration. Darren looked very handsome,
she observed approvingly. The hired dinner jacket fitted

him well, and gave him an air of distinction that he – to be perfectly honest – lacked most of the time. Today, at least, he was not unworthy of her.

Alison, trailing in her sister's wake with the two little girls, felt a peculiar sort of detachment from the momentous occasion, as though she were an observer rather than a participant. Each face she passed was crystal clear to her, distinct in every detail. At the back of the church, the gawpers and general members of the congregation, most of them dressed in their Sunday best. Farther up, Jacquie's friends and co-workers from the Mini Mart. Two of them were wearing very short skirts – *not* the sort of thing one usually saw within the sacred precincts of the Free Baptist Fellowship. A few assorted cousins and aunts and uncles, on both sides of the aisle. The bridesmaids' parents, beaming fondly. Darren's friends. Darren's parents and younger brothers. And at the front, her own mother, resplendent in a new dress and hat, her face shining with pride in her daughter's achievement. To be married, and married well, was the pinnacle of Joan Barnett's ambitions for her girls, and Jacquie was acquitting herself admirably in that department. That belief was as evident to Alison as if her mother had spoken the words aloud. In a few minutes Jacquie Barnett would be Mrs Darren Darke, with the status and financial security that came with that title. For her younger daughter, a failure thus far in the marriage stakes, Joan Barnett spared not a glance.

All the while, too, Alison was aware of Jacquie's triumphant back in front of her, sailing up the aisle. She was getting what she wanted. And her father, erect and proud, walking carefully at her side.

Waiting for them at the front were Darren and his best

man. Alison had never warmed much to Darren, and he did not impress her now, in his hired finery. *Would* he make her sister happy? He had, Alison noticed, nicked himself shaving that morning; a minute spot of blood marred the whiteness of his shirt collar.

And Reverend Prew, front and centre; fierce-browed and black-bearded, like an Old Testament prophet. Even today, on such a happy occasion, he didn't smile; his face bore its customary expression of gravity.

The church was very hot, Alison noted as they took their places at the front. All of those bodies radiating heat.

Bodies and heat. She closed her eyes for a moment.

Was there something she was supposed to do? Her eyes flew open as her sister nudged her. The veil – that was it. She was meant to help Jacquie to put back the veil. Carefully she lifted the net from in front of her sister's face and arranged it behind, then took the bouquet which Jacquie handed her.

The two little girls, in awe at the beginning, quickly became restless as Reverend Prew intoned the words of the marriage ceremony. They were three and five years old; too young, really, to be expected to stand still, thought Alison. Especially in this heat.

'Who gives this woman to be married to this man?' demanded Reverend Prew, and Frank Barnett passed his daughter's hand into the sweaty palm of Darren Darke.

Alison watched her mother's face, hearing in her head the echo of her mother's thoughts. 'I've done it – got her to the altar a virgin. Pure and untouched.' Alison almost laughed aloud.

Reverend Prew droned on. Vows were made. Reverend Prew asked for the ring, and Darren's best man – as gormless and unprepossessing as Darren himself, in Alison's opinion – fumbled it into the minister's hand.

The ring. Alison looked at her own ringless finger. A sound – like the wings of many birds, like the waves breaking on a Grecian beach – whooshed in her head. She closed her eyes, and crumpled gracefully to the floor.

'She's fainted,' announced the five-year-old bridesmaid in a ringing voice. 'Alison has fainted. Maybe she's dead!'

For an instant everything stopped, Reverend Prew frozen in the act of handing the ring to Darren. Then Darren reached for the ring and dropped it; hitting the floor with a metallic clang, it made more noise than Alison's fall had done. He knelt down to retrieve it, but it had rolled some distance away.

Frank Barnett, who had taken a seat in the pew beside his wife, rushed back to the front and knelt over his recumbent daughter.

Jacquie took charge. 'Get her out of here,' she hissed to the best man, who stood staring in slack-jawed amazement.

He jumped into action and moved round to the other side, managing to step on Jacquie's train in the process. With the help of Frank Barnett, he hoisted the unconscious girl up and carried her towards the back of the church.

'Be careful,' ordered the distraught father. 'Don't drop her, mind.'

Nicola, Jacquie's friend from the Mini Mart, and one of those who was now scandalising the Free Baptist Fellowship by the brevity of her skirt, took it upon herself to join the awkward procession. She'd always had a soft spot for Alison, and during Jacquie's 'hen night' the week before, when she'd happened to be in the ladies' room at the same time as Alison, had begun to form some idea of what was wrong with the girl.

Alison began to regain consciousness shortly after they'd reached the vestibule. Her eyes fluttered open, then closed again, and she moaned. In a moment she struggled into a sitting position. 'The loo,' she whispered urgently.

'I'll take her,' said Nicola firmly as the two men helped the girl to her feet. Nicola supported her with one arm and guided her to the ladies' room.

There was no place to sit in the ladies' room, but Alison headed for one of the stalls. Without stopping to shut the door, she sank to her knees and retched into the toilet.

Nicola went to the basin and moistened some paper towels. When, eventually, Alison leaned back, exhausted, Nicola crouched down and bathed the girl's face. 'Alison,' she said kindly, 'are you all right?'

Alison closed her eyes. 'I'm better now.'

She didn't look very much better: her pale face had an unhealthy sheen of sweat, and her eyes seemed almost sunken. Nicola, most emphatically not a member of the Free Baptist Fellowship, had had more experience of the world than both of the Barnett girls put together, and by now she was sure that she knew what ailed Alison Barnett. It was the time, she decided, for bluntness. 'You're pregnant, aren't you?' she asked.

It was unfortunate that Alison's mother should have chosen that moment to check on her daughter's state of health. She opened the door of the ladies' room just in time to hear Nicola's question, and Alison's faint, reluctant assent.

'Pregnant?' Joan Barnett shrieked in a voice that carried all the way to the front of the church.

* * *

He had never written, had never rung. Mike, the fulfil-
ment of Alison's romantic fantasies, her knight in shining
armour, had walked – or flown – out of her life on that
fateful April morning and had not contacted her since
then.

She didn't even know his surname.

For the first week, even the first fortnight, she'd
managed to convince herself that it was only natural that
there should be some delay. After all, his father was gravely
ill, and he wouldn't have the time to worry about anything
else. No time for phone calls or letters, even to the girl
he loved.

He *did* love her; she was sure of it. How could he have
said the things he'd said, done the things he'd done, unless
he loved her, as she loved him?

She pictured him at his father's bedside, a solicitous
son. But all the while he would be thinking of her, taking
solace from the love they'd shared and the promise of a
future together.

As soon as his father was better, he would write to her.
Or perhaps he would come in person, turn up one day on
the doorstep, ready to claim her as his bride. They would
live happily ever after. That dream sustained her: the
fantasy of hearing the doorbell and opening the door to
see his beloved face, falling into his arms in a swoon of
joy. Or coming home from work and finding him there,
ensconced with her parents in the seldom-used front
parlour, cosily drinking tea, having already asked them for
her hand in marriage.

Every time the phone rang, or the doorbell chimed, or
the post clattered through the letter-box, her heart lifted

in anticipation. She had to play it cool, of course; Jacquie was watching her, with her mocking, knowing smile.

But the days turned into weeks, and there was no word. Then the morning sickness started.

The truth didn't dawn at once. Alison was an innocent, inexperienced in the ways of such things. Her exposure to pregnant women had been minimal; her mother was old-fashioned enough to believe that such things were not appropriate for polite discussion, and the Free Baptist Fellowship, though it advocated reproduction within the bonds of marriage, did not encourage its members to flaunt that condition. Eventually, though, she came to realise the truth, even as her clothes began to get snug.

It was fortunate that by that time Jacquie was caught up in the plans for the approaching wedding, self-absorbed and unobservant when it came to her sister. Ordinarily her eagle eyes would have spotted the tell-tale signs, but her thoughts were full of invitations and flowers and dresses and cake. Away from her notice, Alison slunk off to the bathroom frequently and started wearing the clothes that she'd worn before she lost all of that weight.

She was glad that she didn't have to share a bedroom with Jacquie. Tossing and turning, sleepless through the night. When would he come? Would he be angry about the baby?

Still she could not admit to herself the possibility that he might not come, might not even write. It was unthinkable. If only she could hold on till he did come, without her parents or Jacquie finding out about the baby, then maybe it would still be all right. They could elope, have a quiet wedding, leave Sutton Fen so that no one would ever know. They could tell people that the baby was premature. Her parents would be so delighted to have a grandchild that perhaps they wouldn't stop to count.

As the weeks turned into a month, and then two, Alison faced the dreadful thought that perhaps he had lost her address. What if the napkin had fallen out of his wallet at, say, the airport? He might have searched in vain for it, tried to remember what it said. He might even now be looking for her, searching phone-books and ringing door-bells. 'Are you any relation to . . .?' 'Do you know a girl called . . .?'

The possibility that Mike had forgotten her, had deliberately abandoned her, would not be admitted. That, Alison told herself, was out of the question. He *did* love her; they *would* be together. Somehow, and soon. That was the thought that got her through.

Somehow the wedding was concluded; somehow Darren Darke and Jacqueline Barnett were pronounced to be husband and wife. But afterwards no one remembered that sacred moment. All that anyone remembered was the moment when Joan Barnett's voice rang through the church, and the things that had happened in the after-math.

Through sheer determination, Jacquie had brought events back on track, had insisted that the ceremony be concluded and that everyone move on to the reception in the fellowship hall as though nothing had happened. Even Joan and Frank Barnett, after a whispered consultation at the back of the church, agreed that for Jacquie's sake, they would put this other matter aside and deal with it later.

It still might have been all right if the Reverend Mr Prew hadn't interfered. But he felt that as pastor of his flock he had a moral duty to take a stand. And he felt a special responsibility for Alison Barnett, who was, after all, his secretary.

Alison had wanted to go home, to slip away from the church and hide herself. But Nicola, in a long pep-talk in the ladies' room, had talked her out of taking the cowardly way out. 'You've got to face them,' she insisted. 'You can't avoid them for ever, you know. Just go out there and hold your head up. What can they do to you?'

Alison allowed herself to be carried along by the other girl's stronger personality and persuasive skills, though with many misgivings. Nicola, after all, did not know the elder Barnetts very well, and she knew nothing, except by repute, of Reverend Prew. But Nicola refused to go back to the wedding festivities without her, and Alison felt guilty enough about that to give in at last.

With Nicola at her side, she walked into the fellowship hall, where groups of people chatted and sipped fruit punch. For a moment the buzz of conversation died down, then started up again in a self-conscious way. People looked at her out of the corners of their eyes, but no one stared.

No one, that is, except for the Reverend Mr Raymond Prew. He strode across the room to confront her face-to-face, planting his legs in a defiant stance. 'Is this infamy true?' he demanded in the voice of thunder in which he declaimed from the pulpit on Sunday mornings. 'Are you with child?'

She had never seen him so fierce. His black beard bristled with emotion, and spittle had collected at the corners of his mouth, the pink fleshiness of which seemed at odds with his flesh-denying words. Alison quailed; her voice failed her, but she managed a nod of assent. After all, what good would it do to lie to Reverend Prew, to compound her sins with yet another?

By this time everyone was watching; everyone in the room had fallen silent and turned to observe the drama.

'You have committed fornication?' he questioned her further, his voice still at top volume.

Such a word. 'It wasn't like that,' she protested faintly. 'I love him.'

'Oh, *love*,' he sneered. 'Carnal lust is what it was. No better than animals!'

'But . . .'

'Harlot!' he proclaimed, pointing his finger at her. 'You are unworthy to call yourself a member of this fellowship. You have brought shame upon us all! You wilful, wicked girl!'

Alison felt as though she'd been punched in the stomach. Tears sprang to her eyes, but she had no words with which to defend herself.

'How could you do this to your parents, when they've done so much for you? Ingrate! And I've given you a job, taken you under my wing, put my trust in you! Is this the way you repay such kindness?'

She wished that the floor would open and swallow her up, and would have fled at that point if it hadn't been for Nicola holding on to her.

'From this day forward, you are no longer a member of this fellowship,' declaimed the minister. He turned his head to look for Joan and Frank. 'And I think I can speak for your parents in saying that you are no longer a daughter of theirs. You have brought shame upon their house, and you must remove yourself from it.'

Remove herself! Through her tears, Alison focused on her parents' faces. 'Please,' she whispered. 'Please don't.'

Frank Barnett looked agonised but said nothing. Joan, however, after a moment gave a brisk, decisive nod. 'Reverend Prew is right,' she said. 'You'll have to go.'

'Today,' the minister proclaimed, breathing heavily. 'Now. And you must never darken their door again, you sinful Daughter of Eve.'

A wave of nausea overcame Alison. She pulled away from Nicola's grasp and ran for the ladies' room.

Once again, then, Nicola found her crouched over the toilet, retching. 'Oh, God!' Nicola said. 'I had no idea! That bloke is from the Stone Age, isn't he?'

'What am I going to do?' Alison moaned into the toilet bowl.

Nicola paced up and down in the small space outside the cubicle. 'Jacquie,' she said at last. 'She's your sister. She loves you. *She* won't turn you away. You can move in with her and Darren, at least for a while. Until you get yourself sorted.'

'Do you think so?' Alison lifted her head, seeing a glimmer of hope. Jacquie and Darren would be going on their honeymoon. Their house would be empty; it would be a possible solution, for a fortnight anyway.

'I'll find Jacquie right now and bring her here,' Nicola offered. 'You'll see. She'll come up trumps.'

Jacquie Darke, as she now was, was all too happy to follow her friend Nicola to the ladies' room: she had a thing or two to say to her sister. Majestic in her wedding gown, and cloaked in righteous anger, she swept in.

By this time, Alison had come out of the cubicle and

was leaning over the basin, daubing at her face with a wet paper towel. She turned as the door swung open.

'How dare you!' Jacquie began. 'How dare you ruin my wedding, you stupid little slapper!' She was glad to see the tears in her sister's eyes; she wanted to make her cry, wanted to make her sorry for her inexcusable behaviour.

'Jacquie, please. Help me.' Alison's voice was little more than a raw whisper.

Jacquie stared at her sister in astonishment. '*Help* you?'

'Let me stay at your house. Just until you're back from your honeymoon. Please. I don't have anywhere else to go.' Alison clasped her hands together. 'I don't have a job, I don't have a home. But I'll get myself sorted out. I promise.'

'You must be joking!'

'Please, Jacquie. Just a fortnight. Please.' Alison went down on her knees in supplication, reaching out to touch the skirt of her sister's dress.

Jacquie took a step backwards, as if wishing to avoid contamination. 'You can forget it,' she stated coldly. 'You ruined my wedding. I'll never forgive you for that. Never.'

Alison whimpered. 'But what can I do? Where can I go?'

'You can go to hell for all I care,' Jacquie said, turning away, then had a malicious inspiration and turned back to face her sister. 'Why don't you go to *him*?' she suggested, almost facetiously. 'Your precious Mike, who got you up the spout?' She enjoyed seeing Alison flinch at the mention of his name, so she went on, twisting the knife still further. 'You said that he loved you. You insisted that he'd write to you, come for you. So where has he been all of these months?'

'He loves me,' Alison insisted.

'Then he should be glad to see you.' Jacquie flashed a cruel smile. 'You and the little surprise he left you to remember him by. Why don't you go and find him?'

As her sister slammed the door behind her, Alison sank back on to the floor. Yes, she thought. She *would* go to him. She would find him. And he *would* be glad to see her. It would be all right after all.

Through her tears she smiled up at Nicola. 'I'll find him,' she said. 'The father of my baby.'

Nicola, who was after all Jacquie's friend and not hers, couldn't have been nicer or more helpful. She drove Alison home, and waited while the girl put a few things in a suitcase.

It was the lovely new case that she'd bought for the Grecian holiday. Alison had kept it ever since on the top of her wardrobe, as a sort of talisman of that watershed in her life, and a guarantee that Mike would come for her. Now she dragged it down from its perch and thought about what to take with her.

A few dresses – her larger ones, enough to get her by until she needed to go into maternity clothes. A nightgown, some knickers. Her hairbrush, her toothbrush. The little journal, given to her many Christmases ago by her father, and left blank until so recently, when she'd begun pouring out her feelings about Mike and the baby into it, in her rounded handwriting. And Grace, the worn plush rabbit which had shared her bed every night since she'd been a baby. Except for those nights in Greece . . .

There was something else from her bed as well, and she now slipped it out from under her pillow and into her pocket. Her most treasured possession of all: a beautiful old-fashioned silver cross on a chain. She had found it in her bed that momentous morning, after Mike had been with her. *His* cross, left behind after their night of passion, either by accident or design. She told herself that he'd meant her to have it, as a token of their love. But she couldn't wear it: jewellery of any sort was proscribed by Reverend Prew and the Free Baptist Fellowship. Not even a cross was allowed. And besides, if she were to wear it, her parents would want to know where she'd got it.

Now, though, she *could* wear it. As soon as she was out of Sutton Fen, she could put it on.

She would need money. Alison took her building society book from her top drawer and slipped it into her handbag, checking how much cash she had. Very little: that could be a problem, on a Saturday. Perhaps Nicola could loan her a few pounds for her fare. She would promise to send it back just as soon as she could.

Her destination was Westmead: that much she knew.

Alison was amazed at how long it took her to get to Westmead, and how complicated the journey was. First the bus from Sutton Fen to Ely – that was a trip she'd made before. And after that, the great unknown, as she boarded the train to London.

The London train was crowded, and it was hot, as temperatures soared outside. All of the windows were open, but the packed bodies nullified the effects of the hot air which blasted into the carriage. A kindly man helped Alison to lift her suitcase on to the overhead luggage rack, and even gave up his seat for her.

Once seated on the train, she drew the cross from her

pocket and fastened the chain round her neck, enjoying the unaccustomed heaviness of the chunky silver as it rested in the hollow between her breasts. She fingered it like a talisman, pleased that at last she didn't have to hide it as though she were ashamed of it. A visible and tangible reminder of Mike, it allowed her to focus her thoughts on him rather than on the unfortunate events of the day, as the train sped towards London.

Alison had never been to London before, and could scarcely have imagined the bustling immensity of King's Cross station. A guard at the ticket barrier pointed her towards the Underground. 'Paddington, love,' he said. 'Metropolitan or Circle Line to Paddington.'

If she'd thought the train was hot, the Underground was an inferno. Hordes of people thronged the platform and pressed forward to jam into the carriage. Tourists, shoppers; all ages and all nationalities. Where, wondered Alison, had they all come from? And where were they all going? The smell of so many bodies packed in such proximity assaulted her, threatening her with another attack of nausea, but she managed to control it by concentrating on her goal.

Paddington was older than King's Cross, and more confusing. But she found her train, and on it a seat by the window for the journey to Bristol. The landscape whizzed by: fields and trees, cows and sheep. It was so green, even in the shimmering heat of the summer day, and nothing at all like the flat grey countryside around Sutton Fen.

In Bristol, yet another leg of the journey awaited her. Alison listened to the announcement on the Tannoy and carried her suitcase across to another platform for the branch line to Westmead. There was a bit of a wait, and she suddenly realised that she was hungry: she hadn't eaten anything since breakfast, and that had come back up again. So she bought a bun and a cup of tea, and felt revived for the last part of her journey.

It was still daylight, and still hot, when she arrived in Westmead – one of the long, light evenings of midsummer, that first Saturday in July. Alison knew that, sensibly, she ought to seek out some accommodation for that night: she felt hot and sweaty, and could badly use a shower. But she didn't want to waste precious time doing that. She came out of the station and into the High Street, taking greedy deep breaths of the air of Westmead – so different, she was sure, from the impoverished fenland air. This was the air that Mike breathed. Even now, she thought, she was close to him. He might be standing on the pavement, or sitting in any one of these houses.

Now, though, came the difficult part: how to find him? Alison had had the whole journey to think about how that might be achieved, and in the shortest possible time. Where might she even begin to look?

She began to walk, searching the faces of the people she passed. Fortunately her suitcase was not heavy, but it bumped against her legs as she moved through the streets of Westmead.

Alison knew something about Westmead. In the months since she'd met Mike, she had made it her business to find out about it, first by visiting the library, and then by writing off for a brochure from the Tourist Information Office. So she had a rough idea of the layout of the town, and its scenic attractions.

She was aware, then, that there was a cathedral in Westmead; considered by many to be the finest cathedral in the West Country. But she was unprepared for the impact of that building, and the way it dominated the town. Without realising consciously that she was doing so, Alison walked towards the cathedral, drawn to its imposing bulk. She didn't expect it to be open – not at nearly eight o'clock at night.

For a few minutes she stood on the green at the west end of the cathedral, just taking in the magnificence of it. She had, of course, seen Ely Cathedral before – from the outside only, as her parents didn't approve of such manifestations of the Established Church – but this one was different. She couldn't put her finger on it – perhaps it was the colour of the stone, or the richness of the carving. Its silhouette against the evening sky was breathtaking.

Then she became aware that people were going into the cathedral, through a small wooden door on the west front. It must be open.

'Open till dark,' a tourist read aloud from the noticeboard in an American twang. Alison followed the man through the door.

She had expected, perhaps, a numinous silence inside the cathedral. What she hadn't expected was the drop in temperature, like plunging into a cold, dark cave. Alison gasped at the pleasure of the cool air on her warm skin.

She put down her suitcase and stood for a moment, letting her impressions wash over her. Soaring height, golden stone. A space so vast, yet so embracing. Not really dark, once her eyes adjusted to the difference from outside: the sun streamed through the stained glass of the great west window above and behind her, splashing the stone flags of the floor with brilliant colour. And it wasn't really silent, either; several men in long black garments were putting out chairs in rows across the body of the cathedral, purposefully lining them up one by one. The sound of the chairs on the stone echoed all the way to the vault and back down again.

The other end of the cathedral seemed very far away, and looked darker and more mysterious, partially blocked by a stone screen. Alison picked up her suitcase, drawn towards it.

One of the black-garbed men seemed to be supervising the others, standing in the middle of the central aisle by the wheeled trolleys of stacking chairs rather than hustling back and forth. He was also speaking to the tourists, answering questions asked and unasked in a rather self-important manner. 'Petertide ordinations tomorrow,' Alison overheard him saying to the American man as she moved up the aisle towards him. 'So we're working overtime tonight.'

She didn't know what he meant, and he must have seen the confusion on her face. 'Can I help you, Miss?' he asked her.

What, she thought, could she say? That she was looking for someone called Mike, surname unknown, who was the father of her baby? 'Um, no,' she faltered, dropping her eyes. When she raised them again, a moment later, the man hadn't moved, but was looking at her with what she might almost describe as a stare. Something in the intensity of his gaze made her uncomfortable, as it travelled from her face down to her feet and back up again.

He stated the obvious, indicating her suitcase. 'You're visiting Westmead?'

'Um hm.'

'Have you been here before? Or is this your first visit to our fine cathedral?'

Her nod could have been a yes to either question.

The man glanced over his shoulder at his fellows, labouring away with the chairs. 'Shall I give you a bit of a tour, then?' he suggested in a hearty voice, almost playful. 'They can get on without me for a few minutes.'

It was the last thing she wanted, but her parents had brought her up to be polite, especially to her elders. 'If you're sure it's no trouble,' she capitulated reluctantly.

He wasn't put off. 'Shall I take your case for you? I can lock it in my office – just over here – while we're walking round. Then you won't have to carry it.'

She didn't want to relinquish her case. It was, though, starting to feel heavy to her, in her state of exhaustion, so she let him take it from her. He made rather a show of taking out a huge ring of keys and unlocking a little door tucked under an arch. 'It will be safe in here,' he promised her.

Then he led her round the cathedral, pointing out architectural details which meant nothing to her. A tomb here, a window there: Alison nodded obediently as he explained their significance, taking very little in. All she wanted was to escape from him, to find Mike. Barring that, to find a place to stay for the night, where she could have a shower and fall into a clean bed.

'And of course you must see Quire Close,' the man said. 'Apart from the cathedral itself, Quire Close is the glory of Westmead. If we go out of this side door here—'

At that moment he was interrupted by one of the chair-moving men. 'What shall we do by the font, then? If we put the chairs behind it, people won't be able to see a thing.'

Her guide frowned, displeased at the intrusion but unable to resist the opportunity to exercise his authority. 'Wait here a minute,' he said to Alison. 'I'll be right back, as soon as I've dealt with this.'

It was, she realised, her chance for escape, however temporary. She went out through the door he'd indicated, trying to get her bearings. Since she'd gone into the cathedral, dusk had begun to gather as the sun dipped in the west. Ahead of her she saw an arched entryway; she walked towards it.

For a moment she stood beneath the arch, transfixed with wonder. A long double row of houses faced each other across the narrow cobbled pavement, their chimneys reaching high into the darkening sky. It was beautiful. It was nothing like Sutton Fen.

Drawn irresistibly towards she wasn't sure what, Alison Barnett stepped forward into Quire Close.

Chapter 7

The day that Sophie went up to London to keep her appointment with the fertility specialist was a rare and beautiful early autumn day, one of the golden days of September. The previous week had been damp and unseasonably chilly, but on this day the sun emerged as if to show what autumn ought to be like, causing people to shed their cardigans, jackets, and anoraks.

It was Sophie's first trip to London since their move to Westmead. That had been a more-or-less conscious decision on her part: Westmead was now their home, and she realised that it would only slow the settling-in process if she were to flit back and forth between her old home and her new one. And perhaps she recognised as well that at this point, Westmead would suffer in the comparison, and that would only lead to discontent. Why put herself in a position where she would have cause for regret?

Chris had wanted to drive her to London for her appointment, and in some ways that would have been a good thing: he was part of this process too, as he kept reminding Sophie, and he would have provided some company for her, as well as support. But a major choir commitment had made that impossible. Chris apologised profusely that a television company had chosen that very day to film their special Christmas programme of lessons and carols at Westmead; there was no way that he could get out of it.

So she was taking the train instead, preparing herself for the ordeal in solitude. She found that she wasn't really disappointed to be on her own; Chris's chatter might have been a welcome distraction from her own thoughts, but she didn't really want to talk about this with him or anyone else. Chris was so sure that everything was going to be all right, that this famed fertility specialist could work miracles. The day that she had received the letter about the appointment, the day when she'd been so sick with disappointment about the non-pregnancy, he had remained upbeat and even excited, trilling out a verse from one of the Psalms: 'He maketh the barren woman to keep house: and to be a joyful mother of children.'

Barren woman. Thanks, Chris, she'd thought. That was just what she needed. She was feeling bad enough without adding an emotive word like 'barren' to her burden.

She'd never told him about those few days when she'd thought she might be pregnant.

Up till today, Sophie had tried not to dwell too much on the details of what lay ahead of her at the end of this trip: the pokings and the proddings, the invasive medical procedures, the inevitable questions prying into her most intimate moments with her husband. And to her surprise, it had not been too difficult to concentrate her thoughts elsewhere: it had been an eventful fortnight in Westmead, providing a number of welcome distractions from her absorption with the functions – or non-functions – of her own body.

Even now, Sophie's thoughts shied away from the purpose of this trip; deliberately she emptied her mind as she settled back in the compartment and looked out at the landscape moving gently by. The branch line from Westmead to Bristol utilised old-fashioned carriages, and she had a compartment all to herself: there was not much in the way of commuter traffic, as Westmead was proud to consider itself self-contained and self-sufficient. A few women bored with the shops of Westmead might travel to Bristol to take advantage of the possibilities for shopping, but London was outside of the experience and imagination of most of the citizens of Westmead; as far as they were concerned, it might as well have been on a different planet. There were indeed a considerable number of them for whom it was a matter of some pride that they had never been to London, and had no desire to go there.

From Bristol onwards, of course, it was another matter. The Intercity Great Western train, its sleek carriages filled with businessmen deploying mobile phones, whizzed through the countryside. What, Sophie wondered, had they ever done before the invention of mobile phones? Had people *really* travelled in silence then, communing with their own thoughts, or perhaps quietly with a travelling companion, rather than with the outside world at large? 'Hi, it's me. Just outside Bristol now – we should be into London by half ten.' 'Bob? Tell John the meeting will have to be delayed by a quarter of an hour.' 'Honey? I've gone and left the bloody report on the printer. Could you fax it to the office for me?' And it wasn't just people phoning out; all over the carriage, phones rang constantly, blaring out annoying little tinny tunes. 'Oh, hi. Not to worry – I've got it.' 'Yes, I'm on my way. Tell him I'll be there by eleven.'

It wasn't even as if there were any interesting conversations that one could listen in on, or speculate about the other half of. No romantic assignations being made, no words of love being cooed into a handset. All business.

As the man next to her made one phone call after another, Sophie looked out of the window and thought about the topic of conversation which was dominating Westmead at the moment: Canon Peter Swan. The Precentor had returned from the trip about which Sophie and Jeremy had speculated so frivolously, and the truth was even more bizarre and unexpected than they had imagined. He had returned, not with a suntan or some inappropriate souvenir, but with a wife.

Peter Swan, bachelor canon – now a married man.

Needless to say, Quire Close was agog with the news. Sophie had heard about it from Chris, one night after his visit to the pub. Jeremy was his source, of course.

'A wife!' said Chris. 'He's gone and got himself a wife!'

Sophie didn't believe it. 'You must be mistaken.'

'I swear it's true. Jeremy says so – Canon Swan told him so himself.'

'But who *is* she?' demanded Sophie.

'She's called Miranda. That's about all I know.'

That was the problem: no one seemed to know much about her. Only, presumably, Canon Swan himself, and he wasn't talking.

She *had* been seen by now, and people had met her. Peter Swan, in fact, went out of his way to introduce her to everyone they encountered. 'My wife, Miranda,' he would say, beaming with uxorious pride. And she would smile charmingly, murmur a few words. But neither of them was forthcoming when it came to divulging any information about where she had come from, or how they had met.

'We've known each other for years,' was the most that even Jeremy had been able to pry out of Peter Swan, and that only after considerable effort.

It was all extremely frustrating.

Sophie had had only one glimpse of Miranda Swan, strolling down Quire Close arm-in-arm with her new husband, a week or so after the news had broken. That glimpse piqued her curiosity: the new Mrs Swan was not what she'd expected, conforming to neither of Sophie's contrasting preconceptions about her. She was not an elderly faded spinster of the sort who often hung about the clergy, living in hope. Nor was she a young *femme fatale* type, who might have laid a trap for an unsuspecting bachelor canon. The woman she saw holding the canon's arm was nothing like either of those stereotypes. In age she fell between the two, seeming to be somewhere in her mid-to-late forties. And her appearance was ordinary in the extreme – not the sort of woman who would turn heads in the street. Curly brown hair touched with grey, a nice smile. A reasonable figure, clad in trousers. And just outside of Sophie's house they stopped to say something to each other. It was clear from the expression on her face as she turned towards her new husband that she adored him. He, just as clearly, was utterly besotted with her, his ugly face transformed by love: he was looking at her as if he'd just won the lottery, and she was the winning ticket. It was the Peter Swan that Sophie had had an intimation of, those months ago when he had smiled at her.

'He's like a different person,' Jeremy Hammond marvelled, one afternoon when Sophie ran into him in town. 'He should have got married years ago – it's almost made him human!'

'I saw them in Quire Close,' Sophie revealed.

'Oh, that's the latest – they're moving into Quire Close,' Jeremy told her with relish. 'The big house down at the end, next to Priory House.' He went on to explain that previous precentors had always lived there, amongst the men of the choir. But the last precentor, a family man with a tribe of children, had left the house in an uninhabitable state, or at any rate badly in need of redecoration. Since at the time of his appointment Peter Swan was a bachelor, and didn't require quite that much space, he had opted to move instead into a flat attached to the Subdeanery. Now, though, his circumstances had changed, and the house was being done up for the newlyweds.

'Do you know anything about her?' Sophie, in spite of herself, was curious about the newcomer. What sort of woman was she, to see beneath Peter Swan's hangdog exterior to find a man worthy of such adoration? And if anyone would know, it would be Jeremy.

But he shook his head regretfully. 'I haven't been able to find out a thing,' he confessed. 'Neither of them is saying a word, and no one else seems to know. I mean,' he added in a burst of frustrated pique, 'the man goes off on holiday and comes back with a wife! And then not even to have the decency to tell us where he's got her from!'

Leslie Clunch, too, was interested in the newlywed pair, and just as much in the dark about the bride. 'No one at the cathedral has ever seen her before,' he reported to Sophie on one of his frequent visits. 'So where he's found her, I can't imagine.' He drew his brows together disapprovingly. 'A man of his age – it's just not seemly. Picking up women like that.'

'We don't know that he's picked her up, exactly,' Sophie pointed out, feeling somehow defensive on behalf of the couple. 'After all, he *did* tell Jeremy Hammond that they'd known one another for years.'

'Hmph. That's what he *would* say,' he stated. 'And if that's true, why hasn't anyone ever seen her before? Why won't she say who she *is*?'

Sophie had had another visitor during the past fortnight – a rather unexpected one. It happened one afternoon around teatime, when she was feeling particularly low. She'd seen Trish Evans in the close, with her pushchair, and the baby from two doors down had started screaming; both served as a painful reminder to her of the looming visit to the fertility specialist. She was just thinking about putting the kettle on for tea when the doorbell rang. Sighing in anticipation of the unwelcome sight of Leslie Clunch at the door, she was surprised instead to see a fresh-faced, fair young man with an eager expression.

'Dominic, isn't it?' she recalled. 'Dominic Verey?'

'That's right.' He was wearing his school uniform, which made him seem younger than he'd appeared in the tennis whites in which she'd previously seen him, and he shifted back and forth from one foot to another, evidently tongue-tied.

Sophie waited, unsure what he wanted. Perhaps, she thought, he was selling something – raffle tickets or

Christmas cards. 'Can I help you with something?' she encouraged him.

'Is it true that you're a photographer?' he burst out. 'One of the chaps said that Mr Lilburn had mentioned that his wife was a photographer, and I wondered whether you could possibly be *the* Sophie Lilburn?'

'I *am* Sophie Lilburn,' she affirmed, flushing with pleasure. 'You've heard of me?'

'Heard of you? Of course I've heard of you! You're brilliant!'

After that, of course she invited him in and gave him tea. It transpired that Dominic Verey was a keen amateur photographer, with aspirations towards a career in the field. He was thrilled to make her acquaintance, delighted that she had her own darkroom, and horrified that she'd not yet unpacked all of her photographic equipment. 'I'll help you,' he offered eagerly. 'I'll help you to get it all set up.'

And so he had. On several afternoons after school he had stopped by and, after a cup of tea and a plate of Jaffa cakes, had helped Sophie to get her darkroom in shape. He was a bright young man, self-possessed, used to being around adults, and thus not at all ill at ease in her company, with an engaging personality and a refreshing way of looking at things. His enthusiasm and energy were infectious; Sophie found that she liked him very much, and had already begun to look forward to his visits.

Thinking about him now, Sophie smiled out of the train window. Dominic, so eager and so sweet. She hadn't told him that she would be away today: that would have required too many explanations, presumed too much on what was still a very new friendship, and a friendship of unequals at that; he was, after all, only sixteen. But she hoped that he wouldn't worry that she wasn't there when – if – he stopped by after school.

The man beside her finished one phone call, and before he embarked upon another, he took a newspaper from his briefcase and scanned the headlines. The lead story, Sophie saw, was an unsolved murder: 'Police appeal to public for clues'. And that reminded her of the other, altogether darker, distraction which had kept her from dwelling on what was ahead of her today.

The murder. Sophie didn't want to admit to herself how much time she'd spent thinking about the murder of that young girl in Quire Close. Leslie Clunch had shown her the newspaper cuttings; he'd brought them round one day and doled them out to her one by one, clucking to himself as she read them. 'A terrible thing,' he muttered. 'So young. And so pretty.'

'How do you know she was pretty?'

'I saw her, of course.' He told her, then, that he had been the last known person to see the girl alive. He'd given her a tour of the cathedral. He'd been interrupted, had turned away for a moment, and the girl had . . . disappeared. There one minute, gone the next. And in the morning her body had been discovered, dumped at the far end of Quire Close. Discovered, the newspaper cuttings revealed and Leslie Clunch reiterated, by a pair of workmen who were carrying out renovations on Priory House, as they arrived early for work.

The body was in the close, in front of the Precentor's House and not far from the entrance to Priory House. That house was unoccupied at the time, and no one in any of the other houses in the close had heard anything or seen anything – or so they told the police. They hadn't seen the girl coming into Quire Close, they hadn't heard screams. They hadn't witnessed anyone bringing a body in and dumping it.

She'd been strangled, possibly with her own scarf. The police concluded that the body had probably been moved after death. There was no evidence of sexual interference.

And there was no indication at all of the girl's identity. No handbag, no purse. Whoever killed her had made sure of that.

Leslie Clunch had recalled, when it became clear that he had been the last person to see the girl, that she'd carried a handbag. He had also come forward with her abandoned suitcase; unfortunately that had failed to yield any further clues to the girl's identity. It was a cheap new suitcase, without a baggage tag and devoid of any distinguishing marks. Even its contents were anonymous – the clothes, home-made or from chain stores, the worn stuffed animal.

It was that animal, the well-loved plush bunny, that Sophie found the most poignant. The bunny had featured in the newspaper coverage; there had even been a photo of it. 'Do you know this bunny?' said the headline, in the hopes that someone would recognise it and come forward. There were no photos of the dead girl, evidently too disfigured by the manner of her death – only an artist's sketch was provided, to show vaguely what she might have looked like.

But no one had come forward, no one had identified the dead girl as having been known to them, been loved by them. A few people, following the lead of Leslie Clunch, recalled having seen her in Westmead that evening, near the station or in the cathedral precincts. Someone in London even thought they'd seen her on the Underground earlier in the day, but that was never proven, and was not in itself highly significant or greatly helpful. She might have come from anywhere. She might have been anyone.

And anyone might have killed her. There was no seeming motive; there were no evident suspects.

At first the police had concentrated on the two workmen who had found the body. But once the post-mortem examination revealed that the girl had died during the evening hours – certainly before midnight – they had both been ruled out. Their alibis were iron-clad: one had been at home all evening with his wife and baby, and the other had been at the pub with his mates, several of whom could vouch for his whereabouts for the entire time in question.

The other workmen who were engaged in renovating Priory House were also questioned, and eventually everyone in Quire Close was scrutinised as a possible suspect. Nothing at all had come to light. Physical evidence at the scene was slight; there was nothing to link the dead girl to anyone.

Eventually, then, the case had been put on the back burner. The murder of an unidentified girl by person or persons unknown. Ancient history.

Thinking of her now, of the bland, ingenuous face in the police sketch, Sophie shivered and closed her eyes.

The post-mortem examination had revealed, the newspaper cuttings said, that she had been in the early stages of pregnancy.

The consultant's office was lavishly furnished: no straight-backed chairs here, but plush armchairs to cradle the posteriors of the patients. It wasn't the standard of the furniture that Sophie noticed as she sat in one of those comfortable chairs, facing Mr York across his desk: it was the nature of the wall decorations. Apart from the obligatory diplomas and certificates, every square inch of wall seemed to be covered with pictures of babies: babies in cots, babies in prams, babies in their mothers' arms. 'Our successes,' said Mr York with a certain justifiable pride. 'People like to send us photos of our successes.'

Would *she* be sending him a photo of her success? Sophie wondered. In a year's time, would her baby be up there on the wall?

'Not that we can make any guarantees,' he was saying. Sophie refocused her attention on him: Mr York was a man of middle years, his well-cut hair sprinkled with distinguished grey. She watched his mouth moving, heard the words coming out in a soothing stream, without absorbing much of the content. Then he asked her a number of questions, many of them – as she had expected – of an intimate or embarrassing nature, to which she made automatic reply as he jotted notes on a thick pad in front of him.

Finally he folded his hands on the desk: beautiful hands, she noted. Hands that might belong to a concert pianist, white and long-fingered. Hands that she would love to photograph, disembodied in just such a pose. She was, Sophie told herself, in good hands.

'It's very early days yet,' he said. 'And there doesn't seem to be any obvious cause for your difficulties, at the moment. But certain possibilities do suggest themselves, and I'd like to investigate those first.'

'I'm not getting any younger,' Sophie blurted.

Mr York's smile told her that he'd heard that one before, probably many times. 'We'll get to the bottom of this as quickly as we can, Mrs Lilburn,' he said in a reassuring tone. 'First a blood test, to measure your progesterone levels. That's a simple first step, to make sure that you're ovulating. And I'm going to schedule you for an ultrasound. It's a non-invasive procedure,' he added. 'We'll soon begin to get a picture of what's going on – or not going on – in that body of yours.'

A few minutes later Sophie was out on the street, a sheaf of papers in her hand. Instructions, appointments, helpful brochures containing more information than she ever wanted to know. There was no turning back now, she realised with a vague feeling of panic. She was in the clutches of the medical establishment; she would come out of all this with a baby, or . . . not.

And how strange it seemed to be back on the streets of London, with the heedless traffic and the crowds of people. In some ways it was as if she'd never been away, yet at the same time she viewed it all through a haze of nostalgia. This had once been *her* place, her milieu. She had moved about its streets confidently, taking it all for granted.

Taking so much for granted, she now knew.

For some reason, Sophie had not told any of her friends that she would be in town. Was it because she was unable to choose which of them she would most like to see, and was afraid of offending all the rest? Or was it that she missed them *too* much, that it would be painful to see them and be reminded of how much her life had moved on, away from this place, in just a few weeks?

For whatever reason, she had, instead, rung her sister and arranged to meet her for lunch after her appointment with Mr York.

If it had been up to her, Sophie would have chosen to lunch at one of her favourite bistros or wine bars. But she'd left the choice to her sister, and Madeline – not surprisingly – had opted to meet in the rather more splendid surroundings of Fortnum and Mason. Madeline didn't get up to town very often, and when she did, she liked to make the most of it.

Sophie was on time; she checked her watch as she entered the food emporium, crossing the thick carpets through aisles of expensive delicacies and heading towards the restaurant at the back. Madeline was waiting for her at the entrance to the restaurant, already laden with a mint-green carrier bag.

'Sophie, darling,' her sister said, giving her a hug. 'It's been ages. You look wonderful.'

Madeline always said that, no matter how Sophie looked; Sophie wondered, with a part of her brain that didn't seem to come into operation except where her sister was concerned, whether it wasn't just Madeline's way of pointing up how wonderful *she* looked.

Madeline always looked wonderful; she always had. She was six years older than Sophie, and as long as Sophie could remember, Madeline had been impossibly glamorous, providing a role model and a standard of beauty that Sophie could only envy and yearn for. She was naturally slim, and had always been able to eat anything she wanted, never putting on an ounce of weight. Her hair was a fair, silvery blonde, and had remained that colour without recourse to the bottle; it would, Sophie was sure, shade eventually into a stunning and sophisticated silver as Madeline grew older. Her clothes sense was impeccable, and she could afford to indulge herself with the sort of elegant garments that she loved.

Next to Madeline, Sophie always felt a frump. No matter how carefully she dressed, how good she felt about herself when she looked into the mirror, how much sincere approbation she had from others, as soon as she saw Madeline, she would know that she'd got it all wrong. She could never aspire to Madeline's style; it had been years since she'd tried. Sophie had, she told herself, developed her own style, and most of the time it worked. Except when she was with Madeline.

'I've booked a table,' said Madeline. 'Near the string quartet, but not *too* near.'

They went through and sat down facing each other across the white linen tablecloth. 'I've done my shopping,' Madeline announced as she settled the carrier bag beside her. 'Earl Grey tea. Geoffrey insists on F and M's Earl Grey. Nothing else will do.' Her silvery laugh was indulgent, complacent. 'And Jamie wanted me to get him some special American sort of peanut butter, of all things. One of his school friends is American, and has convinced him that British peanut butter is rubbish.'

'Nothing for Victoria?' asked Sophie.

Madeline rolled her eyes. 'Not a thing. Nothing suits Tori these days. I'm sure that *we* weren't like that when we were teenagers.'

Sophie smiled grimly; she suspected that her memories of their teenage years would be substantially different from Madeline's. For one thing, there was the age gap between them. She'd still been a little girl, playing with her dolls, when Madeline had been a teenager. And by the time she was into her teen years, Madeline was on the brink of marriage and motherhood.

And Madeline had been one of those fortunate people for whom the years of adolescence provide no angst, no trauma. She'd transformed, seemingly overnight, from a beautiful child to a lovely young woman. No acne or spots, no mood swings, no problems with boys. She had been admired and sought after by every boy at school; she'd had her pick of the lot. And she'd chosen Geoffrey – good-looking, intelligent, ambitious. They made a perfect couple; everyone agreed that they were made for each other.

Their life together had gone very much according to their plans, and everyone else's expectations. They had married just out of university; after a decent interval Victoria had been born, and then James. Geoffrey had been called to the bar, then had gone into the Civil Service and was now under-secretary for something-or-other in Whitehall. They lived in the country, not far from Guildford, in a seventeenth-century farmhouse of mellow brick and half-timbering, and were accepted members of the county set. Madeline had never had a career, or indeed a job of any sort at all, except as a wife and mother.

Sophie did not envy her sister her life, nor did she understand it. On the occasions that she and Chris had gone to stay at weekends, she had found herself bored with the pace of life in the country, with the seeming lack of things to do and sources of stimulation, and always longed for the weekend to be over so that she could return to London. She didn't know how anyone could live like that, content to go up to London once or twice a month to stock up on tea at Fortnum and Mason.

What Sophie *did* envy was the certainty, the sense of direction that Madeline had always had. Her life seemed preordained, perfect, all of a piece.

Sophie had reinvented herself, had transformed herself from a fat, self-doubting teenager into an attractive and admired professional woman with a successful career and a lifestyle to match. But it had all been such hard work.

And as long as she was secure in the life that she had built for herself and Chris, flourishing in her career in London, Sophie could deal with Madeline, could even feel sorry for her, stuck in her rural idyll with her perfect children and her successful-but-dull Geoffrey.

Now, though, things were different. Now she herself was banished to the country, even farther from London than Madeline was, out of popping-up-for-a-packet-of-tea range. And she had failed – so far, she had failed dismally – at the one thing that Madeline had achieved without any problem at all: motherhood.

For years, Madeline had nagged gently at Sophie that she ought to start thinking about having children. For years Sophie had ignored her, secure and even superior in the certainty that she was making the right choice for herself, and that when the time was right, it would all fall into place. But it hadn't turned out like that.

Why, she asked herself, had she suggested meeting Madeline for lunch today? Why was she putting herself through this? Her sister's very presence was a reminder of her own failure.

And there was worse to come. Self-absorbed as she was in her own life and that of her family, Madeline never missed an opportunity to remind Sophie that time was moving on and she ought to have children before it was too late. She held back until they'd finished their lunch and were waiting for coffee, but having finished her recitation of the latest events in the life of the Arden family – Tori's prowess in the horse trials, Jamie's achievements at school, Geoffrey's latest pay rise – she moved unerringly on to the topic that Sophie had been dreading.

'Now that you're in the country,' she said, 'don't you think it's about time to think about having a baby? I hate to say this, Sophie, but you're not getting any younger.'

Sophie's defences went up; she clenched her jaw. She wanted to tell her sister, as she had so many times before, to mind her own business. Instead she found herself saying, 'Maybe it's not as easy as that.'

Madeline's brows drew together. 'Do you mean you've been trying?'

Why had she said that? Sophie knew that it was too late now to un-say it. 'Yes,' she admitted, looking away.

'Oh, Sophie, why didn't you say?' Madeline reached across the table with ready sympathy and touched her sister's hand.

It all came out then: Sophie confessed that they'd been trying for well over a year, that it wasn't Chris's fault, that she'd just visited the fertility specialist. 'Early days yet, he said,' she concluded with a shaky laugh. 'So I suppose I mustn't give up hope.'

'Oh, Sophie! I had no idea!' Madeline's air of superiority had vanished; she was all sympathy. 'You should have said something before. But I'm sure he's right, you know. They can do marvellous things these days, with all of those *in vitro* techniques. And Mr York has such a wonderful reputation. You and Chris – you'll get through this. You'll see.'

Chris. He was waiting for her at Westmead station, with a bunch of flowers in his hand and a hopeful, supportive smile on his face. He took her home, opened a bottle of her favourite wine, then asked her what Mr York had said.

'Early days yet,' she repeated, wanting to believe it.

But later that night in bed, when he put his arms round her and drew her close, she pulled away, turning her back to him. 'No,' she said. 'I just . . . can't.'

Chapter 8

It was over.

Jacquie Darke watched while the nurses did all of those quiet, efficient things that follow a death – a death not unexpected, not untimely. Wearily she leaned her head back against the wall; for a moment she even closed her eyes. The death had come, as these deaths often do, in the small hours of the night, though the waiting had gone on for days.

'You can go home now,' one of the nurses suggested at last. 'It looks as though you could do with some sleep, Mrs Darke.'

'Thanks.' It was the impetus she needed, and she was grateful.

When had she last had some real, uninterrupted sleep? Jacquie couldn't remember. A week ago, perhaps longer. It seemed that she had been at that hospital bedside for ever. A few hours of sleep, snatched here and there, had been the best she'd been able to manage. Now the idea of falling into her bed, pulling the blankets up around her and sinking into dreamless oblivion, sounded like the most wonderful thing imaginable. Bliss.

But her bed was some distance away. Could she stay awake on the drive home, through the treacherous fens, in the dark?

Jacquie went to the car park, paid some astronomical amount for the privilege of having left her car there, and headed out of Cambridge.

Home, towards Sutton Fen.

She concentrated on her driving, on the sudden twists and acute angles which indicated the positions of the drainage ditches – the levels – beside the road. She knew the dangers; one had heard, all too often, of people who drove their cars off the road and weren't found for days, submerged in a watery grave.

There were no other cars, no comforting tail-lights to follow: no one drove into the fens at four o'clock in the morning. And of course there were no lights on the road, nothing to illuminate the darkness. At least, though, it meant that she could fill her mind with the mechanics of driving, trying to remember and anticipate each twist before she reached it. She ought to be able to remember; she'd driven this road often enough, though not so often at night. And it did look different at night. A turn here, by the shadowy filling station; another just up the road. If she thought about that, she wouldn't have to think about anything else.

At last she reached Sutton Fen. Half-past four, by the clock on the dashboard. Relieved to see that there was an available parking space in the street right in front of the house, Jacquie pulled up to the kerb, locked the car, and let herself into the house with her key.

One foot in front of the other, up the stairs to the bedroom.

She didn't bother to put the light on; she didn't really need to. Quickly she shed her clothes, dropping them on the floor, and climbed into bed. Her body relaxed as the tension of the drive evaporated; her limbs felt weighted, incapable of further movement, beneath the covers.

And now, oblivion.

Jacquie closed her eyes.

But the thoughts which the concentration of the driving had held at bay crowded into her mind, and refused to be stilled.

There would be no sleep for her tonight.

An hour ago, just before he died, her father had looked her in the eye and spoken his last words. 'Alison,' he had whispered. 'I want my Alison.'

Alison.

In the eleven years since she had walked out of their lives, it was the first time, as far as Jacquie knew, that he had mentioned her name.

No one mentioned her name, not ever. And Jacquie tried not to think about her, not to remember that she had ever had a sister.

It wasn't always easy.

The first few years hadn't been so bad. Jacquie had had her new life to settle in to, with its new routine to establish and its new role to fulfil. Mrs Darren Darke. The name gave her status in Sutton Fen; it brought with it certain expectations.

How she had enjoyed it, that first year or two. No more parents looking over her shoulder and telling her what to do. No boring job at the Mini Mart: no demanding customers, or long hours. She could stay at home and make a home for Darren, fulfilling her divinely ordained role as wife and mother.

Except that the babies hadn't come.

She didn't mind at first; she didn't really worry. Getting used to taking care of Darren was enough of an adjustment in the first year, and it was all right with Jacquie if it took a bit longer to have that first baby.

It was ironic, in the light of what happened later, that at the beginning Darren wasn't bothered about the delay either. He was enjoying the unlimited, legal access to the joys of the flesh, and wasn't particularly anxious that it should be curtailed or halted by the arrival of a baby. There was plenty of time for that, he said.

And at first her mother was patient as well. 'Babies are God's gift,' she said. 'They come when he wants to give them to us. Just look at your father and me – we waited so long for you. For our little girl, our bundle from heaven.'

Later, though, as her mother grew older and more frail, she became less patient. 'My grandchildren,' she would say. 'I'm ready for them. And I don't know how much longer God will spare me,' she would add pathetically.

Her father never said a word.

Not so, however, the Reverend Prew. One day when Darren was at work, he dropped by for a pastoral call. After a cup of tea and a few neutral remarks, he got round to the reason for his visit.

'God has not yet blessed you with children,' he said bluntly.

Jacquie wasn't sure what he was driving at. 'No,' she agreed.

He put his teacup down. 'Are you interfering with God's plan? Using some sort of birth control?'

Stunned, she shook her head, biting back a furious retort that it was none of his business.

Clearly he felt that it *was* his business. 'I'm relieved to hear it,' he said in a more moderate tone. 'So many young women today think that they know best. *They* want to be in charge, rather than putting God in charge.'

'More tea, Reverend Prew?' Jacquie said brightly.

'No, thank you. I never have more than one cup.' The minister sat back and pursued his enquiries. 'If you're not doing something unnatural, then we have to get to the bottom of the problem, and I'm afraid, Jacqueline, that it means that you're not right with God.'

'Not right with God?'

'Because if you were right with him, and desired above all things to be a mother, he would honour that desire and give you a child. You know what the Psalmist says: "He will fulfil the desire of them that fear him: he also will hear their cry, and will help them." And St Paul says, "Fear the Lord, and he will give you the desire of your heart."' He stroked his beard in the unconscious way that he did when quoting Scripture. 'And think of Deuteronomy, Jacqueline. When God tells the people of Israel through Moses what he will do for them if they follow his laws and obey his commands: "And he will love thee, and bless thee, and multiply thee: he will also bless the fruit of thy womb, and the fruit of thy land. Thou shalt be blessed above all people: there shall not be male or female barren among you, or among your cattle."'

'But what does that have to do with me?' she was moved to say.

He fixed her with his fervent dark eyes. 'Obedience, Jacqueline. Obedience to God. Think of Jacob and his wives. "And when Rachel saw that she bare Jacob no children, Rachel envied her sister; and said unto Jacob, Give me children, or else I die. And Jacob's anger was kindled against Rachel, and he said, Am I in God's stead, who hath withheld from thee the fruit of the womb?" Don't you see? It was the sin of envy that God was punishing by withholding children from Rachel. It wasn't until later, when she put herself right with God, that he gave her the child that she wanted. "And God remembered Rachel, and God hearkened to her, and opened her womb. And she conceived, and bare a son; and said, God hath taken away my reproach." Reproach, Jacqueline. Think about it. Childlessness is God's reproach upon you. You must pray about this.'

Thus had started the years of worry and self-doubt, the niggling fear that perhaps Reverend Prew was right: perhaps God *was* punishing her.

And at the heart of her fear was Alison.

Alison, her sister. Her sister, as Leah – the fecund Leah – had been barren Rachel's sister.

Alison had needed her help, had begged for her help, and she had denied her. She had turned her face away in anger and refused to help her sister in her moment of direst need.

But was it only anger that had motivated her? The anger, as she maintained, that her wedding, the most important day of her life, had been ruined?

In the bleakest moments of her darkest nights, Jacquie came close to admitting to herself that there had been more to it than that. Not just righteous, understandable anger, but fear: unworthy fear.

Fear of exposure.

As long as she, Jacquie, was the only one who knew about Alison's fall from chastity, she had some sort of hold over her. They were even; they both had secrets and they both knew it. It was a mutual, unspoken pact. Alison wouldn't dare to say a word to anyone – to their parents, to Reverend Prew, to Darren – about Jacquie's escapades in Greece, because Jacquie could just as easily tell them about Mike. It gave Jacquie a sort of power, an insurance policy.

But when Alison's pregnancy made it all too evident that she had sinned, where did that leave Jacquie?

How long would Alison manage to keep quiet about those men in Greece? She'd always had a tender conscience; perhaps she would have felt it necessary to say something, for Jacquie's own good. Or something might just have slipped out, when she no longer had such a strong motive of self-preservation to keep her mouth shut.

And so she'd let Alison walk out of their lives, taking her dangerous knowledge with her.

Her dangerous knowledge, and her unborn baby.

That baby, and her sister's face, haunted Jacquie's dreams, if not her waking moments.

Jacquie admitted this, just now and again, to herself. But never to anyone else. How could she? How could she tell Reverend Prew?

The next morning, still groggy with lack of sleep, Jacquie spent most of her time on the phone, taking calls from people who had heard, somehow, about her father's death. By now she took for granted the fact that in a place like Sutton Fen, nothing of significance could remain a secret. The news spread, saving her the necessity of ringing round.

Most of the calls were from expected sources: people who had known and respected her father, people from the Free Baptist Fellowship, Reverend Prew himself, suggesting that he call round to discuss funeral arrangements.

One call, though, was unexpected. It was from Nicola, her old friend from the Mini Mart.

Jacquie hadn't seen Nicola in years; Darren hadn't approved of her friendship with Nicola any more than her parents had, and after her marriage, the friendship had withered quickly. Jacquie had immediately quit her job at the Mini Mart, where she'd once been in daily contact with Nicola, and their paths ceased to cross. She recalled, now, that she'd heard that Nicola had moved away from Sutton Fen. Evidently she was back.

'I'm working at the florist's,' said Nicola. 'That's how I heard about your father. I'm really sorry.'

'Thanks,' Jacquie said automatically. It seemed an odd thing to say, but what else *could* she say? 'He was old, he was sick, he was ready to go'? 'He hasn't been the same since my mother died'? Or the truth: 'He hasn't been the same since Alison left'?

'I wondered whether I might drop by to see you,' Nicola suggested impulsively. 'It's been ages. I thought we might . . . well, I'd like to see you.'

'That would be lovely.' As she said it, Jacquie realised how true it was. She could use a friend right now; she didn't really have anyone that she could call a friend. There had been some once, but they had been friends of both of them: couple friends, hers and Darren's.

'Shall I stop by when I get off work this afternoon?'

'I'd like that,' agreed Jacquie.

'You're living . . .?' There was a delicate pause on the other end of the phone.

'At my parents' house. You remember where it is?'

'Yes, of course.'

When she arrived, after just a minute or two of awkwardness as they each adjusted to how the other had changed physically in eleven years, it was as if they'd never been apart. 'I'll put the kettle on,' said Jacquie, as Nicola followed her into the kitchen. The Barnetts had always spent far more time in the kitchen than in the sterile front parlour.

Nicola sat down at the kitchen table as Jacquie filled the kettle. 'I suppose your sister will be coming for the funeral,' she said. 'Alison. Where is she living now?'

Glad that she had her back to Nicola, Jacquie found it difficult to keep her voice steady. 'I don't know where she is. We've . . . lost touch.'

'Lost touch?'

'I haven't seen her since . . . that day. You know. The day she left.' The words 'my wedding day' were too painful; they refused to come out. 'She's never written,' Jacquie added, a bit more robustly.

'I had no idea.' Nicola seemed to be waiting for Jacquie to say more, but when no more words came, she fumbled in her handbag. 'Do you mind if I smoke?' she asked.

Jacquie remembered, now, why her parents had always considered Nicola to be 'fast', not a proper friend for their daughter: short skirts and cigarettes. And in Nicola, somehow, through the mists of time she caught a glimpse of herself as she had once been, carefree and rebellious. That was a Jacquie she scarcely recognised, and wondered whether Nicola now felt as old as she did, as defeated, as beaten down by life. At least Nicola still had her fags. But Jacquie – she was a different person: not only older, but sadder. She wasn't at all sure about wiser, though she felt that her experiences over the past years had given her a sort of wisdom that she'd lacked in her youth; she hoped she was, at least, kinder than she'd once been.

'Go ahead,' she said, looking round for something that might serve as an ashtray and settling for a saucer.

'I shouldn't.' Nicola gave a guilty laugh as she lit up. 'I'm not supposed to – Keith would kill me if he knew I was smoking.'

It was said as if Jacquie was supposed to know who Keith was. 'Keith?' she repeated.

'Oh, I forgot – you haven't met Keith.' Nicola sucked hungrily on the cigarette and the tip glowed red. 'My husband.'

'He's worried that smoking is bad for you?' Jacquie hazarded.

Nicola gave a humourless laugh. 'No, just bad for our budget. He says that we can't afford an expensive habit like smoking.'

Jacquie couldn't think of anything to say to that without being rudely inquisitive. 'Oh.'

'So I do it whenever I can, behind his back,' Nicola stated defiantly. 'Whenever I can squeeze a packet of fags out of the housekeeping money. It's my little rebellion. One way to get my own back.' She tipped her head back and exhaled a long, slow stream of smoke. 'That's money that the Bitch isn't getting her greedy little hands on, even if it means that we'll be eating beans on toast tonight.'

'The Bitch?' echoed Jacquie, shocked.

'Keith's ex-wife. Also known as the blood-sucker.'

While the tea brewed, she told Jacquie the story, filling her in on the past ten years of her life.

She had met Keith Jeffries not long after Jacquie had married Darren. He was from out of town, a few years older than Nicola, charming and good-looking – irresistible, in fact. He was also divorced, with a small child.

At first that hadn't been a problem at all; if anything, it had added to his glamour. A man of the world, one who had been around. She was swept off her feet.

Nicola had given up her job at the Mini Mart and moved to Cambridge to live with him. After a couple of years they had married.

At first, Nicola said, it had been wonderful. They were mad about each other; they lived in a charming flat in a desirable part of Cambridge. Keith had a good job with a good salary, as a sales rep covering the East Anglia region. Nicola did volunteer work with the Citizens' Advice Bureau, which she'd greatly enjoyed. And she'd had very little contact with Brittany, Keith's young daughter; Brittany lived nearby with her mother, who did not approve of Nicola, so Keith always took her out on his own.

After their marriage, though, things had begun to change. Mostly due, Nicola said, to the Bitch. Keith's ex-wife, jealous of his new-found happiness, had increased her demands on his time and on his money. She was constantly ringing him up, asking him to come round for one reason or another: something needed doing in the house, or there was some crisis with Brittany, often involving the necessity for the expenditure of money. She wouldn't leave him alone, and that didn't do the marriage any good. Nicola was resentful of the time he was away from home, of the incessant nature of the Bitch's demands and her seeming hold over her ex-husband.

Then, Nicola said, a couple of years ago, the Bitch had turned really nasty. She had taken Keith to court, claiming that the money he paid her in maintenance and child support was inadequate. The court had agreed, more than doubling the amount that he was to pay.

It had crippled them financially. No longer could they afford the flat in Cambridge; no longer could Nicola afford to do voluntary work without a salary coming in. They had found a cheap, run-down house in Sutton Fen, and Nicola had managed to get a job at the florist's.

At least, Nicola said, the move from Cambridge had put Keith out of reach of the Bitch's constant calls asking him to drop everything and come over. Sutton Fen was too far for him to be at her beck and call.

But it was a mixed blessing, as it also meant that Nicola had to see more of Brittany. The girl now came to stay with them for extended periods, for weekends and even for weeks at a time in the school holidays. That, Nicola told Jacquie, was hell: Brittany was spoiled rotten, and she had been schooled by her mother in hatred of her father's second wife. She was rude, she was deliberately cruel. And, to make it all worse, she was now thirteen years old, a teenager. Nicola dreaded her visits with a passion.

'She's *his* child,' she finished moodily, stubbing out her third cigarette. 'Not mine. But who has to take time off work to look after her? Not him.'

'That doesn't seem fair,' Jacquie agreed. 'How does he get on with her, then?'

Nicola grimaced. 'Oh, he thinks the sun shines out of Brittany's bum. But that doesn't mean that he wants to spend time with her.'

The tea had gone cold. Jacquie swirled the dregs in her cup, then got up to make a fresh pot. Her back was to Nicola when she spoke. 'Didn't you ever want to have children of your own, then?'

'Oh, yes.' Nicola's voice was unexpectedly bitter. 'But that's never been on the cards.' She fingered another cigarette out of the diminishing packet and contemplated it without lighting it. 'The Bitch got pregnant to trap Keith into marrying her. Then she decided that she didn't want any more kids, so she made Keith get a vasectomy. Then, of course, she divorced him.'

Appalled, Jacquie turned back to face her. 'I understood that those things – vasectomies – could be reversed.'

'Oh, they can, sometimes.' Nicola played with the cigarette. 'But even if Keith wanted another child, which I don't think he does, there's no way we could afford it. Not now. Not with the lovely Brittany and her mother sucking us dry.'

'That's terrible!'

'That's life.' Nicola sounded old and world-weary. Now Jacquie could see past the image of the Nicola she'd once known, and the remnants of that carefree young woman, to a reality that was no more glamorous, or even more tolerable, than her own life.

'How about you?' Nicola asked. 'Any kids?'

'No,' Jacquie said shortly, turning back to fuss with the kettle and the teapot.

'You didn't want any, then?'

'Oh, we wanted them, all right.' It was Jacquie's turn to sound bitter, though she tried to keep her voice steady. 'It just didn't happen.'

'I heard . . .' Nicola paused delicately, her eyes focused

on the cigarette as she lit it. 'I heard that you and Darren had . . . split up.'

'Yes.'

There was a long pause. 'Do you want to talk about it?' Nicola invited. 'You don't have to if you don't want to.'

The kettle had boiled at last. Jacquie concentrated on pouring the water into the teapot, then covered it with an ancient, stained tea cosy. 'Mother always used this tea cosy,' she said. 'Always, as long as I can remember. I've always hated it.'

'Then why do you keep it?'

'I don't know, really.' Jacquie stared fixedly at the tea cosy, then with a decisive gesture she whipped it off the pot and dropped it in the bin. 'There.'

Nicola clapped her hands. 'Good for you.'

'Mother died last year,' Jacquie said with seeming abruptness. 'Cancer. It wasn't very nice. She needed a lot of care, a lot of looking after. Luckily for her I'd moved home by then. My father certainly couldn't have coped with her on his own. He wasn't well himself. And now . . .' She sat down, staring at her clasped hands. 'Now he's dead. And I'm on my own.'

'But you have the house. You have a place to live.'

'I hate this house.' The passion in her voice startled her almost as much as it must have startled Nicola. 'I've always hated it. The walls – I feel like they're closing in on me. I couldn't wait to get away from this house. When I married Darren.'

She'd spoken his name. Jacquie caught her breath in surprise: she'd sworn never to mention his name again, and till now she had kept that promise to herself.

Darren. Now that she'd said it, there was no reason why she shouldn't tell Nicola the rest. After all, Nicola had confided her problems with painful honesty. Why shouldn't she do the same?

'How much do you know about the Bible?' Jacquie asked.

Nicola shrugged, bemused; this wasn't what she'd expected. 'Not a great deal. You know I was never one of your Bible-thumping friends. That's why your parents didn't like me, remember?'

'Well, then, it's difficult to explain what went wrong between . . . us. Between me and . . . Darren.' Jacquie poured them each a fresh cup of tea.

'But you both went to that church.'

'Yes.' That church. Painfully, Jacquie's thoughts went back a few hours to Reverend Prew's visit, to discuss plans for the funeral. They had sat in the cold, unfriendly front parlour; she had not met his eyes. For her father's sake, she had continued her faithful attendance at the Free Baptist Fellowship, but she was determined that his funeral would be the very last time she would darken its door. After she'd got through that day, never again would she sit on the unforgiving pitch-pine pews, surrounded by ugliness, drowning in Reverend Prew's words. She would be free of it. Free of Darren, free of her parents, free of Reverend Prew.

Or could she *ever* be free?

Stirring a spoonful of sugar into her tea, Nicola waited patiently for her to continue.

'Reverend Prew believes in the Bible,' Jacquie continued at last. 'And he believes that if we're not right with God, then God will punish us for it.'

'I don't get it. What does this have to do with you and Darren?'

'Barrenness,' said Jacquie in a bleak voice. 'That has been my punishment. Like all those Old Testament women. Sarah. Rachel. Samuel's mother.'

'Samuel who?'

'Samuel in the Bible. His mother was called Hannah.' She closed her eyes and recited the words; she'd had them quoted at her so many times by Reverend Prew and Darren that she knew them by heart. 'Her husband loved Hannah, "but the Lord had shut up her womb. And she was in bitterness of soul, and prayed unto the Lord, and wept sore."' Bitterness of soul – in that passage was distilled, thought Jacquie, all of the pain of childlessness, as Hannah went to the Temple and encountered the priest, who mistook her excesses of grief for drunkenness. 'I am a woman of a sorrowful spirit,' Hannah had told him. 'I have drunk neither wine nor strong drink, but have poured out my soul before the Lord.' But God had heard Hannah's prayer, and had given her a son.

Jacquie had had no son, no daughter.

And Darren had grown impatient.

She tried, now, to explain it to Nicola: how Reverend Prew had counselled Darren, had convinced him that there was something wrong at the heart of their marriage, or else God would surely have honoured their prayer for a child. As he had with Hannah, with Rachel, with Sarah, and even with Elizabeth, the mother of John the Baptist. 'Thus hath the Lord dealt with me in the days wherein he looked on me, to take away my reproach among men.'

The reproach of barrenness, a continual reproach.

Primed and coached by Reverend Prew, Darren had

begun quoting Scripture at her. 'Lo, children and the fruit of the womb: are a heritage and gift that cometh of the Lord. Like as the arrows in the hand of the giant: even so are the young children. Happy is the man that hath his quiver full of them: they shall not be ashamed when they speak with their enemies in the gate.'

Darren had been ashamed. His manliness, his virility were in question. A barren wife was a curse, Reverend Prew told him. A sign of a cursed marriage.

Reverend Prew had, a few years ago, started a support group for men, especially those who suffered from troubled marriages. True Men, the group was called, espousing and embracing the Biblical teachings on the headship of men within marriage. Reverend Prew taught his followers that until they assumed their proper places at the heads of their families, God would not honour their marriages. They learned the words of St Paul by heart, and quoted them at their wives: 'Wives, submit yourselves unto your own husbands, as unto the Lord.'

Jacquie, inwardly rebelling, had tried to submit. Month by month, year by year, she had submitted, and waited, feeling her soul shrivelling. But still there were no children.

In her darkest moments, Jacquie had begun to believe that Reverend Prew was right. That heady fortnight in Greece, all of those men – she'd put it all firmly behind her when she married Darren, had ceased to think of it at all; it was almost as if it had been a dream. Every now and again, though, she'd remembered, and with the memory came the horrible thought that perhaps God *was* punishing her for her youthful indiscretion. Over and over again, she had prayed to God for forgiveness. Still there was no baby.

And then had come the blow: God had told Reverend Prew, who passed it on to Darren, that theirs had been no true marriage in God's eyes, or else their prayers would have been answered by now. It was Darren's duty to put his barren wife away from him, to enter into a true marriage for a True Man, a marriage where he could exercise his headship with a woman who was not as stubborn as Reverend Prew knew Jacquie to be. 'She has an intransigent heart,' Reverend Prew told Darren. 'God knows the secrets of our hearts, and she will never be a true wife to you.'

Given God's express permission, Darren had lost no time in divorcing Jacquie. The Bible didn't sanction divorce; even Jacquie, whose thoughts always wandered during Reverend Prew's sermons, knew that. But Reverend Prew explained it to them: this wasn't really divorce, except in legal terms – it was 'putting her away'. Their marriage had clearly not been a true marriage, so its dissolution was not really divorce.

And close on the heels of the divorce had come the new wife, the *true* wife, according to Reverend Prew's lights. Young, pliant, devout. And fertile. In two years of marriage she had already given Darren two babies.

He no longer had cause to be ashamed when he spoke with his enemies in the gate.

Darren flaunted the new wife, and the babies, in the congregation of the Free Baptist Fellowship. On the strength of this exemplar of a marriage, he had become a leader of the True Men group, working with Reverend Prew to spread the message.

Sunday after Sunday, Jacquie had had to take her father to services, to be confronted by the evidence of her own inadequacy.

Never again, she told herself, though she didn't say it to Nicola.

Nicola's brows were drawn together, as if trying to absorb what Jacquie had told her. 'That's really weird,' she said bluntly. 'It sounds to me like you're better off without him, quite frankly.'

She should have known that Nicola wouldn't understand. No one understood. No one who hadn't grown up in the Free Baptist Fellowship, in this household, could possibly understand.

Alison. The name pierced through her with unexpected sharpness. Alison would have understood.

'Wait a minute,' said Nicola, still frowning. 'I *have* heard something about this True Men rubbish. Did you ever know Miranda Forrest?'

Jacquie shook her head. 'The name doesn't sound familiar.' She certainly wasn't a member of the Free Baptist Fellowship. 'Was she at school with us?'

'Oh, no. She's quite a bit older than us. Closer to my mum's age, really. But I knew the Forrests because I used to baby-sit for their little girl. Years ago, when I was at school.'

'I don't know them,' Jacquie stated. 'What do they have to do with the True Men?'

Nicola lit another cigarette and told her the story.

Emma Forrest, she said, had been a lovely little girl, an only child. Bright, pretty, sweet-natured, a joy to baby-sit for. And Nicola, at one time, had spent a lot of time looking after Emma, after school and during school holidays especially: her mother, Miranda Forrest, had a job in Cambridge, and hadn't always been able to co-ordinate her work schedule with her daughter's school timetable.

Mr Forrest, Kenneth, wasn't too much at home either, but they had always seemed – to the young Nicola, anyway – a happy family, a perfect family. They had a nice house, they had lovely possessions, and they had each other.

But things had gone wrong. Emma Forrest, when she reached her teens, had fallen in with a fast crowd, had gone a bit out of control. Her parents had worried about her, had tried to set rules, but hadn't been very successful in curbing her rebelliousness. Then one night, just before her seventeenth birthday, she'd gone out with her friends and hadn't come home.

They found them the next day. Three of them, a boy and two girls, high on drink, had stolen a car and gone for a high-speed drive in the fens. Not surprisingly, the inexperienced and intoxicated driver had missed a sharp curve and had gone off the road into one of the deep levels.

The driver and one of the girls had not worn seat-belts. Miraculously, they had either been thrown clear of the car or had managed to crawl out of it as it sank. They were still alive when the passer-by found them.

Emma Forrest was not so lucky. Belted into the back seat, her reflexes dulled by drink, she had drowned. Drowned in the deep, cold water of the level.

'I'm surprised you didn't hear about it,' Nicola said. 'It was in all the papers. Even in Cambridge. And on the news.'

'We've never taken a newspaper,' Jacquie reminded her. 'And we've never had a television.'

'Of course.'

In spite of herself, Jacquie was caught up in the story of the Forrest family. 'So what happened then?'

she asked. 'And what does it have to do with the True Men?'

'Her parents never got over Emma's death. It knocked them both for six,' she went on. 'I've seen things like that at the Citizens' Advice Bureau. Something that should bring people together, and it drives them apart. They can't talk to each other about it, they can't deal with it.'

Jacquie nodded. Alison's departure had been something like that: they'd all tried to pretend that it hadn't happened, that she'd never existed, but the hole she'd left in the family had never been filled.

'They'd always been churchgoers, the Forrests. The parish church, that is. But Mr Forrest – Kenneth – stopped going to church after Emma died.'

He blamed God, thought Jacquie. And why not?

'Then,' said Nicola, 'he found the True Men. I'm not sure how he got hooked up with them, but he did. And then, the next thing you know, their marriage broke up.'

Jacquie closed her eyes; it was all so horribly familiar. She could fill in the missing pieces of that puzzle for herself.

'Apparently, Reverend Prew told him that it was his wife's fault that Emma had died,' Nicola went on.

'Because,' Jacquie supplied, 'she had had a job and hadn't stayed at home looking after her family the way she should have done.'

'Exactly! How did you know?'

'I know Reverend Prew. That's what he *would* say. That's what the True Men are all about.' She sighed, then roused herself. 'So what's happened?'

'Well, I think it's all been going on for a long time,' Nicola said. 'Emma died five or six years ago. But a few weeks ago, I heard the latest gossip about the Forrests.' She paused for effect. 'They got a divorce.'

'And he's got himself a new wife,' Jacquie extrapolated in an acid voice, before Nicola could finish. 'Some nice young thing who can give him more children. What a surprise.'

'No, that's not it at all. She's the one who's just got married again. Miranda.' Nicola shook her head in wonder. 'And what do you think? She's married the vicar!'

'The vicar?'

'The vicar of the parish church! Well,' Nicola amplified, 'he's not the vicar any longer. He used to be, when Emma died. Now he's gone to be a canon in a cathedral somewhere. And she's married him and gone off as well!'

She'd managed to escape from Sutton Fen, was Jacquie's thought. In spite of Reverend Prew. Lucky Miranda Forrest. People didn't often manage to do that. But Miranda Forrest had.

And so had Alison.

That night, as had happened so many other nights, she dreamed of Alison. Not of Alison as she would be now, that unknown creature – mother, possibly wife – but of Alison as a girl. The two of them together against the world, bold Jacquie and timid Alison. Sisters, best of friends. As long as they'd had each other, they hadn't needed anyone else.

And when she woke, there were tears on her pillow. When her mother died, Jacquie hadn't cried. Her father's death had left her weary but dry-eyed. Even Darren's desertion hadn't brought her to tears. But for Alison – lost Alison – she wept.

The tears were warm and salty, shocking her into wakefulness. And it was a different sort of wakefulness, sharp and aware. She felt as if she were emerging from years of sleep, years of numb acceptance of her fate, of muzzy-headed passivity. With the tears came new resolution: she would find Alison. No matter what it took, she would find her sister.

Chapter 9

Dominic Verey sprawled on the sofa, totally at ease. 'Is there any more tea in the pot?' he asked.

'I think we've drunk it all.' Sophie lifted the lid of the pot and peered inside. 'I'll make some more.'

'Never mind. I'll do it,' offered Dominic. Rising gracefully, he collected the empty pot and headed for the kitchen.

Sophie smiled fondly at his retreating back. He had become a part of her life in such a short time; unless he had something else on after school, he almost always stopped by for a cup of tea and a chat. She looked forward to his visits, which were always enlivening and enjoyable. He made no demands on her, and seemed to expect nothing from her other than her company.

They had photography in common, of course. He could talk about it for hours, and with great enthusiasm. She was flattered that he was so interested in her own work, which he asked about and pored over. They talked about other things, as well: about his school work, about his family, about the close and the people in it.

The more she heard about his mother, the more Sophie realised why her home was a more inviting place than his own for him to spend his after-school hours. Elspeth Verey must be a difficult person to live with, she decided. Dominic wasn't openly critical of his mother, but it was clear that the scene Sophie had witnessed between them, on her one visit to Priory House, was not atypical. Elspeth Verey's standards of behaviour were very high, and she expected her son to live up to them in every way. At Sophie's he could put his feet on the furniture, he could eat his fill of Jaffa cakes, all without fear of criticism – or comparison to his brother.

Sophie had not met Dominic's brother Worthington, nor did she particularly want to. She had heard enough about him to have formed the opinion that he was truly his mother's son: opinionated, conformist, and convinced of his own importance. Dominic spoke of him with rueful understanding, and a determination *not* to follow in his footsteps, however much their mother might wish it.

She *did* wish it. Elspeth Verey, with all of her considerable resolve, was insistent that he would be a priest, like his grandfather, like his father, like his brother. The fact that he felt no sense of vocation, no call in that direction, seemed to make no difference to her. It was the family business, she said, as if they had been shoemakers or butchers or shopkeepers.

Dominic talked frankly with Sophie about it. He was depressed by his mother's insistence on the matter, but he was not intimidated. He, too, had a streak of the Verey – or was it Worthington? – strong-mindedness, especially when it came to his own future.

Sophie knew better than to offer advice. She could only

listen, and express her concern. She couldn't stop herself, though, giving him encouragement to follow his own path when, eventually and shyly, he showed her some of his own photographs. They were good: more than competent technically, and displaying a flair and originality of vision that reminded her of her own early efforts. Every word of praise she uttered – and she tried not to gush or be over-enthusiastic – was taken in by him and stored away; Sophie was sure that one day they would be brought out when he had an argument or show-down with his mother about it. That worried her slightly. She didn't necessarily want Elspeth Verey as a friend, but she wasn't anxious to have her as an enemy, either.

Sophie wasn't sure how much his mother was aware, at this point, about the amount of time that Dominic spent with her. Elspeth Verey wasn't the sort of mother who had to know where her child was at every given moment – there was a certain amount of trust involved there, given his maturity – but she *did* like to know who his friends were, and keep general track of his movements. Dominic stopped by nearly every day after school. Where, exactly, did his mother think that he was? Sophie was afraid to ask.

She did ask him once, when he was talking about his family, a question about his father, the late Dean. His father, it turned out, he scarcely remembered. Dominic had been born into the Deanery, but he had only been five at the time of his father's death, and even when his father was alive, he was a remote figure. 'He was kind,' Dominic said. 'But I didn't see him all that much. He was a very busy man. And then, before he died, he was a very sick man. And old. He was almost sixty when I was born.'

'More tea,' Dominic announced now, bearing the refilled pot into the sitting room. In his other hand he had a fistful of Jaffa cakes. 'And I helped myself to a few more biscuits,' he admitted, stating the obvious.

Dominic was always hungry, no matter how recently he'd eaten. Sophie found herself thinking of him when she did her shopping, and buying things that she knew would please him. Jaffa cakes were a favourite. So were Marmite sandwiches; he'd already consumed a plate of those.

'You'll spoil your supper,' Sophie said in half-hearted protest.

Dominic grinned. 'No fear.' He put the biscuits on his empty plate and licked the chocolate from his fingers. 'My mother would kill me if she saw me doing that,' he admitted cheerfully.

Sophie didn't doubt it. She was pleased, in an odd sort of way, that Dominic felt comfortable enough with her to be himself, to do things that he couldn't do at home. 'Just don't tell her that I let you get away with it,' she said, smiling.

He pulled a face. 'How stupid do you think I am?'

'Point taken.'

Sophie leaned back and watched as he poured them each another cup of tea. He was not her first visitor that day: Leslie Clunch had been to see her late in the morning. She hadn't mentioned it to Dominic; he was inclined to accuse her of being too much of a soft touch.

As if reading her mind, he said, 'I saw two coffee cups in the sink. Has old Clunch been here again, then?'

'You're quite the detective, aren't you?'

'Inspector Morse – that's me.' He grinned at her. 'I

don't know why you put up with him,' he added severely. 'He's a boring old fart. You should just chuck him out. Or tell him you're busy, and not let him in in the first place.'

'Easy for you to say.' Sophie was defensive; she couldn't explain to herself why she accepted the man's visits, let alone explain it to Dominic.

And then there was Chris. Once she had mentioned to Chris that she found Leslie Clunch's visits onerous, and that Dominic had urged her to be firm with him.

She had tried to make a joke of it, but Chris had frowned. 'He's an important man round here, whether you like him or not,' he'd said. 'I don't think Dominic understands that.'

'But I don't like him. He makes me uncomfortable.'

'I don't think you can afford to offend him,' stated Chris. 'He has fingers in too many pies.'

And so Sophie continued to put up with Leslie Clunch, suppressing her increasing feelings of revulsion as his small, hard eyes raked her legs and his tiresome voice droned on. If only he were *just* boring; she could deal with that. But there was more to it: something under the surface, barely glimpsed, with a whiff of unpleasantness about it.

'Speaking of boring old farts,' Dominic went on, 'I saw old Swan today. In the cathedral. With his new wife. And when he thought no one was watching, he kissed her. Behind a pillar.' He rolled his eyes.

Sophie laughed. 'You needn't look so disapproving, young man,' she said playfully. 'One day you'll have a girl-friend, and you may want to kiss her. Maybe even in the cathedral. Maybe even behind a pillar.'

Dominic lowered his lids and gave her a strange look;

he seemed about to say something, when the phone rang.

'Just a moment.' Sophie sighed and picked up the cordless handset from the table. 'Hello?'

'Mrs Lilburn?' said a voice at the other end. 'This is Mr York's office. We've had the results through from your scan.'

Sophie's chest tightened; she suddenly found it difficult to speak. 'Yes?' she managed breathlessly.

'Mr York would like to see you to discuss it,' the impersonal voice went on. 'Can you manage a day next week?'

'Next week? Can't it be sooner?' Sophie's free hand clenched and her fingernails dug into her palm. 'Tomorrow?'

There was a pause. 'Tomorrow isn't possible.' Another pause. 'The earliest I can squeeze you in is Thursday. Eleven o'clock.'

Thursday. Three days away. Sophie couldn't bear it – couldn't bear the not knowing. 'Then tell me,' she demanded. 'There's something wrong, isn't there? I want to know.'

'I'm afraid that I can't . . .'

'Then let me speak to the doctor, to Mr York,' Sophie demanded.

'I'm sorry, Mrs Lilburn, but that's not possible.' The voice was firm. 'He isn't in the office. He'll tell you everything that you need to know on Thursday.'

Sophie didn't bother with any niceties; she pushed the disconnect button, and when she put the phone back down, her hand was shaking.

'What is it?' asked Dominic, concern on his face. 'Is something the matter?'

Sophie's head drooped. 'Nothing.'

'But it's *not* nothing,' he protested. 'The doctor. You're upset. Tell me what's wrong.'

She hadn't wanted to tell him. Sophie looked down at her trembling hands, at the red crescent marks that her fingernails had made on her palm. 'I'm trying to have a baby,' she said, struggling to keep her voice steady. 'We're trying. Chris and I. We're . . . having trouble. Nothing's happened. We're seeing a consultant, a specialist. A fertility specialist. Or I suppose it would make more sense to call him an *in*fertility specialist.' Her laugh was as shaky as her hands.

'I've seen programmes on the telly,' he said in a voice knowing beyond his years. 'Those baby-making doctors. They can do all sorts of things these days. Don't worry, Sophie. It will all come right in the end.'

She bit her lip, and squeezed her eyes shut as tears threatened; his sympathy, and his assurance, were almost more than she could bear. 'That's very sweet of you, Dominic, but I'm not at all sure that it will.'

'Do you want to talk about it?' he invited.

'No.' Again she clenched her hands. 'Yes. Oh, yes.' After a shuddering sigh, she went on. 'You just can't imagine how awful it is. The things people say. Unthinking, cruel things that hurt so much. "Don't you think it's about time you started a family? You're not getting any younger, you know." That's what my sister says. And other people, too. People who . . . well, it's none of their business.'

'That's horrible!' he said indignantly. 'And rude, as well.'

Now that she'd started, she couldn't stop. 'And there are babies everywhere. Everywhere I go, babies in prams and pushchairs. Pregnant women and babies. It's like . . . a reproof. A visible reproof to me, and a reminder of . . . my failure. My failure as a woman. As a wife. Chris wants children so badly – he always has done.' She couldn't go on. It was too painful. Sophie gulped and stared down at her hands.

'Don't blame yourself,' Dominic said. 'It's not your fault.'

'Oh, but it is! There's nothing wrong with *him*. And I'm the one who wanted to wait. Maybe if we'd started earlier, like he wanted to . . .'

'You can't know that.'

'All I know is that there's something wrong with me. I'm not . . . normal.' Her voice was passionate.

There was a long silence; no more reassurances came from Dominic. After a moment Sophie raised her head to look at him. His face was white and set; his eyes looked enormous, and they were filled with tears. At once she stopped thinking of herself. 'Dominic, what is it? What's the matter?'

'I'm not normal, either,' he said in a low voice. 'There's something wrong with me as well.'

'What do you mean?' She was alarmed: surely the boy wasn't ill with some incurable disease?

He wouldn't look at her. 'You must know. You must have guessed.'

'Dominic, what are you talking about? Tell me.'

The boy got up and began pacing from one end to the other of the small room. 'I can't say it,' he stated.

Sophie had to turn her head to see him. 'You're not ill, are you?'

'Ill?' He gave a shaky laugh. 'Some would say so. My mother, for one. And my holy brother, I'm sure. They would say I was sick. Sick, sick, sick.'

Bafflement had now joined Sophie's alarm. 'But what is it? If you're ill, I'm sure that your family would—'

'I'm gay,' he announced baldly. He had stopped pacing, and grabbed on to the back of the sofa for support. 'Homosexual. Whatever you want to call it. Now I suppose you'll hate me.'

Sophie felt as if the wind had been knocked out of her; for a moment she was unable to speak. Of course. She didn't question the truth of what he'd said. Now that he'd spoken the words, she realised that she wasn't in the least surprised. If she hadn't been so wrapped up in her own woes and concerns, she would have guessed, would have acknowledged the truth to herself, a long time ago. It made sense of so much about him, like the last piece of a jigsaw puzzle falling into place and making a coherent picture of the whole. 'No, of course I don't hate you,' she said carefully.

'You believe me, then?'

She smiled in spite of herself. 'It's not something you'd make up. Just to make me feel better.'

'No, but . . .' Abruptly he threw himself down on to the sofa. 'But sometimes people think it's just a phase. Something that all boys go through, and grow out of. At public schools, especially. You know.'

'I *have* heard such things, certainly. And I suppose there's some truth in that, for some people. Experimentation, and all that.'

Dominic's fair skin flushed. 'It's not a phase,' he said insistently. 'I've always known. Always. That I was . . . different. As long as I can remember.'

She believed him. He *was* different. 'Is that what your mother says?' she asked. 'That it's just a phase?'

'My *mother*?' He stared at her, as if she'd just sprouted a second head. 'My mother? You can't possibly think that I've told my mother?'

Later that evening, after supper, when Chris was out at the pub with the choir men, Sophie's thoughts returned to Dominic and their painful conversation.

He hadn't told his mother. Of course he hadn't told her. How could he, when she was so set upon him becoming a priest? And however anyone might feel about the justice or the wisdom of it, the Church of England still refused, officially, to ordain gay people as priests.

Sophie had pointed out to Dominic that telling his mother was perhaps one sure way to convince her, once and for all, that the priesthood was not for him. But he hadn't agreed. 'In the first place, she wouldn't believe me,' he said. 'She'd think I was just saying it to get her off my back. And anyway,' he went on, his voice tinged with bitterness, 'everyone knows that it doesn't mean anything. What the Church says and the Church does are two different things. It's a nonsense, really. Officially there are no gay priests. What a joke. There are hundreds of them, thousands of them. But as long as they don't tell their bishops, or get caught in a public lavatory, everyone turns a blind eye.'

Hypocritical sophistry, then.

In her ignorance of the Church, Sophie had always been a bit cynical about it. Until she'd come to Westmead, to dwell in the all-pervasive shadow of the cathedral, her attitude towards the Church could have been described as indifference rather than hostility, disinterest rather than antipathy. Now that the Church was always there, at the edges of her consciousness, she found that she could no longer avoid thinking about it.

An institution that said one thing and did another. Like the Government, like any other institution that was made up of fallible human beings. In the Church, though, this hypocrisy seemed to be magnified through the lens of its ostensible holiness. People in the Church *ought* to be better than other people, ought at least to be more honest. But they were still people, after all, and people falling short of an ideal always seemed worse, more reprehensible, than if there were no ideal to fall short of.

She found that Dominic's bald assertion about gay priests had shocked her. She'd been aware that there were such things, but she had always assumed that they were in a tiny minority. Thousands, he'd said. And, he'd added, they were some of the best priests, too.

Still, Sophie was sure that his mother wouldn't see it that way. She might not consider her son's sexual orientation as an absolute bar to the priesthood, but she would certainly not be overjoyed about it.

'You must tell her,' Sophie said. 'It's not fair to her if you don't.'

'I can't.' Dominic's face was white, his lips compressed. 'Not now. Not yet. I just can't.'

She could see his point. Elspeth Verey had, till now, imposed her will upon her son in virtually every aspect of his life. She had moulded him, shaped him, as she had his brother. But this fundamental thing was something over which she had no control. Elspeth Verey could not wave a magic wand over her son and make him heterosexual. She might still hold out firm hopes that she could wear down his resistance to the priesthood, but this was something she could not change.

And, in many ways, Sophie could empathise with her. It was not the life one would choose for one's child.

Inevitably, moving in London's artistic circles, Sophie had known a great many gay men. Some of them, indeed, she had counted amongst her closest friends. So there was no shock there, no revulsion. She loved camp humour; she was fully tuned in to the gay sensibility.

And yet, she realised, she would not choose it for a child of hers. Even now, in the supposedly enlightened twenty-first century, it was a lifestyle fraught with dangers, and with problems that heterosexual people could never fully understand.

If it seemed so to her, how much more so would it seem to Elspeth Verey? Conventional, proper, upright Elspeth Verey? Elspeth Verey, the control freak?

It didn't bear thinking about.

The next day, a Tuesday, Sophie went out shopping in the morning, hoping to avoid a visit from Leslie Clunch, and encountered Trish Evans by the entrance to Quire Close. She was in no mood to talk to fecund Trish Evans, but by the time she saw her, bearing down eagerly, it was too late.

'Oh – I've been hoping to see you,' Trish greeted her. 'And I've been meaning to ring. But I just haven't . . .'

Sophie tried not to look at Trish's protruding abdomen, nor at the squirming toddler in the pushchair.

'I was wondering whether you might come to our little get-together on Friday morning,' Trish continued. 'As I've told you before, it's just a few of us choir wives – or should

I call us choir widows,' she giggled, 'who get together for a cup of coffee and a good old moan.'

It wasn't the first time that Trish, in such random encounters, had offered the invitation; always before Sophie had had a legitimate excuse. But though the idea of a group of moaning choir wives did not particularly appeal to her, she was beginning to feel the lack of female companionship.

'I've invited Miranda Swan as well,' Trish added, in the manner of one proffering an irresistible lure. No doubt Trish, like everyone else in the Close, was desperately curious about the Precentor's new wife, and was sure that Sophie would share her curiosity. 'She's said that she'll come, if she can manage it.'

'I can't promise,' Sophie evaded. 'But I'll try to make it.'

'Oh, that's brilliant. It's at mine this week. Ten o'clock, or a bit after.'

'All right. I'll try.' That, Sophie reflected, didn't commit her unalterably; she could always change her mind, or come up with a subsequent engagement. But perhaps she would go. It would be interesting to meet Miranda Swan, in any case.

Laparoscopy. 'Just a bit of keyhole surgery,' Mr York said in his calm, reassuring voice. 'Not much to it. We'll just have a little look inside, and you can go home the same day.'

The scan, he explained, his beautiful hands folded on the desk in front of him, had indicated some possible irregularities. The only way to be sure of the true situation was to perform a laparoscopy, inserting a tiny probe into her abdomen.

'What sort of irregularities?'

He was ever the diplomat, smooth and unforthcoming. 'I can't say, really. Not without having a look. It's quite routine. Nothing to worry about,' he added. 'And then we'll have a much better idea of what we're dealing with.'

'When?' said Sophie, wanting to get it over with, dreading what it would discover.

'As soon as possible.' He smiled at her, a professional smile. 'You'll be getting a letter with an appointment, Mrs Lilburn. I promise you that you won't have to wait long.'

How long was not long? And what on earth had the scan revealed, to spur him on to this next step? Sophie fretted about it during the long train journey back to Westmead. This time Chris had offered to drive her to the appointment, to arrange for a supply teacher and a choir deputy, but she had refused. Of course it involved both of them, but she'd wanted to face the doctor alone, to hear what he had to say and have time to absorb it before she had to tell Chris.

And by the time he met her at the station, she had managed to arrange her face into a cheerful smile, as reassuring as that of Mr York. 'Nothing to worry about,' she repeated. 'A little keyhole surgery. Home the same day.'

'You're sure you're not worried?' he asked, looking relieved.

'He says it's routine.'

Routine for him, perhaps. Sophie scarcely slept that night, going over and over the conversation in her mind, probing for shades of meaning behind the doctor's words.

Something was wrong with her, seriously wrong. If he didn't suspect that, why wouldn't he tell her what he *did* suspect? If it really was nothing to worry about, why was he scheduling it as soon as possible? Not just to reassure her, but because he knew there was something wrong.

Just as she was about to drift off to sleep, in the small hours of the morning, the baby from two houses down began to cry. The volume must have been ear-splitting; even with the windows closed and that much distance between, Sophie could hear its wails clearly. She buried her head in her pillow, but the shrieks echoed painfully in her head.

In the morning she continued to put on a cheerful face for Chris's sake, at least until he was out of the house. But she would not, she determined, go to Trish Evans's. She didn't have the will to face anyone; she couldn't continue to pretend that everything was as it should be.

At five minutes to ten, though, she happened to look out of the front window, to see Leslie Clunch bearing purposefully for her front door.

Leslie Clunch was an infinitely worse prospect than Trish and her chums. His company, his conversation, were relentless and unavoidable. Once he was in her house, she wouldn't be able to get rid of him for at least an hour, unless she faked a headache or the onset of some other mystery ailment. And that would only elicit his concern, thinly masking his curiosity. He would probe and probe to get to the bottom of it.

Sophie made a sudden decision. Grabbing her handbag and her jacket, she opened the front door before he could ring the bell, and fixed an expression of surprise on her face as she saw him. 'Oh, hello,' she said. 'I was just going out.'

He stood his ground. 'I was wondering if you were all right,' he said. 'When I called yesterday, you were out.

And you weren't home all day. You didn't get back until after Evensong.'

She suppressed a shiver; it was as if he knew her every movement, and that realisation made her deeply uneasy. She would *not* give in to it; she would *not* tell him where she'd been. Sophie made a show of consulting her watch. 'Yes, I'm all right, thank you,' she said briskly. 'But I'm going to be late if I don't go now. Trish Evans is expecting me.'

'Oh, yes.' He gave a dismissive snort. 'The young mums. Not quite your sort of thing, I wouldn't have thought.'

Not her thing, she was sure. *You've driven me to it*, she wanted to say. She hated herself for her cowardice. Why was she resorting to this? Why couldn't she just tell him to go away?

Leslie Clunch still hadn't moved from his central position, blocking her escape. 'Perhaps I'll see you later, then,' he said. 'Teatime, perhaps.'

'Someone may be coming later.'

'Oh, yes.' He gave a knowing nod. 'Young Dominic Verey, that will be.' His smile bared his crooked yellow teeth. 'What does his mum think of him spending so much time here, then?'

'I don't know,' Sophie said, barely civil, and stepped into the garden to get round him. 'Why don't you ask her?'

By the time she had reached her destination across the close, under his watchful eye, she was regretting her rudeness, as well as her rashness in saying that she was going to Trish's. It was the first thing that had come into her head, and now she was committed to it. He was watching;

she couldn't very well go anywhere else. If only she'd thought to say that she was meeting someone *outside* the close . . .

'Sophie, you've come!' Trish enthused, opening the door.

At least, Sophie thought, it seemed a genuine welcome. Maybe it wouldn't be so bad.

'Come on through. We're still missing a few. But I'm so glad that you've come.'

The room into which Trish led her was small; three or four people would have filled it, and there were already half a dozen women crowded into the space. Most of them were strangers to Sophie, though she'd seen some of them coming and going from the close, usually laden with shopping and children. They were all much of a type, virtually interchangeable. Trish made some rapid introductions.

The children were there, as well; Sophie hadn't expected that, though of course she should have done. This was really, she realised, a sort of glorified playgroup, the mums drinking coffee and keeping each other company while the toddlers played.

Katie Evans, as the resident child, held court bossily in the centre of the room, doling out her toys to the other children. 'You can have Doggie,' she said to a fair-haired boy in a tiny denim overall, handing him a moth-eaten, one-eared stuffed animal.

'Want blocks,' he announced.

'No.'

He threw the scorned toy to the floor. 'Want blocks!'

Sophie had already forgotten which of the women was Jennifer and which was Louise. But Miranda Swan was there, sitting on the low-slung sofa, and there was an empty spot next to her, as though the others were shy of her. Sophie squeezed in beside her, trying to ignore the fracas that was now taking place over the disputed blocks. 'Want blocks!' the boy was now bellowing, red in the face.

None of the mothers paid any attention. 'I'll put the kettle on, shall I?' Trish suggested happily.

Sophie turned to Miranda Swan. Up close the woman seemed perhaps a bit older than when seen from a distance, the lines under her eyes etched clearly in the glare of the harsh overhead light. But the eyes were a warm brown, and their corners crinkled when she smiled. 'Your husband is in the choir, then?' enquired Mrs Swan; her voice was low and pleasing.

'Yes. Chris Lilburn. He sings tenor,' she confirmed.

'Dark hair? Sits at the end of the row on the Decani side?'

'I don't know where he sits,' confessed Sophie. 'I don't go. I've never been.'

The tone of Miranda Swan's reply was incredulous rather than censorious. 'You've never been? You're missing a real treat. The choir are so good, you know.'

'The cathedral . . .' Sophie trailed off; how could she explain it? 'Well, it's Chris's thing, not mine.'

'I love it,' confessed Miranda, as though she were making a shameful admission. 'Evensong, especially. There's nothing like it. This time of year, in the twilight, getting dark, with the candles – it's like magic. And the choir are wonderful, and Peter sings the Office so well.' She smiled as she spoke her husband's name; it was said almost with reverence.

Sophie felt a pang that was akin to envy. When was the last time she had spoken of Chris like that, her face alight with the joy of her love for him? Had it *ever* been like that for her? She could scarcely remember. 'I hear that you're moving into Quire Close,' she said.

'Yes, Peter and I are looking forward to it.' That wondering, radiant smile again, coupled with a shy hesitation as she linked herself with his name, as if still marvelling at the conjunction. 'The flat is quite small. It will be lovely to be in a proper house.'

By now, thought Sophie, Miranda Swan must be sick of all the probing questions; apparently, from all Sophie had heard, she was skilful at deflecting them. 'How do you like Westmead, then?' she asked, trying for a neutral subject.

Miranda's reply was prompt and sincere. 'It's wonderful. The town – city – has so much character, such a history. The shops are excellent. And then there's the cathedral, which is so splendid.' She twisted the thick gold wedding band round her finger, smiling to herself, and Sophie could read on her face the unspoken corollary: Peter. Peter is here.

'But it's not London,' Sophie said, before she could help herself.

'London? Oh, I wouldn't want to live in London. Far too dirty and crowded. And all that traffic. No, Westmead seems just right to me.'

'You've never lived in London, then?'

'Good heavens, no.' Miranda shook her head, but volunteered no more information.

Just then the confrontation between the toddlers escalated into drama, as the little boy grabbed one of Katie's blocks and threw it at her. It clipped her on the side of the head, and she shrieked, more in rage than pain. Her mother was out of the room, but the boy's mother – Louise? Jennifer? – scooped him up on to her lap. 'You know what I've told you about playing nicely,' she said to him, while he struggled and glowered.

'You don't have children, then?' Miranda addressed Sophie. 'Or are they in school?'

It was Sophie's turn to be evasive; she tried to keep her voice even. 'No. No, we don't.'

Miranda turned her head away slightly, but Sophie could see that tears had sprung to her eyes. 'I did,' she said in such a quiet voice that Sophie had to strain to hear. 'I had a daughter. But she's dead.'

This was so unexpected that Sophie hardly knew what to say. Miranda Swan had been a widow, then, when she married the Precentor – not a spinster, as Sophie had assumed. 'Oh! I'm so sorry,' she managed.

Just then the doorbell went, and there was another flurry of activity a moment later as Trish re-entered the room with a tray of coffee cups, followed by another woman carrying a baby.

'Sorry I'm late,' announced the woman. 'He was making a terrible fuss.'

As if on cue, the baby screwed up his face, opened his mouth and howled. The noise was like fingernails on a blackboard, only much louder.

It was, Sophie realised immediately with an involuntary clenching of her stomach muscles, the baby from two doors down whose cries haunted her waking moments and interrupted her sleep.

She couldn't bear it; Sophie blundered to her feet. 'I'm sorry,' she said to Trish, moving towards the door. 'Forgive me. I have to go.'

Chapter 10

The days following Frank Barnett's death were busy ones for Jacquie. The condolence calls continued, and then there were the practical things to be seen to: obtaining the death certificate, registering the death, making funeral arrangements.

She'd been through it all before with her mother, so the routine was not unfamiliar to her. And her father had left very clear instructions, indicating his wishes; he'd even chosen the hymns for the funeral service, which would of course be held at the Free Baptist Fellowship. After the funeral he was to be laid to rest beside his wife in the burial ground.

Jacquie went through it all on autopilot. 'Isn't she brave?' agreed everyone who knew her. 'And now she's alone in the world.'

In her numbness, that realisation took a while to dawn on her. She *was* alone now, she told herself. No ties, no responsibilities. No function in life. She could sell the house. Leave Sutton Fen, even, if she wanted to. She could go anywhere, do anything.

All the while, though, she lived with a nagging sense of unfinished business.

Alison. Alison should be here. Her sister should be at her side, helping her with the arrangements. Together they should be making plans for the future – a future without their parents.

It was during this week – the week between the death and the funeral – that Jacquie's determination to find her sister took hold. There was now nothing to stop her, she realised: no frosty disapproval on the part of her mother, no wistful longing from her father. The idea which she'd had on that first night after her father's death lodged in her mind like a gritty little seed, and once lodged she couldn't get rid of it. The seed sprouted, sent up thin green tendrils, and entwined with all of her conscious and unconscious thoughts. Alison.

Later, she was glad that the idea had been her own, that she had already set her mind to finding Alison, even before she'd seen the solicitor.

Mr Mockler, her father's solicitor, was, of course, a leading light of the Free Baptist Fellowship. Additionally, he was a member of the True Men, carrying out the precepts of that movement in his own life. Jacquie didn't know him well, but from what she knew of him, she had no reason to like him. He had teeth like tombstones, fingers like sausages, and a manner of supreme self-importance.

He called on her a few days before the funeral, bringing with him two shocks.

The first he imparted almost immediately, over a cup of tea in the front parlour. 'I am the executor of Mr Barnett's will,' he announced, his voice as pompous as his expression.

'But I thought that *I* would be the executor,' Jacquie protested.

'Oh, no.' He smiled, baring his tombstone teeth. 'Mr Barnett might not have been a member of the True Men, but he knew that such matters should never be left to women. Originally he had named your then-husband, Mr Darke, as executor, but that, of course, is no longer appropriate.'

'No,' said Jacquie numbly.

'So I suggested that I might serve in that capacity, and Mr Barnett agreed. With Mr Prew's blessing, I might add.'

What did it have to do with Reverend Prew? Jacquie wondered. But she kept her face impassive, focusing on the sausage-like fingers as the solicitor raised the teacup to his lips and took a sip. 'How long will it take to sort things out?' she asked. 'I think I'd like to sell the house.'

Mr Mockler lowered his cup and exploded the second bombshell. 'Oh, you won't be able to do that,' he said. 'Not without your sister's permission, at any rate.'

'What?' Jacquie stared at him, stunned.

'Didn't you know?' He favoured her with another baring of the tombstone teeth. 'Your sister Alison is the joint beneficiary of your father's will. Half of the house belongs to her. Half of everything, in fact.'

'But Alison . . .'

'Left Sutton Fen some years ago. Yes, I know.' He put the teacup down on the table and laced his fat fingers across his abdomen.

She couldn't take it in. 'But my mother . . .' she protested. 'She always used to say that when they were gone, everything would be mine. The house and everything.'

'Mrs Barnett didn't know. Mr Barnett didn't want her to know. But he insisted until the end – and I saw him in hospital, less than a week before his death – that Alison was to receive half of his estate.'

Jacquie's hands were shaking; she put her cup on the table to avoid spilling her tea. 'But it's been over ten years! We've never heard from her in that time. I don't have any idea where she is.'

'Then I suggest,' said Mr Mockler smoothly, 'that you find her.'

She *would* find her; she *must* find her.

But how?

Late that night, sleepless, she went over and over the same ground in her mind. How did one find a person who had been missing for eleven years? Someone, presumably, who had no wish to be found? How would one even begin?

She remembered, then, something that Nicola Jeffries had mentioned to her just a few days before: the Citizens' Advice Bureau. Could they help her? Nicola had worked with them for a time; perhaps she would even be able to offer some advice herself.

With that in mind, Jacquie went to the florist's shop the next morning, hoping to find Nicola working there.

Nicola was behind the counter, and there was a queue. 'I'd love to chat,' she said to Jacquie, 'but I can't at the moment. Why don't I come round to you after work?'

'Yes,' Jacquie agreed, adding impulsively, 'Come for a meal. If your husband doesn't mind, that is.'

'Oh, bugger Keith,' Nicola said with a humorous shrug. 'He has his precious Brittany there tonight – they can eat baked beans together. I'll look forward to it.'

'So will I.' Jacquie discovered, as she left the shop, that she was looking forward to it already. And it gave her something to do, something to occupy her for the rest of the day. It had been quite a long time since she'd done any entertaining – years, in fact. Not since she and Darren had split up. Once she'd enjoyed having their friends round of an evening, preparing nice meals for them, but those days were long gone. All of the cooking she'd done since she'd moved back home – and she'd done quite a lot – had been of the utilitarian variety, and for invalids at that.

This would be different; this would be fun.

Feeling more cheerful than she had in a long time, Jacquie went along to the Mini Mart.

She would give Nicola something special, she decided – Nicola, who had to scrimp and save, and eat baked beans so that her spoiled stepdaughter could have everything that her heart desired. She would give her something more like supper than tea.

The Barnetts had always had their big meal – their dinner – at midday, followed by a simple tea in the evening. These days, Jacquie didn't eat much of anything, midday or evening: an egg, usually, or a tin of something. But tonight would be different.

Darren had always enjoyed her steak and kidney pie, had always praised it, and she admitted to herself that she *did* have a light hand with pastry. Her father couldn't digest steak and kidney, so she hadn't made it for at least two years, but it would be fun to have a go. Perhaps that would be the thing to do. She made a detour into the butcher's, and came out with a parcel of stewing steak and kidney.

Everything else she needed would be available at the Mini Mart: a few nibbles, veg, and something nice for pud.

The Mini Mart was crowded that Friday morning, with people doing their shopping before the weekend. Jacquie took a basket and threaded her way through the shop, round the pushchairs of the young mums and the trolleys of the old dears. Concentrating on her cooking plans, debating between single and double cream for the pudding, she failed to notice one of the young mums until it was too late.

'Hello, Jacquie,' said the woman, with what could only be described as a smirk.

It was Darren's wife, the second Mrs Darke.

She was manoeuvring an unwieldy double pushchair containing her two young progeny, and it was evident that yet another child was on the way.

'Hello,' Jacquie muttered, not bothering to be gracious, but too well-brought-up to be deliberately rude.

'I was *so* sorry to hear about your father. And Darren is devastated. Simply devastated. He always thought of him as a second father, he told me.'

Yes, I'll bet, thought Jacquie sourly. She hadn't had a word of condolence from Darren himself. Not that she would want to. Not that she cared.

'We'll both be at the funeral, of course. Darren will probably have to close the garage for an hour or so. But it's the least he could do, he says. For dear Mr Barnett.'

The older of the infants in the pushchair began grizzling. Jacquie tried not to look at the child, but her eyes were drawn to it. Both babies had Darren's colouring, Darren's nose; it was too painful to look at them. They should have been hers, she thought, her useless womb contracting.

She ought to say something; she *must* say something.

Something neutral. 'Steak and kidney,' she stated irrelevantly, holding up her parcel. 'Darren's favourite.'

The second Mrs Darke laughed. 'Don't I know it. But he doesn't get it from me,' she said, almost as if she were proud of the fact. 'Too much work. I don't have time for that sort of thing, so I just give him Fray Bentos instead. The babies keep me far too busy,' she added smugly, then patted her swollen abdomen. 'And at the moment, just the thought of kidneys makes me queasy. I'm always like that when I'm pregnant.' *But then you wouldn't know about that.* Her look said it as clearly as if she'd spoken the words.

Unbidden, a Bible verse popped into Jacquie's mind: 'And her adversary also provoked her sore, for to make her fret, because the Lord had shut up her womb.' Tears stung her eyes; she turned away, not caring now whether it seemed rude, and fled with her basket to the checkout.

The encounter had destroyed all of her pleasure in the anticipation of entertaining. Apathetically she rolled out the pastry and prepared the filling. In her agitation she had come away without the ingredients for the trifle she had intended to make for pudding. It would have to be fruit, or ice-cream from the freezer.

'Mm – something smells divine,' Nicola enthused when she breezed in a few hours later.

In spite of herself, Jacquie felt her spirits lift. 'Steak and kidney.'

'Oh, yum.' Nicola proffered a bottle of wine. 'Open this straight away,' she ordered. 'I need a glass right now.'

Jacquie took the bottle. 'You shouldn't have.'

'Oh, I know. It's only plonk, the cheapest bottle I could

find. But as long as it has alcohol in it,' Nicola added with a grin, 'I don't care.'

It had been years since Jacquie had touched alcohol – not since her marriage to Darren. Not, in fact, since that holiday in Greece. The holiday with Alison. She pushed the thought of the holiday, of Alison, from her. 'But I'm sure we don't have a corkscrew in the house,' she said.

'Corkscrew?' Nicola laughed. 'I told you it was cheap plonk. You don't need a corkscrew for a screw-top bottle.'

'That's all right, then.' Why not? thought Jacquie defiantly. There was no longer anyone left to disapprove. Her parents were dead, Darren was gone, and Reverend Prew no longer had the power to control her life. But as she fetched the water tumblers – there were, needless to say, no wineglasses in the house – it was her sister's face she saw: Alison's shocked expression, when she had ordered wine at the bar in the Greek hotel.

She sloshed the wine into the tumblers, suddenly urgent for the distantly remembered feeling of release that the alcohol promised. 'Here, then.'

'Cheers.' Nicola clunked her tumbler against Jacquie's and took a gulp. 'Oh, that's foul,' she sputtered with a grimace. 'But I don't care.'

They settled down in the kitchen. On the table, Jacquie had placed bowls of peanuts and crisps, and the makeshift ashtray. Nicola helped herself to a handful of crisps and reached into her handbag for her packet of cigarettes. 'Would you like one?' she offered, holding out the packet to Jacquie.

Jacquie was tempted: now that she had started down the path towards damnation, what was to stop her? But common sense prevailed, as well as a realisation that in taking one she would be depriving Nicola of a valued treat that she could ill afford. She waved the packet away. 'No, thanks, I won't.'

Nicola lit up and drew in the first breath, then exhaled slowly. 'That's better,' she sighed. 'God, I needed that.'

The wine was enough for Jacquie. Unused to its effects, and on an empty stomach, she found that it only took a few swallows for her to feel a bit peculiar, but in a very pleasant way. 'It was nice of you to bring the wine,' she said.

'Oh, don't mention it. It was selfish, really. After the day I've had, I needed it.' Nicola launched into an account of her day: the difficult customers, the demanding boss looking over her shoulder. 'But at least I had this to look forward to,' she finished. 'You don't know how nice it was to think that I wouldn't have to sit across the table from Brittany's sarky face tonight.' As if realising that her words might have sounded ungracious, she added, 'And it's great to see you, Jacquie. I really enjoyed visiting you the other day. I was hoping that it wouldn't just be a one-off. This is really kind of you.'

Jacquie remembered the reason for the invitation, and might have felt a bit guilty, if the wine hadn't been affecting her, and if Nicola hadn't herself just confessed to selfishness. As it was, she came clean straight away. 'It's great to see you, too. But I had a reason for wanting to talk to you.'

'Oh?'

'You mentioned that you'd done some work with the Citizens' Advice Bureau,' Jacquie said. 'And I wondered what advice you might give to someone who was looking for . . . well, for someone who'd gone missing. You know.'

'You want to find your sister,' Nicola guessed, with a shrewd look at Jacquie's down-turned face. 'You want to find Alison.'

'Yes.' For a moment Jacquie struggled for control, biting her lower lip. Then she took a deep breath. 'I may as well tell you. The solicitor says that I have to find her, because my father has left her half of everything. But I'd already decided, before that. For myself. I need to find her.'

Nicola smoked thoughtfully for a moment. 'I'm sure that the solicitor will be making enquiries, you know. That's what they do. They hire private detectives and things like that to find missing heirs. Especially if there's much money at stake.'

'Not that much money,' Jacquie said. 'Not what a solicitor would consider a huge estate, I'm sure. Though my parents were very frugal, and saved as much as they could. So there's a bit in the building society.' No holidays, no alcohol, no luxuries: it all added up over the years. 'And there's the house, of course.'

'The house.' Nicola looked round her at the drab kitchen.

'I want to sell it. I want to leave this town.' There was more passion than she'd intended in Jacquie's voice.

'And you can't sell it until you've found Alison,' said Nicola shrewdly.

It was the truth, but it was crucial to Jacquie to make Nicola understand. 'But that's not the most important thing. I need to find her. For myself.'

'Yes.'

'She's my sister. She's all I have. We used to be . . . so close.' Jacquie lowered her head. 'I miss her,' she added softly. 'And I need to . . . make things right between us.'

Nicola took a long draw on her cigarette. 'I was at the wedding,' she said. 'I understand.'

Nicola had been there: Jacquie remembered now. She had been with Alison in the ladies' toilet when they'd had that last, dreadful scene, the scene that haunted her dreams though she managed to avoid thinking about it in her waking hours. Was that, she asked herself now with painful honesty, why she had avoided Nicola all those years? Why they had so quickly grown apart?

They had never talked about it.

And Jacquie had managed to forget Nicola's presence at that final confrontation, had erased her from her memories of the scene. Now it all flooded back with dreadful clarity: Alison grovelling on the floor, her face pale and tear-streaked, her dress stained. And Nicola, there beside her.

She didn't want to know, didn't want to hear it, but she knew that she must. 'Tell me what you remember,' Jacquie asked.

'I've never forgotten it,' said Nicola reflectively. 'She was . . . a wreck. Hysterical. And you were . . . well, I've never seen anyone so angry. I didn't know that you could be like that. But you were upset,' she added, as if she feared that Jacquie might take her words as criticism of her. 'It was your wedding day, for God's sake. Anyone would have been upset to have their wedding ruined like that.'

'I was awful,' admitted Jacquie, swallowing hard. 'There's no excuse for the way I behaved.'

Nicola tapped a long snake of grey ash into the saucer. 'I'm sure she's forgiven you,' she said.

'Do you think so?' Jacquie raised her face with a pathetically eager expression. 'Do you think she could have done, after the things I said to her?'

'It's been so many years.' Nicola looked at her fingers, as if counting them. 'Ten years? Eleven? She knew that your wedding was important to you. She was terribly sorry that she'd ruined it. And she knew that you loved her.'

'She did? How do you know?'

Nicola took her time replying as she concentrated on the end of her cigarette, holding it between her thumb and forefinger to extract the very last bit of goodness from it before stubbing it out in the saucer. Then she exhaled slowly. 'She told me so. Afterwards. When I took her home.'

Jacquie stared at her. 'You took Alison home? After the wedding?'

'How did you think she got home?'

'I . . . didn't think,' Jacquie admitted. 'At that point I didn't care what happened to her, I'm ashamed to say. I was only thinking about myself.'

'I took her home – brought her here – and waited while she packed her suitcase. Then I took her to catch the bus. I even loaned her twenty pounds, since she didn't have enough cash for her fare. She said she'd pay me back – that she'd send it to me,' Nicola added, with a wry smile. 'But she never did.'

Revelation upon revelation: Jacquie was astonished. Why had she never asked Nicola about this? How could she not have known that Nicola was the last person in Sutton Fen to have seen Alison? Then another thought occurred to her. 'But where was she going? Didn't she say? She must have said.' Her voice was urgent, pleading.

'To Ely, in the first instance. I was with her when she got on the bus.' She extracted another cigarette from the pack and lit it. 'She was planning to catch a train at Ely.

But she didn't say where. Just that she was going to the father of her child. Mike, was he called? I think it was Mike.'

'And she didn't say where?' Jacquie didn't want to believe it. Surely, surely she must have said. She twisted her hands in a gesture of supplication. 'You're sure?'

Nicola shook her head as she exhaled a stream of smoke. 'I asked, but she didn't want to tell me. Evidently she knew where he was, though. She seemed confident enough that she could find him.'

Jacquie squeezed her eyes shut to hold back the tears of frustration. If only Alison had said!

'But there *are* ways of finding people, you know,' Nicola said quickly. 'It was a question we often got at the Citizens' Advice Bureau.'

'Tell me! Tell me what to do,' Jacquie demanded.

Nicola became a detached professional. 'The first port of call should be the Salvation Army,' she said.

'The Salvation Army?'

'They have a great deal of experience, and success, at finding missing persons. Quite a phenomenal success rate, in fact. Something over ninety per cent, I believe.'

'But why? How?' Jacquie wanted to believe her, but it sounded too good to be true.

'They've been doing it for years, apparently. Only family members, though,' she added. 'Not long-lost lovers or anything like that. Just immediate family.'

'Alison is my immediate family,' stated Jacquie, as if fearing that there might be some doubt.

'Of course. And the thing is that the Salvation Army, because they've been doing this for so long, have access to all sorts of records and sources of information that even the police don't have. Like DSS records. If someone is drawing benefits, or paying National Insurance, the Sally Army can find that out.'

It was too easy, thought Jacquie, trying to quell the bubble of hope. 'But she's probably married. She won't have the same name.'

'They'll find her,' stated Nicola confidently. 'If she's still in this country, they can find her. People leave paper trails – banks and building societies, National Insurance, the DVLA, the Inland Revenue. Most people, when they disappear, even voluntarily, take all of those things with them, all of those numbers. Those numbers follow you everywhere, all your life. It's very difficult to establish a new identity, with the best will in the world.'

It all sounded very plausible, the way that Nicola put it. Feeling more positive than she had in days, Jacquie took another sip of wine. Cheap plonk it may have been, but it tasted delicious to her.

'A toast,' announced Nicola, raising her glass. 'Here's to finding Alison.'

The meal was consumed in a mellow alcoholic haze. The wine smoothed the edges off any awkwardness they might have felt; they relaxed with each other and began talking about old times, reminiscing about their carefree days together at the Mini Mart.

'And speaking of the Mini Mart,' said Jacquie as she cleared their plates, 'I was in there today. I meant to get the ingredients to make a trifle for tonight. But . . . well, I didn't. We'll have to make do with ice-cream.' She rummaged in the freezer compartment and pulled out an ice-encrusted box. 'It doesn't look very nice,' she pronounced ruefully. 'Sorry about that.' It had, she realised, been in there for quite a long time.

'Never mind. Do you have any chocolate sauce?'

Jacquie shook her head. 'No, sorry. How about some tinned fruit cocktail?'

'Yes, all right.'

She opened the tin and spooned the fruit over the gummy, unappetising-looking ice-cream, then handed a bowl to Nicola.

Nicola looked at it without enthusiasm, but gamely tucked in. 'What happened at the Mini Mart, then? Did you just forget about the trifle?'

'Not exactly.' Jacquie took a spoonful of ice-cream, let it melt on her tongue, then found herself telling Nicola about her encounter with the second Mrs Darke. 'The little . . . bitch!' she finished explosively, and realised that she felt better for having said it.

Nicola laughed. 'Atta girl, Jacquie. Don't let them get to you. Here,' she added. 'There's a drop left in the bottle. I think you deserve it.' She held the bottle over Jacquie's glass and poured the last dribble of wine into it. 'What a cow.'

Jacquie tilted her glass and drained the wine. 'She's supposed to be so holy,' she stated in a bitter voice. 'Like all of them. All of those pious cows. And yet she was so cruel. On purpose. She wanted to hurt me.'

'Of course she wanted to hurt you. Just like I want to hurt the Bitch, Keith's ex. But at least I'm honest about it,' Nicola grinned. 'But then, I'm not supposed to be holy. Nobody expects me to be.'

'I'm not going back there.' Jacquie gave a rebellious scowl. 'Not ever.'

'What, to the Mini Mart?'

'No, to the Free Baptist Fellowship!' They both found that inordinately funny, and giggled over it for minutes as they finished their ice-cream.

'And Reverend Prew can just . . . go to hell!' Jacquie added with wine-induced daring.

'Oh, that old windbag.' Nicola grimaced, setting them both into fresh fits of giggles.

She would find Alison, Jacquie was now convinced. Nicola's practical advice had encouraged her. There were resources, there were ways. Alison would be found, and it would be a new beginning for both of them.

For the first time in as long as she could remember, she slept soundly, and woke refreshed.

And during the night, another idea had taken hold of her, one which till now had never even crossed her mind.

She would cut her hair.

One of Reverend Prew's tenets – promulgated to his flock, and accepted without question – was the Biblical injunction that women should never allow scissors near their hair. '"But if a woman have long hair, it is a glory to her: for her hair is given her for a covering,"' Reverend Prew often quoted.

This had never bothered Jacquie before; after all, her hair was one of her best features, wavy, glossy, and thick and dark as a raven's wing. Darren had always said that he loved her hair.

As a young girl, and a young wife, she had worn her hair loose, framing her face in a dark cloud. Latterly she had taken to plaiting it or bundling it into a coil on the back of her head. But she had never considered cutting it.

Now she rose and sat before her dressing-table mirror, and freed her hair from its plait. Dispassionately she contemplated it: still wavy, still shiny, still not a hint of grey, in spite of what she had been through. A glory to her, according to the Bible and Reverend Prew.

And a symbol of the bondage to which she had been subjected for so many years.

With resolution she picked up her nail scissors and held out a lock of hair. But before she could snip it, an unexpected memory assaulted her: she and Alison, as young girls, no more than five or six. One rainy day, bored and restless, they had borrowed their mother's sewing scissors and cut each other's hair. No mischief had been intended, no rebellion; it was merely an act of experimentation. But to hear their mother's cries, you would have thought that the world was about to end. Wicked girls, she'd screamed, her eyes going to Alison. She'd had no doubt that it was Alison's fault, Alison's idea. Alison would go to hell; perhaps they both would.

Of course, in the fullness of time, their hair had grown out, and that earlier incident was completely forgotten.

The memory, strong and painful, strengthened Jacquie's resolve. But instead of the nail scissors, it seemed right that she should once again use her mother's sewing scissors.

They were where they had always been, in Joan Barnett's sewing box, kept on top of the wardrobe in the parental bedroom. Jacquie went next door, pulled the box down and blew the dust off, then opened the lid. Everything in its proper place: pins, needles, thread, thimble, scissors. She took the scissors, returned the box to the top of the wardrobe, and went back to her dressing table.

The first cut was the hardest, and Jacquie sat for a moment with the heavy lock of hair in her hand, weighing it. Then she dropped it in the bin and continued with the task.

She hadn't made a very expert job of it, she realised even before she'd finished. She'd tried for a chin-length bob, but one side was higher than the other, and the fringe had an uneven, hacked look. Remembering back to the day when she and Alison had sat on their parents' bed, mingling golden curls with black waves in the middle of the candlewick spread, she knew that in trying to repair the damage, she would undoubtedly make it worse.

But it was done. That was the main thing. She shook her head, enjoying the lightness, the freedom.

Later that morning she went along to Shear Excitement, Sutton Fen's only hairdressing salon, where a gum-chewing slip of a girl squinted at her critically and then went to work. With a few deft snips she transformed the botched bob into a short, bouncy cap of hair.

'Not bad,' said the girl when she'd finished, and held up a mirror so Jacquie could see the back. 'Suits you, like.'

Yes, thought Jacquie, smiling at her image. It suited her very well.

Chapter 11

Dull September had given way to dreary October; in Quire Close, the cobbles were slick with drizzly rain and the sky seemed to press down on the mediaeval rooftops, in spite of the efforts of the soaring chimneys to hold it at bay. Sophie was torn between conflicting instincts: she wanted to escape, to get out of the close, yet she also wanted to hibernate in her house, to burrow in and hide from the world. Leslie Clunch often drove her to do the former; leaving the close seemed to be the only way to avoid his visits. Her refuge, once she had exhausted the limited delights of the shops, was the coffee bar, where she could sit for an hour or two, nursing a caffe latte. Leslie Clunch was not likely to frequent the coffee bar; she felt safe there.

He didn't very often come in the afternoons. That, at least, was something. Afternoons seemed to be his time to do other things, to look after his wife or carry out errands on her behalf, or even to act as a volunteer tour guide in the cathedral. In the afternoons, Sophie could answer the doorbell without the horrible sinking feeling in her stomach that even the thought of Leslie Clunch now elicited – with, indeed, a lifting of the heart and raising of her spirits. In the afternoon, at teatime, her visitor was likely to be Dominic.

As the evenings drew in, and the afternoons were increasingly dark and chilly, she would close the curtains in the sitting room and light a fire. She and Dominic would toast crumpets over the fire, using an ancient toasting fork which he had produced one day with a mixture of shyness and triumph. Toasting crumpets was his idea; it quickly became a part of their ritual, accompanied by pots of tea.

After that day in which he'd made his painful confession about his sexuality, they didn't discuss the matter, or refer to it directly. Yet it informed everything that passed between them, her unspoken understanding and sympathy creating an increasing bond. He trusted her, and she began to rely on him for companionship. On the days he didn't come, for whatever reason, she found that she missed him dreadfully.

The only other person within Quire Close with whom she felt that she had any sort of relationship was Jeremy Hammond. Occasionally she would run into him in the coffee bar, and he would impart to her the latest gossip which had come his way.

One day, though – on the Friday before her laparoscopy, when she had escaped to the coffee bar to be alone with her thoughts – he came looking for her there, and found her at the corner table which she favoured. 'Sophie! Thank goodness you're here!' he said with a theatrical gesture, folding himself gracefully into the chair across from her.

She looked at him, startled. 'What is it? Has something happened?'

'Has something happened? Oh, my dear Sophie. I wanted to be the first to tell you, before you heard it from anyone else.'

Chris, she thought. Something's happened to Chris.

Her panic must have shown on her face, because Jeremy laughed. 'It's nothing like that, my dear. Nothing sinister. Just the best gossip to hit this place for years!'

Sophie relaxed. 'I'm agog.'

'You will be, believe me.' After that, he made her wait; he went up to the counter and ordered a double espresso, then brought it back to the table and made a show of stirring just the right amount of sugar into it.

'Well, tell me,' Sophie demanded.

He sat back in his chair and folded his arms across his chest. 'She's divorced,' he said, with the manner of one bestowing a precious jewel.

Sophie was beginning to get tired of his dramatic game-playing. '*Who's* divorced?'

Jeremy leaned forward and cast his eyes in either direction, as if afraid that he would be overheard. 'Miranda Swan,' he breathed in a stage whisper.

'But she's only just married him! She can't have divorced him already!' blurted Sophie. 'And she loves him. I'm sure of that.'

'Ah, Sophie, Sophie.' Jeremy took her hand and gave it a light squeeze before dropping it back on the table between them. 'What a goose you are. I mean that she's divorced from someone *else*, not from old Swan.'

For a moment Sophie didn't grasp what he was driving at. 'So? Lots of people are divorced.'

'Perhaps lots of people that *you* know are divorced,' he said severely, 'but this is a cathedral. May I remind you, my dear, that the Church of England may have eased up a bit, but divorce amongst the clergy is still a no-no.'

'But *he's* not the one who's divorced,' she pointed out.

'That doesn't matter. Marrying a divorcée is just as bad as being divorced oneself, according to the Church.'

'Oh.' Sophie thought about it for a moment. 'So what will happen? Will Canon Swan be defrocked, or whatever it is they do to them?'

'Nothing so dramatic as that,' he laughed. 'But there's going to be the most almighty kerfuffle when it all comes out. Fur will fly. Heads may roll.'

'How did you find out?' she asked. Obviously, if it were such a major issue, they had tried to keep it quiet; no wonder Miranda Swan evaded questions from all and sundry about her origins and history.

'Now *that's* rather delicious.' He leaned forward again. 'He wrote a letter to the Dean and told him everything.'

'The Dean? Then how . . .'

'The Dean left the letter on his desk yesterday. His housekeeper read it, and told the woman who does for me, and she lost no time in spilling every detail to me. Isn't that choice?'

Sophie was rather appalled, but her curiosity got the better of her. 'What did the letter say, then?'

Again Jeremy became coy, prolonging the moment by sipping his espresso. 'You must remember that the Dean and Peter Swan have known each other for yonks. They're old chums, from theological college days. That's how Swan got the job here. I mean, let's be honest – he's not a bad singer, but he's a bit long in the tooth for a precentor.'

'Yes. You told me.'

'Apparently the letter was written as an apology, because

he hadn't informed the Dean of his intentions to marry, or sought his permission as a member of Chapter. He wrote it from his honeymoon – from Venice, no less.'

So they'd gone to Venice on their honeymoon. In her mind's eye, Sophie conjured up a picture: Peter Swan and his new wife in a gondola, his arm round her shoulders, framed for a moment by an arch as they passed under the Bridge of Sighs. How romantic, she thought.

'So he came clean,' Jeremy went on. 'He explained that he couldn't say anything before, because her divorce hadn't been finalised.'

'You mean that they knew each other *before* she was divorced!' This, Sophie grasped immediately, was rather more serious than what she had assumed at first – that somehow, somewhere, Peter Swan had come across a woman with a divorce in her distant past, and had fallen in love with her. Evidently that was not the way it had happened.

'They did indeed. And what's worse, he was her vicar!'

Even Sophie, with her limited knowledge of the Church, realised that this was not quite the done thing. 'She was a member of his congregation?'

'Exactly.' Jeremy nodded and lifted an eyebrow. 'You're beginning to catch my drift.'

'Are you saying that they were having an affair while she was married to someone else? That he was implicated in her divorce?'

'He claims not,' Jeremy admitted begrudgingly. 'But then he *would* say that, wouldn't he?'

Hating herself, but thoroughly intrigued, Sophie demanded, 'What *did* he say, then?'

'He insists that it was an honourable relationship. That

she was having marital problems and he was counselling her, and they fell in love, but they didn't have an affair. That he'd waited for her for two years or more, while her divorce was sorted out, and then as soon as he could, he married her. He said that they were deeply in love, and very happy, and he hoped that the Dean would understand and be able to wish them well, and forgive him if he hadn't been entirely honest with him about his situation or his intentions.'

Sophie thought aloud. 'So he already knew her when he came here . . .'

'Exactly. He probably left his parish to put some distance between himself and the situation – it could have been a major scandal in a parish. He used his friendship with the Dean to get the post here, without telling him why he needed to leave his parish. And all the while that he's been at Westmead, he's never said a word.' Jeremy shook his head. 'You've got to hand it to the old bird. He's been one cool customer.'

'But won't there be a scandal *here*? Will he get the sack, or have to resign?'

Jeremy drained his cup of espresso before replying. 'I shouldn't think he'll have to resign. The Dean will protect him, I reckon. But there certainly will be a scandal. No matter what he says, and no matter what the truth of it is, people will believe the worst.' He grinned. 'Before you know it, the rumour mills will be working overtime. People will assume – just as you did – that he broke up her marriage. Hanky-panky at the Vicarage, and all that sort of thing.'

'Oh, dear.' Sophie realised that she felt protective towards the couple, wishing that she could fend off the destructive gossip and allow them to get on with their lives in peace. She thought about what Miranda Swan had told her: that her daughter had died. For some reason, she hadn't passed that information on to anyone – not to Chris, not to Dominic. Certainly not to Jeremy, who would have turned a personal tragedy into a matter for speculative gossip. And she wasn't about to tell him now, though she could see how it fitted into the story he'd shared with her. Probably the death of the daughter – how old had she been? how long ago had it happend? – had triggered or exacerbated the marital difficulties, possibly had driven her to seek counselling and advice and even comfort from her vicar. And they'd fallen in love. Miranda had seen past the grim exterior to the caring man inside; he had come to know a woman, vulnerable and bereaved, and had loved her. What was so terrible about that?

'I'm having another espresso,' said Jeremy. 'Can I get you a refill?'

'Caffe latte,' Sophie said automatically. 'Yes, please.'

Jeremy leaned back in his chair and turned his most charming smile on the woman behind the counter, gesturing to their empty cups. She returned his smile, and though she didn't usually leave her post, she nodded and a moment later set fresh cups in front of them.

'You've gone awfully quiet,' Jeremy remarked. 'I've dished up the choicest morsel of gossip in years for you, and you don't have much to say about it.'

Sophie stirred her coffee. 'I just feel sorry for them,' she admitted. 'Why can't people leave them alone to get on with their lives?'

'Because, my dear, people aren't like that.' He repeated his sugar-sprinkling ritual. 'Life in Westmead would be frightfully dull if it weren't for a nice bit of goss. You know it's true, Sophie. What would we have to talk about?'

Sophie remembered the way the Swans had looked at each other, that time she'd seen them together, and the expression on Miranda's face when she'd uttered her new husband's name. 'But what *will* happen?'

'Oh,' he predicted, 'it will die down eventually, when the next thing comes along. But life isn't going to be easy for them in the mean time. As I said, I don't think he'll lose his job, if the Dean is inclined to protect him, which I suspect he will be. But they'll probably be ostracised. All of those invitations will dry up. They'll be cut off from Westmead society, such as it is.'

'Elspeth Verey,' said Sophie involuntarily.

He raised an eyebrow. 'Ah, yes. Our Elspeth.'

'Does she know?'

'Probably not yet, with any luck,' said Jeremy. 'But as soon as I've finished my coffee, I'll pay a call at Priory House.'

Sophie frowned, dismayed. 'You'll tell her?'

'Of course. She's going to hear it from someone, and soon. Why not from me? Why deny me the pleasure of being the one to tell her?' His smile was heartless.

She remembered, then, what he'd said at their first meeting, when he'd told them the story of Elspeth and her family: Elspeth Verey found him amusing. No doubt he kept her well supplied with cathedral gossip, kept her entertained with the stuff of other people's lives.

Jeremy lowered his voice, and the expression on his face altered as he leaned forward across the table. 'Speaking of Elspeth, my dear. A word to the wise. People are beginning to talk about a certain young man who's been seen coming to your house rather often these days. When your husband isn't there.'

Sophie felt herself flushing. 'Dominic,' she said. 'Don't be ridiculous, Jeremy. He's sixteen years old. We're just friends.'

Jeremy's eyebrow went up again. 'Just friends? How many times have I heard that one?'

'But it's true,' she insisted. 'There's nothing . . .'

'Oh, I know. I believe you.' He paused, watching her face. 'But Elspeth may well take a different view.'

'Does she know? Has she said anything to you about it?' Had *he* said anything to Elspeth? Sophie wondered. Tendered it as an amusing titbit?

'She hasn't mentioned it.' Jeremy reached across the table and lightly touched her fingers. 'That's why I'm telling you, Sophie. I know what she's like. Elspeth would not be amused. Take care.'

His words, and his tone, chilled her. 'But . . .'

'Be careful, Sophie,' he repeated, more serious than she'd ever heard him. 'Be very careful.'

The laparoscopy was to take place in a London hospital, first thing on Monday morning. This time there was no question of her going up by herself, even if she'd wanted to: although she was being admitted as an out-patient, the procedure would be carried out under a general anaesthetic, and she would need to be driven home afterwards. Fortunately for Chris, the appointment coincided with half-term week, so that he didn't have to worry either about his teaching or the choir.

It was a long drive, the traffic heavy on the motorway even that early in the morning. Chris wanted to talk about what lay ahead that day. Sophie did not.

'It will all be fine,' he said, in his most reassuringly cheerful voice. 'You'll see.'

His unquenchable optimism irritated her; she turned away from him and looked out of the car window as they crawled towards the M25. It was still dark; rain slashed across the headlights of slow-moving lorries. Don't be ridiculous, she wanted to snap at him. If everything were fine, there would be no need for this to happen at all.

'And isn't it lucky that it's happening this week? And on Monday, as well? I'll be able to look after you all week. No school, no choir, no pub in the evenings.'

'Lucky,' she muttered, hoping that he was as oblivious to her irony as he usually was. The idea of Chris fussing round her in the aftermath of today's ordeal did not fill her with joy, though she wasn't proud of the fact.

There was only one other topic which contained enough interest to distract her from her own problems, and by some good fortune Chris alighted on that. 'Lucky for the Swans, too, that half-term week has come along just now. Maybe things will die down a bit by next week.'

'Maybe.'

Quire Close, and the whole cathedral community, had been a-buzz with the news at the weekend. Miranda Swan's past – and the couple's future – was the subject of endless speculation in countless conversations. Why had she divorced her husband? Was he unfaithful? A drunkard, abusive? Or was she the one at fault? Had he found out that she had been carrying on a clandestine affair with the vicar – Peter Swan – for years? The letter, the contents of which everyone in the close knew by now, had said not, but there was a general opinion that there was no smoke without fire, that perhaps Canon Swan protested too much.

'And to think that I invited her to my house,' Trish Evans had said with unconcealed indignation when Sophie ran into her in Quire Close at the weekend. 'She sat on my sofa and didn't say a word. Bold as brass, taking advantage of my hospitality like that.'

Sophie didn't see how accepting an invitation could be construed as an abuse of hospitality, and said so. 'Surely you don't blame her for not announcing it to the world,' she argued. 'After all, whose business is it, anyway, but hers and her husband's?'

Trish bristled at the implied criticism. '*Which* husband?' she snapped sarcastically. 'In a place like Westmead, it's everyone's business. Standards of morality . . .'

Katie, in her pushchair, shrieked for attention, but Trish was distracted only for a moment, handing her a dummy. 'Divorce and infidelity,' she went on. 'Things like that are important, especially for the clergy. Especially in a cathedral. I mean, think of all those choirboys.'

Her fractured logic was beyond Sophie, and the mention of choirboys was genuinely baffling. Surely no one had ever suggested that Peter Swan had longings, expressed or unexpressed, in that direction? 'What do choirboys have to do with it?'

'I mean,' said Trish, with a certain dignity, 'it was as good as lying. Trying to keep it all quiet like that. Not telling the truth. What sort of example does that set?' She clamped her lips together and frowned. 'When you have children, you have to think about things like that.'

Sophie flinched.

'And I, for one,' Trish added, 'will never have her in

my house again. Louise and Jennifer say the same. No one will. No one *decent*.'

She would, Sophie decided at that moment, her sense of fair play and instincts for the underdog coming to the fore. She would invite the Swans for a meal. A dinner party, perhaps, if anyone else would come. Jeremy probably would, she reckoned; his insatiable curiosity would probably outweigh his concern for what other people might think.

'I want to invite them for a meal,' she said to Chris now, in the car.

He wasn't following her train of thought. 'Invite who?'

'The Swans. Canon Swan and Miranda.'

Chris frowned. 'Whatever for?'

A lorry screamed past them, spattering the windscreen with spray. 'To show them some support,' she said, surprised that she should have to explain it to him. 'To show them that not everyone is against them.'

'That's very sweet of you.' He was still frowning. 'But do you think it's a good idea? Right now, I mean. Maybe in a few months, when things have settled down a bit . . .'

'But that's exactly the point! Now is when they need the support, need to know that someone is on their side.' Sophie felt exasperated, almost angry. Since when had Chris been so concerned with appearances and what other people might think of him, so afraid to stand up against hypocrisy? It was Westmead that had done it, she realised: that damned cathedral. It had changed him. She bit her lip.

'I'm thinking about *you*, as well,' he said defensively. 'With everything up in the air about the baby.'

The baby? thought Sophie bitterly. When would Chris accept the fact that there wasn't going to be a baby?

Sophie had never had a general anaesthetic before. The oblivion it brought was immediate and complete; the waking up from it proved to be gradual, as she floated back to consciousness by stages.

She was in a bed: that was the first thing she knew, remembering nothing of how she had come to be there, or why. Then she became aware that Chris was there as well, but not in the bed. He sat beside her, holding her hand between both his own.

That was when she remembered. The hospital, the doctor. The baby.

There was no feeling in her body; it floated, weightless, on the bed. Perhaps that was just as well. No feeling, no pain.

'Chris?' She whispered, summoning her voice. It sounded strange to her own ears, as if coming from a long distance, from a mouth other than her own.

He leaned towards her. 'Sophie! You're awake!'

Not really, she wanted to say, but couldn't form the words.

'Don't try to talk,' Chris said, squeezing her hand.

The other hand, the one he wasn't holding, had a needle going into the back of it, she now saw, connected to a clear tube. She tried to lift it; unlike the rest of her body, it was as heavy as lead, a dead thing resting on top of the sheet.

Sophie closed her eyes again and drifted off. The next time she surfaced, a nurse leaned over her, where Chris had been, cool fingers on her wrist to take her pulse. 'Vital signs,' the nurse said as Sophie's eyes fluttered open. 'I'm monitoring your vital signs.'

She managed a weak smile. 'I'm still alive, then.' This time her voice came out sounding stronger.

'Oh, you're alive, all right,' grinned the nurse.

'How long?'

The nurse dropped her wrist and laughed. 'A good few years yet.'

'Till I can go home?' Every word was an effort.

'A few hours, Mrs Lilburn. No more than that. As soon as you're able to sit up in bed and drink a cup of tea, and Mr York says it's all right, we'll be sending you home.'

Chris resumed his place beside her and reclaimed her hand. He didn't say anything, and when she focused her eyes on his face, Sophie could see the strain there, and the evidence of tears.

It was bad news, then. She couldn't bear to ask him, couldn't bear to hear him tell her. She squeezed her own eyes shut, feeling the tears prickling.

'Soph! Does it hurt?' he asked urgently, his grip on her hand tightening. 'Are you in pain?'

A pain that will never go away, she wanted to say to him. She wanted to shout it, in fact, to scream the words that had thrummed at the back of her brain for months: there is something wrong with me! I will never have a baby!

Instead she shook her head, not trusting her voice.

'Mr York will be here soon,' Chris assured her. 'He wants to talk to you. To both of us. Together.'

The expression on the consultant's face was as professionally caring as always. This time, though, there were a few added elements: a certain bafflement, a tinge of regret, and a large measure of sympathy. That expression told Sophie everything that she needed to know. Still, she had to hear the words.

'I'm afraid it isn't very good news, Mrs Lilburn,' he said. 'Endometriosis.'

'Endo . . .'

'It happens when cells from the endometrium – the lining of the womb – escape into the pelvic cavity and begin growing there, attaching to other organs,' he explained.

'But how . . .'

'No one knows what causes it,' he went on. 'Or just why it so often results in infertility. And often, if it's caught in time, it can be treated quite successfully. With drugs, in the first instance. Or with surgery, to incise the lesions.'

'Then there *is* hope,' Chris interposed eagerly.

Mr York turned to him, and his voice was grave. 'I would like to say so. But in this case, Mr Lilburn, I would be lying, and doing you both no favours, if I held out false hope.'

Chris's face crumpled. 'But you said . . .'

'I said if it's caught in time. But,' he added baldly, 'this is probably the worst case of it that I've ever seen. And I've seen quite a lot of it over the years.'

There was a lump in Sophie's throat, blocking any words that might have come. She couldn't bear to look at Chris, as the hope died in his face; she couldn't bear to look at the sympathy in the doctor's eyes. Instead she focused on his beautiful hands, the nails short and clean and as shiny as if he'd had a manicure. Perhaps he had done.

'The lesions are black, and widespread,' he went on relentlessly. 'Both ovaries are badly damaged. This has obviously been going on for years. The thing that puzzles me,' he added, 'is the fact that it's remained undetected for so long. I would have expected to have seen more symptoms in a case this severe. Pain, particularly, if nothing else.'

'Sophie *does* have painful periods,' supplied Chris.

Mr York frowned. 'You didn't mention that during our interviews. I should have thought . . .'

Sophie struggled to defend herself. 'But I thought that was normal,' she said. 'I've always had painful periods. Always, as long as I can remember. I thought everyone did.'

She had a sudden vision of herself, a fat thirteen-year-old, curled into a cumbersome foetal ball and hugging a hot-water bottle; her mother bending over her and saying, 'It's part of being a woman, sweetie. It happens to all of us. And men will never understand.'

Men. Sophie turned her back on both of them and buried her face in her pillow.

On Tuesday, Sophie didn't feel like getting out of bed, but that meant suffering Chris's ministrations. He hovered round her, keeping her supplied with cups of tea and grating on her frayed nerves with his relentless chirpiness. That chirpiness, she realised, must be artificial, which made it all the more annoying.

'I think we must get a second opinion,' he said. 'Mr York might be wrong.'

'He's a top man in his field,' Sophie pointed out.

Chris leaned over and fluffed up her pillow for probably

the twentieth time in the space of an hour. 'That doesn't mean he can't be wrong.'

'Black lesions,' she repeated bleakly. 'I don't think he's made a mistake about that. A sure sign of advanced endometriosis.'

'I don't mean wrong about the endometriosis.' He smoothed the covers at the end of the bed. 'But maybe he's wrong about the treatment. Remember, he *did* say that there were drugs available. I think it's worth a try.'

'I am *not* taking drugs.' Hormones, which would make her swell up like a balloon. Porky Sophie, she would be again, and at the end of the day it would make no difference. The drugs wouldn't work; there would be no baby.

'Surgery, then. He *did* mention surgery,' Chris insisted, checking the level in her teacup. 'To remove the lesions.'

Sophie closed her eyes; it wasn't worth arguing with him. Mr York, as far as she was concerned, had been perfectly clear: the disease was so far advanced, the lesions so well established and widespread, that surgery would be pointless, if not impossible.

The only surgery she would have would be to remove her damaged ovaries and her disease-producing womb.

The doorbell chimed.

'I don't want to see anyone,' Sophie stated.

Chris moved towards the door. 'All right,' he agreed. But a moment later, when he returned, he was not alone. 'Mr Clunch,' Chris said apologetically. 'He said he'd only stay a minute.'

Sophie shrank down under the covers, instinctively pulling them up round her shoulders, as he came towards the bed. 'I had no idea you were ill!' he said, his voice reproachful.

She hadn't told him she was going into hospital; she hadn't told him anything. It was, she reminded herself defiantly, none of his business. 'I'm not ill,' she stated.

'A bit under the weather, perhaps?' he probed as his eyes raked the room for clues to her indisposition. 'Damp days like this can be bad. Mrs Clunch isn't doing at all well today, either.'

Sophie clamped her lips shut; she *would* not tell him.

'Would you like some tea?' Chris intervened. 'Coffee, perhaps?'

'No,' said Sophie quickly.

But Leslie Clunch was just as quick. 'Yes, please. White coffee, two sugars. Sophie knows how I like it, don't you?' He winked in the direction of the bed.

Chris was gone for what seemed like for ever, and Sophie was not inclined to make small-talk. She tried to pretend that he wasn't there, that she wasn't aware that he was taking in everything in the room, assessing the furniture and the décor, cataloguing the items on her dressing table, his small black eyes ranging avidly from one corner of the bedroom to the other. Would he go home and tell Mrs Clunch what colour her duvet cover was, what books were on her bedside table, what brand of moisturiser she used? This must be a gift to him, this opportunity to invade her bedroom.

'You weren't at home yesterday,' Leslie Clunch said at last, inviting explanation.

'No.'

He paused. 'And I didn't see you at the weekend.'

'No.'

'So we haven't had a chance to speak about this Swan business.' He shook his head in an exaggerated manner.

'Very sad business. Divorce. At the cathedral! Things like that never happened in *my* day, I can tell you. Dean Worthington would never have allowed it. Nor Dean Verey either, come to that.'

'Times change,' said Sophie.

Unctuously he pressed his lips together. 'Some things *don't* change. Morality, for instance.'

Sophie hoped he wasn't going to go pious on her: many irritating traits he'd displayed in the time she'd known him, but at least piety was not one of them. She needn't have worried; what was on his mind was gossip.

'Jeremy Hammond told me that Elspeth Verey was *livid*,' he went on with relish. 'Especially because she didn't *know*. The Dean should have told her as soon as he had the letter, she said, instead of leaving her to find it out as a matter of common gossip.'

'Like everyone else,' Sophie murmured.

He was oblivious to her irony. 'Exactly! She feels she was made a fool of. She'd planned a dinner party for the Swans, you see. She'd already invited the Dean and Chapter, and the wives, of course. And nothing was said by the Dean, though by that time he knew. It was to be the social event of the year in the close, I can tell you. And of course it's had to be cancelled.'

'Cancelled!'

'Well, she could hardly go ahead with it, could she? It would be rude to un-invite the Swans, but under the circumstances she couldn't very well go on and just pretend that nothing had happened.'

Sophie didn't see why not: Elspeth Verey seemed to have made a career of pretending that things hadn't happened. Her husband's death, for instance; she still acted, thought Sophie sourly, as though she were married to the Dean of Westmead, as though her word could not be challenged.

'Just as well, really,' Leslie Clunch went on, his tone of voice belying his words, 'that Mrs Verey has gone away this week. Half-term week. She and young Dominic have gone to Tidmouth to stay with her other son, Worthington.' Then his voice changed as a note of sly insinuation crept in. 'But you would know about that, of course.'

'I'd heard,' Sophie replied, struggling to sound noncommittal and uninterested.

She missed Dominic already. Of all the times for his mother to drag him to Tidmouth, she thought . . . He was the one person that she wouldn't have minded having around her right now, cheering her up with his youthful optimism and making her laugh with his wicked sense of humour. Dominic could have made her forget, if only for a while, that her body was diseased and useless, that she would never have a baby. As it was, she wouldn't even be able to tell him about it for nearly a week.

Seemingly unable to draw her out on the subject, Leslie Clunch returned to his former theme. 'It reminds me,' he went on, 'of one other time that Mrs Verey had to cancel a party. Years ago, it was. She'd been planning it for months. To celebrate Worthington's ordination. Then Dean Verey died, not long before, and she didn't think it would be the done thing to go ahead with the party.' He gave a regretful sigh, shaking his head. 'Everyone was invited. Though of course it would have been difficult for me to get away from the cathedral, the night before the ordination. So much to be done, what with getting the chairs set out and everything in the proper place. An ordination is a busy time for a verger, believe me.'

'Like the night that poor girl was murdered,' Sophie said slowly. He'd told her about it more than once: how he'd probably been the last person to see her alive. He'd been overseeing the set-up for the ordination, he'd said; that was why he was in the cathedral so late. And that was why he'd had to abandon her so abruptly, leaving her to walk out of the cathedral and to her death.

He looked surprised that she'd remembered, and gratified. 'It *was* the night she was murdered, as a matter of fact. *That* would have cast a damp squib on the party. Though of course they didn't find her till the next morning,' he recalled. 'And maybe,' he went on, a speculative glint in his eye, 'it wouldn't even have happened if the party had gone on as planned. All those people about, in Quire Close. The murderer might not have taken the chance – she might still be alive today, if Elspeth had had that party.'

'But the party wouldn't have been in Quire Close,' Sophie pointed out. 'Didn't you say that the workmen were still in the house? That it wasn't occupied?'

He smacked himself on the head and gave a self-deprecating laugh. 'Of course. The Vereys were still at the Deanery then. The party was to have been at the Deanery.' He laughed again. 'I'm getting forgetful in my old age.'

'Here's your coffee, Mr Clunch,' announced Chris, coming back into the bedroom. 'And more tea for you, Sophie.'

Sophie sank back into the pillows and opted out of the ensuing small-talk. Her mind's eye once again was filled with the horrifying picture that had haunted her for weeks, imprinted there as clearly as a photographic image. It was as if she had seen a photograph of the girl's body, but she knew she had not; her brain had constructed it, and produced it in excruciating detail, always the same: the rain-slicked cobbles of Quire Close, the convulsed face, half-covered by a veil of blonde hair, the crumpled body, the arm thrown across the plump abdomen, as if protecting the baby that would never be born.

Chapter 12

'I'm sorry. We've had no luck at all.' To her credit, the woman looked genuinely regretful as she shook her blue-bonneted head.

'Nothing?' Jacquie echoed, dismayed.

'As I've told you, we have a very good success rate indeed. Our failures are rare. But in this case . . . nothing.' Again the woman shook her head.

Captain Gregory, her name was. She had driven all the way from Cambridge to see Jacquie in person, to convey the bad news face-to-face rather than over the phone.

Jacquie felt numb. She'd counted so much on the Salvation Army, trusting their track record, their success rate, their confidence that if Alison Barnett were anywhere to be found, they would find her. At her first interview with Captain Gregory, a few weeks earlier, Jacquie had gone home cheered, buoyant with hope and anticipation. They *would* find Alison; it was only a matter of time.

And now . . . nothing.

'Are you sure you've checked everything?' Maybe,

Jacquie told herself, there was something they'd over-looked, some little avenue of enquiry that would lead them to her sister.

Captain Gregory took a piece of paper from her brief-case and consulted it. 'There is no record of her having paid any National Insurance contributions since June of 1989.'

'The month before she left,' Jacquie said numbly.

'Nor has she paid any income tax, by PAYE or as a self-employed person. She didn't have a driving licence, you said?'

'No. Alison never learned to drive.'

'And there is no indication that she has applied for or received one since then, at least not under the name of Alison Barnett.'

'But if she'd married . . .' Jacquie suggested, a spark of hope flaring.

'She might have applied for a driving licence under a married name,' acknowledged Captain Gregory. 'But the National Insurance and Inland Revenue are a different matter.'

There had to be an explanation. 'But say she hasn't worked since she left Sutton Fen,' said Jacquie. It was possible, she told herself. If Alison had gone to her lover, and he had married her, she might never have needed to work again. She could be a full-time mother, with a ten-year-old child and who knew how many others; the realis-ation gave Jacquie a real twinge of pain. 'If she hasn't had any income . . .'

'Then we wouldn't be able to trace her through the Inland Revenue,' agreed Captain Gregory. 'Though, inci-dentally, she hasn't claimed any benefits from the DSS, either, so she would have had to have been supporting herself by some other means.'

Was this woman suggesting that Alison was living on unreported income? That she was a prostitute, perhaps, or a street person? 'If she's married . . .' Jacquie repeated, in her sister's defence.

'That's certainly possible. But a change of marital status, and a change of name, would only account for some of it.' She checked her paper again. 'You've given me some information about her building society account.'

'It was at the Sutton Fen branch,' Jacquie reiterated. 'In the High Street.'

'Yes. We've checked with the building society, and your sister's account is still intact.'

'Intact?'

'She hasn't drawn any money out of it,' amplified Captain Gregory. 'Not since April 1989.'

'That was for our holiday.' Jacquie remembered, with a sharp pang, the day that they had gone together to draw out some cash. Alison had been so excited about the imminent holiday; they'd *both* been excited. 'How much money do you think I'll need?' Alison had asked her, eyes shining.

Captain Gregory gave her a sympathetic look. 'Nor,' she added, 'has she paid anything into the building society account. Are you sure that she didn't have any other accounts? Perhaps there was one that you didn't know about. At a bank, or another building society?'

Jacquie shook her head. 'There might have been, I suppose. She never mentioned it to me.' She swallowed a lump in her throat. 'We were . . . close. She told me everything.' Feeling the need to be honest, to explain, she went on, 'At least . . . until near the end. Near the time she left. I was involved in plans for my wedding. We sort of . . . grew apart.'

'So there might have been another account.'

A glimmer of hope; another avenue to explore. 'Maybe,' said Jacquie.

'Is there anyone you could ask? Her employer, perhaps?'

Reverend Prew. Jacquie gave an involuntary shudder. No, she thought. Not that. She couldn't bear it. Wordlessly she shook her head.

Captain Gregory slid the paper back into her briefcase and snapped it shut. 'If not, then I don't really know what else to suggest. We've gone as far as we can on the information you've been able to supply.'

'What happens now?' asked Jacquie, her voice thick.

The woman reached out and touched her hand. 'We've gone as far as we can,' she repeated gently. 'If you *should* come across any further relevant information, or something else that might give us a new lead, please do feel free to ring me. You have my number. I'm very sorry, Mrs Darke,' she added. 'But it looks very much as if your sister doesn't want to be found.'

For two days Jacquie brooded over what Captain Gregory had told her, and the possible implications.

There was no trace of Alison. Her sister had not drawn any benefits, or reported any income. The alternatives were marriage or . . . the unthinkable. Alison living on the streets, begging strangers for money, selling her body.

It was that thought, ultimately, that led her to do what she wouldn't have believed herself capable of doing: Jacquie went to see the Reverend Raymond Prew.

There was just that chance, she told herself, that he

might know something. Something that Alison hadn't told her sister or her parents, during those final few weeks. Something important. Jacquie would have said that Alison could not have kept an important secret from her, but that was obviously not true: Alison had been pregnant and had not told her. So there might have been something else. And no matter what Jacquie's opinions were of Reverend Prew, Alison had respected and trusted him, right up to the very end, when he had turned on her and cast her out.

She had to see him in person; it was part of her self-imposed punishment. It was, after all, she told herself, *her* fault that Alison had left Sutton Fen. She was the one who must make amends, must put things right, and if that meant looking into Reverend Prew's eyes and saying so, then that was what she must do. She owed that much to Alison.

But it took all of her courage to do it.

And as she pulled a concealing hat over her shorn head, she told herself that it was not cowardice which motivated that action, but pragmatism: Reverend Prew would go purple if he saw what she'd done to her hair, and there was no need to antagonise him unnecessarily. He was her only hope; she needed his co-operation, not his wrath.

Mr Prew lived at the Manse, just across from the Free Baptist Fellowship, with his wife and children. It was there that he worked, there that Alison had gone five days a week for several years to type his letters and file his papers, and there that Jacquie went to see him now. She walked up and down the road several times, screwing up her nerve to ring the bell, to face his glowering countenance on the doorstep. It was a raw November day, with the sharp, cold winds blowing the rain almost horizontally across the fens, plastering wet leaves to her legs as she walked. Even Mr Prew's face would be better than that, she told herself at last.

When she did ring the bell, though, it was Mrs Prew who came to answer it, with a little Prew hanging on her skirts.

'Jacquie!' Esther Prew looked surprised to see her, as indeed she must have been.

'Hello,' said Jacquie, almost defiantly. 'I want to see Reverend Prew.'

Esther Prew glanced towards the closed door of her husband's study. 'He has someone with him at the moment,' she said. 'Would you like to come back later?'

Jacquie would dearly have loved to flee at that moment, postponing the encounter as long as possible. But that would be too easy. 'Could I wait?' she suggested. 'I can just sit here in the hall until he has time to see me.'

'I'm not sure when he'll be free . . .' Mrs Prew hesitated, then said, 'Why don't you come through to the kitchen and have a cup of tea while I peel the potatoes?'

'All right.' Peeling potatoes, thought Jacquie in disgust as she followed her. That just figured. Esther Prew was the exemplar of the true wife, the sort of which Reverend Prew preached. He often sermonised about his own wife, in fact, holding her up as the perfect model of all that a wife should be: subservient, obedient, submissive. Having no life of her own, devoting herself entirely to the care of her husband and children. And in this case there were many of the latter, as she had proved herself to be as fertile as she was dutiful. Eight little Prews, ranging in age from fifteen down to two, and there was no telling how many more there might be before she left her child-bearing years behind her. Esther Prew seemed to rejoice in her voluntary bondage to her husband, almost wearing it as a badge of honour.

In spite of that, though, or perhaps because of it, Jacquie had never had anything against her. Esther Prew had always been kind to Jacquie, insofar as Reverend Prew had allowed her to be, even when Darren left her. If anything, Jacquie felt desperately sorry for Esther; she had always sensed that under that joyously downtrodden exterior was an unhappy woman, too intelligent to be pretending that she had no brain, too insightful to leave all of the decisions to her husband. But she clearly did what she had to do to survive.

'Do you want to take your coat and hat off?'

Jacquie shook her head. 'No. I'm all right.'

'Is herbal tea all right?' Esther asked as she filled the kettle. 'Raymond has decided that ordinary tea has too many stimulants in it, that it isn't good for you.'

She looked as if she could use a stimulant or two, Jacquie decided. Esther had always been a rather wan woman, but now she seemed paler than ever, and thinner, almost insubstantial. Perhaps Reverend Prew had cut her rations as well, Jacquie speculated. Quashing an impulse to demand proper tea, she acquiesced. 'Whatever,' she shrugged, perching on a high stool at Esther's gesture of invitation.

'Want bicky,' announced the till-now-silent toddler.

'Yes, all right, Aaron,' sighed Esther. She took a digestive biscuit out of a tin and gave it to him; after her child's needs were catered for, she put two more on a plate and slid it in front of Jacquie.

Jacquie picked up a biscuit, then proffered the plate in her direction. 'This one's for you.'

'No, I won't.' Esther tucked a straggle of long hair behind her ear. 'Raymond thinks I need to lose a bit of weight.'

Bollocks, Jacquie wanted to say; she contented herself with protesting, albeit indignantly, 'But that's silly. I don't see where. There's nothing to you, Esther.'

Esther pinched a tiny bit of flesh on her hips. 'See? Here. I haven't been able to shift this since Aaron was born. Raymond says it's unsightly, almost enough to put him off . . .' She blushed. 'Well, you know.'

I would have thought that would be a positive blessing, Jacquie said to herself sardonically. The thought of marital attentions from Reverend Prew, with his bristly black beard and his wet pink lips, was enough to turn her stomach. And did he quote Bible verses while he did it? she wondered, only half facetiously. Towards the end of her own marriage, it had almost been like that with Darren.

'Where are you, my treasure?' Reverend Prew's voice boomed out from the hall.

Esther started guiltily. 'In the kitchen,' she called.

He came through the door. 'I thought you were going to make us some tea,' he said in a jovial voice which only thinly masked irritation.

'Yes, it's on the way.'

Raymond Prew's eyes narrowed as he spotted Jacquie. At the same time, she saw who was behind him: none other than Darren, his faithful deputy.

'Hello, Jacquie,' said Darren Darke, grinning. 'Fancy seeing you here.'

'Hello.' Her voice was as cold as she could make it. Although she ran into Darren occasionally – that was inevitable in a place as small as Sutton Fen – she had nothing to say to him, and no desire to engage in small-talk with him.

'How's it going?' he asked easily, as he might ask anyone he happened to meet, from a casual acquaintance to a customer at the garage.

'All right.' That took a great effort on her part; she wanted to tell him to go to hell.

'You don't sound very cordial, Jacqueline,' Reverend Prew reproved her. 'May I remind you that you're in my house, and I expect a certain standard of behaviour from my guests?'

That nearly did it. She wanted to tell them *both* to go to hell, if not somewhere worse, and slam out of the house. But she remembered Alison, and the reason for her visit; that silenced her. She pasted a large, artificial smile on her face and turned to the men. 'Hello, Darren. Hello, Reverend Prew.'

The minister nodded. 'That's better,' he said. 'And to what do we owe the honour of this visit? I was under the impression that you had left our fellowship.'

She gulped; this was going to be even more difficult than she'd thought. 'I'd appreciate a word with you, Reverend Prew,' she said as meekly as she could. 'In private, please.'

He looked gratified, and Jacquie could tell what he was thinking: she had repented of her sins, was regretting her rash behaviour, and wanted to return to the Free Baptist Fellowship.

In your dreams, she said to him silently as, ignoring Darren, she followed him to his study.

Reverend Prew gave himself the advantage by taking a seat behind his desk, gesturing her to a chair. 'Now,' he said, turning a beneficent smile on her, 'what can I do for you, Jacqueline?'

She wouldn't lead him on, tempted as she was to do so, just for the fun of it. She would come to the point. 'It's about my sister,' she said bluntly. 'Alison.'

The smile fled from his face as abruptly as if a cloud had blotted out the sun. 'Alison?' he whispered in an ominous hiss. 'I know no one by that name.'

'My sister,' Jacquie repeated, her tone distinct. 'I'm trying to find her, and I'm hoping that you might be able to help me.'

'I don't think you understand me.' He leaned back in his chair and folded his arms across his chest.

Jacquie remained calm, refusing to be intimidated. 'I understand you very well, Reverend Prew. You'd like to pretend that my sister never existed. That was one of the things that drove her away. It was partly your fault that she left Sutton Fen. Partly my fault, as well – I'm not denying that. But now it's time to make amends. It's time to find her, to bring her back home.'

She'd been staring down at her clasped hands; when she looked up at him after a long silence, she saw that he had turned purple and could barely contain his choler. 'How – dare – you!' he thundered at last.

Jacquie went on with the speech she had prepared, as if he hadn't spoken. 'My sister worked for you for several years. So you knew her as her employer as well as her pastor. And I'm wondering whether there is anything at all that she might have said during those last few months that would help us to find her. Perhaps she asked you to pay her some of her wages in cash, for example. Or she might have mentioned something about . . . well, about a man called Mike. Where he lived, or something like that.' That seemed improbable to Jacquie; if Alison hadn't said anything about him to *her*, she was scarcely likely to have discussed him with Reverend Prew. But it was worth asking. Alison was such an open person, not used to keeping secrets, and she had always trusted Reverend Prew.

'How – dare – you!' he repeated, at a higher volume, his face going even more purple. 'Why would you think I would want to find that – that – harlot? That Jezebel? Who betrayed my trust in her, and betrayed your parents as well? Good riddance, I say!'

Her parents. 'My father never stopped loving Alison,' Jacquie said. 'He would have wanted us to find her.'

'That little harlot broke Frank Barnett's heart!' shouted Reverend Prew; spittle had collected at the corners of his fat pink mouth. 'She killed him, as surely as if she'd stuck a knife into his heart! "Honour thy father and thy mother"! Where's the honour in what she did to him? To him and your dear mother?'

'He forgave her,' stated Jacquie. 'He never stopped loving her, and he forgave her at the end. Doesn't the Bible talk about forgiveness as well as all that "thou shalt not" rubbish?'

Reverend Prew narrowed his eyes at her and spoke in a softer, almost threatening, voice. 'Don't you go quoting the Bible to me, Jacqueline. You've cut yourself off from this fellowship. You have no right.'

'You don't own the Bible,' she snapped back. 'You may think that you do, but you don't.'

The minister rose majestically from his chair; he had never, thought Jacquie, looked more like an Old Testament prophet than he did at that moment, pointing his finger towards the door. 'Get out!' he roared, spittle spraying. 'Leave my house this instant, you stiff-necked and disobedient woman! And don't come back, until you're ready to repent of your wickedness!'

This time she said it aloud. 'In your dreams.' She rose, turned her back on him, and walked out. As she passed through the door, she pulled off her hat to reveal her shorn head. His gasp was audible; she didn't allow herself to turn around to witness his reaction to her defiance.

Though outwardly calm, inwardly Jacquie was in despair. There was no one else to help her, nowhere else to turn. If she couldn't come up with another lead, no matter how slender, the Salvation Army could do no more for her; Captain Gregory had said so.

And then, a day or two later, on Sunday afternoon, she had another little idea.

There was, perhaps, just possibly, a third alternative to the two scenarios she had constructed. Alison might be married, she might be on the streets. Or she might have gone abroad. That would account for the absence of a paper trail. She had a passport, obtained for the holiday; she'd had enough cash to get her as far as France.

Nicola had been the last person in Sutton Fen to see Alison. Though it had been a long time ago, and Nicola claimed that Alison hadn't said where she was going, there just might be some little thing that her sister had revealed which Nicola wouldn't have thought was important but which could now make all the difference.

In this case, she had nothing to lose, Jacquie realised. She had faced the lion in his den; this would be easy.

So she rang Nicola straight away, hoping to catch her at home.

She was in luck. Nicola *was* at home, and would be happy to come over. 'I'll have to bring Brittany with me, though,' she warned. 'Keith has gone off to play football with his mates, and left me to look after his darling daughter.'

'If it's inconvenient . . .' Jacquie said reluctantly.

'Oh, no. A change of scenery will do us *both* good,' Nicola assured her.

They arrived a short while later. 'This is Brittany,' said Nicola. 'Brittany, my friend Jacquie.'

'Hello, Brittany. Nice to meet you.'

The girl shrugged, not making eye contact, and followed her stepmother into the house, putting one foot in front of the other carefully so she wouldn't fall off her platform shoes as they moved back towards the kitchen.

Nicola had not exaggerated about Brittany's lack of charm, Jacquie apprehended at once. She had no manners and no social skills. She also, evidently, had no sense: on this raw November day, she was wearing no coat. The top part of her body was covered – if one could call it that – by the skimpiest of black Lycra tops, exposing her bra straps and stopping well short of her navel, which was pierced and adorned by a double-headed rhinestone stud. Below the waist she wore low-slung and skin-tight black jeans, and the ridiculously elevated shoes, her painted toenails sticking out.

The girl's hair was streaked and hacked into an unbecoming style, one lock of which hung down to obscure an eye. She was carefully made up, with thick mascara and purplish-black lipstick, and her fingernails were painted a dark sludge colour to match her toes. Evidently, though, she bit her nails; they were short, almost to the quick, and the polish was chipped.

'Would you like a cup of tea?' Jacquie offered.

Nicola agreed quickly. 'Oh, yes, please.'

'D'ya have any Coke?' asked Brittany, flicking her hair out of her eye with her hand.

'Coke?'

The girl repeated it impatiently. 'Y'know. Coke. Coca-Cola.'

'No, nothing like that,' apologised Jacquie. 'I could give you some orange squash, or some lemonade.'

Brittany rolled her eyes and flicked her hair. 'Don't bother,' she muttered, plopping down on a chair and folding her arms across her chest.

Nicola glanced at Jacquie in mute apology. 'Brittany didn't want to go to watch her father play football,' she explained brightly.

'Football is dead boring,' Brittany announced, pulling a face.

Jacquie decided to make an effort. 'What do you like to do, then, Brittany?' she asked as she filled the kettle.

The girl shrugged. 'Go to the cinema. Shop. Hang out with my friends.' Again she flicked her hair. 'That's why this place is such a dead loss. All my friends are in Cambridge. There isn't even a cinema in this stupid town. And the shops are the pits.'

'Life is tough,' said Nicola in an ironic voice.

Brittany shot her a baleful look. 'I don't know why I have to come here, anyway. The house is grotty. Dad is always too busy to spend time with me. And you hate my guts. Why can't I just stay at home with Mum?'

Ignoring her, Nicola addressed Jacquie. 'Isn't she charming? She spreads such sweetness and light into our lives.'

'Oh, sod off,' muttered the girl. She got up and went over to the television set and switched it on, then returned to her chair with the remote control in her hand and concentrated on the screen, apparently tuning out the presence and the conversation of the grown-ups.

After a life without television, and not even knowing what she was missing, Jacquie had installed a set in the kitchen and one in her bedroom following her father's death. It had been done as an act of rebellion against Reverend Prew and the Free Baptist Fellowship, but she'd found that she enjoyed it, and now spent hours watching practically anything that was on, making up for years of lost time. It was the television, in fact, and a programme she'd seen a few nights before, which had given her the idea for what she wanted to do with Nicola.

'You're probably wondering why I wanted you to come over this afternoon,' she began when the tea had been made and poured.

'You said that it had something to do with Alison.' Nicola stirred sugar into her tea. 'Have you found her, then? Did the Sally Army come through for you?'

'No. But I've had a little idea.' Jacquie explained it to her eagerly. 'I was watching one of those crime programmes, where they reconstruct a crime in the hopes that it will jog someone's memory. That's what I want to do.'

'I don't understand.'

'You were the last person to see Alison before she left Sutton Fen,' Jacquie said. 'You said that you came into the house with her. Were you with her when she packed her case?'

Nicola frowned, trying to summon up the past. 'Yeeees . . .' she replied slowly. 'I went into her bedroom with her, to see if I could help.'

'Brilliant!' A smile spread across Jacquie's face. 'That's just brilliant!'

'I still don't get it,' Nicola admitted.

'That's what I want to reconstruct,' she said, clasping her hands together with excitement. 'As soon as we've finished our tea, I want to go into Alison's bedroom. I'll pretend to be Alison, and pack a case. You tell me what you remember, and maybe it will help you to remember more. Something important, even.'

'But it's been so long,' Nicola protested.

Brittany turned towards them, demonstrating that she had been eavesdropping on their conversation. 'Cool!' she said, with more enthusiasm than she'd shown about anything that afternoon. 'Just like *Crimewatch*. Can I come?'

'No,' said Nicola, automatically.

Jacquie spoke at the same time. 'Yes, if you like.'

A few minutes later she took Nicola upstairs to Alison's bedroom, with Brittany tottering along precariously behind them.

Although as children and adolescents the two sisters had been in and out of each other's rooms constantly, Alison's room was not a place where Jacquie had spent much time in recent years. After Alison left, and while their parents were alive, her room had been kept locked, its contents untouched. It had always thrown up too many painful memories for Jacquie, so she had continued to keep

it locked, going in only once: after her initial contact with
the Salvation Army, she had conducted a search of the
room, looking for Alison's building society passbook or
any other records or papers which might help to lead to
her current whereabouts. That had been a painful exercise, and a fruitless one; she had found nothing that seemed
to her to be of any importance. But, she recalled now with
rising excitement as she turned the key in the lock, she
had not found Alison's passport. That fact, that absence,
could be significant.

'It's dusty,' said Brittany, wrinkling her nose.

'It hasn't been dusted in about eleven years,' Jacquie
explained. 'That's when my sister left.'

'You mean no one ever comes in this room?' the girl
demanded.

'No.'

She gave her hair a flick and looked round. 'That's cool.
Like something in a film! It's like an old lady's room,
though – how old was your sister when she went away?'

'She was only twenty,' said Jacquie, who could just
about imagine what Brittany's room must be like: bright
colours everywhere, a garish throw on the bed, posters
of pop groups on the walls, an up-to-date stereo system
with huge speakers, probably a television set and a video
as well. Alison's room bore no resemblance to that. The
walls were a rather insipid shade of pale pink and the
bedspread was candlewick, once white but now grey with
dust; the furniture, all in cheap laminated white wood,
consisted of a single bed, a wardrobe, a bookcase, a
bedside table, and a chest of drawers. On the wall above
the bed hung a simple wooden cross, and another wall
was adorned with a framed sampler of the Ten

Commandments, worked by Alison herself when she was about twelve. Jacquie remembered well the months when Alison, who was not a natural needlewoman, had laboured over that sampler, shedding tears and drops of blood equally until it was finished, framed, and given pride of place in her room. Looking at it brought a lump to her throat. Even more poignant was the framed photo on the chest of drawers: two little girls, one dark and slender, the other blonde and chubby, dressed in their Sunday best, their arms round each other's waists.

Jacquie turned away. 'Let me get my case, so we can do this properly,' she said to cover her discomfiture. She went down the hall and returned with it a moment later. 'Now. Were you standing or sitting while she packed, Nicola?'

Nicola pondered for a moment. 'Sitting,' she remembered. 'On the bed.'

'Then do it,' Jacquie directed.

Nicola complied, and Brittany lowered herself to the floor, watching curiously.

'She took the case down from the top of the wardrobe, and put it on the bed next to me,' said Nicola.

'Excellent.' Jacquie put the case on the bed and opened it up.

For a moment Nicola sat thinking, cupping her chin in her hand. 'She opened her wardrobe first,' she said. 'She took out some dresses and put them in the case.'

Jacquie opened the wardrobe. It still held some of Alison's clothes – the best Laura Ashley frock, the sundress that they'd chosen together in Greece, the newer things that Alison had bought when she'd lost all that weight before the holiday. Shut up for so long, they exuded a concentration of Alison's natural scent. Jacquie gasped, her eyes filling with tears.

'Oh, wow,' said Brittany. 'That stuff is, like, really old. Did people really wear weird clothes like that?'

Jacquie was glad of the distraction. 'We did,' she assured her without irony, taking several dresses off the hangers and folding them into the case. 'Like this?' she asked Nicola.

'Yes. Like that.' It was coming back to her. 'Then she opened the middle drawer, there, and took out a folded nightgown, and some pairs of knickers.'

Jacquie pulled the drawer out and saw that Alison hadn't emptied it completely. Another nightgown was there, and some underwear, so she put them into the case.

'Right,' said Nicola. She closed her eyes and thought herself back eleven years. 'Then she went off, to the bathroom, I suppose, and came back with her toothbrush and face flannel. No, wait. First she threw her hairbrush in with the clothes. I think it was on the top of the chest of drawers.'

'All right.' Jacquie pretended to pick up and pack a nonexistent hairbrush, then left the room and came back with her own toothbrush and face flannel.

'Perfect,' Nicola approved.

While Jacquie was away, Brittany had moved to the bookcase and was pulling books out. 'Look,' she said. 'Enid Blyton.'

'Alison and I loved Enid Blyton,' Jacquie said, smiling.

'So did I,' Brittany admitted, with a certain amount of chagrin. 'When I was really little, that is. Enid Blyton is so uncool.'

'I don't think Alison ever stopped reading Enid Blyton. They were her favourite books.'

'There are lots of Mills and Boons here as well,' reported Brittany. 'Soppy romances. Gross.'

'A book,' said Nicola suddenly. 'There was some little book that she put in the case. Like a diary, or a journal, or something like that – I think it had a lock on it. She got it out of the drawer of her bedside table, I think.'

Jacquie frowned. 'I don't remember anything like that.'

Nicola's eyes were screwed shut. 'And something else. A stuffed animal. She took it off the bed and put it in her case, right on top.

'Grace,' breathed Jacquie as tears stung her eyes. 'Oh, God. Grace.'

'Grace?' queried Brittany.

'Her stuffed rabbit. She loved that rabbit, from the time she was a baby.' Somehow it cheered Jacquie to think that Alison had Grace with her, even now. A reminder of her childhood, of their years growing up together. Jacquie had had a stuffed dog called Bob; she had no idea what had happened to him. Had she taken him with her when she married Darren? She couldn't remember.

'And she got her building society passbook out of the top drawer,' Nicola went on. 'She put it in her handbag, not the case. That's when she said that she didn't have any cash, and I offered to loan her some money for her fare. I gave her twenty pounds – that was what I had on me.'

Jacquie brought herself back to the present. 'And then?' she asked. 'What happened then?'

'Then she closed the case and we left. I drove her to the bus stop.'

'That's all?'

Nicola shrugged. 'All I can remember.'

Jacquie bit her lip in disappointment. Nothing new,

then. Nothing that would help her to find Alison. No indication of where she'd been planning to go, and whether her destination might have been out of the country.

'Wait a minute.' Nicola stopped in the act of getting up from the bed and sat back down. 'There *was* something else. At the last minute, after she'd closed her case, she was looking for a map. She couldn't remember where she'd put it, and spent a few minutes looking for it. Finally she gave up. She was afraid she was going to miss the bus.'

Jacquie forgot to breathe. 'A map?' she said at last.

'I'm sure it was a map.'

'A map of what? Of where?'

Nicola shrugged. 'She didn't say. Sorry.'

Brittany was leafing through the books. 'Did you say a map?' she asked suddenly. 'I just saw a map. In one of these books.' She pulled a Mills and Boon novel out of the bookcase and riffled through it. 'Here. Do you suppose this is what she was looking for?' She stretched her hand out towards Jacquie.

As if in a dream, Jacquie reached down and took it. 'Westmead,' she said in a peculiar voice. 'It's a map of Westmead.'

Chapter 13

A week after Sophie's laparoscopy, in the afternoon at about the time she was expecting Dominic, she had a phone call from Mr York. He rang himself this time, and the fact that it was his voice on the line rather than that of the nurse was enough to warn Sophie that this was probably something she didn't want to hear, even before she heard what he had to say.

'I wanted to tell you this right away,' he said. 'It would have been better, of course, if you could have come to my office, but that would have wasted valuable time.'

'What is it?'

There was a pause, and when he spoke, Mr York's voice was grave. 'As you know, I wasn't very happy about what I saw when I had a peek at your insides last week.'

'The endometriosis,' she said, wishing he would get on with it.

'I'm afraid that it's worse than I thought. I took some tissue samples, as a matter of routine, and have just had the results back from the lab.'

'And?' Sophie held her breath.

'Now, this is nothing to get into a panic about,' he said in his most reassuring professional tone. 'But there were some very dodgy cells there in the sample. Pre-cancerous cells.'

Sophie felt her stomach plummet. 'Cancer!'

'No, I said *pre*-cancerous. Not life-threatening, Mrs Lilburn. Not at this stage, certainly. But we want to prevent things from progressing any further. Surgery is indicated.'

Why was he beating about the bush so? Why couldn't he just come out and say it? 'A hysterectomy,' Sophie said, trying to keep her voice calm. 'That's what you're talking about, isn't it?'

Mr York cleared his throat. 'Yes, I'm afraid so. And I think it should be done sooner, rather than later. Before things have a chance to get really nasty. I've rung the hospital. They can fit you in next week.'

She wasn't sure what she was meant to say. Should she thank him? Curse him? Instead she said nothing, holding the phone to her ear as though frozen.

'Mrs Lilburn? Are you still there?'

'Yes.'

'I'll be sending you a letter,' he continued, 'and it will all be in there, in writing – the details of your hospital admission, and so forth. After you've read it, we'll talk, and I'll try to answer any questions you might have at that time.'

'Thank you.'

'Is there anything you'd like to discuss further now? Any questions about what I've told you?'

'No. It's all quite clear.' She walked towards the window with the cordless phone and looked out into the close, at the ragged trees, almost bereft of leaves now, silhouetted against the darkening sky. Already the cathedral was little more than a black shadow, blotting out the corner of her vision.

'I'll be talking to you soon, then,' he said in a more business-like voice. 'After you've had the letter, and have had a chance to talk everything over with Mr Lilburn.'

'Yes. Thank you.'

The phone went dead, but she continued to hold it to her cheek as she stood at the window, her forehead pressed against the glass. The room was growing dark; she'd not yet lit a fire, and she found that she was shivering in the gathering chill.

Chris. What was Chris going to say?

She had to talk to Chris. More than anything she wanted to share this burden with him, to allow him to comfort her. 'In sickness and in health.' Wasn't that what marriage was all about?

Sophie wasn't sure how long she'd stood there, clutching the phone as tightly as she was clutching her grief. She squinted at her watch: it was just after four.

Chris would have finished his teaching by now; his last lesson ended at half-past three. The school was on the other side of the cathedral from Quire Close, and though occasionally he would pop home for a cup of tea before returning to the cathedral for choir practice and Evensong, more often, especially since Dominic had become a frequent visitor at teatime, Chris would have his tea in the cathedral refectory with Jeremy and some of the other lay clerks. It was nearer, he explained, and that made a difference in the cold, wet weather they'd been having.

Choir practice started at half-past four, and Evensong an hour later. He might come home after that; more likely he would go to the pub. So it might be hours before she had a chance to see him, to tell him.

Unless she went looking for him.

Sophie had not been into the cathedral since the day of Chris's interview, and she did not want to go there now. But if she wished to see Chris, she had no choice.

She couldn't allow herself to stop and think about it. Wrapping herself in her coat, she walked quickly through Quire Close towards the bulky presence beyond it.

Outside of the protection offered by the twin terraces of the close, the wind whipped cruelly round the walls of the cathedral. Sophie clutched her coat and circled round to the massive west door, where a smaller arched door was let into it. Unfamiliar with the mechanism, she struggled for a moment with the great iron ring before it turned and the door swung inwards.

Dark and bleak as it was outside, nothing had quite prepared Sophie for the vast empty gloom within the cathedral. On her other visit, in the spring, it had been much lighter, and far more populated. Now it seemed almost as if she were alone in that huge blackness. And it was cold, with a deep-to-the-bone damp chill emanating from the stones, striking up through her feet.

Far in the distance, towards the other end of the cathedral and beyond the carved stone screen, there shone a glimmer of light, and she moved towards it as though drawn by a beacon.

Beyond the screen, in the Quire, she discovered the source of the light: candles were being lit in their glass-sheathed holders along the stalls in preparation for the choir's arrival. The area itself was, if anything, wrapped in a more profound darkness than the rest of the cathedral, with carved stalls and panelling and canopies of age-blackened oak on either side. The pools of light shed by each candle were self-contained, little oases of comfort. A solemn man in a black cassock moved through the stalls with a taper, lighting one after another.

'Will the choir be here soon?' Sophie asked him, her voice echoing in the emptiness.

He nodded. 'They'll be arriving to practise in five or ten minutes.' Then he moved on without pause, so there was no opportunity for further conversation, even if Sophie had wished for it.

Five minutes. Ten at the most.

'Sophie!'

She started and looked about, but saw no one who might have called out her name; she was beginning to think that she had imagined it, when an arm waved at her from a higher level, from the top of the screen, and Jeremy leaned over the parapet.

'What are you doing here?' he called.

Sophie shaded her eyes from the glare of the candles and looked up at him. 'Waiting for Chris.'

'He'll be along in a few minutes.'

'How did you know I was here?'

'Saw you on the camera,' Jeremy explained briefly, then disappeared; a few seconds later the organ boomed out in a deafening chord, followed by a series of gentler, indefinite ones.

'The organ console is up there,' said a soft voice close to her ear.

Sophie jumped and spun round.

It was Leslie Clunch.

'I saw you heading for the cathedral,' he said. 'You

seemed to be in a hurry. I wondered if everything was all right.'

He had followed her, Sophie realised with an unpleasant feeling in the pit of her stomach. Of all the people she didn't want to talk to at that moment, he topped the list. How could she get rid of him without causing a scene? 'I'm fine,' she said abruptly, turning her back to him.

'I thought it might have something to do with a certain young man.' His voice was sibilant, insinuating.

Dominic. Dominic hadn't come, she realised suddenly.

'Because I saw him leaving Quire Close with his mother, in the car,' Leslie Clunch went on. 'About three-quarters of an hour ago.'

Sophie wrapped her coat more closely round her. 'I was looking for my husband,' she said coldly.

'Oh, he won't be here for a few minutes yet.' He gave a confident nod. 'The organist always warms up for a bit before the choir arrive.'

Jeremy was here, Sophie reassured herself. She wasn't really alone in the cathedral with Leslie Clunch. 'He said that he could see me on the camera,' she said, as much to herself as to her unwelcome companion.

'Most people don't know there's a television monitor up there,' he chuckled. 'But how else would the organist see the choir?' He pointed to the glinting eye of a video camera, above their heads and well hidden in the rich wooden carving. 'Of course,' he went on, his voice dropping to a more confidential tone, 'it has other uses as well. Once when I was Head Verger, there were some people over there, a man and a woman, hanging round the Bishop's throne.' His pointing finger indicated the over-sized wooden chair.

Involuntarily, Sophie's eyes followed his finger.

'They were acting rather suspiciously, in my opinion. They kept looking round, and looking at me, as if they were waiting for me to leave. So I obliged them. I nipped up the stairs to the organ loft, and switched the camera on so I could see what they were up to. I thought maybe they were going to try to nick something, or carve their names on the Bishop's throne, or some such mischief.'

He was waiting for her to encourage him, Sophie knew: to ask him what they'd done. She pressed her lips together; he could wait until Christmas, as far as she was concerned.

'And what do you think they were doing?' he asked, after a long pause. His voice dropped to a stage whisper. 'They were *having sex*. Right there, on the Bishop's throne!'

His small black eyes shone lasciviously at the memory. Sophie took a step away from him, feeling contaminated and sickened.

Just then half a dozen choirboys clattered in, all talking at once. Rosy-cheeked, high-voiced, they brought with them an air of normality, and suddenly the cathedral seemed populated, less threatening. They slid into their places in the stalls, still talking, as they arranged their music in front of them, and were soon joined by another half dozen.

And just a moment later, Chris followed them into the Quire, deep in conversation with another lay clerk. Sophie hurried to meet him.

'Sophie!' he said, alarmed to see her there in such an unfamiliar setting. 'Is something wrong?'

She put her arms round him and buried her face against his shoulder, oblivious to the sniggers of the choirboys. 'Hold me, Chris,' she whispered. 'Just hold me.'

*   *   *

If October in Quire Close was dreary, then November was dank. Wet leaves loosed their tenuous hold on the trees and fell in profusion, covering the already treacherous cobblestones of the close with another slippery layer. The days drew in rapidly; the sun, when it was seen at all, was in full retreat by mid-afternoon, dipping behind the hulking presence of the cathedral long before Evensong.

But it was not to Quire Close, not to the cathedral, that Jacquie Darke planned to go when she arrived in Westmead for the first time. It was to the Tourist Information Office.

She had a map.

The discovery of the map had been electrifying, a moment of revelation. It had triggered a long-buried memory of a morning in Greece: Alison's tear-stained face, her wails of abandonment. And a letter, scribbled in haste and briefly glimpsed. 'I must return home to Westmead'.

Alison had known, then, as Jacquie had forgotten, that Mike lived in Westmead.

Another memory, even more unwelcome, surfaced unbidden. The fateful wedding day, Alison grovelling on the floor, tear-stained once again, begging for her sister's help. Jacquie's own incandescent anger, her hateful words: 'You can go to hell for all I care. Why don't you go to *him*?'

Alison had gone to Westmead to find him. That was the answer, inevitable and incontrovertible, and as evident to Jacquie in that instant as was the certainty that she must go there as well.

'Ally has gone to Westmead,' she said aloud, in a strange

voice, as if it had happened no more than a day or two before. 'I'll find her in Westmead.'

Nicola and Brittany were staring at her.

'You're going to Westmead?' said Nicola.

'Of course. I have to find her. 'That's where she's gone. I'm positive.'

Nicola shook her head. 'Get a grip, Jacquie. She left here eleven years ago. Even if she *did* go to Westmead, and you can't know that for sure, there's no guarantee that she's still there. She's had plenty of time to go elsewhere.'

Jacquie wouldn't listen; she didn't want to believe that her intuition could be wrong, so forcible and unshakeable was her conviction that she had at last got it right. She wanted to leave immediately, on the spot, but Nicola managed to convince her that she should wait till morning. 'One more day won't make any difference, after eleven years,' Nicola said sensibly. 'You don't know the way, and it's already dark. Get a good night's sleep. In the morning you might feel differently about it.'

Jacquie knew that she wouldn't feel any different; she knew as well that there was no chance of a good night's sleep, or indeed of any sleep at all. But she admitted the sense of Nicola's argument about driving in the dark on unfamiliar roads. It was raining; the roads were slick as well as dark.

So that evening she packed her case, making sure to put in a photo of Alison. Then she studied the driving atlas, as well as the map of Westmead.

And as she lay awake in bed, she planned her strategy. Once she got to Westmead, she would go to the Tourist Information Office, where they should be able to find her some accommodation: a nice centrally located bed-and-breakfast with parking available for the car. And then . . . she would find Ally. One way or another, through luck or intuition or hard work, she would find her.

Nicola rang early in the morning, while Jacquie was making sure that all of the windows and the back door of the house were locked and secure, to wish her friend success in her search and a safe journey. 'I've thought of something, as well,' she said. 'Remember when I told you about Miranda Forrest? Well, I'm almost positive that it's Westmead she's moved to. With her new husband. Some coincidence, huh?'

Jacquie, anxious to be away, made a noncommittal noise.

'I was just thinking that if you get stuck, or need some help, she'd be a good person to know,' Nicola explained. 'She's very nice. I'm afraid I don't remember her new married name, but I'm sure you could find her. Her husband is a canon at the cathedral.'

'Thanks,' said Jacquie, then promptly put Miranda Forrest out of her mind as she wrote a note to the milkman, asking him to stop deliveries until further notice, and stuck it in an empty bottle on the doorstep. After that, she locked the front door, and without a glance at the house in which she'd spent so much of her life, she carried her case to the car.

The one-way system in Westmead came as an unpleasant shock to Jacquie, at the end of a fairly arduous journey.

The weather hadn't improved, and negotiating the sharp turns in the fens with the narrow roads slick with rain required all of Jacquie's concentration. Reaching the motorway, she might have anticipated an easier time, but she wasn't really accustomed to motorway driving; Monday morning traffic on the M11 towards London was horrendous, and the M25 was even worse. On the M4, going towards the West Country, the traffic improved even as the weather worsened, and just as she turned off the motorway towards Westmead, she ran into extensive road-works and a long tail-back. As a result of all that, the journey which shouldn't have taken longer than five hours, even allowing for a much-needed midday break at a Little Chef for a sandwich and a cup of coffee, ended up taking the better part of the day.

It was already beginning to get dark when Jacquie reached Westmead and discovered the one-way system which had come into effect in the years since her map was published. Eventually she got her bearings, and after whizzing past the Tourist Information Office on the first time round, she took the drive more slowly on her second circuit of the town.

Parking, too, was difficult; the car park which her map had indicated was most convenient for the Tourist Information Office had disappeared, and there was a new building in its place. But luck, eventually, was with her, as a car pulled out from the kerb just in front of her, and she slotted into the space.

The woman at the tourist office was helpful when Jacquie asked for a bed-and-breakfast recommendation. 'You'd like something close to the cathedral, I imagine?'

'Cathedral?' Jacquie shrugged. 'It doesn't really matter. Just something clean and reasonably priced, with car parking available.'

The woman consulted her list. 'Well, the Cathedral View Guest House is very nice, or so I'm told. And they have their own car park. It's just off the High Street.'

'That sounds ideal.'

A phone call was made, and a short while later Jacquie found herself in an immaculate bedroom on the first floor of a narrow Victorian house. The room boasted a double bed, tea-making facilities, a basin with hot and cold running water, and a window overlooking the cathedral. The downstairs lounge was equipped with a television; a bathroom and shower were at the end of the corridor.

The first thing Jacquie did was to fill the kettle and switch it on, then she flopped down on the bed, exhausted.

Her mind, though, was racing. She was in Westmead, where she was convinced that she would find her sister. But how should she go about looking for her?

The library seemed the most logical place to begin. They would have directories, and knowledgeable librarians who might even know Alison, if she showed them the photo; she couldn't have changed all that much in eleven years.

The kettle switched off, and she made herself a reviving cup of tea. While she drank it, she looked at the map and located the library. She would have loved to have given in to her exhaustion and taken a nap, but couldn't bear to lose the whole day. Her watch said that it was half-past four; she could probably just about make it to the library before it closed, and ask a few preliminary questions.

Finishing her tea in one scalding gulp, Jacquie put her damp coat back on, retrieved her dripping brolly from the basin, and made sure that she had the map and the key to the room.

According to the map, the library was in the High Street, the other side of the cathedral and before the

Tourist Information Office. It shouldn't be difficult to find, as long as she kept the cathedral to her right; she passed the ancient gatehouse which led into the cathedral precincts, reassured that she was headed in the right direction, but when she reached the Tourist Information Office, she knew she'd gone too far. It must be the rain, she told herself ruefully, then retraced her footsteps.

This time she reached the cathedral gatehouse again, and realised that something was wrong.

The woman in the Tourist Information Office looked concerned when Jacquie came back in. 'Isn't the Cathedral View suitable, then?' she asked. 'I'm sure I can find something else for you, if that one isn't any good.'

'The library,' said Jacquie. 'I'm looking for the library.' She spread her map out on the counter and pointed to the elusive location. 'I thought that if I walked along the High Street, I would be sure to pass it, but I've managed to miss it three times.'

The woman frowned and studied the map closely. 'Where did you get this old map?' she laughed. 'It's way out of date. The library moved to new premises about six years ago. On the outskirts of town, it is. The old library has been turned into one of those theme pubs.'

Jacquie felt foolish. 'Oh, that explains it.'

'Here,' said the woman. 'Have one of these new maps. I'll mark the new library for you.' She glanced up at the clock. 'But there's not much point going there now. They'll be closing by the time you get there.'

'Thanks,' said Jacquie. 'Thanks very much.'

Deflated, she headed back towards the Cathedral View Guest House. At least, she thought, it had stopped raining. Maybe tomorrow would be a better day.

But just as she reached the cathedral gatehouse, the skies opened in the worst cloudburst yet, and she realised that she had left her umbrella on the counter in the Tourist Information Office. She dashed under the shelter of the open arch and prepared to wait out the storm.

While she was there, though, she peered out of the other side of the gatehouse towards the cathedral. It was huge, she saw, floodlit and sitting in the middle of a spacious green. The side that was facing her, which looked to her untrained eye as if it must be the front, was covered with intricate carving, like stone lace, and there were life-sized statues in niches above the great wooden door.

She had never been inside a cathedral before. Her parents had drummed into her their belief – Reverend Prew's belief – that the Church of England, the Established Church, was corrupt and probably not Christian at all – little better, in fact, than the Catholics. Once, when in Ely, she had asked her mother if they might go in the cathedral; her mother had reacted with horror. All of those statues – idolatrous, heathen things, Joan Barnett had said. Forbidden in the Bible. Graven images. Thou shalt not.

Perhaps, then, it was a subconscious impetus towards rebellion against her mother and Reverend Prew that drew her out of the protection of the gatehouse to make a dash towards that imposing façade.

It was probably closed, she told herself. The door would be locked, and she would have got soaked for nothing.

But it wasn't locked. She twisted the iron ring, and the little door in the middle of the big door swung open.

Her imagination had not prepared her for the reality of the cathedral. It seemed to stretch endlessly, magical and mysterious in the dark. Lights twinkled far off, and an unearthly sort of music floated over the stone screen. Beautiful, clear, soaring, like angels singing. More wonderful than anything she'd ever heard before. Jacquie stood transfixed, hardly breathing, oblivious to her drenched state.

'Will you be attending the service?' said an official-looking man near the door, not unfriendly.

'Yes,' she replied, but didn't move.

The music stopped.

'Evensong will be starting in about ten minutes,' the man informed her. 'If you go up to the chancel, someone will help you to find a seat.'

Jacquie's feet carried her through the immensity of the cathedral, towards the place where the music had come from. She was vaguely aware of soaring pillars, of carved stone, of vast darkened windows, but she was intent on reaching her goal.

'This way, please,' said another man who stood at the arch which led through the screen. 'This way for the service. You can sit anywhere except the choir's stalls, the ones with the music.'

'Will they be singing?' she asked the man, hardly daring to hope.

'Oh, yes.'

There were a few people seated in the carved wooden stalls, scattered here and there. Old ladies with brollies and shopping, a few tourists, identifiable by the cameras round their necks. A middle-aged woman on her own, with a kind face and curly hair, kneeling to pray. Jacquie chose a seat on the opposite side from the woman and leafed through the unfamiliar book on the ledge in front of her, then stared at the altar at the very end of the cathedral. Sumptuous embroidery, silver candlesticks and a big silver cross with a little man on it. Reverend Prew would have a fit, she said to herself with satisfaction.

There was an unnatural hush. One old lady coughed and rustled in her handbag for a cough sweet; a tourist whispered to his companion. Somewhere a clock ticked loudly.

And then the organ began to play: a sweet, reedy sound from the pipes behind Jacquie. Everyone stood, Jacquie following their example, and a double line of red-robed choirboys processed under the arch of the screen. Their little faces were solemn above their starched and pleated white ruffs; they moved to their places, with the men following into the rows behind them, bowed in unison towards the altar, then turned to face each other.

'O Lord, open thou our lips,' sang someone behind Jacquie.

'And our mouths shall show forth thy praise,' the choir responded, full-throated and joyful; the hair on the back of Jacquie's neck stood up.

The exhaustion and the excitement caught up with Jacquie; that night she slept soundly and dreamlessly in a bed more comfortable than the one at home. She slept so well, in fact, that she almost missed breakfast in the morning. She rushed through a cold shower – earlier risers had used up the hot water – then towelled her short hair dry, dressed quickly and hurried downstairs.

'I thought you weren't coming,' said the proprietress, a jovial West Country woman.

'I don't usually eat much breakfast,' said Jacquie, helping herself to cereal from the sideboard. 'I'll just have this.

And perhaps some toast and coffee, if it's not too much trouble.'

'Oh, no.' The woman put her hands on her hips and looked critically at Jacquie. 'You look like you could do with feeding up, love. You'll have a full cooked breakfast, and I don't want any argument from you.'

'All right.' Jacquie smiled, inexplicably happier than she'd felt in a very long time. When the cooked breakfast came, she ate every bite, greedily mopping up the last of the egg yolk with a triangle of wholemeal toast. Then she lingered over a second cup of coffee and thought about her plans for the day.

The library, of course: that would be her first destination. After that she wasn't sure; it depended on what information the library yielded up. If possible, she would go back to the cathedral at some point.

Amazingly, the weather had cleared; when Jacquie went back upstairs for her coat, her handbag and the new map, she spared a moment to look out of her window. The cathedral basked beneath a pale blue November sky, astonishing in its mellow beauty. 'First nice day we've had in weeks,' the landlady had said. 'You must have brought it with you, love.'

On a day like this, Jacquie said to herself with a smile, how could anything go wrong?

This time she found the library with no difficulty, and the fifteen-minute walk was no hardship on such a lovely crisp day. She enjoyed her walk through Westmead, making a mental note of shops which she might want to visit at a later time. After she'd found Ally, she would probably stay in Westmead for a while. She might even move there to be close to her sister; after all, there was nothing to keep her in Sutton Fen any longer, and Ally was now all that she had. Westmead seemed a civilised sort of place, far more interesting than Sutton Fen, with friendly inhabitants – nothing like the sour, insular, nonconformist fen-dwellers she'd always known. And then there was the cathedral.

The librarian at the reference desk was as helpful and cordial as the other people she had met so far. Jacquie explained to her that she was looking for her sister, who had moved to Westmead some eleven years earlier; the librarian suggested checking the telephone directory.

Jacquie told her that she had already done a quick check of the Westmead telephone directory at the bed-and-breakfast, and had ascertained that there was no one by the name of Alison Barnett listed. 'I think she's married,' she said. 'To someone called Mike, I think, but I don't know his other name.'

'That will make it more difficult to find her,' the librarian warned, her voice sympathetic.

Jacquie was not discouraged. She got out the photo of Alison and showed it to the other woman, who shook her head. 'No,' she said. 'I don't know her. At least I don't remember ever having seen her.'

'Well, then,' said Jacquie. 'What do you think I should do to find her? Should I take out an advert in the local newspaper, maybe? In the Personal column, asking her to contact me?'

The woman looked thoughtful, tapping her teeth with a polished fingernail. 'The newspaper. Now, that's given me a little idea.'

'Yes?' Jacquie prompted eagerly.

'Do you know when she moved to Westmead, then? Exactly, or even approximately?'

'Oh, yes.' How could she ever forget? 'It was at the beginning of July, 1989. Saturday, the first of July.'

'And do you know,' the librarian went on, 'when she got married?'

Jacquie shook her head. 'I'm afraid not. But probably,' she added, remembering Alison's pregnancy, 'not too long after she arrived.'

'Never mind.' The librarian rose from her desk. 'You could always go to the Family Records Centre, in London, and check the marriage records from around that time. But the thing is, if she got married in Westmead, there would have been something in the newspaper. As a matter of public record, you know.'

Jacquie's spirits rose even further. 'Of course! What a wonderful idea!'

'And we have all of the old newspapers here, on microfilm. If you don't mind going through some old papers, you just might be able to discover her married name.'

'Of course I don't mind!'

The librarian took her to a bulky microfilm reader and explained its operation. 'The newspapers are on these rolls, three months per roll. January to March, April to June, and so on. So this roll,' she said, producing the relevant one, 'happens to start with the first of July.' She threaded it on the machine and switched on the light. 'In those days, the *Herald* was a daily paper. Now it's only published once a week.'

Jacquie turned the crank and the pages of the newspaper whizzed by in a blur. 'Like this?'

'Slowly. Take your time,' the librarian added, smiling.

'We don't get much call for microfilm any longer, in these days of the Internet. Everything is on-line now. But the *Westmead Herald* has never got as far as that. Microfilm is the best we can offer, I'm afraid.'

Jacquie thanked her abstractedly, already absorbed by her sudden plunge back to 1989. It was so easy to get distracted by things like the adverts, to forget her objective. For nearly an hour she pored over the first paper, page by page, losing track of the time in her fascination with the minutiae of the past. Eventually, though, she realised that this would not do: she would be here for weeks, giving herself eye-strain in the bargain, if she read every word of every paper. When she reached the edition for Sunday the second, she forced herself to scan the pages in a disciplined way: the front page, then straight to the list of weddings without lingering along the way. Not, she realised, that Alison's wedding could possibly have been reported or even have taken place *that* soon, but she might as well establish the routine. It wouldn't take her long to reach a more likely date, perhaps late July or early August, depending on the banns.

So there was nothing, of course, on the Sunday, and she whizzed through it quickly. When she reached Monday, though, her attention was caught by the front-page headline: 'Murder in Quire Close'.

Jacquie frowned, disturbed. Murder was something that happened in London, not in an idyllic place like Westmead. She skimmed the article, which was small in relation to the headline, and not very informative. 'The body of a young woman was found yesterday in Quire Close, near the cathedral. According to police sources, she had been strangled. The body was discovered in the early morning by workmen, who have not been named. Police have not released the identity of the victim, pending notification of next of kin.' There was little more than that.

Interested but not alarmed, she cranked ahead to the front page of the next day's paper. This time there was quite a bit more information, written in a far more emotive style. The young blonde woman, it said, had not yet been identified; if anyone had any information which would help police to establish her identity or to apprehend the person responsible, they were to come forward. Jacquie had just begun to read the details when her eye was caught by the photo which illustrated the article. 'Do you know this bunny?' said the caption, and the grainy photo depicted a worn plush rabbit, with one eye missing and one ear ripped.

It was Grace. Without a doubt, it was Grace.

Jacquie's cry – piercing, instinctive, inconsolable – shattered the silence of Westmead Library.

Chapter 14

There was no question of Jacquie being allowed to find her own way to the police station; the kind librarian at the reference desk turned her post over to a deputy and took Jacquie there herself.

'She's had rather an upset,' she said to the perky young woman on duty at the desk. 'There was a murder here a few years back. She thinks that the victim might have been her sister.'

'It *was* her,' Jacquie insisted, rigid with shock. 'It was Grace.'

The young woman, who would have been very young indeed when the murder took place, shook her head. 'I'll get someone,' she offered. She scurried off and was gone for several minutes.

The person who appeared in her place was a man, tall and thin, with curly ginger hair. He spoke to the librarian for a moment; she gave him a concise account of what had happened, and he nodded to show that he understood. 'Thank you,' he said to her. 'You've been very kind. I'll deal with this now, if you need to get back to the library.'

The librarian departed; Jacquie hadn't moved. The man bent over and looked into her face. 'I'm Detective Sergeant Merriday,' he said. 'Could I ask you what your name is, Miss . . . Mrs?'

Jacquie unclenched her jaw with an effort. 'Darke. Jacquie Darke. Mrs.'

'If you would come with me, Mrs Darke,' he said. 'This way.'

She lifted one foot and put it in front of the other. 'It was Grace,' she said.

He guided her down a corridor, up some stairs, and into an office. 'Please sit down, Mrs Darke.' Jacquie sat as he lifted the phone and gave a concise order. 'Sweet tea, please, Liz. Plenty of sugar. Right away.'

Sergeant Merriday turned back to Jacquie. 'Now, Mrs Darke. When you're ready, I'll need to ask you a few questions.'

She nodded.

'You have reason to believe that a body which was found some years ago was that of your sister Grace?'

'No.' She shook her head. 'Ally. Alison.'

He leaned towards her, puzzled. 'But you said Grace.'

Jacquie gave a shuddering sigh and made an effort to explain. 'Grace was her rabbit. Her stuffed bunny. In the picture. But my sister is . . . was . . . called Alison.'

'Oh, God, the rabbit.' He slumped back in his chair; until that moment, he had only half believed her. But the rabbit . . .

'Your tea, Tim?' said the girl from the front desk, hovering at the door with a steaming mug.

'Thanks, Liz, that was quick. It's for Mrs Darke. And I'd better have a cup myself,' he added, realising that the pit of his stomach had dropped.

Jacquie looked at the mug of tea as though she didn't know what she was meant to do with it. Sergeant Merriday helped her to cup her hands round it and guided it to her mouth. 'Here, take a sip,' he said gently. 'It will help.'

Her teeth chattered against the side of the mug, but she gulped, then sputtered. 'It's hot,' she said. 'And sweet. I don't take sugar.'

'Trust me,' he said.

Jacquie looked at him properly for the first time, and found that she did. He wasn't at all handsome, but he had such a kind face. She focused on the details: on his pale eyes, with eyelashes so light that they were almost invisible, and on his slightly crooked nose. Then she looked down at his hands, still cupped around hers. They were covered with freckles, and the knuckles were red. 'Your hands are warm,' she said.

'And yours are frozen.' He withdrew his hands and put them palms down on his desk. 'Just take your time,' he said. 'There's no hurry, Mrs Darke. I'm not going anywhere.'

She closed her eyes and concentrated on drinking the tea. Sweet tea, the time-honoured treatment for shock. A moment later another mug was brought. The sergeant took a gulp from the mug, and sighed. 'I know that I shouldn't have it with sugar,' he said confidentially, 'but I just can't seem to give it up.' He picked up the phone again and spoke into it, something to do with files. 'Look under Jane Doe,' he said. 'July, 1989.'

Why did people think that tea would make things

better? Jacquie wondered. Nothing would bring Alison back – not tea, nor all the wishing in the world. Nothing would ever be right again. 'My sister is dead.' She said the words aloud, trying them out – words that she knew she would repeat again and again. 'Ally is dead.'

Sergeant Merriday put down his mug of tea and drew a pad of paper towards him, selecting a sharpened pencil from a holder on his desk. 'Are you ready to talk about it, then?' he said. 'You don't have to until you're ready, Mrs Darke.'

'Call me Jacquie,' she said. 'Please.'

'Yes, all right. Jacquie.'

She moistened her lips with her tongue and tried to put the words in the right order. 'Ally left home on the first of July, 1989. I never saw her again.'

The dates fitted, the detective realised; there couldn't be any doubt, then. 'Your sister's full name?' he asked, pencil poised.

'Alison Barnett. Alison Rebekah Barnett.'

He wrote it down. 'And do you know her date of birth?'

'She was my sister. Of course I know her date of birth,' Jacquie said sharply, then sighed. 'Sorry. I didn't mean that. Her birthday was the third of April, and she was twenty when she . . . left. So that means she was born in 1969.'

His pale skin flushed. 'I'm sorry, Jacquie. I'm not trying to patronise you. This is difficult for me, as well.'

Why should it be difficult for him? she wondered. He was just doing his job. He hadn't known Ally, hadn't grown up with her, hadn't loved her for twenty years . . .

'Who murdered my sister?' she asked abruptly, putting the mug down on his desk. 'Tell me who killed her.'

It was his turn to sigh. 'I wish I could.'

She stared at him. 'Do you mean you don't *know*?'

His pencil began moving over the pad of paper in an elaborate doodle which turned into a cat. 'Your sister's murderer was never caught,' he said, keeping his voice as neutral as he could. 'It wasn't as if we didn't try, believe me.'

The efficient Liz appeared in the door again with two heavy box files, which she proceeded to dump on his desk. 'There. Now I've had my exercise for the day – I won't need to go to the gym this evening.'

'Thanks,' he said again, smiling at her, then he turned a grave face back to Jacquie. 'Now,' he said, 'before we start going through all of this, I have a question for *you*. Why didn't you report your sister missing? We spent an awfully long time trying to put a name to her, and we never managed to do that, either. Why now, Jacquie? After all these years, why now?'

Jacquie opened her mouth, then closed it again. She couldn't tell him; she couldn't look into those sympathetic pale eyes and tell him that she had driven her sister away, had not in all those years tried to find her. Instead she answered obliquely. 'I can't understand why she wasn't identified. She had her building society passbook with her – that had her name in it. And her passport – that must have been in her handbag as well.'

His reply was straightforward. 'There was no handbag with the body. Nothing at all to identify her. Just the . . . just Grace.' He looked down at the pad, where his latest doodle was transforming itself into a rabbit. 'Believe me, Jacquie. We tried. And,' he added, 'not just locally, either. Every police department in the country was notified, every missing person list was checked. All of the national papers ran stories, with the photo of Grace, and a description of . . . the dead woman. It was even on the evening news. I don't understand why you never saw any of that.'

This, at least, she could address. 'We didn't take a newspaper,' she stated. 'We never had a telly. My parents . . . were very religious. They didn't believe in being corrupted by the outside world.'

Tim Merriday nodded, satisfied with her answer. It was one of the many things about the case that had haunted him for years: unless she came from abroad, how could a young woman appear from nowhere, and have no one who would, eventually, miss her, and connect her with the unidentified dead girl in Westmead? And it was evident that she had not come from abroad; when her case had been found, it and all of its contents were of domestic manufacture or origin. 'Your parents . . .' he said, leaving it open-ended.

'They're dead,' she said baldly.

At least they would be spared the agony of discovering that their child had been murdered, he thought. Had been dead for years without them knowing.

'That's really why . . . now,' Jacquie went on, gulping. 'Alison is all I have left. Or I thought so.'

He found the pain on her face, in her voice, unbearable; he wished there was some way to comfort her. 'Your husband?' he said. 'Mr Darke?'

'I'm divorced,' she stated. 'And I have no children.'

Worse and worse. 'Mrs Darke,' he said, 'Jacquie, we don't have to do this now.' He dropped his pencil and put his palm down on the bulky box files. 'This will wait. Would you rather come back tomorrow, when you've had a chance to assimilate the fact of your sister's death? It may be too much for you now to hear all of the details.'

'I want to know,' she insisted. 'I *need* to know. I need to know how my sister died, and what the police did to try to find the person who killed her. I need to know everything. Do you think I could sleep tonight, not knowing?' She raised her eyes to meet his and saw that his eyes were swimming with tears; that was almost too much for her. Why, she wondered again, did he care? This was just part of his job, dealing with situations like this. They probably didn't have many murders in Westmead, but still . . .

'All right, then. If you're sure.' He opened the top file and adopted a business-like tone; it was the only way, he realised, that he would be able to get through this. 'The body of a young woman was found in Quire Close, north of the cathedral, at approximately 7 a.m. on Sunday the second of July, 1989. The people who found her, and who rang us to report their discovery, were two workmen, on their way to do some work at Priory House, at the north end of the close.'

'On a Sunday?' Jacquie interrupted sceptically; Reverend Prew had always drummed into them the sacredness of the Sabbath Day, and surely at a cathedral it would be the same.

'They were running behind, and planned to spend all day Sunday putting in some overtime,' he explained, not fazed by her question. 'The house was being renovated for the retiring Dean of the cathedral. Or for his widow, at any rate.'

'So how do you know that the workmen didn't kill her?' Jacquie demanded. 'One of them, or both of them? Maybe they tried it on with her, and when she wouldn't have it . . .'

'She was killed some time the previous evening,' he said. 'Not that morning. She probably wasn't killed where the body was found, but was dumped there later. We were never able to discover where, exactly, she was murdered – no forensic evidence turned up to indicate that.'

'They still could have murdered her,' insisted Jacquie. 'The night before. Then pretended to find her body. Isn't that what happens sometimes?'

'Yes, and that was the obvious line of enquiry.' DS Merriday flicked through the files, then plucked out a piece of paper. 'Alibis,' he said. 'They both had them. Detective Inspector Crewe, who was in charge of the investigation, interviewed both men for hours. He had their alibis checked, rigorously. Sid Nelson, aged twenty-nine, a joiner: he was at home with his wife and baby all evening. His wife swore to it. And the other one, Terry O'Connor, aged twenty-two, was at the Blacksmith's Arms pub from six o'clock till closing time, with six friends, all of whom said that he never left the pub. After that he went home with one of his mates to sleep it off.'

'Alibis can be faked,' she said stubbornly.

'There was no evidence of that in this case. And we checked, as well, into the backgrounds and alibis of all of the other workmen at Priory House. There were several of them. They all came up clean.' He ticked them off on his fingers. 'The plumber, the electrician, the decorator. None with any obvious motives, all with reasonable alibis.'

'Motives?' said Jacquie. 'Surely it's obvious what the motive must have been. My sister was an attractive girl, on her own in a strange town.'

The policeman shook his head. 'It's not as simple as that. She wasn't . . . raped, if that's what you're thinking. No evidence of sexual interference, is what the post-mortem report says.'

Jacquie shuddered, thinking of Alison on a slab in the mortuary, being probed and prodded.

'She was fully dressed,' he went on. 'Her clothing wasn't ripped or disturbed.'

'Ally was pregnant,' Jacquie stated, trying to make sense of it in her own mind. 'Maybe some man came on to her, and she told him she was pregnant, and . . . well, I don't know.'

He tried to get back on track. 'Everyone in Quire Close was interviewed,' he said. 'All of the people who live there have something to do with the cathedral, which made it much more difficult. The powers-that-be at the cathedral threw up all sorts of barriers. But we interviewed them all, and searched every house for forensic evidence. It was a logical assumption that she was killed there, in Quire Close, perhaps in one of the houses. But it was a washout. No one knew her, no one had seen her. No one had seen *anything*. It would have helped,' he added, 'if we'd known who she was. It was difficult to try to establish any sort of personal motivation behind her murder, when we didn't even have a name. She was a stranger in town. We couldn't interview her old boyfriends or any other likely contacts, because as far as we were concerned, there weren't any.'

Jacquie was frowning. '*Someone* must have seen her,' she said. 'She must have come in by train. She must have walked to the cathedral, or taken a taxi. A pretty girl, walking through the town with a suitcase . . .' She stopped and leaned forward. 'What about the suitcase? It was with her . . . body? When they found it?'

'No.' He picked up his pencil and resumed doodling: flowers this time, growing up round the cat and the rabbit. 'The suitcase didn't turn up until a day or so later. And you're right, of course. Several people *did* see her, on her way to the cathedral. And someone even spoke to her: the Head Verger at the cathedral. Apparently she'd gone into the cathedral, and he met her there. Talked to her, gave her a little tour. Chatted her up, I reckon.' He thought of Leslie Clunch and gave an involuntary grimace. 'He offered to lock up her case while he was giving her the tour, to save her carrying it. He put it in his office, he said. Then he was called away on urgent business, and by the time he got back, she had disappeared. He never saw her again, he said, and he forgot about the case until he heard about the murder and realised that she must have been the victim.'

'He said. He said. Surely he could have been lying?' suggested Jacquie sharply. 'What if *he* killed her? That's just the story he would have made up.'

'Leslie Clunch is a highly respected member of the cathedral community,' said DS Merriday. 'I'm not saying that there wasn't some suspicion attached to him at the time, but once again there was no evidence. Apparently he was in the cathedral for most of the evening, and then he went home to his wife. Mrs Clunch confirmed that he didn't go out again that night. And,' he added, 'there was no reason for him to have come forward with the suitcase, if he was guilty. He could have destroyed it, or chucked it in a skip somewhere, like the murderer presumably did with her handbag. Clunch could have kept out of things entirely, instead of drawing attention to himself.'

'But,' Jacquie pointed out, 'other people would have seen her with him. They would have seen the case, seen her carrying it or him taking it from her.'

'Point taken,' he admitted. 'But the fact is that he *did* come forward. He was interviewed for hours, and never changed his story.'

Jacquie was silent for a moment, trying to take it all in. When she spoke, her voice was bitter. 'And so, in a few weeks, or a few months, you forgot all about it. You buried my sister in an unmarked grave, I suppose, and put the files away. You let them get away with it – whoever killed her. She's dead, and he's still out there. But the police won't do anything about it. After all, she was just a stranger.' She knew, as she said it, that she was being unfair, that she was projecting her own guilt on to them. She didn't care; she couldn't help herself.

'No,' he said, quietly but with an intensity that dragged Jacquie's unwilling eyes to his face.

'No?'

'I didn't forget all about it. I've never forgotten it, not for one day.'

She stared at him. Sergeant Merriday was young, certainly no more than a few years older than she herself. Thirty-five, perhaps, at the outside. Alison's murder had taken place eleven years earlier. Surely he hadn't been a sergeant then, or even a detective; he couldn't have been involved personally in the investigation. She had assumed, all along, that his 'we' was a corporate one, not reflecting anything more than the fact that he was a policeman, and that he knew about the case because there weren't many murders, especially unsolved ones, in Westmead. 'What do you mean?'

'I was the one,' he said, looking away. 'I was the constable who was first on the scene. I saw her, before anyone else did.'

'Oh, God.' Jacquie closed her eyes, but it didn't blot out the picture that was now imprinted on her brain, as if he had transmitted it to her by some sort of telepathy: her sister's dead body. Sprawled limbs and tumbled blonde hair.

Downstairs, Liz Hollis, the perky young woman at the desk, was gossiping with a middle-aged WPC. 'Some old murder,' she said. 'The woman said it was her sister Grace. Before my time, it was.'

The WPC nodded. 'Yes, I remember that one. Quite a nasty one, as I recall. Never solved, and no one ever turned up to claim the body. Fancy someone coming forward, after all these years.'

'Tim asked for the files,' Liz revealed. 'Jane Doe.'

'That's right. Identity unknown. I suppose now they can at least put a name to the poor thing. Grace. That's something, anyway.' The WPC shook her head. 'Tim has always had a bit of a thing about that case. A bee in his bonnet. I think he found the body, or some such. And I think he goes and gets those files out and looks at them, every so often. Just in case they missed something.'

'Oh, really?' Liz Hollis was not a member of the force, but a civilian employee, and a fairly recent one at that, so there were huge gaps in her knowledge. To be truthful, she wasn't particularly interested in the mechanics of police procedure. But she *was* interested in people, and in gossip. And, having recently split up from her long-term boyfriend, she fancied her chances with Tim Merriday. He might not be the world's greatest catch, but he was personable and kind and conscientious; she had hopes that he might be interested in her. Once after work he had asked her, on the spur of the moment, to go for a drink at the new theme pub. She'd had to say no, as she had another date that evening, and the invitation hadn't been repeated, but she was biding her time and waiting for her chance. So anything to do with Tim Merriday was potentially useful information. She filed it away in her head.

'You don't want to hear this,' DS Merriday said.

'Tell me.'

His pencil flew over the paper, adding a bird. A hawk, perhaps: a predatory creature, with wings outstretched and curved beak. 'It was a sight I'll never forget,' he said. 'She was so . . . young. So . . . vulnerable.' So still, he didn't add. So dead. It was the first time he had seen death; he had been moved to tears then, and still was when he allowed himself to remember that moment.

'But you didn't know her,' Jacquie stated, her voice harsh, questioning his right to claim any ownership in this matter. 'She was a stranger to you. She was *my sister*. Nothing to you.'

'She reminded me,' he said softly, 'of my wife. Blonde, pretty. All I could think was that it might have been her lying there instead. Gilly, my wife.'

So he was married, then. Jacquie was conscious of an absurd twinge of disappointment at the realisation.

'We hadn't been married that long at the time,' he said,

as if he needed to explain, to excuse his weakness. 'And then, when I found out that the girl – your sister – had been expecting a baby . . .' He averted his face. 'Gilly was pregnant, too. It was a few months before Frannie was born. My daughter Frannie.'

Frannie. Jacquie felt as if a knife had twisted inside her; she hadn't believed that the pain could be any worse, but this was too much. Frannie, his daughter was called. If things had been different, *she* might have had a daughter Frannie, named after her own father.

'I've got to go,' Jacquie said abruptly, standing up.

He rose as well, and put out a hand to stop her. 'I'm sorry. I shouldn't have said that. You didn't need to hear it. What you said is true – she was *your* sister, and it has nothing to do with me. I have no right to care about her, and what happened to her. I just . . . do. But that's my problem, not yours.'

'No,' said Jacquie. 'That's not it.' She had, just a moment before, been thinking that very thing, resenting his seeming emotional stake in her sister's death. Now it seemed to her touching; it made her like him even more. 'I just . . . can't cope with any more. Maybe another day. Maybe tomorrow. Not now.'

'I'll come with you,' he said. 'You've had a terrible shock – you shouldn't be by yourself just now. Where are you staying? I'll take you there.'

'You're not responsible for me,' she protested. But his concern moved her deeply, even in her pain, and he was right about one thing: she didn't want to be on her own. To be alone in that immaculate but unfamiliar bedroom at Cathedral View Guest House, alone with her thoughts and her memories of her sister, alone with the final and ultimate realisation that it was too late to put things right.

Alone with Ally's ghost.

'I'm coming with you,' he said firmly, and Jacquie allowed him to take her arm, to lead her downstairs and out of the door, past the front desk with the perky Liz, who stared at them suspiciously. 'I'm taking Mrs Darke home,' he said to Liz. 'Don't expect me back for a while. If anyone is looking for me, tell them I've signed out for the afternoon.'

They were out on the pavement. 'Now,' he said, turning to face Jacquie. 'Where are we going?'

'I don't think I'm ready to go back . . . there,' she said shakily. 'To my bed-and-breakfast. Not yet.'

'Right.' He paused for a moment, thinking. 'A drive, perhaps. A drive in the country. How does that sound?'

'You're supposed to be working,' she protested.

'I *am* working.'

'Your boss – Detective Inspector Crewe, did you say? – might not think so.'

He gave a mirthless laugh. 'Old Crewe retired years ago. He's moved to Eastbourne. I'm not worried about *him*.' He would not, Tim Merriday told himself, mention, or even think about, the Superintendent.

'Whatever, then.' Jacquie shrugged, too drained to make any decisions. 'It's very kind of you, Sergeant.'

'Please, Jacquie,' he said. 'If we're going to be spending the afternoon together, at least you can call me Tim.'

'All right, then. Tim.' It was a nice name; it felt good on her lips.

They went behind the police station to his car. Then he concentrated on negotiating the one-way system to get out of the town, looking over at her once or twice to make sure that she was all right. Jacquie leaned back against the head rest, her eyes shut.

Once out in the country, though, she opened her eyes as she sensed that they were climbing. 'Oh!' she said. 'It's hilly.' She'd never seen hills quite like this before, green even in November, and rolling gently from one fold to another, dotted picturesquely with sheep. The sun still shone: it had, she realised, been only a matter of hours since she'd set out from the Cathedral View Guest House with such high hopes, brimming with optimism.

He glanced curiously at her. 'You call this hilly?' he said. 'Where on earth do you come from, then? You never did say.'

'From Sutton Fen,' she said. 'You won't have heard of it. Not too far from Ely. North of Cambridge. In the fens.'

'I've never seen the fens,' he admitted. 'Flat, are they?'

'Very.' Flat and featureless and grey, she wanted to say. Oppressive and horrible and inward-looking. And I never want to go back there again. But she left it at that, looking out of the windscreen at the shifting light on the undulating fields.

'In case you're wondering,' he said after a while, 'I'm taking you to get some lunch. To a nice pub I know, right out in the country. We'll soon be there.'

The number of cars in the pub's car park attested to its popularity, but Tim Merriday was known by the publican, who managed to find them a tiny table in a corner.

'What would you like to drink?' Tim asked Jacquie.

'I don't care. You decide.'

'And what would you like to eat?'

She shrugged. 'I'm not hungry.'

'We'll see about that.' He left her and went to the bar to order, returning with a pint of bitter and a gin and tonic.

Jacquie looked doubtfully at the drink. 'What is it?'

'G and T. Drink up.'

In her moments of rebellion, Jacquie had drunk wine, but she'd never had gin before. The first sip shocked her with its astringency; the second warmed her all the way down. 'It's good,' she said, pulling a face.

He laughed. It was the first time she'd heard him laugh. Part of her resented the fact that he could laugh when her sister was dead; the rest of her relaxed a bit, helped by the gin.

'Tell me,' said Tim Merriday, his expression serious once more, 'about your sister. Tell me about Alison.'

'I can't,' said Jacquie. But after two more sips of the gin and tonic, she opened her mouth and the words came out. 'Alison was . . . lovely. She was more than just a sister. She was my playmate, she was my friend. There was only a year between us, you see. And our parents didn't like us mixing with other children. Worldly children. We were . . . set apart, Ally and I. Just the two of us.'

He leaned back into the corner and listened, maintaining eye contact and making encouraging noises.

Once she'd started, though, Jacquie didn't need much encouragement. The words poured out of her; for more than three hours she talked, stopping only to take bites of food. She didn't even notice that she was eating, let alone what it was.

She needed to talk, needed to tell him, needed to make him understand what it had been like. She told him everything she could remember about their childhood, about their teenage years: Jacquie as the bold tomboy, Alison as the timid little sister, playing with her dolls. She told him about Reverend Prew, and the Free Baptist Fellowship, and about their parents.

He was a wonderful listener, she discovered. No one but Ally had ever listened to her like this before. Not Darren – certainly not Darren. Not Reverend Prew, who never listened to anything but the sound of his own voice. Not her parents, who thought that *she* should be the one listening, that children should be seen and not heard, even when they were no longer children. Not Nicola, who had problems of her own to deal with. No one but Ally.

The stories followed one on another, out of sequence, jumbled as a box of old snapshots. They finished lunch, and started on coffee; still the stories came, and still he listened.

There was just one thing she didn't tell him, couldn't tell him. Her account stopped short of the holiday in Greece, and all that followed. How could she bring herself to admit – even to a man she'd never met before today – that it was her fault that her sister was dead? If she hadn't talked Ally into going on that holiday, if she hadn't pushed her into Mike's arms, if she hadn't driven her away from Sutton Fen . . . If, if, if . . .

'And then?' Tim Merriday prompted. 'What happened then?'

She looked down into her empty coffee cup. 'Then I got married,' she said lamely. 'And Alison . . . left. She left Sutton Fen that day.'

Had Alison been jealous of her sister's marriage? he wondered. Had she run off in an envious strop? Was she, perhaps, in love with the groom herself? Who was the father of her child, then? There was much, he sensed, that Jacquie wasn't saying, things that she was keeping back. Perhaps in time she would tell him. But he wouldn't push her. Not until she was ready.

All of the other guests had left the pub long before; the landlord wiped the surrounding tables and asked them if they'd like anything else.

'I think that's a hint,' Tim said.

Jacquie looked at her watch. 'Is that really the time?'

'Don't they say that time flies . . .' He stopped, embarrassed, without finishing his sentence. 'Fun' was hardly an appropriate word to use in the circumstances, and yet he *had* enjoyed the afternoon. 'The evening crowd will be arriving pretty soon,' he added quickly.

'You won't be going back to work, then.'

'No.'

She kept her voice light. 'Your wife will be wondering what's happened to you, as well. Will she give your dinner to the dog?'

'My wife?'

'Gilly,' she prompted him.

He gave a little laugh. 'Didn't I say? Gilly and I split up years ago.'

'You're divorced?'

'She couldn't cope with the job,' he said. 'My job. The same old story that policemen always tell. Long, unpredictable hours. And you never leave the job behind. Sort of like being a vicar, I suppose.'

Jacquie smiled, imagining Tim Merriday in a dog collar; the mental picture was an incongruous one.

He was delighted at the smile, which transformed her face. 'Penny for them?' he prompted.

'I was just trying to picture you as a vicar.'

'Oh, heaven forbid! A policeman is bad enough. Gilly probably would have murdered me if I'd been a vicar.' As soon as he said it, he realised what he'd done; he could have kicked himself. At the mention of murder, the smile died from her face and the light from her eyes. 'Oh, God, Jacquie. I'm sorry,' he apologised quickly.

But it was too late. She was silent in the car, all the way back into Westmead.

It wasn't only Alison that occupied her thoughts, though. She was thinking about Tim Merriday, and what a nice man he was. A nice, unattached – as far as she knew – man.

She couldn't believe that she was thinking like this, and feeling the way she felt. Yes, she was unused to drinking spirits, and the gin might well have something to do with it. But he was so extraordinarily sympathetic. Such a good listener.

It had been a very long time since Jacquie had even thought about men. Those days before her marriage, when she had been so anxious to sow her wild oats, to experience as much as she could, seemed a lifetime away; the holiday in Greece was like something that had happened to a different person, some other Jacquie, read about in a book and dimly remembered. Once she had taken her vows to Darren, she had kept them, had been a faithful wife. Darren had hurt her badly; since he'd left her, she had certainly not gone out looking for anyone else. Love – and sex – were things of the past, she had come to believe. And worse than that: a snare, a trap for the unwary. Evanescent, ultimately unsatisfying. She was beyond all that; it wouldn't happen to her again.

Tim, for his part, was thinking how much he had enjoyed the afternoon, in spite of the grim and terrible circumstances. Jacquie was a survivor, no matter what she said; she'd had a pretty horrible life, but it hadn't defeated her. She had a good sense of humour, she was articulate, she was good company. And she was attractive, with her cap of short dark hair and her angular face. She didn't, he thought involuntarily, look anything like her sister. Her dead sister, who had reminded him so painfully of Gilly.

Gilly, who had left him.

He hadn't given up on women after his divorce, but he hadn't exactly had time to pursue them either. He'd thought that Liz, at work, was a nice, sparky girl, if a bit young for him; once, on a whim, he'd invited her out for a drink, but she'd turned him down. There hadn't really been anyone else he'd felt strongly enough about to bother with.

He parked the car at the back of the Cathedral View Guest House.

'You've done enough,' said Jacquie. 'You don't need to come in with me.'

'I insist,' he said. 'And besides, I could do with a cup of tea. You do have tea-making facilities, I assume?' he added ironically. 'Isn't that what these places advertise?'

Her mouth twitched into a smile. 'Along with hot and cold running water. All the mod cons, in fact.'

There was no one about as they climbed the stairs to the first floor and she unlocked her door. It seemed, she thought, at least a week since she'd left the room that morning. Now it was dark, but it was still the same day.

Tim crossed to the window while she filled the kettle

at the basin. 'Nice view,' he said, looking out at the cathedral. 'Hence the name, I assume.'

'There's only one cup,' Jacquie noted. 'Shall we share it, or shall I go and try to find another one?'

'We can share.'

She put a tea bag in the solitary cup and poured the boiling water over it, then handed it to Tim. He fished the tea bag out with a plastic spoon, and dumped in the contents of a tiny tub of UHT milk. 'Now,' he said, 'we have a problem. Sugar, for me, or no sugar, the way you like it?' He pondered the dilemma. 'I know. You drink half the cup. Then I'll put sugar in the rest.'

Jacquie gulped down half of the tea, then passed it over to him. When he'd finished it, he rinsed the cup at the basin. 'I suppose I'd better go now,' he said. 'I've seen you safely to your room. I've had my tea. I don't have any more excuses to hang about.'

'Thank you,' Jacquie said. 'Thank you for everything, Tim. I can't tell you . . .'

'No need to thank me,' he protested. 'You'll come back in to the station tomorrow? I'm afraid there are some things we still need to clear up, a few questions I need to ask you. Paperwork,' he grimaced. 'You'll come?'

'I'll come.'

As he opened the door to go, though, she found that she couldn't bear it. In just a few seconds she would be on her own. 'Don't,' she said in a low voice. 'Don't go.'

Tim turned back. 'What?'

'Don't go, Tim. Don't leave me.' She shut her eyes and moved close to him.

His arms went around her; she made him feel strong,

protective. She made him feel like he hadn't felt since Gilly left him.

'I can't bear it,' she murmured against his chest. 'I don't want to be alone.'

He felt powerless to resist. Nor, he discovered, did he particularly want to, as her hungry mouth reached up to seek his. Half pulling and half being pulled, they moved together towards the bed.

Chapter 15

From her bed, Sophie could see the towering chimney of the house across the close; she could see the bare branches of a tree. She could not see the cathedral, for which she was, at least, grateful. That meant that there were moments when she could forget its hateful proximity.

For the first few days after her return from hospital, weak as a newborn kitten and low in spirits, Sophie stayed in bed, ministered to by Chris. He'd taken leave from work, and could devote himself to looking after her.

Chris hovered excessively, attentive and sympathetic, though he scarcely seemed to know what to say to Sophie. And she had nothing at all to say to him.

Just before she'd gone into hospital, she and Chris had had the biggest row of their marriage. Up until then, in all of ten years they had never shouted at each other; Chris's sanguine and nonconfrontational temperament had precluded any such displays of anger.

But one day he had returned from Evensong to find her redecorating the nursery. She had already ripped off the frieze on which the teddy bears marched to their picnic, and was in the process of slapping a coat of paint on the walls.

'What are you doing?' Chris asked.

Sophie's voice was tart. 'I should think that's fairly obvious.'

'But why, Soph?'

She didn't pause. 'I wouldn't have thought I'd need to spell it out for you.'

'But . . .'

'Listen, Chris.' She threw down the paintbrush and turned round to face him. 'There isn't going to be a baby. We know that now. So why should we have a perfectly good room going to waste? We'll be able to use it as a guest room. I've ordered a bed – it will be delivered on Thursday.'

He looked distressed. 'But Soph. Aren't you rushing things a bit? I mean . . .'

'Rushing things?' Impatiently she picked up the brush again. 'There isn't going to be a baby, not now, not ever. What part of that sentence do you not understand?'

'Maybe we can't have a baby of our own,' he said. 'But that doesn't mean—'

'*We* can't have a baby?' Sophie interrupted him in an aggressively bitter voice. 'You mean *I* can't have a baby. I'm the one who's defective, remember?'

'I don't think of it like that,' he protested. 'We're in this together. And I've been thinking—'

'There's nothing to think about,' she snapped. 'I can't have a baby. That's that.'

'Listen to me, Soph.' He grabbed her arm. 'There are other ways.'

She tried to shake his hand off, and glared at him with

something approaching hatred. 'You can have a baby with someone else, you mean? If you want to divorce me, just say so. I'm sure there's some nice, willing young woman in Westmead who can give you babies.'

He stared at her for a moment, his jaw slack with amazement, then laughed. 'You must be joking!'

That seemed to infuriate her even more. 'Don't laugh at me!' she shouted. 'It's not funny!'

Chris dropped her arm and retreated a step; he tried to speak calmly. 'I'm not laughing at you. I love you. I don't want anyone but you. All I'm trying to say, Soph, is that we could always adopt.'

'Adopt?' She said it as though it were a foreign word which she'd never heard before. 'Adopt? You just don't get it, do you?'

'I don't . . .'

Sophie spaced out her words deliberately, in the manner of one talking to a slow child. 'There . . . is . . . something . . . wrong . . . with . . . me.'

'But . . .'

'I'm not meant to be a mother,' she stated with more bitterness than self-pity. 'This is nature's way of telling me that I'm not fit to be a mother.'

'But that's ridiculous,' Chris assured her. 'Lots of women – lots of couples – can't have children of their own. And there are so many children who need good homes, who need love.'

She glared at him. 'You want me to take some other woman's baby into my home.'

'I don't see why not. It wouldn't make any difference. It would be *our* baby – you'd see.' He took a step towards her. 'At least it's something to think about, Soph. You don't have to decide right now. But think about it.'

'There is nothing to think about.' Again she turned her back on him.

Chris moved up behind his wife and put his arms round her. 'Come on, now, Soph,' he said softly into her ear. 'Let's forget about all this. Let's go to bed.'

She jerked away from him. 'Bed?' she cried. 'Is that all you can think about? And what's the point?' she added caustically.

Instead of retreating, he stood his ground. 'The point is that I love you. That I want to show you how much I love you, and I want to comfort you. I keep saying, Soph, we're in this together.'

'And *I* keep saying that I'm the one who can't have a baby. I'm the one with the body that won't do what it's supposed to do.'

Chris's face changed. 'Aren't you being just a little bit selfish about this?' he challenged her.

'Selfish? All you want is to drag me off to bed, all you're interested in is sex, and you call *me* selfish?'

'Now you *are* being ridiculous.' Again he took a step towards her.

'Don't touch me,' she warned. 'Just don't even try to touch me.' She wielded the paintbrush in his direction like an offensive weapon, fending him off.

'I wish you'd let me—'

'You wish I'd let you have sex!' she shouted. 'Well, you can just forget it! Not now. Not ever. There's just no point.'

Chris's face had gone red. 'You just won't listen to me, will you?' he said in a voice she'd never heard before, hot with anger. 'All you can think about is yourself! You, you,

you. *You* can't have a baby. *You* don't want me to touch you. What about me? What about what *I* want?'

'Oh, that's rich,' snapped Sophie sarcastically, knowing she was hurting him and past caring. 'Talk about selfish. You're the one who dragged me off to this God-forsaken place. You're the one who spends all your time with the bloody choir and leaves me on my own. I hate it here. I never wanted to come here, and I hate it.'

He stood still for a moment, looking as if he'd been slapped; the colour had drained from his face and he was now as white as a corpse. When he spoke, at last, his voice had a deadly calm about it which was far worse than the heated anger. 'I hated London. I stayed there all those years for you, hating it. I put *you* first. You and your precious career.'

'Oh, bully for you,' she sneered. 'Aren't you the noble one?'

'And the baby,' Chris went on inexorably, putting into words at last that which had never been spoken between them. 'You're the one who wanted to wait. Your precious career again. If we'd had a baby years ago, when I wanted to, then maybe you wouldn't be in this condition. Maybe we'd be a family, instead of two people who—'

She didn't let him finish the sentence; she didn't want to know how he was going to finish it.

'Oh, just go away,' said Sophie coldly, turning her back on him.

He went.

A moment after he'd gone, her anger left her abruptly, and Sophie realised how unfair she'd been, how hurtful her words. She wept a bit, sick with remorse, but it was too late. The words could not be unsaid.

*   *   *

'My sister is dead.' Jacquie said the words calmly, almost conversationally, to the proprietress of the Cathedral View Guest House.

'Oh, my dear! Will you be leaving us, then?' The woman's kind face creased in concern and she crossed the breakfast room to pat Jacquie's arm. 'Your family will be needing you, won't they?'

'She hasn't *just* died,' Jacquie explained. 'Years ago, it's been. And I didn't even know she was dead.'

Now the woman looked confused. Jacquie poured milk on her cornflakes. 'I don't think I'll have a cooked breakfast this morning,' she said. 'Just toast, please. And coffee.'

It was the only way she could handle it. No hysteria, no tears. Just that simple acknowledgement: her sister was dead.

After what had happened last night . . .

Remembering, she crunched a mouthful of cornflakes.

She had thrown herself at Tim Merriday. Shamelessly, needily, she had thrown herself at him.

And he had rejected her.

Dear God, he had rejected her.

At first he had seemed as keen as she, had responded with unmistakable enthusiasm as she kissed him and pulled him on to the bed.

But then, after a few minutes, he had drawn away from her.

Unprofessional, he had said, flushed to the roots of his ginger hair, clothing in disarray. Unthinkable. He couldn't, they mustn't.

And he had left her then, left her alone in the bed.

How could she have been so foolish? How could she

have thrown herself at a man like that, on such short acquaintance?

He must think she was cheap. Desperate. A lonely divorcée, grabbing at the first man who came along and treated her kindly.

But he *had* encouraged her, she reminded herself. He had taken her to a pub, he had plied her with alcohol when he knew that she wasn't used to it, he had urged her to talk. He had created a bond between them, a feeling of closeness and understanding.

And when she'd kissed him, he had responded.

That was no excuse, though.

What must he think of her? A bereaved woman, who has just discovered that her sister is dead, and she tries to drag a man into bed.

Shameless.

Was she any better than she'd been eleven years ago?

All she wanted to do this morning was to pack her bag, get into her car, and drive back to Sutton Fen. Back to the lonely house where she would be for ever on her own, for ever trapped with her own inadequacies.

Alone with Alison's ghost.

Trapped with the knowledge that she had been responsible for her sister's death.

And it was that realisation – that if she hadn't done the things she'd done, if she hadn't driven Alison away, her sister would be alive today – that convinced her of the impossibility of that scenario.

She owed it to Alison to stay in Westmead.

No matter what the personal cost, she owed it to Alison.

She would stay in Westmead until the police found out who had killed Alison.

It was the least she could do. It was the *only* thing she could do.

The girl Liz was on the front desk again. Was it her imagination, Jacquie wondered, or did Liz look at her suspiciously when she asked, in the calmest voice she could muster, to see Sergeant Merriday?

'Tim?' said Liz, in a protective, even proprietary, way. 'Is he expecting you? Do you have an appointment?'

'No, but he asked me to call in to answer some questions.'

'I'll see if he's available. Your name again?'

Jacquie swallowed the lump in her throat. 'Mrs Darke.'

'Oh, yes. Mrs Darke.' Liz picked up the phone and punched in a number. 'Tim? Mrs Darke is here to see you. She doesn't have an appointment. Shall I send her up?' A smile played round her lips as she listened to his answer, then she put the phone down and turned to Jacquie. 'He says he'll come down for you, Mrs Darke. In a few minutes. Would you like to take a seat?'

Jacquie perched on the edge of a hard chair with a fake leather seat, her hands clasped in her lap to keep them from shaking. She *must* remain calm, she told herself. She mustn't show any emotion at seeing him. She must act as if nothing had happened. A memory stirred, unbidden, of how soft his lips had been and how warm and comforting his body, how exciting it had been to be in his arms for just those few minutes; she flushed and squeezed her hands even tighter.

Upstairs, Tim sat for a moment at his desk, taking deep breaths to compose himself, before going down to find Jacquie. He'd been at his desk for nearly an hour, with papers spread out in front of him, but he had no consciousness at all of what was written on them, or even what they related to.

What, he asked himself, had he done? How had he allowed himself to behave in such a thoroughly unprofessional manner?

Whatever must she think of him?

He *had* been unprofessional. He'd told himself that he was being kind to a distressed woman; a good Samaritan, acting above and beyond the call of duty. But he *had* urged her to drink, and he had encouraged her to talk, to develop a rapport and a closeness that were both premature and inappropriate.

He was a policeman. She was the sister of a murder victim.

But, God, how he had wanted her.

In those few minutes on the bed, before common sense struggled to reassert itself, he had felt alive again, a real man making love to a real woman.

Pulling away from her, leaving that bed, had been one of the hardest things he'd ever had to do.

It was the right thing, he was sure, but it was no easier for that.

And now she was back.

After the row, Chris had slept on the sofa, and as soon as the new guest-room bed arrived, he moved there. Sophie's status as an invalid, just returned from hospital, had fostered the continuation of that arrangement. No night-time closeness, then, holding each other in bed and enjoying each other's warmth, with or without anything more than that. None of that: just two people living in the same house, tied together, the one utterly dependent on the other, yet isolated from each other.

They had, of course, never again referred to the row, at least not directly. Sophie had tried, early on, to offer an apology, but Chris had rebuffed the attempt, and that had made things worse. The row hung between them like a poisoned cloud, colouring everything they said to each other. The unspoken had been spoken, and it seemed that things would never be the same, however bitterly they both regretted it.

And so it was with some relief that Chris took a phone call from Sophie's sister Madeline, a few days after Sophie came out of hospital. 'I really feel that I ought to come down and look after poor Sophie,' she said.

Under other circumstances, Sophie wouldn't have been keen. She would, in fact, have done anything to keep Madeline away from her, especially when she was feeling low and vulnerable. But being alone with Chris, having him treat her with elaborate courtesy, moving about as if he were treading on eggshells: it was taking its toll on her. Anything, even Madeline, would be a welcome change.

'I *do* think it would be a good idea,' said Chris, unaware that she wouldn't require much convincing. 'She's family, after all. And a woman. She could look after you better than I can.'

If he was expecting to be contradicted by Sophie, then he waited in vain. 'And you really ought to go back to work,' she said. 'You've had a week off already.'

'We're coming up to the end of term,' he agreed, almost eagerly. 'Advent and Christmas will be here before we know it. And things are going to get incredibly busy for the choir. Not to mention school.'

So Chris made arrangements to go back to work, and Madeline arrived.

She came by car, bringing with her enough luggage to sustain a visit of at least six months. Chris helped her to bring it in, carrying it up to the guest room; he would now return to sleeping on the sofa. Meanwhile Madeline went into the bedroom to hug Sophie and rhapsodise about Quire Close. 'I had no idea it was so wonderful,' she enthused. 'Sophie, you didn't say. You gave me the impression that you were living somewhere awful and grim, but it's utterly charming!'

'It may look that way to you, but you don't have to live here,' Sophie retorted.

'But it's ancient! Far older than *my* house, and that's Elizabethan!' Madeline moved to the window and looked out into the close. 'All of that lovely warm stone! And the chimneys. And the cobblestones. It's delightful, Sophie. You can't say that it's not. Most people I know would give their eye-teeth to live here.'

Madeline had already, within minutes, managed to put her in her place, Sophie realised: she was obviously an ingrate, unworthy of the splendid house that had been bestowed upon her. She bit her lip and resolved not to argue with Madeline, no matter what the provocation.

'It *is* lovely,' Chris agreed, coming into the bedroom. 'We're very lucky to live here.' He was careful not to look at Sophie as he said it, but Madeline didn't notice. 'Of course,' he added, 'not all of the houses are the same inside, even though they look quite similar outside. Some of them have been modernised and redecorated to a very high standard. And they vary in size. This one is a bit small, and hasn't had much done to it for quite a few years.'

'All part of its charm,' said Madeline, with her silvery laugh.

Sophie gritted her teeth. Her sister was getting on her nerves already, and she hadn't even been there for five minutes.

'You came on a good day,' Chris went on. 'You're seeing Quire Close at its best. It seems like it's been raining for weeks. Maybe,' he said, smiling, 'you've brought the good weather with you.'

Madeline returned his smile. Chris had always got on better with Madeline than Sophie herself did; this was a long-standing source of irritation to Sophie.

'Well, I'm afraid I haven't come to sightsee, or I'd ask you to give me a little tour of Westmead. The cathedral looks splendid – I'd love to see it.' Madeline sounded wistful.

Chris glanced at his wife. 'I'm sure Sophie wouldn't mind if we had a quick tour.'

'Oh, go ahead,' she said, making an effort to be gracious. 'I'll be fine on my own for a bit. I should have a nap now, in any case.'

She *did* sleep, but awoke on their return, as they came into the house laughing. For several minutes she lay grog-gily half-awake, waiting for them to come up to the bedroom, but it was some time before Madeline put her head round the door. 'Come in,' said Sophie.

'You're awake?'

'Since you got back.'

Madeline grimaced. 'Were we being noisy? Sorry. That husband of yours does make me laugh.'

Something that could never be said of the stolid Geoffrey, Sophie thought sourly, then was ashamed of herself.

'I was wondering if you'd like a cup of tea,' Madeline offered. 'I've put the kettle on.'

'Yes, please.'

Madeline brought the tea, and sat by the bed while Sophie drank it. 'The cathedral is beautiful,' she said. 'A real treasure. And how lucky you are to have it right on your doorstep.'

'Lucky,' echoed Sophie ironically.

Her sister ignored the interruption. 'And we met the most delightful man. The organist – Jeremy.'

Yes, thought Sophie. Madeline would love Jeremy. And he would be enchanted by her. She wasn't surprised when Madeline told her, with some satisfaction, that Jeremy would be calling in the next morning for a cup of coffee. 'He wants to see you, of course. He said he'd been staying away, out of consideration for your invalid state. But Chris assured him that you were quite ready to receive visitors.'

'I think I am,' Sophie agreed, her heart lifting at the prospect of seeing someone different. It would be good to see Jeremy, who always raised her spirits, and she had really missed Dominic. He had stopped by a few times in the afternoons, just to check how she was, but her afternoons were always spent sleeping, and Chris, protective of her rest, had sent him away with progress reports.

Then, unbidden, another thought surfaced. 'I just have one thing to ask,' she said. 'If someone called Leslie Clunch comes to the door, please don't let him in.'

'Leslie Clunch? What a peculiar name!' Madeline laughed. 'Who is he, then? And why don't you want to see him? I'm intrigued.'

'He *is* peculiar,' Sophie said emphatically. 'He's horrible.

Chris thinks he's all right, but I . . . I hate him. I don't want him anywhere near me.'

'Now I really *am* intrigued.' Madeline gave her a curious look.

'Just promise me, Maddy. If he comes, promise me that you'll send him away.'

He would take his cue from her, Tim Merriday decided as he came down the stairs. He would wait for her to say something. His heart constricted when he saw her, sitting upright on the edge of the chair, looking brave and determined. He wanted nothing more than to go to her and take her in his arms, to say that it had all been a terrible mistake, but he managed to keep his face impassive.

Jacquie rose as he approached, swallowing a lump in her throat. She would *not* say anything about last night. She couldn't. Not with that cheeky girl watching. 'Good morning, Sergeant,' she said stiffly. 'I'm sorry to bother you, but could I have a few minutes of your time?'

That was how it was, then, thought Tim. Easier, in a way, to play it like that. And he, too, was conscious of Liz's curious eyes on them. 'No bother at all, Mrs Darke,' he said with the courtesy he would show to anyone who made that request. 'Would you like to come up to my office?'

'Thank you.'

Silently they ascended the stairs, keeping a distance between them. In his office, he went behind the desk to distance himself even further. 'Mrs Darke. Would you like to take a seat?'

'Thank you.'

As she sat, she bowed her head, and that defeated gesture, along with the sight of the nape of her neck, was enough to bring words to Tim's lips which he'd had no intention of uttering. 'Jacquie,' he blurted. 'About last night. I'm so sorry . . .'

She didn't look at him. 'I don't want to talk about it, Sergeant.' Her voice was emotionless.

'Yes. All right.' With an effort he pulled himself together and sat down.

'I'm here to talk about my sister,' Jacquie went on in the same flat voice. 'Alison. I want to know what you're going to do about her.'

'Do?' That startled him out of his embarrassment. 'What do you mean, *do*?'

'About catching her killer. The man who murdered her,' Jacquie stated.

He stared at her for a moment, then found his voice. 'I explained this to you yesterday, Mrs Darke. Eleven years ago we tried very hard to do just that.' The bulky files were still on his desk; he put his hand on them. 'We explored every possibility. We conducted scores of interviews. And at the end of the day, we . . . weren't successful. We weren't able even to come close to discovering who killed her.'

'That's why you need to do it now.' She crossed her arms across her chest, and the set of her jaw was stubborn. 'To reopen the case.'

'Unsolved cases are never closed,' he said. 'Just filed, pending further investigation. And periodically reviewed and re-examined, as a matter of fact. But I'm just trying to be realistic.'

'You have to try to find her killer,' Jacquie insisted.

'I'm not saying that we won't try.' Tim tried not to feel exasperated. 'The case will certainly be reviewed, now that we have an identification. But what makes you think that we'd be any more successful now than we were eleven years ago? The trail is cold. People have moved away. Died, even. There is no new evidence. We don't know one single thing that we didn't know then, to make any difference.'

'You know who she was,' Jacquie said quietly. 'You just said it yourself.'

He looked into her eyes; she maintained eye contact, unflinching. 'Yes,' he said at last. 'We *do* know that.'

'And that *does* make a difference.'

It made a difference to Jacquie Darke, certainly, and Tim admitted to himself that it made a difference to *him*. But he couldn't see that it had advanced things in the least. There was still no new evidence, no new avenues of enquiry. Alison Barnett, not Jane Doe, had come as a stranger to Westmead and had been murdered. That was the only difference. And to be perfectly honest with himself, he knew that the Superintendent wasn't going to look at it the way he did. Apart from the fact that the two of them had never seen eye to eye, there was the little matter of resources. Tim could allow himself to get excited over things, but with the Superintendent it always came down to pounds and pence. Limited officers, limited time, limited finances. It was November, with over a month to go in the year and most of the annual budget spent already. Tim could imagine what the Superintendent would say if he were to go to him at this moment and say that he wanted to reopen the investigation of an eleven-year-old murder.

He picked up a pencil and began to doodle. Houses this time, one after another, with tall, soaring chimneys like those in Quire Close. 'Your sister,' he said, not looking at her, 'didn't know anyone in Westmead.'

'I never said that.'

Tim dropped his pencil. 'What?' Once again he stared at her.

'I never said that she didn't know anyone in Westmead. You didn't ask.'

In their conversation of the day before, they had both been assuming that she'd been killed by a stranger. He tried to put this into words. 'But . . .'

Jacquie was well aware of what she hadn't told Tim, and why. It was time to put that right, painful as it might be. 'The father of her baby,' she stated. 'She knew that he lived in Westmead. That's why she came here.'

This *did* change everything; this was the lead he'd been waiting for all these years. Why hadn't she mentioned it till now? 'But who was he?' Tim demanded eagerly.

'He was called Mike – I never knew his other name, though Alison might have done.'

'Mike.'

'That's all I know,' Jacquie admitted.

Mike. Tim cast his mind back over the files, those reams of paper which he'd perused for so many years, waiting and hoping for something to pop out at him. Was there a Mike there? Someone in Quire Close? One of the workmen? He restrained himself from pulling the files towards him there and then. 'How did it happen?' he asked bluntly. 'How did she know this Mike, then?'

'They met on holiday,' said Jacquie. 'In Greece.'

One of those holiday flings, thought Tim; it explained a great deal. That was something that had been niggling at him, that didn't make any sense: how a girl with the sort of religious – one might almost say repressive, if not oppressive – upbringing and timid nature that Jacquie had described to him could have found herself pregnant. That one fact, the fact of her pregnancy, just didn't fit in with everything else that Jacquie had told him about her sister, and he'd hesitated to ask, fearing to upset Jacquie, sure that she would have told him if she hadn't had a very good reason not to mention it. 'And she didn't tell you any more about him,' he said slowly. 'What he looked like, or anything like that? Short, tall? Young, old?'

Jacquie hesitated, but it was too late now – and too important – not to tell him. 'I saw him,' she admitted. 'I was with her when she met him.'

Exasperation mingled with excitement; Tim wasn't sure whether he wanted to hug Jacquie, or throttle her. Instead of either, he said as calmly as he could, 'Can you describe him to me, then?'

It had been a long time, and Jacquie had spent those years repressing memories of that holiday. She hadn't, she realised, paid that much attention to Mike when he had been the object of Alison's interest. She'd been far more interested in his friend – Steve, was he called? – and the more attractive men about the place; she'd scarcely looked at Mike, dismissing him as a non-starter. She closed her eyes and tried to picture him, but failed. 'Tall, I think,' she said vaguely. 'Young. I think his hair was blond. Or it might have been light brown. I don't think it was ginger.'

'Oh, that narrows it down,' said Tim, trying not to sound too sarcastic.

'Glasses,' Jacquie added suddenly, as a memory came to her. 'Round, I think they were. Or maybe square.' More than the glasses themselves, she remembered saying something to Alison about them.

Tim had picked up his pencil and was drawing a face; he put a pair of round spectacles on it. 'Anything like this?'

'Yes. I think so.' But she didn't sound convinced.

'All right, then.' He left it.

'I'd recognise him if I saw him,' she said, still somewhat doubtfully.

Tim rubbed both hands over his cheeks; his voice was regretful. 'It's not really enough to go on. I wish I could say otherwise.'

At last Jacquie realised what he was getting at, and gasped. 'You don't think he killed her, do you? Mike?'

He gave her a twisted, humourless smile. 'I've learned a few things as a policeman. One of them is that when someone is murdered, it's always much more likely that they've been killed by someone they know, than by a complete stranger. Most of the time, in fact.'

'I don't remember much about him, but he didn't seem the type at all,' protested Jacquie. 'Pretty meek and mild, in fact. And why would he kill her?'

Tim shook his head. 'You tell me. An argument that got out of hand? Or maybe she told him about the baby, and he wasn't happy about it.'

'That seems awfully far-fetched.' Jacquie frowned.

Tim remembered, as if it were yesterday, how he had felt when Gilly told him that she was pregnant. The pregnancy hadn't been planned; at first he'd been distinctly ambivalent about it. But he'd been in love with Gilly, anxious to please her. He'd quickly accustomed himself to the idea of a baby and before long he was as pleased as Gilly was about it; when Frannie was born, he felt himself to be the luckiest, and the happiest, man on earth. Now, of course, Frannie was the joy of his life; he couldn't imagine being without her. That, though, was hindsight: he recalled the sinking feeling in the pit of his stomach when Gilly had broken the news. It took some stretch of the imagination to contemplate that feeling as a prelude to murder, but . . .

He shook himself out of his reverie. 'Not as far-fetched as her being murdered by a stranger for no reason at all,' he pointed out.

'If he killed her . . .' Jacquie said with sudden passion. 'You *will* find him, won't you? Please say that you will.' She fixed on him a gaze of fierce entreaty.

He wanted to do as she asked; he wanted to say that he would find Alison's killer, whether it was Mike or someone else, no matter what effort it took. Single-handedly, if necessary. But he knew that he owed it to her to be realistic. 'I can't promise that,' he said at last, with reluctance.

Jacquie looked down at her clasped hands and her voice was bitter. 'I should have known.'

'I *will* try, though,' he heard himself saying, with a sudden mental picture of himself as a knight on a steed, slaying dragons on her behalf. 'The thing is, it isn't up to me. I never have been officially involved with this case. I'll do my best to get the investigation properly reopened, and to get myself assigned to it. But it's not up to me. I'll have to go to my boss and convince him. And he won't be easy to convince.'

'Thank you,' said Jacquie, and smiled for the first time that day: a trusting smile, confident that he could deliver.

That smile, thought Tim, was worth it all. If he had to go down on his knees to the Superintendent, it would be worth it. 'I'll do my best,' he repeated, feeling idiotic.

'I know you can do it,' she stated, and made as if to leave.

He didn't want her to go. 'There *is* one other thing,' he said, reaching for the files. 'This isn't going to be pleasant, Mrs Darke, but I'll need you to make a formal identification.'

The smile left Jacquie's face, wiped off in an instant. 'Identification?'

'I'm going to have to ask you to look at a photo,' he said, looking at her gravely, gauging how his words were affecting her.

Jacquie swallowed. 'Yes. All right.'

Shielding the files from her eyes, he flipped through the photos until he found one that was less distressing than the others. It was a close-up of the girl's face, stopping short of the cruel marks on the neck, missing out the twisted limbs. As many times as he'd looked through the photos, as vivid as his own memories of the crime scene were, they never failed to move him, sometimes to tears; there were tears in his eyes now as he silently passed the photo across to Jacquie.

She steeled herself to take it. Up till this moment, although in her heart she knew that Alison was dead, she had allowed herself to hold on to the tiniest scrap of doubt. Perhaps there was some mistake; perhaps it was, after all, some other girl. Now the moment of reckoning had come, as she forced her eyes to glance at the photo. A glance was enough. 'Yes,' she said. 'Yes, that's Ally. That's . . . my sister.'

Chapter 16

Now that Sophie's sister had come, Chris was able to go back to work with a clear conscience.

He didn't need to be so transparently cheerful about it, thought Sophie sadly as he came into the bedroom to get dressed on that first morning. It was obvious that he couldn't wait to get out of the house and away from her, and it was her fault.

'And it's about time for you to be up and about,' he said to her. 'I spoke to the surgeon about it, and he says that you've been in bed long enough. You should be getting dressed, going downstairs. It doesn't do your recovery any good for you to spend the day in bed – the sooner you're up and about, the sooner you'll be back to normal.'

Normal? thought Sophie. She would never be normal again. There was no reason for her to get out of bed.

She had, until that moment, fully intended to get up that day, to get dressed and go downstairs to welcome Jeremy for coffee. Now, though, she couldn't face it – couldn't face Jeremy's sympathy, Madeline's chatter. 'I don't feel like getting up,' she said. 'Not this morning.'

And when Madeline looked in on her after Chris had gone, Sophie told her the same thing. 'I just don't feel up to it. I think I'll stay in bed this morning. Maybe this afternoon I'll get up.'

'But Jeremy,' said Madeline, her face showing her disappointment. 'He's meant to be coming.'

'You're quite capable of entertaining him on your own,' Sophie stated. 'While I have a nap.'

But in the event, she couldn't sleep. The voices downstairs were too loud, too full of laughter. She couldn't hear their words, but the buzz of conversation and the laughter carried up the stairs and kept her awake. Her incision hurt; she was thirsty. She tried not to feel sorry for herself, without much success.

Before he left, Jeremy came upstairs to bring her some flowers. That hadn't been part of the plan: Sophie didn't really want him to see her in such a state. She knew that she looked a fright, with her hair unwashed and even uncombed, but he was insistent, and Madeline couldn't say no to him.

'Sophie, my dear,' he greeted her, flourishing a bouquet of overpoweringly fragrant lilies. 'They couldn't keep me away from you a moment longer. Your sister tried to tell me that you didn't want to see me, but I didn't believe her for an instant.'

Sophie couldn't help smiling at that. 'It *is* good to see you, Jeremy. And thank you for the flowers. But I look awful.'

'Nonsense,' he said, as she'd hoped he would. He sat down at the side of the bed while Madeline went off to find a vase for the lilies.

'And why haven't you told me about your sister?' Jeremy

went on. 'She's a delight. An absolute delight. We just couldn't stop laughing.'

'I heard,' said Sophie.

'Oh, my dear! Have we been keeping you awake, then? How naughty of us.' He took her hand and squeezed it. 'I'm so sorry. But we couldn't help ourselves. Why hasn't she been down here before, then? Why haven't you invited her?'

Why, indeed. Sophie didn't reply.

Jeremy didn't seem to notice. 'I was filling her in on all the gossip,' he continued. 'She doesn't know any of the people – yet – but she was frightfully interested. We must get her down here often. Once you're back to normal, my dear, we must have a party. So that Madeline can meet everyone in the close. She'd make a great hit with the Dean. Not to mention Elspeth. She'd be just Elspeth's cup of tea.'

Oh, no doubt, thought Sophie. Madeline would be welcomed in circles where she herself was not. The great and the good of Westmead would take Madeline to their bosoms. Not, she told herself, that it mattered. What, after all, was Westmead society?

When Jeremy had gone, Sophie felt cheered and a bit stronger, in spite of herself. She threw back the duvet. 'I'm getting up now,' she announced. 'I'm going to have a shower, and I'm going to wash my hair.'

'Let me help you,' offered Madeline, moving to her side.

Sophie shrugged off her sister's hand. 'I can do it.'

'Are you sure? You seem a bit wobbly to me.'

'I can do it,' insisted Sophie, making slow but resolute progress towards the bathroom. But once she'd shed her nightgown and stepped into the shower, she discovered that, for all of her protestations of independence, she barely had enough strength to turn the taps to adjust the water.

'How are you doing?' Madeline called from the other side of the door.

'All right.' Gritting her teeth with determination, as though willpower could see her through, Sophie reached for the bottle of shampoo. It slipped through her fingers and landed at her feet; she found that she couldn't even bend over to retrieve it. 'I can do this,' she said to herself.

But it was beyond her limited strength. Eventually she had to admit defeat. 'I need some help,' she called at last, furious with herself for her weakness.

Madeline was only too happy to oblige, shampooing Sophie's hair, helping her into her dressing gown, and guiding her back to the bedroom.

'I can dry my hair myself,' Sophie stated, reaching for the hair-dryer. Again, though, her resolve exceeded her abilities, and she had to acquiesce to her sister's unwelcome assistance.

Madeline expertly wielded the hair-dryer on Sophie's hair, chatting all the while over the noise. 'Have you thought about having your hair cut a bit shorter?' she suggested. 'It would make it easier to care for. And some of the short styles these days are quite attractive. Short hair wouldn't suit *me*, of course, but I think it would suit *you*.'

'I like my hair the way it is,' stated Sophie. She would *not* let her sister dictate the length of her hair.

'Victoria's recently had her hair cut,' added Madeline. 'I must say, it does look nice. Of course, Tori would look nice no matter what she did with her hair. Though I don't suppose one ought to brag about one's children like that.'

Madeline's pride in her children had never bothered Sophie before; after all, they *were* lovely children, and Sophie was very fond of them. But now things were different: Madeline had children, and she never would. It was extraordinarily difficult to listen to Madeline, and pretend she didn't mind.

'I was telling Jeremy about the children,' Madeline went on. 'How musical they are. James, especially. He has a wonderful voice, and he loves singing in the school choir. Jeremy said that though they usually look for boys a bit younger than James, it's not too late to audition him for a cathedral choir,' she added. 'Maybe even Westmead. Wouldn't that be fun?'

'Fun.'

'Though he'd hate leaving his school,' Madeline mused. 'It's a bit late in the day to uproot him from there. But I'd like Jeremy to hear him sing, just to get his opinion.'

Sophie couldn't bear it, and made an effort to change the subject. 'What else did Jeremy talk about?'

Madeline smiled teasingly. 'You, of course. He says that you're the talk of Westmead these days, with a young man paying court to you. What's this all about, Soph?'

'Paying court? Don't be ridiculous!'

'He says that he comes round here all the time, that everyone's talking about it. What does Chris say, then?'

Sophie sighed. 'Dominic is a friend of mine. Why don't people understand that?'

'I expect people are jealous,' mused Madeline. 'Sometimes I think I wouldn't mind a toy boy myself.' She laughed her silvery laugh. 'Just kidding, of course.'

* * *

Tim was at his desk early that morning. He hadn't slept well; the events of the previous day had seen to that.

His interview with the Superintendent, carried out just a few minutes after Jacquie had left his office, had not been a success.

Not that he had ever expected it to be. But it had been even worse than his imaginings.

In the first place, the Superintendent had been furious that he hadn't been told straight away, as soon as Jacquie Darke had come into the station and identified the dead girl as her sister.

And then there was the little matter of resources.

'There's just no money left in the budget,' he'd said bluntly, tapping his letter opener on the desk blotter. 'And if you think that I'm going to go cap-in-hand to the Chief Constable and ask him for more, just because some old case has been raked up . . .'

Oh no, thought Tim bitterly. The Superintendent wasn't about to do that. Nothing to rock the boat. Nothing to jeopardise that knighthood he was hoping for, once he'd retired in a year or two. Everyone at the station knew that was his ambition, and between now and then, a quiet life – that was all he wanted. Tim longed to say exactly that; instead he said, 'But you can see Mrs Darke's point.'

The Superintendent turned the letter opener over with his fat fingers, not looking at Tim. 'We're not here to see her point,' he stated. 'We're here to make the best possible use of the taxpayer's money. And in this instance, there isn't any.'

'But we have a substantial lead, sir,' Tim dared to remind him. 'The identification of the victim, and a lead on her local connection. She knew someone in Westmead. Someone called Mike.'

The Superintendent snorted. 'Oh, that narrows it down, Merriday.'

'Just a few officers, sir,' Tim persisted. 'That's all I ask for.'

'Absolutely not.' He slammed the letter opener down on the desk and stood, glaring across his desk at Tim. 'You can keep the file on your desk, Merriday. That much I'm giving you. For now. But don't you dare waste any time on it. Not yours, and certainly no one else's. You have more important things to do. We all do.'

'But Mrs Darke . . .'

'Attractive, is she?' The Superindendent narrowed his eyes at Tim and spoke in a cutting voice. 'You fancy her, do you, Merriday?'

Tim felt himself flushing to the roots of his hair; he opened his mouth but no words came out.

'Well, fancy her all you like. Good luck to you. But not on police time.' The Superintendent turned his back on Tim and looked out of his window. 'That will be all, Merriday.'

And that was that.

No hope, no room for manoeuvre.

But what, Tim asked himself now, was he going to say to Jacquie Darke? How could he bear to tell her?

The whole of the previous day, after his disastrous interview with the Superintendent, he had agonised over it, had been unable to bring himself to pick up the phone and convey the bad news.

Now, though, sitting at his desk with the files in front of him, he was gripped with a new resolution.

The case was his, just as he'd hoped. As long as he didn't neglect his other work, as long as he didn't draw any attention to himself, nothing could stop him from doing a bit of investigation. On his own time, if necessary. But he *would* find Alison Barnett's killer. And when he'd done it, the Superintendent would be happy enough to claim the credit, to see it as one more triumph in his long and distinguished career. One more thing to propel him towards that knighthood.

Or so Tim told himself, pulling the files closer.

In a few minutes he had forgotten about the Superintendent, engrossed in the task at hand. So many times he'd been through these files, but this time he was looking for something different: this time he was looking for the name 'Mike', or any variant of it.

One of the workmen who had been employed on the renovations to Priory House was, he discovered, a plumber who went by the name of Mickey. A possibility, if not a strong one; Mickey Murphy sounded as if he were Irish, and Jacquie Darke had said nothing of an Irish accent. Besides, Tim doubted very much that eleven years on he would be able to find or even trace Mickey Murphy.

A more promising lead was one of the lay clerks in the choir: a Michael Thornley. Mr Thornley had, at the time of the murder, lived in Quire Close, and he had been interviewed.

Tim pulled the sheet of paper recording the interview from the files and held it under his Anglepoise desk lamp, studying it carefully. It was a bit of a disappointment: Mr Thornley's interview had apparently been little more than perfunctory. He claimed that he had been home by himself on the night in question, and he had no alibi, no one to back up his version of the evening. But there had been no particular reason to suspect him, other than the fact that he – like numerous others – lived in Quire Close, so nothing had been done to follow up on him.

Now, he thought, was the time to do that. Tim wondered whether he dared to pay an informal call to Quire Close. As long as the Superintendent didn't find out about it, that was . . .

The phone on his desk rang; he picked it up. 'Merriday.'

It was Jacquie Darke; involuntarily he caught his breath. 'I was just wondering how you were getting on,' Jacquie said. 'What did your boss say?'

He opened his mouth, and found that he couldn't tell her.

'Well . . .' Tim doodled as he spoke: a sabre-tooth tiger emerged from his pencil, a crude representation of what he thought of the Superintendent. 'I haven't talked to him yet,' he lied. 'I'm trying to get all the facts together, so I can present them to him in the best possible way.'

'Oh.' She sounded disappointed. 'I'd been hoping . . .'

'Sorry. Sorry. It's going to take a day or two,' Tim said. 'Even if he agrees with my proposals, it's going to take a bit of time.' He'd let her down gently, he told himself, trying to justify his lies; he'd give her time to get used to the idea of official opposition. And who knows, he thought – maybe there *would* be that breakthrough. Maybe he would find Mike, and both the Superintendent and Jacquie Darke would be impressed and delighted.

Jacquie sat down on the hard, old-fashioned chair in the passageway at the Cathedral View Guest House, clutching the receiver of the pay phone, her eyes welling with unexpected tears. She had been so sure that he'd have good news for her, that things would begin to happen immediately. Now the prospect of days of inactivity loomed before her.

She couldn't bear it: couldn't bear sitting about at the Cathedral View, waiting for something to happen. Waiting for days, possibly longer.

'I'm sure I'll be able to win him over in the end,' Tim embroidered.

Jacquie was gripped by a sudden resolution. She would *not* sit around waiting. She would go back to Sutton Fen and put Alison's affairs in order. She would get things settled with the solicitor, she would put the house on the market. But first . . .

'I want to go to Quire Close,' she said abruptly. 'I need to see . . . where she was.'

'I'll take you there,' Tim offered, his heart lifting at the prospect of seeing her again, whatever the circumstances.

'No,' Jacquie said. 'I'd rather go on my own.'

'But I could show you the spot. How will you find it, otherwise?'

She hesitated, half longing for his company and half dreading it. 'All right,' she said at last. 'I could meet you there.'

They arranged to meet after lunch, at the entrance to Quire Close.

Sophie made it downstairs for lunch, a fact which Madeline regarded as a personal triumph. 'You're looking much better,' she pronounced. 'It's amazing what a difference clean hair can make. And getting into some proper clothes for a change.'

'I *feel* better,' Sophie admitted. 'And I'm hungry.'

She sat on the sofa while Madeline put together something in the kitchen. 'Your kitchen is just a wee bit inconvenient,' Madeline admitted as she brought their sandwiches into the sitting room on a tray.

'It's dreadful,' Sophie said bluntly. 'It's poky, it's dark, it's antiquated. It should have been gutted and done up years ago. But I don't suppose they're going to do anything about it now.'

'Who's the person in charge?' Madeline wanted to know. 'I suppose it's the Dean. Maybe if you had a little word with him . . .'

The doorbell chimed.

'Are you receiving visitors?' Madeline asked. 'Or shall I say that you're having your lunch?'

Sophie thought rapidly. It wouldn't be Dominic; he would still be at school. Trish Evans, perhaps. Or Clunch. 'No,' she said. 'No. Tell them I can't see them.'

Tense, she waited while Madeline went to answer the bell. Through the closed door of the sitting room she could hear a murmur of voices: Madeline's, high and silvery, and another, more low-pitched. Clunch.

A moment later Madeline reappeared. 'It was your friend Mr Clunch,' she laughed. 'And I must say, he was persistent.' She thrust forward a bouquet of stiff rust-coloured chrysanthemums, wrapped in clear polythene. 'He wanted to give you these in person, and promised that he wouldn't stay long. I had to be quite firm with him.' Again she laughed.

'Put them in the bin,' ordered Sophie. 'Ugh – they're horrible. I *hate* chrysanths, and especially ones that colour.'

'You can't just throw them away,' Madeline protested. 'What if he comes back?'

Sophie shuddered. 'Oh, he'll come back, all right. I don't care. I don't want them.'

But when Madeline returned a second time, a few minutes later, she was bearing a vase in which she had artfully arranged the chrysanthemums. 'See?' she said. 'They're not so bad, once they've been titivated a bit. It's all in knowing how to do it.'

'I don't want them,' Sophie stated.

Madeline ignored her and put the vase on a table in the front window. 'There. Now he'll be able to see them when he goes past. You don't want to hurt his feelings, Soph.'

'I don't care.'

Her sister's voice held a mild rebuke. 'It's not like you to be so rude, Sophie. I'm sure he's a perfectly nice man. He seemed rather sweet to me.'

Sweet? Sophie's memory conjured up a picture of his hard little eyes, staring at her legs. 'He's horrible,' she stated. 'I hate him.' Summoning all of her energy, she got up and crossed to where Madeline had put the flowers, but found that she was unable to lift the heavy vase. She pulled the flowers out and stuffed them in the wastepaper basket. 'There,' she said, before collapsing back on the sofa in exhaustion, 'that's where they belong.'

Tim worked at his desk until the last minute, continuing his perusal of the files. If he'd been running the investigation at the time, he thought, even without the benefit of hindsight, he probably would have handled things differently. For one thing, he would have spent a bit more time asking questions of the Precentor, in front of whose house the body had been found. Not that the Precentor had ever been a suspect, even remotely, but surely he could have provided a bit more information than he had done. It seemed, though, that the inspector in charge of the case had not wanted to ruffle cathedral feathers; he had trodden very lightly indeed where the Chapter and other official personnel were concerned.

Tim looked at his watch and realised that unless he left immediately, he was going to be late. Bundling the files into a drawer for safe-keeping, he grabbed his coat and hurried down the stairs.

Liz was at the desk, and her eyes were shining with resolution. 'Tim . . .' she said.

'I'm in a bit of a hurry,' he apologised. 'Can it wait?'

But she had summoned up her nerve, and she was not to be deflected. 'I was just wondering about tonight,' she said. 'Whether you were busy. Whether you might like to have that drink you invited me for a few weeks ago, when I couldn't go. Maybe even dinner.'

Tim glanced at his watch, and in his mind's eye he saw Jacquie, waiting for him in Quire Close. In that instant of imagination, he remembered her as she had been in the pub, sitting across from him, devastated by her sister's death yet glowing. Liz, with all of her sparkle, seemed a poor substitute. 'I don't think so,' he said. 'I think I'll be busy tonight. Maybe another time.'

'Yes. All right.'

But he didn't even hear her as he pushed the door open.

It was raining, he realised: thin, cold needles of rain pitched down from a grey sky. But he didn't want to go back for his umbrella; he would have to pass Liz again, coming and going, and he would be delayed yet further. Pulling up his collar, he sped towards Quire Close.

She was waiting for him, just as he had imagined; as Tim approached he saw her huddled desolately under the arch, clutching a bouquet of flowers. Rust-coloured chrysanths, the colour of dried blood . . .

'Jacquie . . .' he began to call out, then corrected it to 'Mrs Darke . . .'

She turned.

'I'm sorry I've kept you waiting. In the rain. And without a brolly.'

'Never mind.' She shrugged and pulled her coat more closely round her.

Tim felt compelled to explain. 'I was delayed. I'd meant to be here earlier, but . . .'

'Never mind,' Jacquie repeated. She stepped out from under the arch, into the close. 'Let's get this over with, shall we?'

'Mind the cobbles,' he said. It was treacherous walking in Quire Close, and he had an impulse to take her arm, to keep her from stumbling over the uneven stones. But something in the set of her shoulders warned him that his help would not be welcomed.

'I want to know where you found her. The exact spot,' Jacquie said.

'This way. It was almost at the far end.' He went on, a step ahead of her, until he reached the pavement a few yards in front of the Precentor's House. 'Here.'

Jacquie stood for a moment, staring at the spot as if picturing that lifeless body on the cobbles. Her lips moved soundlessly, and rain ran down her face like tears. Then she stooped and placed the flowers on the precise spot. After another moment of standing, her head bowed, she turned abruptly and moved away. 'I'm going now,' she said over her shoulder. 'Thank you, Sergeant. You don't have to come with me.'

But he hurried to catch her up. 'You're drenched,' he said. 'How about a cup of tea? In the cathedral refectory? Or there's a nice teashop—'

'No, thank you.' Her voice was as cold as the rain.

'Later, then?' Tim suggested. 'We could meet for a drink. We could talk about the investigation.'

Reaching the shelter of the archway, Jacquie hesitated for just a second, and turned to face him. 'No,' she said. 'I'm going back to Sutton Fen. Today. This afternoon. I'm going to sort out Ally's affairs at that end.' She searched her handbag for a scrap of paper and a pen, then scribbled her details and proffered the paper towards him. 'Let me know,' she said. 'About the investigation. About what your boss says. Ring me.'

He took the paper from her, allowing his fingertips to brush hers; she snatched her hand away as if she'd been scalded. 'I'll be in touch,' he promised. 'But you shouldn't go without a cup of tea.'

'You're very kind,' she said, and he thought that her face softened for a split second before she once again turned from him. 'But no, thank you.'

He stood under the arch and watched her go, her back straight and her head high, heedless of the rain.

Madeline was talking about her favourite subject, apart from herself: her children. She had explored but by no means exhausted the latest exploits of her son James, then moved on to give equal time to her daughter Victoria.

Sophie tried not to listen, but certain facts percolated through.

Victoria, it would seem, had a boyfriend. He was called Simon, and Madeline approved of him: he came from a good family; he was polite and presentable. 'Not like some of these scruffy boys you see these days,' she said. 'He has a decent haircut, he dresses well. And he calls me "Mrs Arden".' She gave a light laugh. 'Though I must admit, that makes me feel ancient.'

Sophie knew that she was meant to assure Madeline that she was nothing of the sort, but she didn't have the energy; she managed to summon a faint smile, which more or less served the same purpose, so, encouraged, her sister went on.

'I must say it's about time for Tori to have a proper boyfriend. Up till now it's been horses, horses, horses – with no time at all for anything else, even boys.' She ran an unconscious hand over her silver-blonde hair. 'You know what I was like when I was her age, Soph. I was surrounded by boys.'

'Like bees round a honey-pot,' Sophie murmured, remembering.

'Exactly. And Tori is a pretty girl. Not a great beauty, perhaps, but she's very pretty. No spots to speak of, nice hair, and she has beautiful eyes.'

As she talked, Madeline had been watching idly out of the front window; now she broke off her discourse on her daughter's attractions to remark, 'There's a woman walking by with some chrysanths just like the ones you threw away,' adding facetiously, 'They must have them on special offer somewhere.'

Sophie, who was sitting with her back to the window, wasn't sufficiently interested to turn round and look to see who it was. 'One of the choir wives, I expect,' she said.

'She has a man with her,' Madeline reported. 'And they seem to be headed down towards the end of the close.'

Still Sophie didn't turn. 'It's probably the Swans. They'll be moving in soon. Or tourists – we do get quite a lot of them, coming into the close to gawp at the houses.'

'Elspeth Verey lives at the end of the close, doesn't she?' Madeline commented. 'Jeremy told me all about her – your little friend Dominic's mother. But this woman is too young to be Elspeth.'

Sophie declined to rise to the bait.

Once the couple were out of sight, Madeline resumed the one-sided conversation where she'd left off. But a moment later she reported, 'They're coming back now. And she doesn't have the flowers any longer. Neither of them has a brolly – they're getting drenched.'

They'd been taking flowers to someone in the close, then; that was of sufficient interest to cause Sophie to twist round and look. She saw a tall, ginger-haired man and a slender dark-haired woman, picking their way over the cobbles with some distance between them. 'I don't know them,' she said. 'I've never seen them before.' They didn't, somehow, look like tourists. Intrigued now, and welcoming the respite from Madeline's child-centred monologue, she watched them making their way towards the archway, then saw the man coming back on his own. He was walking slowly, in spite of the rain, and seemed to be checking house numbers.

'He's stopping,' observed Madeline. 'He's looking at this house. I think he's coming here.' And a few seconds later, in confirmation of her words, the doorbell chimed. 'I'll get it,' she said.

Sophie heard the murmured voices at the door; in a

moment Madeline was back in the room, closely followed by the man. 'This is Detective Sergeant Merriday,' Madeline announced, her eyes sparkling with excitement. 'He's investigating a murder, and he'd like to have a word with you.'

The man stood dripping just inside the sitting-room door. 'I'm sorry to bother you,' he said. He smiled his apology. 'And I'm not at all sure whether you can help me or not.'

'Would you like to sit down?' Sophie suggested. 'Excuse me for not getting up, Sergeant, but I'm . . . recovering from an operation.'

He nodded his sympathy, then indicated his wet coat. 'As long as you don't mind . . .'

'Take your coat off, if you like.'

He complied, perching on the edge of the sofa with the wet coat across his lap.

'Would you like a cup of tea, Sergeant?' Sophie offered. 'You look as if you could use something to warm you up.'

'If it's no trouble, that would be lovely.'

'My sister was just about to put the kettle on. Weren't you, Maddy?' She gave Madeline a sweet smile, gratified in spite of herself to see her sister's look of frustration at having to miss out on the excitement.

When Madeline had gone, however reluctantly, Sophie turned her attention to the policeman. 'Now. How can I help?'

'Perhaps you can't,' he admitted. 'I'm trying to trace someone called Michael Thornley, who lived in this house some eleven years ago. Your sister tells me that you've been here for just a few months.'

'Since August,' Sophie confirmed. 'And I don't know

Michael Thornley. Not at all. I've never even heard the name.'

'He was a lay clerk in the choir,' said the policeman.

'You might ask my husband, then,' she suggested. 'He's only been in the choir since the beginning of this term, but he knows a lot of musicians. He might be able to help you. I'm sorry that I haven't been any good to you.'

The policeman shook his head. 'Never mind. It was a bit of a long shot, I admit. I'm sorry to have disturbed you, Mrs . . .'

'Lilburn,' Sophie supplied. 'Sophie Lilburn.'

'But I will have that cup of tea, Mrs Lilburn.' The man gave her a wry smile, and the corners of his eyes crinkled. Sophie found herself smiling back at him, liking him instinctively.

Murder, Madeline had said. And he'd mentioned eleven years having passed. The penny dropped; Sophie caught her breath with the shock of it, as though she had been thrust out of her cosy sitting room into the cold rain; her skin prickled with goose flesh. 'The murder,' she said. 'It was that girl, wasn't it? At the end of the close. The one who was never identified.'

Reluctantly he nodded. 'You've heard about it, then.'

'Everyone in the close knows about it.'

'Yes, I suppose they would.' He sat for a moment, his head bowed and his freckled hands dangling between his knees, before speaking again. 'Listen, Mrs Lilburn. I probably shouldn't have mentioned the murder at all – but I didn't think that your sister was going to let me in, until I said it was to do with a murder investigation.'

'Oh, I don't mind,' she assured him.

'You don't understand.' He gave Sophie a sheepish grin.

'The thing is, my boss doesn't know I'm here. I've done this off my own bat. He might think I've been a bit . . . rash.'

Sophie shrugged, returning his smile. 'I'm certainly not going to tell him, am I? In the first place, I don't know him. And in the second place, I'm not going anywhere.'

The policeman sighed, and his shoulders relaxed. 'Thanks.'

'So the least you can do,' Sophie pursued, 'is to tell me why you're asking questions. Why now? After all these years?'

'Yes.' He gave another sigh, not looking at her. 'She's been identified,' he said.

Sophie's arms prickled again, and the hairs stood up on the back of her neck. 'The girl?'

He nodded. 'Her sister turned up at the police station two days ago, and has made a positive identification.'

Sophie felt as if she'd suddenly shed the skin of ennui and sluggishness which had engulfed her since well before her operation; for the first time in weeks, she felt alive, and her mind seethed with questions. 'But why now?' she repeated. 'It's been eleven years, for God's sake. Where has she been all of that time? Why didn't she come before? Didn't she ever report her sister missing? And who is she?' The woman in the close, she realised: the woman with the flowers, just a few minutes ago. She'd been with the policeman. That must have been the sister.

He shook his head; his voice was regretful. 'I'm afraid I can't tell you any of that. Not now.'

'Who *was* the murdered girl, then?' Sophie, undeterred, went on. 'And what about Michael Thornley? That was the name you said, wasn't it? He lived in this house, you said. What did he have to do with it? Is he a suspect, then?'

'A suspect? Who's been murdered, then?' Madeline, bearing the tea tray, pushed the door open, her face avid with curiosity.

The policeman grimaced. 'This is very kind of you, but I really think I ought to be going.' He rose and shrugged on his wet coat. 'I'm sorry to have put you to the unnecessary trouble. And sorry to have bothered you.'

'Oh, please don't go,' Madeline urged.

'I'll see myself out,' said DS Merriday.

His shoulders hunched against the rain, Tim Merriday exited Quire Close and hurried past the cathedral, towards the police station.

Why, he asked himself, had he mentioned murder? And why had he compounded his mistake by telling Sophie Lilburn that the girl had been identified? It had been a stupid, stupid thing to do. Mrs Lilburn might be discreet, she might not know the Superintendent, but she knew about the murder. And her sister certainly wouldn't rest until she'd extracted every detail; from there it was only a short step to the whole close – the whole cathedral community, for that matter – being a-buzz with the news, rumours spreading like wildfire. The cathedral was notorious as a hotbed of gossip; things festered and grew unchecked in its rarefied atmosphere. It would be only a matter of time before it got back to the Superintendent: that Tim Merriday had been nosing about in Quire Close, asking questions.

If the Superintendent were to hear about it, he would tell him his fortune. He would take the case away from him.

And he, Tim Merriday, would be letting Jacquie Darke down.

That was the last thing he wanted to do.

He hadn't been thinking about where he was going; now he realised that without conscious volition, he was headed not for the police station, but for the Cathedral View Guest House.

He needed to see Jacquie Darke just one more time, to tell her . . . he wasn't sure what. The words would come. He had to see her.

Impatiently he rang the bell; impatiently he waited for the heavy footsteps to approach the door from within.

The door was flung open, and a woman with a face like a currant bun pointed, not unkindly, to the 'No Vacancies' sign in the window. 'No room just at the minute,' she said in a soft West Country burr. 'But if you're not in a hurry, I could have something ready for you in an hour or so. As soon as it's cleaned and tidied.'

His heart sank. 'Mrs Darke?' he said hopelessly.

The woman's face changed. 'Just gone,' she said. 'Not five minutes ago. You've just missed her.'

Tim Merriday turned and made his way to the police station, trying not to think about Jacquie Darke. It was time to forget about her, to put her from his mind once and for all. She was gone; she was out of his life.

Liz, at the desk, raised her head as he pushed the door open and started for the stairs. 'Tim! You're soaked!'

'Am I?' he said indifferently.

'I'll bring you a cup of tea, shall I?' she offered, her eyes bright. 'Plenty of sugar.'

'Thanks, Liz.' He stopped, looked at her. 'And about tonight,' he said. 'I *am* free, after all.'

Chapter 17

The drive back to Sutton Fen seemed, to Jacquie, to take even longer than her trip to Westmead had done; again it was raining, and dark descended long before she reached the M25.

This time there was no hope at the other end of the road.

Three days before – had it only been three days? – she hadn't been able to wait to get away from Sutton Fen. Westmead had beckoned her, holding out the promise of a long-delayed reunion.

She'd thought, then, that she would never go back.

Only three days later, and here she was, driving back in the other direction, like a repeating nightmare with subtle variations.

Jacquie tried to keep her mind blank, focusing on her driving. Not too fast; watch that lorry; mind the cars coming off the slip road.

She didn't want to think about Westmead, and what had happened there. She didn't want to think about Ally; she didn't want to think about Tim Merriday.

And she didn't want to think about Sutton Fen.

At the other end of the road, an empty house waited for her.

As if the day hadn't already held enough for Sophie, that afternoon Dominic stopped by after school. This was one visitor to be welcomed gladly, even with Madeline present; it was the first time she'd seen him in what seemed like weeks.

He didn't come empty-handed. There was an offering from his mother: yet another bunch of flowers, in the form of delicate and fragrant freesias. And from himself there was a book: a rare volume on the early history of photography which he'd seen once in a library and had gone to some considerable trouble to procure for her. Sophie was touched and delighted.

After the preliminaries, and the making of tea, the conversation was dominated by the topic of the murder.

It was one thing she'd never discussed with him before, feeling – misguidedly, perhaps – that it wasn't a suitable subject for a boy who was, after all, just sixteen, and who had been very young indeed when it had happened, possibly too young to remember much about it. The body had been found virtually outside his house; she didn't want to remind him of that.

Over the weeks of their friendship they had discussed many things: never that.

But today it was not to be avoided. With some reluctance, she'd told Madeline what she knew of the murder, and now Madeline brought the subject up, quizzing Dominic.

'You were here when it happened. What do you remember?'

Dominic shook his head. 'Not much. I was only five years old.'

'But it happened practically outside your house, from what Sophie says,' Madeline persisted. 'You must have been aware of it.'

'We hadn't moved into Quire Close yet at that point,' he explained. 'We were still living at the Deanery.'

'Surely people were talking about it.'

'About nothing else, probably,' he grinned. 'Knowing this place. But I think that my mother was trying to protect me from it all. She certainly didn't talk about it. And I *do* recall that once or twice she turned the telly off because there was something coming on that she didn't want me to see. My mother has definite ideas,' he added. 'And I'm sure that she didn't think that I needed to be exposed to all of that.'

Yes, thought Sophie. That sounded like Elspeth, all right. She wondered how Elspeth had felt about the fact that a young girl had had the indecency to get herself murdered in Quire Close, virtually outside her own front door; she wondered whether it had cast a shadow over the move to Priory House, and whether Elspeth ever thought about it now, coming and going from her house.

If she'd been thinking ahead, Jacquie would have made a stop along the way home and bought a bottle of wine, or even gin. But the idea didn't occur to her until it was too late: until she had reached Sutton Fen, and was about to pull up in front of the house. The Mini Mart would be closed by now, and she wasn't about to go into a pub and ask for a bottle.

She would have to make do with tea.

But, she remembered, she had left a note for the milkman. There would be no milk for tea.

Sighing, she let herself back into the house which she thought she had left for ever.

It was just the same, Jacquie realised with a slight feeling of dislocated shock. Exactly the same. So much had happened to her since she'd left; she scarcely felt like the same person. Somehow she had expected the house to reflect that: she'd expected a musty, unlived-in smell, or a film of dust covering everything.

But it had been only three days. Not long enough for anything to have changed.

Even the milk. Jacquie went through to the kitchen, took a half-used bottle of milk from the fridge, and sniffed it. It had been fresh on Monday morning, and it hadn't gone off.

Tea, then.

She put the kettle on and took off her damp coat, intending to drape it over the boiler to dry it off.

The boiler was cold, of course: as a thrifty daughter of thrifty parents, she had switched it off before she left. And now that she'd removed her coat, she realised how chilly the house was. While the kettle simmered, she turned on the boiler and pushed up the thermostat.

But it would take some time for the house to warm up. Jacquie carried her tea through into the seldom-used front parlour and switched on two bars of the electric fire which her mother had reserved for use only when important guests – like Reverend Prew – were being entertained there in inclement weather. Her mother was no longer here to tut-tut at the extravagance of turning on the fire only for herself, Jacquie told herself defiantly. She wrapped herself in a hand-knitted throw from the back of the sofa and cupped her hands round her mug; in a few minutes she was feeling tolerably warm and as comfortable as could be expected in this cheerless room.

The sound of the doorbell was so unexpected, so jarring, that she spilled tea over one of her hands. Who, she thought in panic, could it be? Perhaps it was one of the neighbours, knowing that she was away and concerned at having seen lights on in the house. She wiped her stinging hand with a tissue and went to the door.

It was Darren. His hands were in the pockets of his anorak; he smiled at her. 'Hello, Jacquie.'

'What do you want?' she demanded stonily.

'I was passing and saw your car, and thought I'd call in.' As he spoke, he turned to look over his shoulder at the car rather than at her. 'How is the car, by the way?' he asked, with professional interest. 'Running all right, is she?'

'All right.'

'I thought she was a nice little motor when I bought her,' he said. 'I'm glad she's served you well.'

The car had been a part of the divorce settlement; Jacquie wondered whether he expected, now, to be thanked for it. It wasn't as if it had cost him dear; cars were his business, and it hadn't even been new when he'd bought it. She said nothing, waiting to see what he would do.

Darren shifted from one foot to the other, then kicked

at a pile of leaves which had blown on to the porch. 'Could I come in?' he asked.

'I don't see why.' She folded her arms across her chest.

'I'd like to talk to you for a few minutes. Just a few minutes. I have something to ask you.' Taking his hands from his pockets, he rubbed them briskly together as if to emphasise the silliness of the pair of them standing outside in the chill rain.

'All right, then,' she gave in, and led him towards the parlour.

He slipped out of his anorak and hung it over the bannister in the hall, a habit which had always annoyed her.

'You needn't bother taking that off,' she said coldly. 'You're not staying.'

Now that his eyes had adjusted to the light, he was able to see her properly; he gave a low whistle. 'Jacquie! You've cut your hair!'

She ran her fingers through it. 'What of it?'

'It suits you,' he said appreciatively.

Jacquie flinched. 'It's none of your business,' she snapped. Leaving Darren standing, she went back to her seat by the fire.

'Can I have some of that tea?'

'No.'

'I can get myself a mug from the kitchen,' he offered. 'No.'

Undeterred, he inched closer to the warmth of the glowing bars. 'Does that – the haircut – mean it's true what I've heard? That you've really left the Free Baptist Fellowship?'

'What do you think?' Her voice was sarcastic.

'Has Reverend Prew seen your hair, then?' he asked. 'He certainly wouldn't be happy about that.'

Jacquie raised her chin. 'I honestly couldn't care less.'

'You really hate him, don't you?'

The tone of Darren's voice had changed; Jacquie looked at him, trying to gauge what he was getting at. 'Yes,' she said at last, serious rather than bitter. 'I really hate him.'

Without being invited to do so, he sat down across from her and leaned forward, his elbows on his knees. 'Jacquie,' he said. 'I need to ask you something. And it's not as daft as it sounds.'

'Go ahead.'

'You remember our wedding day . . .'

Jacquie caught her breath. 'If that's what you've come here to ask me about, you can go right now. Of course I remember our wedding day.'

'No, that's not it at all,' he said quickly. 'Your sister. Alison. All the fuss about . . . well, about her being pregnant. You remember.'

'Of course I remember.'

'What I need to ask you is, do you know who . . . well, who did it? Who the father was?' Darren looked away, embarrassed, and Jacquie wondered what on earth he was getting at.

'Maybe I do,' she said cautiously, unwilling to give anything away.

'Because I just wondered if . . .' He stopped, and tried again. 'Was it Reverend Prew?'

Jacquie felt as if the breath had been knocked out of her by a gigantic blow to the stomach. 'Reverend Prew?' she gasped at last.

He rushed on, still not looking at her. 'Because if it

was, it would explain a lot. Why you hate him so much, for one thing.'

I hate him because he took my husband away from me, Jacquie thought, scarcely knowing what to say.

'And she was his secretary. She was alone with him every day,' he suggested. 'She was always an attractive girl, your sister.'

'And Reverend Prew is a married man, who stood – who *stands* – in the pulpit every week and talks about what an unforgivable sin it is to commit fornication, let alone adultery,' Jacquie said vigorously.

'But you haven't denied it.' At last he looked at her. 'So you don't know for sure that it's not true, and that means it's possible. Your sister talked to you. She might not have told you that . . . um . . . she was sleeping with him or anything like that. But she might have said that she was in love with him. Or found him attractive. Or something.'

The suggestion was monstrous, unthinkable. And untrue. Ally fancying Reverend Prew – the idea was so ridiculous that it was almost laughable.

But, Jacquie decided, she would *not* tell Darren that. Let him think what he liked, draw whatever conclusion he chose. If it revised his opinion of his precious Reverend Prew, made him lose respect for his hero, then so be it. That was nothing to her.

It wasn't until late into her near-sleepless night that Jacquie realised the oddity of Darren's visit, and the questions surrounding it. How, she wondered suddenly, had he even entertained the possibility of Ally and Reverend Prew being lovers? What would give him such a ludicrous idea?

And more important, even, than that, was the other question: why did he want to know?

'He's absolutely adorable,' Madeline said. 'Your Dominic. Too young for you, of course, but I can see the attraction. He really is adorable.'

'Oh, stop being silly,' insisted Sophie crossly. 'There's no attraction. He's just a friend.'

Dominic had just gone, and Chris hadn't yet returned from Evensong; the two sisters sat by the fire which Dominic had built. An outsider – a curious tourist perhaps – passing through Quire Close, looking through the window whose curtains had not yet been drawn against the dark, would have found it a cosy domestic scene: two women, their fair hair gilded a deep gold by the glow of the fire, deep in conversation. The artfully arranged freesias in the window, the china tea service on the low table: it made a pretty picture.

'Does he have a girlfriend?' Madeline asked consideringly.

Sophie's reply was short. 'No.'

'Hmm.' She put her head to one side. 'Don't you think you ought to do something about that?'

'Do something?' Sophie was startled by the question. 'Me, do something? Why?'

'Oh, I suppose you want to keep him for yourself,' Madeline teased. 'But he's far too attractive not to have a girlfriend. And at sixteen, he's certainly old enough.'

Sophie bit her tongue, wishing that she could tell her sister the truth. But the secret was not hers to tell, and in any case it was none of Madeline's business.

'He and Tori would make a very handsome couple,'

Madeline went on. 'I can just picture them together.'

'I thought Victoria had a boyfriend. And that you liked him.'

'Oh, Simon.' Madeline shrugged. 'He's very nice, and all that. But you know how short-lived these teenage romances can be. By next week she may be tired of Simon.'

'Well, she's not likely to meet Dominic, in any case,' Sophie pointed out.

But Madeline was not willing to let it go. 'It's not impossible,' she said. 'I was planning to bring James down to sing for Jeremy. I could bring Tori as well. I'm sure they'd both like to see where Aunt Sophie and Uncle Chris live. We could all come down one weekend – or during the Christmas school holidays. And it would be easy to arrange a meeting between them. Who knows? – they might really hit it off.'

I doubt it, thought Sophie wryly, seeing the humour in the situation. How frustrated Madeline would be to witness the failure of her match-making attempts. She just wouldn't get it.

'His father was the Dean of Westmead,' Madeline mused.

It was pure snobbishness, then, Sophie realised. A dean's son: what a catch for Madeline's precious daughter.

But the conversation was interrupted by Chris's arrival home, heralded by the sound of a key in the front door.

'In here,' called Madeline, and Chris came into the room.

He crossed to Sophie and stooped to give her a peck on the forehead. 'How has your day been, then?'

'Fine,' said Sophie. 'Yours?'

'Busy. So much catching up to do.'

'It's been very eventful here,' Madeline interjected. 'The doorbell hasn't stopped. Jeremy, Mr Clunch, Dominic Verey. And you'll never guess, Chris! There was a policeman here, investigating that old murder in the close! You know about it, I'm sure – that girl who was found dead all those years ago.'

'What's this?'

'Apparently they now know who the girl was. And they must have a lead on the murderer, too, because the policeman was asking questions about someone who used to live in this house. A lay clerk. Michael Thornley. Wasn't that the name, Soph?'

Reluctantly Sophie nodded, remembering that the nice policeman had not wanted the news to get round, lest his boss find out.

'Just think – the murderer might have lived in this house! Do you know him, Chris?' Madeline pursued.

He shook his head. 'Before my time, of course. Though I've heard the name. I'll ask Jeremy. And one or two of the others have been in the choir for yonks, so I'm sure that someone will know where he's gone.'

That was it, thought Sophie with resignation. Once Jeremy knew about it, this new development would be a secret no longer.

The evening had gone better than he'd expected, Tim Merriday admitted to himself as he and Liz left the restaurant. He had, at least, been diverted: Liz was a chatty girl, never at a loss for words, and she wasn't stupid. She was a skilled mimic, and had made him laugh with her spot-on – and wicked – impressions of their co-workers, from the lowliest bobby on the beat to the Superintendent himself. For several hours his mind had been occupied; he hadn't had any time to think about Jacquie Darke, about Alison Barnett, or about the Superintendent. That, he reflected, was no bad thing.

They'd started with a drink at the local pub, then gone on to have a meal at a modest Italian trattoria round the corner. After the meal they'd lingered over coffee, so it was past ten o'clock as he drove Liz back to her flat. At her direction, he pulled up in front of a block of modern flats on the outskirts of Westmead. 'I'll see you to your door,' he said.

'Won't you come in?' she urged him. 'Another coffee? A brandy?'

'I'm driving,' he reminded her. 'And tomorrow is a work day, don't forget.'

She looked disappointed, and Tim sighed inwardly; this was what he'd been hoping to avoid. He wasn't sure what Liz had in mind, but it probably wasn't coffee, and he knew that he just wasn't ready for that level of involvement. A meal together was one thing, and that had been fine. But as far as he was concerned, that was enough for one evening. 'I don't have to worry about disturbing a room-mate,' she said, as if that would encourage him, and put her hand on his arm. 'I live on my own, since my ratbag of a boyfriend walked out on me.'

'Another time, perhaps,' he said as they approached her door.

Her key was in her hand, but she had yet to put it in the lock. Did she expect him to kiss her? Tim wondered. And if he did, would that satisfy her, or would she expect it to lead to something else?

Before he could make up his mind what to do, the

mobile phone in his pocket sounded its tinny tune. Relieved at the interruption, he pulled it out and pushed the button. 'Yes?'

'Tim, it's Gilly.'

His heart plummeted. 'What's wrong?' he demanded. 'Has something happened to Frannie?'

'Frannie's fine,' she said. 'But I need to talk to you about something.'

'I told you never to ring me on this number unless it was an emergency,' he said crossly.

Her voice matched his in pique. 'But I've been trying your number at home all evening, and you haven't been answering, or returning my messages. And you weren't at the police station, either, which is a bloody miracle, considering how much time you spend there. So what was I supposed to do? I needed to talk to you.'

Old grievances, Tim said to himself. Would it never be over? 'I'll be home in ten minutes,' he told her. 'I'll ring you when I get there.' Without waiting for an answer he pressed the disconnect button, then smiled apologetically at Liz. 'My ex-wife,' he explained. 'I've got to go.'

If he'd turned around before he got to his car, he would have seen Liz still standing at her door, hands on her hips, and an expression of bitter disappointment on her face. But he didn't turn; he didn't give Liz another thought.

Home, for Tim Merriday, had once meant a cottage in a village a few miles outside Westmead, shared for some years with Gilly and Frannie. Now he lived alone in the top-floor flat of a converted Victorian red-brick semi, not far from the city centre: alone, that is, apart from his cat Watson, a handsome black-and-white tom. He'd always fancied having a cat, but Gilly had been allergic to cats, so as long as they were together, it wasn't an option. The week after he'd moved out of the cottage, desperately lonely in his solitary flat, he had gone to the nearest animal rescue shelter and been shown a number of cats, including one who was abandoned, abused, but undefeated. He'd looked into the cat's impassive golden eyes and it had been love at first sight; they had bonded instantly. Watson, unlike Gilly, never complained about his unsocial hours or his commitment to his job. Watson was always gratifyingly glad to see Tim, but his cat nature dictated that he was fundamentally independent of the need for human contact or human self-justification.

The sleek, well-nourished cat who met him at the door, purring and rubbing against his legs, bore little resemblance to the scraggly specimen he'd brought to the flat several years earlier. 'Watson,' Tim murmured, bending down to scratch his ears. 'The game's afoot, eh?' It was his usual greeting. And as usual, Watson said nothing, but went on purring, his eyes slits of joy.

And the flat which Tim now called home bore little resemblance to the domestic clutter of the cottage. Tim was essentially a tidy person, who liked order in his life; his flat was furnished with the bare minimum of possessions, and everything was in its place. A cynic – Gilly, for instance – might have said that it was because he was so rarely there to mess it up, but his sense of order went deeper than that.

The button on the caller display phone was blinking merrily away; Tim cycled down through the numbers to see that they were all Gilly's. Eight calls that evening, between six and ten. He needn't even bother dialling up his call-minder service to listen to the messages; he knew what they'd all say. And, he decided, he might as well make himself comfortable for this; no matter what it was about, he had a feeling it wasn't going to be pleasant. He took his shoes off, poured himself a drink, and settled down on the sofa. Watson jumped up, kneaded Tim's legs with his paws, then curled up, closed his eyes, and purred.

Tim took a sip of his drink before reaching for the phone and making the call. 'Gilly? I'm home.'

'About time,' she commented.

'Now, tell me what's so important that you had to ring me eight times this evening. Not counting,' he added, 'the one on the mobile, and how ever many calls you made to the police station.'

Quickly Gilly explained: her new boyfriend had booked a last-minute holiday for the two of them, and they would be leaving on Saturday morning, early. They would be gone for a fortnight, and during that time he, Tim, was to have Frannie.

'Wait a minute. You're telling me this *now*, when it's all a *fait accompli*?'

'He wanted to surprise me,' she said, smug rather than apologetic. 'He didn't tell me until tonight, when he got here after work. He handed me the tickets and told me to start packing.'

Tim pressed his lips together. 'And you've just assumed that it would be all right for me to have Frannie.'

'Well, she *is* your daughter,' stated Gilly. 'And you're always saying that you don't see enough of her. Well, now you're going to have your chance to spend some time with her.'

'On *your* terms. When it's convenient for *you*.' It was an old argument, but that didn't stop him. 'What kind of a mother are you, going off to some sunny clime with your lover and leaving your daughter behind?'

'And what kind of father were *you*?' she retaliated. 'Out at work all the time, never home. Never there for Frannie, *or* for me.'

'I'm surprised you can trust your precious daughter with me, then, if you don't think I'm capable of taking care of her.'

'Oh, you're capable, all right. If you can be bothered. If you can fit it into your schedule.'

Tim gulped down the rest of his drink before he answered, and he tried to achieve a more reasonable tone of voice. 'I'm just saying that you're assuming a great deal. It so happens that I'm very busy at the moment, with an important case on the go.'

'Tim, you're *always* busy! It's *always* an important case. That's just the problem, isn't it? That's *always* been the problem!'

He sighed. She just didn't understand; she never had. Most of the time he would have been delighted at the prospect of a fortnight with Frannie, but the timing couldn't have been worse. He was going to have to fit his clandestine investigation of Alison Barnett's murder in with the rest of his case-load, and that was going to mean a lot of extra hours. How was he going to manage, with a ten-year-old girl in his sole charge? 'I take it,' he said, defeated, 'that you want Frannie to come here?'

'Well, I certainly don't want you staying at the cottage,' Gilly stated. 'So you'll have to have her there.'

More complications, then: there was only one bedroom in the flat. When Frannie came to stay – a rare occurrence: he usually had her for the day and took her back to the cottage – he gave up his bed for her, and slept on the sofa. He didn't mind that, but it meant that he wouldn't have any private space. No space to think, no space to organise his papers and his files in the evenings. Frannie would spread her schoolwork over the kitchen table, so he wouldn't even have that. And it would spill from there to the sitting room, to the rest of the flat. She was not, he regretted, the tidiest of children; in that respect, she took after her mother. Worse yet, encouraged or at least tolerated by her mother, she was a fussy eater, with ever-changing food fads dominating her diet. Having her to stay would demand far more time than he usually devoted to shopping and cooking.

As if sensing that some conciliation was in order, Gilly said, 'She'll be in school most of the time, of course. You'll only have to look after her in the evenings, and at weekends.'

'*Only*,' muttered Tim. He picked up the pencil which always rested next to the phone and drew a horned devil on the notepad. Gilly? he wondered. Or the boyfriend?

She ignored him. 'Will you collect her – say, tomorrow evening? Or would you like us to drop her off? We could do it on our way to the airport – Saturday morning at about half-past five? Would that be more convenient for you? Might there be a chance of finding you at home then?'

Tim was determined not to rise to the bait. 'I'll collect her,' he said wearily.

'Tomorrow evening.'

Chris went down to the pub after dinner, for what he promised Sophie would be just a quick drink.

He asked Jeremy about Michael Thornley. Jeremy admitted that eleven years ago had been before his time at Westmead, but called over a couple of men who had sung in the choir for a number of years.

'Oh, yes, I remember him,' said one of the senior basses. 'A counter-tenor. Nice voice, if you like that sort of thing. Rather fancied himself, if I recall. I wonder what's happened to him?'

'I used to hear from him occasionally,' added a tenor. 'He went to Winchester from here. Then he tried his chances at a solo career, and from all I could tell, he sank without a trace. I don't have any idea where he is now.'

'I might be able to track him down,' offered the bass. 'Through various contacts. Friends of friends, you know. Why do you want him, exactly?'

'It's not me who wants him.' Chris grinned. 'Some policeman came to our house today looking for him. It has to do with that murder in the close a few years ago.'

They all stared at him and spoke simultaneously.

'The murder?'

'That girl?'

'The police think that Michael Thornley murdered that girl?'

The clamour drew in a few more curious lay clerks, and Chris was entreated to tell the whole story.

Within a few minutes, everyone in the Tower of London pub knew that the police had identified the dead girl after eleven years, and that Michael Thornley, late a lay clerk at Westmead Cathedral, was the chief suspect.

By the next morning, virtually everyone in Westmead knew.

Chapter 18

Liz Hollis was at the front desk of the police station as usual on Friday morning, and she smiled at Tim Merriday as he came in. 'That was lovely last night, Tim,' she said. 'I really enjoyed it.'

He hadn't given Liz much thought at all since he'd left her at her door; he had other, more important things, on his mind. Now he made himself focus his attention on her. 'Oh, yes. I enjoyed it as well,' he said. 'Thanks for coming out with me.'

Her smile became even brighter, and she toyed with a lock of her hair. 'Listen, Tim. I was thinking. You paid for last night, even though I was the one who did the inviting, so it's my turn to treat *you*. If you're not busy tomorrow night, I could cook you a meal at my place.'

Tim sighed. 'Not possible, I'm afraid. I'm going to have my daughter with me. For the next fortnight.'

'Your daughter?'

'Frannie. She's ten. Her mother is going on holiday, and Frannie's going to be staying with me.'

Liz was not to be dissuaded. 'You could bring her

along,' she said with determination. 'I like children.'

'That's very kind of you. But she's a fussy eater,' he warned.

'I can cope,' she said bravely. 'I have a little sister who wouldn't eat anything but frozen pizzas and oven chips for over a year.'

It would be nice, thought Tim, not to have to worry about feeding Frannie for one night, at least. 'If you're sure,' he said. 'It's very kind of you. And I hope you won't be sorry.'

'It will be fun,' Liz insisted.

'I need to go out and do some shopping this morning,' said Madeline over breakfast. She'd managed to get Sophie up and dressed and downstairs; now she surveyed the contents of the fridge. 'We're almost out of milk. And I used up most of the salad things last night. With the weekend coming up, I must get a few things in. Something for Sunday lunch.'

'Sounds to me as if you just can't wait to get out of the house,' said Sophie in a joking tone. But from the expression on Madeline's face, in the instant before she denied it, Sophie realised that she'd hit closer to the truth than she'd intended.

'You'll be all right on your own for a bit, won't you?' It was more of a statement than a question.

'Of course,' Sophie said staunchly, though she felt a bit apprehensive about being alone at the mercy of the doorbell, without Madeline to intercept callers. But that was being silly: if the doorbell rang, she told herself, she just wouldn't answer it.

Madeline got Sophie settled in the front room with a

cup of coffee and a magazine before she left. It was a glossy home-decorating magazine, and Sophie flicked through its pages without particular interest, restless and frustrated. Her sister hadn't been gone for very long, though, when the doorbell did ring.

Clunch, thought Sophie, suddenly chilled. She wouldn't answer it; she wouldn't move.

After a moment the bell chimed again, and it was another moment before she heard retreating footsteps.

He's given up, she told herself, letting out her breath in a relieved sigh. It had worked. She had not answered the door to Leslie Clunch, and the world hadn't come to an end; the cathedral had not come tumbling down round her ears, as she'd half-expected it to do from Chris's dire warnings of the consequences of ignoring or snubbing the ex-verger. She went back to turning the pages of the magazine.

The phone on the table beside her bleated, and Sophie jumped, then snatched up the receiver. 'Hello?'

'Oh, hello,' said a familiar voice: Clunch. 'You *are* there, then. I thought you must be – I saw your sister go out, but you weren't with her. I tried the bell a few minutes ago – I hope I haven't got you up from a nap?'

'No,' said Sophie through clenched teeth.

'Only I really *did* want to see you. It's been such a long time since we've been able to have a chat.'

She was trapped. He knew she was there; he knew she was awake; he knew she was alone. 'All right,' said Sophie, defeated. 'Just for a few minutes. I *was* about to take a nap.'

'I'll be along straight away,' he said happily.

Opening the door to him, she experienced the familiar

repugnance at his greasy thin hair, his yellow teeth, his avid eyes; it was a visceral reaction, uncontrollable, and he seemed completely unaware of the effect he had on her. She stood back to let him in, allowing him plenty of space so there was no chance of inadvertent contact. She couldn't bear it, she thought, if he were to touch her; the very idea made her shiver inwardly with revulsion.

She would *not* offer him coffee, she was determined. It would only encourage him to stay, and she wanted him out as quickly as possible.

But he settled down on the sofa and came straight to the point. 'Now,' Leslie Clunch said. 'What is this I hear about a policeman coming here yesterday? They've identified the dead girl, I hear.' His beady eyes shone, and there was a bit of spittle at the sides of his mouth.

The first thing on Jacquie's agenda in the morning was a trip into town: she needed to replenish her food supplies. A trip to the Mini Mart provided her with fresh milk and bread, and enough meat and veg to get her through the next few days. That, she discovered, was all she could afford at the moment; she'd spent almost all the cash she'd had on hand in Westmead. So a trip to the building society was in order.

Jacquie had never owned a credit card. It was against the ethos of the Free Baptist Fellowship, and the concept of 'pay as you go' had been drummed into her from earliest childhood. If you didn't have the money for something, her mother had always said, then you didn't really need it.

At the time of her divorce from Darren, she'd been too proud to take any money from him, and her parents had assured her that there was no need: they would give her a roof over her head, feed and clothe her. And that had seemed only right, as she had devoted herself to looking after them. There was always the understanding, as well, that when they were gone, everything would be hers: the house, the tidy sum which two frugal people had accumulated in the building society over a number of years.

At first, her mother had doled sums of money out to her on a weekly basis – never generous, but sufficient for one who had the basics of life provided. In addition she'd had control of the housekeeping money, supplied by her mother. Latterly, after her mother's death and especially in her father's final illness, when he was unable to go out himself, she had been given power of attorney to draw money out of the building society as needed. She'd never abused that; frugality was too ingrained in her by then. But she'd always regarded it as money that would be hers one day, money that she had every right to spend if she so desired.

She went to the counter, to the woman who had been serving her for years. When she slipped the passbook under the partition, though, and asked for a hundred pounds, the woman frowned. 'I'm sorry, Jacquie,' she said. 'I can't give it to you.'

Sometimes, Jacquie knew, they ran low on cash on a Friday, as people did their shopping for the weekend. 'That's all right, then,' she said easily. 'Fifty will do. Or even twenty. I can come back on Monday.'

'No.' The woman looked down, unwilling to make eye contact. 'I can't give you any money at all.'

Still Jacquie didn't understand. 'But why ever not?'

'Mr Mockler. Your father's executor. He's put a stop on

the account until the grant of probate comes through. I'm really sorry,' she added, 'but he was very clear. Your father's account is frozen.'

Jacquie turned on her heel and went straight to Mr Mockler's office, upstairs in an old building not far from the Free Baptist Fellowship. The receptionist was loath to give her access to him, protesting that he was a very busy man, but when Jacquie threatened to sit there all day if necessary, she unbent sufficiently to grant her a quarter of an hour. That, she said, was all that Mr Mockler could possibly spare.

That was fine with Jacquie; what she had to say to him could be said quickly, and she had no desire to linger over pleasantries.

'My sister is dead,' she stated.

Mr Mockler's fat sausage fingers stopped in the act of smoothing his waistcoat over his belly. 'Dead? Miss Alison Barnett is dead?'

'She was murdered. In Westmead. Eleven years ago, just after she left Sutton Fen.'

'My goodness.'

Jacquie could read the expression in his eyes as clearly as if he had spoken: God's judgement, it said. God's judgement on a sinner who had left the fold of the Free Baptist Fellowship. Pregnant, disgraced. Dead. It was no more than she deserved.

She said nothing, waiting to hear what he would say next.

'How very sad,' he intoned unctuously. 'Please accept my condolences, Mrs Darke.'

She wouldn't dignify that bit of hypocrisy with a response. 'Now that we know she's dead,' said Jacquie, aware that she sounded unfeeling but unable to handle it any other way, 'I'm assuming that the legal position is more clear-cut. I am the only one left to inherit my father's estate. Isn't that true?'

'Well, yes.'

'That means that his money belongs to me. And the house. So is there any reason that I can't get some cash today, and put the house on the market immediately?'

He laced his sausage fingers together and favoured her with a humourless baring of the tombstone teeth. 'Two reasons, in actual fact, Mrs Darke.'

Dismayed, she demanded, 'What reasons?'

'First of all, there is the little matter of probate. Until it is granted, none of it is legally yours. Neither the house nor the money.' He leaned back in his chair.

'So how long will that take? And what's the other reason?'

'I was getting to that.' The solicitor picked up a heavy gold pen from his desk and caressed it absently. 'It takes about three weeks for a grant of probate. Once it's been applied for, that is. But I won't even be able to apply for probate, Mrs Darke, until I have a death certificate for your sister.'

'But . . . why?'

'It is my job as your father's executor to see that his wishes are carried out,' he explained in a patronising, pompous voice. 'And his wish was that you and your sister, Miss Alison Barnett, should share equally in his estate.'

'But I've told you. She's dead.'

Again he bared his teeth. 'I'm not calling you a liar, Mrs Darke. But that's exactly the point: you are in effect the beneficiary of her death, and I have only your word that she is, in actual fact, dead. With all due respect, that's not good enough.'

Tim sat at his desk with files spread out round him, but only half his mind was on the task at hand: with the other half he thought about Jacquie Darke, and wondered how she was getting on. The scrap of paper on which she had written her address and phone number was propped up against his phone, and every now and again he picked it up and looked at it, wishing that he had an excuse to ring her, something to report.

Why, he asked himself at last, did he need an excuse? With sudden resolve he picked the phone up and rang the number.

He counted the rings: ten, fifteen, twenty.

She wasn't there, or she wasn't answering. And there was no answering machine.

Sighing, he put the receiver down and tried to apply himself to his work, and had just about succeeded when the phone rang. Abstractedly he picked it up. 'Tim Merriday.'

'Sergeant Merriday?'

It was Jacquie Darke's voice; he became attentive at once. 'Yes, Mrs Darke. How . . . how are you? Did you have a safe trip back?'

'Yes, thank you.' Her voice was brisk, impersonal.

She was wanting to know what progress he'd made, then. 'I'm sorry. There's nothing new here,' he said, then, still cowardly where she was concerned, he embroidered on his previous lie. 'I'm still working out what to say to my boss. I *will* ring you when I've spoken to him.'

'That's not why I've rung. I have a problem, and I hope that you can help me with it.'

Tim picked up his pencil. 'I'll certainly try.'

'I've been told by my father's solicitor that I need a death certificate for my sister. And until I get it, I can't put the house on the market. I can't even touch his building society account. So it's urgent.'

He discovered that he was drawing pound signs; so, he thought, she's hard up for money. 'Now, that's a point,' he said. 'I'll need to talk to the coroner. I'll get on to it straight away, Mrs Darke.'

Encouraged, perhaps, by this promise of efficiency and speed, she thawed a bit. 'I do appreciate it, Sergeant. The sooner, the better.'

'I'll ring you back as soon as I have anything to report,' he promised. Then, not wanting the conversation to end, he added impulsively, 'And as long as I have you on the line, Mrs Darke, I had something to ask you about.' What could he ask her? He reached for the files on the case, opened them up, and said the first thing that came into his head. 'About this chain your sister was wearing. Any idea what it was? Was it, by any chance, valuable?'

'Chain?' said Jacquie blankly. 'I don't have any idea what you're talking about.'

'A necklace, I suppose it was,' he amplified. 'The one she was . . .' He cleared his throat and tried to think how he could put it, then laid out the facts as emotionlessly as he could. 'Your sister was . . . strangled . . . with what would have appeared to be a metal chain. The chain itself was missing when we found her. That was one reason why it was assumed that robbery might have been the motive.

If it was a particularly valuable necklace, a family heirloom, perhaps . . .'

'I don't understand,' Jacquie stated. 'It said in the newspaper that she was strangled with a scarf. I'm sure that's what it said.'

'Oh, that.' With his pencil, Tim fashioned a chain which looped round the paper, adding link after link. 'I'd forgotten. The chain was something that we didn't make public. We always like to keep one or two things like that back – things only the killer would know.'

'But the newspaper said a scarf,' she insisted.

'I'm sure we didn't lie to them and tell them it was a scarf. They probably just assumed it,' he explained. 'And we didn't correct them. The police aren't in the habit of lying,' he added, hoping that she wouldn't hear the guilt in his voice.

'I see.' There was a long silence on the other end of the phone, then Jacquie went on. 'But it's impossible, don't you see?'

'Impossible?'

'Ally didn't wear any jewellery. It's against our religion. No adornment of any kind – no make-up, no jewellery.'

'None at all?' he echoed, unbelieving. 'Not even a simple chain?'

'Nothing,' she assured him. 'The only thing that's allowed is a wedding ring. A plain gold band.'

'But . . .'

Her voice was firm in its certainty, cutting across his surprised protests. 'Ally didn't own any jewellery, Sergeant. I can promise you that.'

*   *   *

Having rid herself at last of Leslie Clunch, Sophie went upstairs to take a nap, falling into an exhausted sleep. She woke at the sound of Madeline's return, and reached for the alarm clock: it was lunch-time. Madeline had been gone for the whole morning, far longer than expected.

Her sister tiptoed up the stairs and peeked in at her. 'You're in bed, then. I hope you haven't been worried about me.'

'I was sleeping,' Sophie said.

'Sorry I was a bit long.' Madeline was smiling in the self-satisfied way that had infuriated Sophie for years. 'But you'll never guess who I met in town.'

Sophie's answer was prompt. 'Jeremy.'

'Well, yes.' Madeline looked a bit deflated. 'I found that lovely coffee shop he'd told me about, and he was there. So we had a coffee together. He was absolutely agog to hear my account of the policeman's visit.'

'You do surprise me.'

'Jeremy wanted to hear it straight from the horse's mouth, as it were. He made me tell him everything – every single detail.' She smiled at the memory.

Sophie refrained from pointing out that Madeline had been absent from almost all of the interview.

'And then he told me that he'd been speaking to Elspeth Verey, and that she wanted to meet me. So he took me to meet her. To Priory House.'

'Oh, yes?'

'What a splendid house it is,' she rhapsodised. 'And she's absolutely lovely, isn't she? Gracious and stately. Just what a Dean's widow should be.'

'Her father was Dean as well.'

Madeline nodded. 'Yes, that's what she said. Dean

Worthington, wasn't it? She showed me his portrait.'

'She rather lives on past glories, it seems to me,' Sophie remarked.

'Not at all,' protested her sister. 'She's very proud of her sons. She has quite a lot invested in both of them. In their futures, you might say.'

Sophie closed her eyes and remembered the day that Dominic had blurted out the truth to her about his sexual orientation, wondering anew how Elspeth would cope with it when she found out – as she inevitably would. 'I just hope,' Sophie said feelingly, 'that they don't disappoint her.'

'Oh, there's no reason why they should. The elder son seems marked out for preferment in the Church. And Dominic is such a bright, personable boy – he'll go far, I'm sure.'

Far, perhaps. But in what direction? Sophie wondered. If he was lucky, he'd go far from Westmead, and escape from the iron-willed control of his mother. But would he have the strength to do that?

Madeline went on at length, about the elegance of Elspeth Verey and the charm of Priory House. Sophie kept her eyes closed and let the words wash over her. Her thoughts were on Dominic. Would he ever escape? She had no desire to come between mother and son, but if there were ever a show-down, Sophie was in no doubt as to whose side she'd be on.

'Tim Merriday.' Expecting a return call from the coroner, who had been unavailable when he'd rung, Tim picked up the phone and said the words automatically.

'Tim? It's Barry. Barry Sills.'

He nearly put the phone down at that point: Barry Sills was the one person – apart from the Superintendent, of course – to whom Tim had no wish to speak.

Barry Sills was a journalist, a reporter for the *Westmead Herald*, with particular responsibilities for the crime beat – such as it was. This usually, in Westmead, amounted to little more than traffic offences and the odd burglary, but over the years he'd built up a relationship with the Westmead CID over such trifles. He and Tim Merriday had often shared a pint at the local pub, and there was respect on both sides – even something approaching friendship.

Sills was known for his integrity as a journalist; Tim had always found that to be true. He checked his facts scrupulously; he didn't fall back on innuendo or sensationalism. Tim had a lot of time for him.

Usually. Not now.

He did not want to talk to Barry Sills.

'Listen, Tim,' said the journalist. 'How about a drink? Or lunch? I'll buy you lunch – I can't say fairer than that, can I?'

'No, thanks, Barry.' Tim tried to keep his voice jovial and noncommittal. 'I'm really busy just at the minute. I'm not leaving my desk.'

'Oh, come on, Tim. You've got to eat.'

'Maybe another day.'

'Maybe,' Sills said, 'you'd rather have me ring the Superintendent? I'll bet he wouldn't refuse an invitation to lunch.'

'I'll bet he *would*,' Tim shot back, but he knew he was beaten. 'All right, then. But that one was below the belt. Don't they teach you anything about playing fair at journalist school?'

'Playing fair isn't the name of the game in this business, old friend.' Sills chuckled. 'One o'clock? At the pub?'

'Make it a quarter to one – so we'll be just ahead of the crowd.'

'Done. I'll see you there.'

The pub where they usually met was a bit scruffy and down-at-heel, well overdue for a make-over. But that was the way its patrons liked it, so it wasn't likely to change; in spite of its appearance, it served good food, and had a loyal clientele. Barry Sills was already ensconced at a corner table when Tim arrived. 'I've bagged the best table,' he said. 'We won't be overheard here. And I've bought you a pint.'

'I should only have a half,' Tim protested. 'I need to keep my wits about me this afternoon. I suppose that's part of your strategy – get me drunk, and loosen my tongue.'

'You've found me out at last,' grinned the journalist. 'Cheers.' He lifted his glass, and Tim followed suit.

'Cheers.' He knew that he was being manipulated, but he couldn't feel any resentment towards Barry Sills: he was just doing his job, after all. And he was, essentially, a decent bloke. Or so Tim reminded himself.

Sills didn't look like most people's stereotype of a journalist, dressed in seedy tweeds; he looked more, thought Tim, like a prosperous solicitor. Well-cut suit, immaculate white shirt, and a stylish haircut that had cost more than a fiver.

'The fish and chips look pretty good today,' Sills said. 'Are you up for that?'

'Why not?' He liked fish and chips, and the pub always had fresh fish on a Friday.

The journalist went to the bar and placed the order; while they waited for their food, they engaged in small-talk of a general nature. Sills was a happily married man who continually urged upon Tim the joys of that state, while still able to commiserate with him about his ups and downs with Gilly.

Tim told him about the phone call from his ex-wife. 'And she didn't *ask* me if I could have Frannie. She *told* me that I was having her,' he complained.

'I don't suppose this is a very good time for that,' said Sills, and suddenly they were drawing close to the subject which they'd been so gracefully skirting.

'No,' Tim admitted, shaking his head. 'It couldn't be worse, really.'

The journalist tackled it head on. 'The old Quire Close murder. The new evidence. You're involved with all that, I hear.'

Tim might have denied it; with anyone but his old friend Barry he almost certainly would have done. But they knew each other too well. He could, though, still play for time, and possibly even discover something as well. 'Where did you hear that?' he asked cautiously.

Sills laughed. 'Where *haven't* I heard it? Everyone in this town is talking about it, mate. If you think it's a secret, think again.'

'Bugger,' Tim said with feeling.

'So what I want to know,' Sills stated, 'is who was she? I've heard that you've got an ID on the dead girl, after all these years. That her sister has identified her.'

In spite of the fact that they were at an isolated table, Tim lowered his voice, and he carefully didn't answer the question. 'The truth is, Barry, that I'm in rather a difficult position with this one. The Super has put me in charge of it, but that's in name only. He doesn't want any attention drawn to it, and he doesn't want me to *do* anything. This case has been dead in the water for eleven years. It wouldn't make him very popular with the higher-ups, you know, to run over budget for something like this.'

'So you've been nosing around without his permission.' The journalist gave him a knowing wink.

Tim shrugged ruefully and admitted, 'That's about it. So you can see why I'd like to keep it out of the papers. For a few days, anyway.'

'You can see *my* problem, though, can't you?' Barry unrolled the cutlery from the napkin and tapped his fork on the table. 'The *Herald* is a weekly paper, as I'm sure I don't need to remind you. We go to press tomorrow. And if I don't have something from you today, it will be too late. By next week it will be old news. Ancient history, mate.'

'I'm sorry. But I really can't—'

'Let's make a deal,' interrupted Sills, suddenly all business. 'I know that you've been going round asking about a Michael Thornley. Formerly a lay clerk in the cathedral choir, I'm told. And presumably he's your new hot suspect.'

Tim gulped; the rumour-mills *had* been busy. 'I can't confirm that,' he said stiffly.

'No, of course you can't. But that doesn't mean I can't print it.'

'Barry! You wouldn't do that!' he protested, horrified. 'The Super would eat me for breakfast. With brown sauce.'

'I won't print it,' promised the journalist. '*If*, that is, you give me the dead girl's name. And the name of her sister. And where they're from. That's all I ask, Tim. It's not a lot to ask.'

'Oh, no. Not much.' Tim knocked back the rest of his pint.

'And the other thing I'll do,' added Sills with a magnanimous smile, 'is help you to look for this Thornley bloke. I have some connections, you know. I'll keep his name out of the paper, and I'll help you to track him down. I can't say fairer than that.'

Tim moved his empty glass round the scarred wooden table top, leaving wet streaks like snail trails, and thought about his options. Any way he looked at it, he was buggered. Barry might be a friend, might be an honourable specimen of his kind, but in the end that wasn't saying much. He had a living to earn, and he wouldn't hesitate to carry out his veiled threat. And in the end, it would be far more damaging to have speculation about the suspect in print than it would be to confirm the identity of the dead girl, which was now a matter of fact.

The journalist must have read the emotions on Tim's face; he smiled in anticipation of victory. 'Do we have a deal, old friend?' He stuck his hand out in Tim's direction.

Tim clasped his hand reluctantly. 'Deal.'

'Then give.'

'Miss Alison Barnett of Sutton Fen, Cambridgeshire,' he stated tersely.

'And the sister?' the journalist prompted.

Why, thought Tim, did he feel that he was betraying Jacquie? 'Do you really need to know that?'

'You promised. Part of the deal.'

Tim sighed, and dragged the words out. 'Jacquie Darke. Jacqueline. Mrs.' The only consolation, he told himself as he drained his glass, was that it wasn't only his head on the chopping block on this one – it wasn't going to do the Superintendent's chance of a knighthood very much good, either. In spite of himself, he smiled.

The word was out, then, and the Superintendent was going to be furious. Tim hurried back to the police station, determined to have a word with his boss as soon after lunch as possible. He would, if necessary, sweet-talk the Superintendent's secretary into squeezing in an early afternoon appointment, he decided. If he could get to him *first*, before he found out from another source, he might be able to explain what had happened, salvage something from the mess he'd made for himself.

But when he got back to his office, there was a message waiting on his voice-mail from the coroner, and that distracted him into a series of phone calls to the coroner, the registrar of deaths, and back to the coroner again.

Should he ring Jacquie with the results, as he'd promised, or should he do the grown-up thing and make arrangements to beard the Superintendent in his den at the earliest opportunity? Tim's hand hovered over the phone in a moment of indecision.

The choice was made for him when the phone rang. He picked it up. 'Tim Merriday.'

'Merriday,' said the Superintendent.

Tim gulped. 'Yes, sir.'

'I'm just back from my Rotary lunch, Merriday. And who do you think I sat next to?' The question was posed in a voice that was reflective, almost gentle.

'I don't know, sir.'

'The Dean of the cathedral, Merriday. That's who I sat next to.'

Unconsciously Tim reached for his pencil and found that he was drawing a hangman's noose. He couldn't think of what to say.

The Superintendent didn't seem to notice the silence. 'And the Dean was telling me something very interesting, Merriday. Very interesting indeed.'

'I see,' Tim managed.

'I think it's time for us to have another little chat, Merriday. Don't you think so?'

Tim wanted to run in the opposite direction, as fast as he could. But his reply was meek. 'Yes, sir.'

'My office. Five minutes. Don't be late.' He didn't shout; his voice was as soft as velvet, as unbending as steel.

'Yes, sir.'

Tim had never been so terrified in all his life.

Jacquie needed something to do to keep her busy while she waited for the phone call from Sergeant Merriday. She would, she decided, employ her time usefully in getting the house sorted out. Eventually she would be allowed to sell it, and while all she wanted to do was to hire a skip and chuck out the entire contents of the house, she realised that it would be more complicated than that.

Her parents' room first, then. She'd scarcely been in there since her father's death, and she was surprised at the emotions the room evoked. In her obsession with finding Ally, Jacquie had not allowed herself to grieve properly for her father; she found herself choking up at the sight of his shoes, all lined up in the bottom of his wardrobe, neatly polished. Frank Barnett had always been particular about his shoes.

Jacquie swallowed the lump in her throat and fetched

a large black bin-liner. Someone could use the shoes; someone could use the clothes. Her mother's clothes were still there as well: Frank Barnett had insisted that they remain. There was no reason to keep them now.

She folded each garment carefully and placed them in the bag, trying not to think about the way they had once clothed living flesh, flesh that was now dead. But the memories were there: of her father wearing this particular tie, his favourite for a Sunday. Of her mother, huddling into this dressing gown on a chill morning, too frugal to turn on the central heating.

The sound of the phone brought her out of her painful reverie, and she hurried to answer it. 'Yes?'

It was, as she'd expected, Sergeant Merriday's voice. 'Mrs Darke?'

'Yes.'

He gave a little laugh, dry and humourless. 'Do you want the good news first, or the bad news?'

Jacquie's stomach muscles contracted; she didn't think that she could handle bad news just now. 'The good news,' she said.

'The good news is that I've sorted out the death certificate. I'm sorry that it took longer than I'd hoped, but it was a bit more difficult than I'd anticipated,' he explained. 'The coroner said that the registrar of deaths had it, and the registrar claimed that the coroner had never given it to him. Eventually, between them, they've managed to track it down.'

'Thank you,' she said, holding her breath for the rest.

'The bad news is,' he went on, 'that it won't be ready for you until after the weekend. They have to amend it, of course. To show her name. And when it comes to that sort of thing, the wheels grind exceeding slow.'

Jacquie let out her breath in a relieved sigh. That wasn't so bad; he'd led her to expect something much worse. 'I've waited this long,' she said. 'A few more days won't matter.'

There was a pause on the other end of the phone, then the policeman said, in a graver voice, 'There's more bad news, I'm afraid.'

'Tell me.'

'My boss. The Superintendent.' He sounded embarrassed, distressed.

'You've told him. What happened?' she demanded.

'I gave it my best shot. I told him how important it was that the investigation should be fully reopened. But . . . well, he just isn't buying it. Finances. Budgets. Resources.' Tim sounded bitter. 'He was so self-righteous about it – the guardian of the public purse. Couldn't justify committing our limited resources, blah blah.'

'So nothing is going to be done?'

'The very minimum. Just as I feared. And the case is being given to someone else – I'm not going to be allowed to have anything to do with it. I wish I could . . .' His voice trailed off. 'I'm sorry, Ja . . . Mrs Darke. I'm really sorry. I can't tell you how sorry.'

Jacquie said nothing; she put the phone down and stood for a long time staring at it, fighting back tears.

He'd failed. Sergeant Tim Merriday had failed. She'd trusted him, and he'd let her down.

She wasn't sure just how long she'd been standing there when the phone rang again. More excuses, she thought furiously, and snatched the receiver up, ready this time to tell him off, to tell him how useless he was.

But the voice wasn't Tim Merriday's. 'Mrs Darke?'

enquired an unknown man in a West Country accent. 'Mrs Jacquie Darke?'

'Yes. I'm Jacquie Darke.'

'My name is Barry Sills,' he said. 'I'm a reporter with the *Westmead Herald*. I apologise for ringing you like this, but I'm preparing a story for tomorrow's edition, about your sister's murder. And I was hoping that you might be able to give me a word. Something that I can quote, perhaps.'

If the call had come a quarter of an hour earlier, she would have put the phone down on him just as she'd hung up on Tim Merriday. But now things were different. Now it didn't matter any longer. She had nothing left to lose, and she might as well vent her bitterness on him as on anyone else. Sergeant Merriday wouldn't like it, but what was that to her?

'Yes,' said Jacquie thoughtfully. 'Yes, Mr Sills. I *do* have something to say.'

Chapter 19

'I don't like Rice Krispies.' Frannie Merriday, her jaw jutting out at a stubborn angle, kicked at the leg of the table.

Her father sighed. 'But Frannie – you've *always* had Rice Krispies for breakfast. "Snap, crackle, pop": those were practically the first words you ever said.'

'That's just it, Dad.' She gave him a pitying look. 'Rice Krispies are for babies. I'm not a baby any more.'

No, thought Tim, looking at his daughter: she wasn't a baby. At ten, nearly eleven, she was on the cusp of growing up; soon she would be a young lady. Already there were moments of extreme maturity, even wisdom, when he found it hard to believe that she was only ten. The next minute, though, she would inevitably revert to childish ways, and he would realise how far she had to go.

She wasn't, he had to admit, a great beauty, nor was she likely to grow into one. Her face was too long and thin, too bespattered with freckles. Frannie was tall for her age, thin, with gangly limbs, and her hair was an unfashionable bright ginger, untameably curly. In short, she took after her father far more than her mother, and sometimes Tim regretted, for her sake, that it was so. But he loved her with the deep love of a father for an only child. And – most of the time – he treasured the rare hours he spent with her.

Now, though, he faced the prospect of entertaining her for a fortnight. Apart from the time she would spend at school, his would be the sole responsibility of keeping her occupied. And, even more germanely, fed.

'If you don't like Rice Krispies any longer, what *do* you eat for breakfast?' he asked patiently.

'Frosties,' she stated. 'And toast with Nutella.'

He was sceptical of the latter. 'Your mother lets you have Nutella for breakfast?'

Frannie gave a self-satisfied nod. 'Mum lets me have whatever I like.'

The course of least resistance, thought Tim: that had always been Gilly's way. She had allowed herself to be swept by him into marriage, but as soon as the marriage had begun to seem like work . . .

'Well,' he said, 'I don't have any Frosties, and I don't have any Nutella. We can go shopping later on and buy some. But I got the Rice Krispies specially for you, so I think you can eat them just this once.'

She narrowed her eyes at him in displeasure, but she crunched her way through a bowl of cereal without another word.

Tim, occupied as he was with Frannie, was one of the few people in Westmead who was not poring over the *Westmead Herald* at the breakfast table. In Quire Close, in the cathedral precincts, in humble Victorian terraces and modern semi-detached boxes across the town, people absorbed the front-page story with varying degrees of avidity. The Superintendent, in his suburban villa, was purple with rage, and took it out on his wife by screaming at her that his eggs were overcooked, while in the Precentor's House at the far end of Quire Close, there was quite a different reaction.

'That poor girl,' said Miranda Swan to her husband with feeling. 'I must do something.'

And a few minutes later, Tim Merriday's phone rang.

'I apologise for ringing you at home,' said a female voice which he didn't recognise. 'But it's rather important. My name is Mrs Miranda Swan.'

He sighed, trying to place her without success. 'How can I help you, Mrs Swan?'

'I'm trying to locate Jacquie Darke, the dead girl's sister. Is she staying somewhere in Westmead, do you know?'

'Wait a minute.' Tim sat up and reached for his pad and pencil. 'How do you know about Jacquie Darke?'

'From the newspaper, of course. The *Herald*.'

Tim clamped his lips over an obscenity, conscious of Frannie as well as Mrs Swan's sensibilities. 'Of course. I'd forgotten about the *Herald*.' How could he have forgotten? he asked himself.

'As I said, it's quite important that I get in touch with Mrs Darke. Can you possibly give me a contact number for her?'

Once again he experienced a surge of protectiveness, all the stronger since he felt he had let Jacquie down. 'No, I'm sorry,' he said. 'That's not possible.'

'Perhaps,' said Miranda Swan, 'I'll have better luck with Mr Sills, the man who wrote the article. She seems to have been quite open and honest with him.'

And he'd told himself that things couldn't get any worse. Tim started sketching a horned devil, and this time he knew exactly who it was: Barry Sills. 'I think,' he said to Miranda Swan through clenched teeth, 'you'd better tell me why you want to talk to Mrs Darke. Maybe I can help you, after all.'

Jacquie hadn't yet forced herself out of bed. What, after all, was there to get up for? She had all the time in the world, and nothing much to do.

She was back where she had been before her trip to Westmead: aimless, rudderless. All of the fight had gone out of her. The past week, in which she had taken action, taken the initiative, seized control of her life, seemed like a dream. The quest for Alison was over, and it had ended with resounding finality. Alison was dead, and Jacquie was powerless to deal with the consequences of that. What, now, did she have to look forward to? What reason was there for her to get out of bed?

Yes, she could spend as many hours as she wanted in cleaning the house, in tidying things up and clearing out the rubbish, but what was the hurry? It would still be weeks before she was able to put it on the market. Maybe she wouldn't even sell the house after all; at the moment it seemed like too much effort. Perhaps she'd just stay there until she died. In this house, in this bed.

It was hunger that eventually did the trick; the night before she had been too upset to eat, and now it was catching up with her. So she wrapped herself in her dressing gown against the chill of the house and went downstairs to make herself some toast and coffee.

The phone rang while the toast was under the grill.

What now? she thought, going to answer it.

'Mrs Darke? You don't know me, but my name is Miranda Swan.'

Miranda, Jacquie repeated to herself. Miranda Swan: that sounded familiar.

'I used to live in Sutton Fen, though I don't think we've ever met. Now I live in Westmead. My husband is the Precentor of the cathedral.'

Oh, yes. The woman that Nicola had told her about, whose first husband had fallen in with Reverend Prew and the True Men. 'I've heard of you,' Jacquie acknowledged. 'From my friend Nicola.'

'And I've heard of *you*. In conjunction with the Free Baptist Fellowship. And the True Men.'

Jacquie didn't want to talk about Reverend Prew. 'Yes,' she said shortly.

'I've just read about you in the *Westmead Herald*.' Miranda launched into the reason for her call. 'And I wanted you to know how desperately sorry I am about what's happened to your sister, and the way that the police have let you down. I think it's appalling.'

'Yes.'

'And,' Miranda went on, 'I wanted to say that I don't think you should give up. I think you should come back to Westmead and fight. The police aren't infallible. They're not God. If you make enough of a fuss, someone will have to listen to you, and do something.'

A spark of hope flared; Jacquie allowed herself, for an instant, to believe that what Miranda Swan had said might be true.

Then she remembered the hard facts about her finances: as long as she couldn't touch the money in her father's building society account, she couldn't afford to go anywhere. The Cathedral View Guest House, reasonably priced as it was, had gobbled up her available resources.

And under no circumstances was she prepared to ask Darren for money: she might be desperate, but she couldn't imagine being *that* desperate.

'I don't think so,' she said. 'It's . . . well, it isn't practical.'

'Do you have a job, then? Family responsibilities?'

'No,' Jacquie admitted. 'Nothing like that. It's just that . . . well, to be perfectly honest with you, Mrs Swan, I can't afford it. My affairs are all tied up at the moment, waiting for my father's estate to be sorted out.'

'So you don't have a place to stay in Westmead,' Miranda Swan guessed.

'No.'

'That's no problem at all, then,' Miranda said with warm impulsiveness. 'We have a huge house, and there are only two of us. There's a lovely guest room, just redecorated.'

'Oh!' Jacquie was overwhelmed; she didn't know what to say. Miranda Swan was a stranger to her, with only the tenuous link of Sutton Fen and Nicola, and she was offering her hospitality. People at the Free Baptist Fellowship were always talking about hospitality – 'entertaining angels unawares', and all of that – but they very rarely offered it. 'It's very kind of you,' she managed at last. 'But I couldn't possibly.'

'Why not, then?' she challenged, then her voice changed. 'Oh, Mrs Darke. I'm really sorry. I should have realised. I suppose I've been really insensitive.'

'Insensitive?'

'Your sister . . . I understand that she was found outside

our house. Where we now live. I don't suppose you could cope with that.'

'No,' said Jacquie. 'It isn't that at all. I just don't see why you should put yourself out for someone you don't even know.'

'Don't be silly,' Miranda Swan assured her. 'Come and stay for as long as you like. And we'll do all that we can to help you. My husband,' she added, 'is not without influence.'

Jacquie felt that she could hardly refuse; the other woman was so insistent, so persuasive, so very kind. To turn her down would be rude and ungracious. 'All right, then,' she heard herself saying.

'Come today. Or tomorrow – whatever is convenient for you.'

And so, before the morning was over, Jacquie found herself packing her suitcase for the third time inside a week.

Madeline was, of course, one of the people most interested in the *Westmead Herald* that morning, feeling that she had a personal stake in the story. 'It's too bad that the reporter didn't ring here,' she said. 'I don't know who his sources were, but he didn't have the whole story. He's missed out the bit about Michael Thornley. I could have told him that.'

'Maybe he *did* know about it, and had a good reason for not printing it,' Sophie pointed out.

Madeline didn't buy it. 'But without that, it's little more than a rehash of old information. The only thing new is the girl's name. Alison Barnett,' she read. 'From Sutton Fen, in Cambridgeshire.'

Somehow, Sophie felt, giving the girl a name *did* make a difference. No longer just an unknown young woman, with no one in the world to claim her, but Alison Barnett of Sutton Fen. Someone with a name, a history, a home, a family.

A sister. Jacqueline Darke.

Sophie tried to imagine what Jacqueline Darke must be feeling. From her quoted words, she was very bitter, and rightly so: the police had bungled the case from the beginning, eleven years ago, and now they were compounding their sins. She had every right to feel aggrieved.

And yet her words raised so many questions in Sophie's mind. Why, for instance, had she waited for more than eleven years to report her sister missing? What had she been doing in those intervening years? Had she never wondered what had happened to her sister? And why Westmead? How had Alison Barnett happened to come there, of all places, to be murdered? Did she know someone in Westmead? If so, why hadn't they come forward? Unless they were the murderer, of course. And if not . . .

Sophie didn't voice any of her questions, though. Madeline was too wrapped up in her own disappointment at having been excluded from the article; she wasn't even listening.

Chris, who had been the last to be allowed to read the article, looked up from the paper and raised some points of his own. 'It's so strange that it doesn't mention Michael Thornley. Everyone in Westmead knows that the police were trying to trace him. I suppose they interviewed him at the time, like they seem to have done with everyone else in the place. Do you suppose this Alison Thingy knew him?'

'Jeremy and I talked about that,' said Madeline. 'And I have my theories.' But they were fated never to know what those theories were; at that moment the phone went.

Chris picked it up, and recognised his brother-in-law's voice. 'Do you want Madeline, then?' he asked, then handed her the phone.

Still absorbed in the implications of the newspaper story, Sophie paid scant attention to Madeline's end of what seemed to be a fairly one-sided conversation. But she did notice when Madeline abruptly left the room, clutching the cordless phone, to continue her conversation in private.

Chris raised his eyebrows. 'I wonder what that's all about?'

'How should I know?' said Sophie tartly.

'Geoffrey sounded really strange. Really upset. I wonder if there's something wrong?'

'I'm sure that whatever it is, Maddy will tell us all about it.'

But Sophie was mistaken about that; when Madeline returned to the kitchen, her face as white and set as a fine marble sculpture, her words were tersely uninformative. 'I have to go home,' she said. 'Now.'

Chris got up and went to her. 'What is it? What's wrong?'

'I can't talk about it. Not now.' She shrugged off his hand, dropped the phone, turned, and fled to pack her case.

Oh, wonderful, thought Sophie. Now it was back to just her and Chris. Madeline, as annoying as she was, at least had provided some relief from that uncompromising formula. Just the two of them. One and one equalled – what? In their case, at the moment, not very much.

She looked at him now, and remembered the unspeakable things they'd said to each other during that row, at the way he'd rebuffed her clumsy attempt to apologise. Could they ever bridge the gap again? Did she even want to? Sophie wasn't sure.

Other people's problems were always more attractive than one's own. She pulled the newspaper towards her again and reread the article, her sympathies firmly on the side of Jacquie Darke. The facts of the case, as always, reached her on a level that she couldn't quite explain, and for a moment she wished that she wasn't feeling so weak and helpless. If only she were a bit stronger, perhaps she'd be able to do something to help Jacquie Darke.

Tim knew that he was being a coward, but he switched his mobile phone off that morning, dreading the inevitable call from the Superintendent, telling him that from now on he would be writing traffic tickets. Technically he was off duty; he was under no obligation to be available. And, he told himself, he had Frannie to think about.

Shopping with Frannie was a useful distraction. They went in the car, to a Sainsbury's superstore a few miles out of Westmead, and spent over an hour pushing the trolley up and down the aisles. Hoping for a quiet life, Tim allowed Frannie to choose whatever she wanted, whether he thought it was a good idea or not: at least, then, she couldn't complain. While she loaded the trolley with appealing treats, he supplemented it with staples, cat litter, and tins of Watson's favourite food.

'And,' he said at the last minute, thinking aloud as they approached the checkout, 'I need to get something to take to Liz tonight. A box of chocolates, I suppose. Or flowers. Or wine.'

Frannie picked up on his words at once. 'Tonight? What's tonight? Who's Liz? Do you have a *date*?' She invested the final word with all the scorn and disapproval she could muster.

'Oh, it's not a date,' he replied quickly. 'Nothing like that, sweetie.'

'Then what?' she demanded, narrowing her eyes at him. 'And what about *me*?'

Tim could have kicked himself; he'd meant to break it to her gently, and now he was at a distinct disadvantage. 'Liz is someone from work,' he explained. 'She's been kind enough to offer to cook a meal for us tonight. For *both* of us, sweetie. It will be fun – you'll see. She's very nice.' He knew, even as he said it, that he was overdoing it.

'Do you love her?' Frannie demanded.

As accustomed as he was to Frannie's directness, the blunt question fazed him a bit; he shook his head. 'No, of course not.'

'Are you sleeping with her?' She made no effort to keep her voice down; if anything, it was growing louder and more shrill with each question.

People were looking at them, smiling. Listening.

Tim crouched down and brought his face level with Frannie's, speaking to her quietly. 'No,' he said. 'I am *not* sleeping with her. Not that it would be any business of yours if I were.'

'Mum is sleeping with Brad,' she announced. 'She thinks I don't know, but I do. They wait till they think

I'm asleep. Sometimes he even pretends to go away, but I can hear him coming back.'

Ten years old, thought Tim with exasperated bemusement, and talking about things like that. When he was ten, he hadn't had a clue. 'It's nothing like that with Liz,' he assured her. 'She's just a friend.'

'Yeah,' said Frannie, unconvinced. 'That's what Mum says, as well. About Brad.'

That afternoon, having packed, Jacquie realised that she didn't have enough money to get her to Westmead. Even though she wouldn't have to pay for accommodation when she'd arrived there, she would need to buy petrol.

By now she'd set her mind on going. In spite of initial reservations, she felt it was the right thing to do: she *must* fight on. If the police weren't going to do anything more than the bare minimum, it was down to her, and she owed it to Alison to go back.

But the money was a problem.

She ran through the possibilities. She could ask Nicola for a loan, but Nicola, she knew, was chronically hard up. She could throw herself on Mr Mockler's mercy, and try to convince him to give her some sort of advance on the inheritance. Not, she reckoned, that he would unbend sufficiently to do so.

And then there was Darren.

Determined as she was not to ask Darren for money, she was beginning to accept that she had little choice.

He could certainly afford it, she told herself. And she'd never asked him for a penny before.

She'd promised herself that she would never stoop so low. But it wasn't for herself: it was for Ally.

Jacquie reached for the phone, fiddling absently with a loose button on her cardigan. At that moment, though, as if in answer to prayer, her subconscious kicked in and she remembered something: her mother's button box.

It had always been kept in her parents' bedroom, in the drawer of her mother's bedside table. She and Ally had been strictly forbidden to touch it, but once in a while, when a special treat was in order, their mother would delve into the button box and come up with a fifty-pence piece or even a pound.

Could there, even now, be money there?

Jacquie went upstairs and found the box exactly where her memory told her that it would be: a cheap tin box, emblazoned with Union Jacks, commemorating the Coronation of the Queen. Just as she remembered it, in those days when its appearance presaged something unexpectedly nice.

She opened it. At first it appeared to contain nothing but buttons. Large and small, old and older. Buttons, and a few small coins. But under the buttons was a piece of card, carefully cut to an exact fit, and when she lifted that she found what she was looking for.

It wasn't a fortune, exactly, but it was certainly more than a few coppers. Five-pound notes, a few tens. More than a hundred pounds, all told. Probably, Jacquie surmised with an intuitive guess, money that her mother had been given as gifts over the years. Her father had never been much of a shopper; he had usually slipped her mother an envelope with a five-pound note on traditional gift-giving occasions like birthdays and Christmas.

And it would be enough to get her to Westmead.

'Thanks, Mum,' Jacquie said aloud, smiling.

* * *

'I would have thought that Madeline would have rung by now,' Chris fretted over tea by the fire, just before he went out to rehearse with the choir for Evensong. 'To tell us what's going on. Or at least to let us know that she's home safely.'

Sophie made no reply. She hadn't forgiven Madeline for running out on her, no matter what the reason. For leaving her alone with Chris, the polite stranger.

'I suppose we could ring *her*,' he suggested. 'Just to make sure she's okay.'

'No,' said Sophie. 'She'll ring. When it suits her.'

And so, when the phone rang a bit later, Sophie assumed that it was her sister. 'Hello,' she muttered.

There was a brief pause on the other end. 'Sophie?' said a hushed female voice. 'Mrs Lilburn?'

'Yes?'

'This is Olive.'

Olive? wondered Sophie.

'Olive Clunch,' she elaborated. 'I hope I'm not disturbing you.'

'Oh, no. I'm not going anywhere.'

'It's just that . . .' the woman's voice trailed off. 'I needed to talk to someone. And I thought of you.'

Sophie was torn between irritation and interest. 'Go on, then,' she said.

'It's about Leslie.'

Yes, it would be, thought Sophie in disappointment.

'Leslie likes you, Mrs Lilburn. Sophie. He talks about you ever so much.'

She couldn't very well say that she liked *him*, so Sophie made a noncommittal noise.

'And he sees a lot of you.'

Sophie wondered, suddenly, if Mrs Clunch was pursuing a round-about way of asking whether she was having an affair with her husband; the idea was so ludicrous as to be laughable, if it hadn't been so nauseating. But how could she say as much, without insulting Olive Clunch?

Mrs Clunch didn't seem to notice her silence, and went on. 'Does he talk much to you about that old murder, then?'

'Why . . . yes. We do talk about it,' acknowledged Sophie, startled out of her suppositions.

'Because ever since that policeman came round the close, he's been acting very . . . well, I don't know. Like he has some secret. Something that he knows and they don't.'

'What do you mean?'

'I can't explain it,' Mrs Clunch admitted. 'But that's how it seems to me. And this morning, when the *Herald* came. He read that article over and over again, sort of smiling to himself. "Alison Barnett," he said. "So now they know." It was as if he already knew it, before they did. How could that be?'

'I'm sure . . .'

'Am I just being silly?' Olive Clunch said. 'I hope so. And I don't know why I'm telling you this, really. I just needed to talk to someone, that's all.'

'That's quite all right,' said Sophie.

But when she'd put the phone down, it was as though Leslie Clunch had invaded the room and refused to go away. As though he were hunkered down in a corner, staring at her. Sophie shivered and moved closer to the fire.

*   *   *

'So this is Frannie,' said Liz brightly.

Frannie handed her a box of chocolates, a stiff smile stretching her mouth. She had insisted on buying the chocolates, and had even chosen them herself, in the not unreasonable hope that she might be offered one before the evening was over. Her father had given her strict instructions on her behaviour; that included smiling, so she was doing her best to comply. 'These are for you, Miss Hollis,' she said, just as her father had coached her. 'Thank you for inviting me.' Already, from the first moment, she knew that she did not like Liz Hollis.

Liz gave a nervous giggle. 'Please, call me Liz. "Miss Hollis" makes me sound so old.'

She *was* old, thought Frannie. Maybe not as old as her dad, but old nonetheless: at least twenty-five. Frannie said nothing.

'And some wine,' Tim said, presenting her with a bottle.

'Come in. Come in.' Liz stood back and let them into her flat.

Obviously her pride and joy, thought Tim: it seemed to have been done up in the style of one of those popular home-decorating programmes on television, with contrasting bright colours on the walls, vivid scatter rugs and cushions, and unusual lighting effects.

Her next words echoed his thoughts. 'I've done it all myself,' she said. 'Sort of a hobby of mine. I love *Home Front* and *Changing Rooms*.'

'Very nice,' Tim assured her.

'Would you like a drink?'

Liz had addressed Tim, but Frannie answered first. 'No, thank you.'

'What do you have?' Tim asked.

'Anything, really. Wine. Sherry. G and T. Whisky. Or some of that beer that you drank the other night. The Czech beer.'

'I'll have the beer, thanks.' Tim was unexpectedly touched that she'd remembered, and had gone to the trouble of getting his favourite beer.

It hadn't passed Frannie by, either. So, she thought, they *had* gone out, and recently as well. Not just work colleagues, then: there was something more to it. She shot her father a baleful glance, which he ignored.

'You're sure you don't want anything, Frannie?' Liz pressed her. 'I have juice, and squash, and Coke, and lemonade, and milk.'

'No, thank you. I'm not thirsty.'

'If you're sure.' Belatedly Liz gestured to the sofa and chairs. 'Please, sit down. I won't be a minute.'

As Liz disappeared into the galley kitchen, Frannie carefully chose a seat in the middle of the sofa. That would prevent them sitting together, she thought. Her father went to one of the chairs, sinking into its overstuffed embrace. 'A bit squishy for my taste,' he whispered to Frannie.

She smiled sweetly. 'Yes, isn't she?'

'Now, Frannie . . .' he warned.

'Yes, I know. You've told me to be nice to her. And I *am* being nice.'

Liz returned with the beer, and a glass of wine for herself. The next few minutes passed in strained conversation, Liz trying to engage Frannie, and Frannie determined not to be engaged.

'What's your favourite subject at school?' Liz asked.

'History.' There was no elaboration. 'And music.'

'Oh, I never cared much for history,' admitted Liz. 'But I like music.' She gestured towards a rack of CDs.

Frannie swept a cursory glance over the collection of pop albums. 'Not that sort of music,' she stated. 'I mean *proper* music.'

'Frannie plays the oboe,' Tim interposed, with a warning glance at his daughter.

'I'd like to play the harp,' Frannie asserted. 'But there isn't enough room at home for a harp. At my mother's house,' she added, making sure that Liz knew she had a mother.

'There wouldn't be enough room here, either,' Liz giggled, with a gesture at the compact room.

Frannie pasted a smile on her face. 'I'm not likely to be moving in here, am I?'

Tim jumped in and changed the subject to something neutral, and Liz gave up on her efforts with Frannie for the time being. But as the time to eat drew closer, she tried again. 'Your father says that you're a . . . well, that you don't like to eat some things. I hope I have something you'll like.' She laughed. 'I was telling him that I have a little sister, and when she was younger, she wouldn't eat anything but frozen pizzas and oven chips for about a year.'

'That must have been boring for her,' Frannie said, watching her father out of the corner of her eye.

Liz smiled. 'And for my mum, as well.'

'*My* mum doesn't mind me eating whatever I want,' Frannie stated.

'What *do* you like to eat, then?'

'It depends,' said Frannie obscurely.

'Well, tonight your father and I are having steak.' Liz

smiled across at Tim, and addressed an aside to him. 'You seemed to enjoy your steak the other night.'

Frannie frowned: the other night again.

'But if you don't like steak, you can have some pasta. Or something else.'

Catching her father's eye, Frannie was docile. 'Steak will be fine. Thank you very much.'

But when it came to it, she mauled the meat round her plate, cut it into tiny bites, and consumed about two of them. She ate all of her potatoes, but none of the other vegetables, and when offered pudding she refused politely. 'I don't care for cheesecake, thank you.'

The chocolates were opened with the after-dinner coffee; those Frannie did not refuse, and it was only after her third one that she paid heed to her father's cautioning glare.

'I've hired some videos, Frannie,' Liz said when she'd cleared the table. 'I thought you might like to watch one.'

Trying to get rid of me, then, Frannie thought. She wasn't having any of that. 'No, thank you,' she said.

Liz sighed. 'You're sure?'

'Sure.'

They moved from the dining alcove back into the sitting room, and Frannie made a dignified dash for the middle of the sofa again. There she sat for the rest of the evening, listening to but taking little part in the stilted conversation of the grown-ups, who were obviously constrained by her presence in the midst of them.

Just the way she wanted it, she thought with satisfaction.

She believed her father when he said that he and Liz weren't sleeping together. But she also trusted in her nascent feminine intuition as she observed the way that Liz looked at her father, and was convinced that if Liz had her way, the situation would change. Clearly, thought Frannie, she had designs on him.

Over my dead body, she said to herself, folding her arms across her thin chest.

Chapter 20

Jacquie stretched, then curled into a ball and luxuriated in the enveloping warmth of the down duvet. In the half-aware state between sleep and waking, she wasn't quite sure where she was; she only knew that she was warm and comfortable, and that she had slept well.

Gradually she remembered: she was in the guest room of the Precentor's House in Quire Close. It was still too dark to pick out the details of the room, but her mind now supplied them. An ancient beamed roof above her, leaded panes in the window, thick-pile carpet on the floor: great age coexisting with modern comfort. And the décor was charming – chintzy, but not too frilly or feminine. Just right.

It was, by far, the nicest room she'd ever slept in; in a different league from the utilitarian austerity of the Cathedral View Guest House; far better, of course, than her spartan bedroom at her parents' house in Sutton Fen, or the one she'd shared with Darren during the years of their marriage. Even on their honeymoon, in the long-ago reaches of history, they hadn't stayed anywhere as delightful and cosy as this.

And her hosts couldn't have been kinder to her if she'd been a close friend or a member of their family. There was no question of her feeling like an intruder, or someone who didn't belong there. She wasn't fussed over – which might have made her uncomfortable – but she was made to feel welcome, and free to stay for as long as she liked. As long as she needed to.

On her arrival, late in the evening, Miranda Swan had given her a simple supper. They had talked for a while, then she'd been shown to this wonderful room and told to sleep as late in the morning as she wanted to – a long lie-in after a tiring journey, if that suited her. Miranda and her husband would be attending services at the cathedral, but Jacquie was under no obligation to join them. If they weren't there when she got up, she was to help herself to breakfast, and make herself at home in the house.

Miranda Swan had looked familiar to Jacquie, as if she'd met her before. Jacquie tried to recall if they had, in fact, met in Sutton Fen, then remembered the Evensong she'd attended at the cathedral the previous week: the pleasant-faced woman across from her. That brought back the memory of that service, and how marvellous it had been, transporting her to another world for an hour. Balm to her soul, it had been, after the ugliness – physical and spiritual – of the Free Baptist Fellowship.

'I'd like to go with you,' she'd said.

'If you're up.' Miranda Swan smiled. 'Don't set your alarm. There will be plenty of opportunities for you to go to the cathedral. Several times a day, if that's what you want to do.'

Jacquie wasn't at all sure, now, what time it was, or what had caused her to wake. It was dark in the room, but that was nothing to go by: the curtains at the window were drawn, and were thick enough to block any amount of daylight.

For a few minutes she snuggled sleepily under the duvet, rejoicing in its embracing warmth. Then she reached for the clock on the bedside table. It was just past eight o'clock. Plenty of time, then, to spare before the service.

Eventually she got out of bed and went to the window, pulling back the heavy curtains. The room faced south, looking directly down Quire Close towards the cathedral. Before she'd gone to bed she'd stood there for a while and contemplated it, flood-lit and mist-shrouded.

Now, though, it was completely different: the weather had cleared. Miraculously, as on her first morning in Westmead, the sky was a limpid blue, and the early sun bathed the cathedral in light, its stones glowing golden. Infinitely beautiful, infinitely welcoming.

Sunday was a day on which Sophie scarcely ever saw anything of Chris, with choral services at the cathedral both morning and evening. Once she had found that regrettable, and had resented it; now it was a relief.

But time, that morning, was hanging heavy on her hands. She was unable to concentrate on reading, and there was certainly nothing on the telly.

Madeline, she thought, her conscience pricking her. She really ought to ring Madeline and find out what was wrong.

Sophie picked up the phone. More than an hour later she put it down again, shaken.

Madeline hadn't really wanted to talk to her, hadn't wanted to tell her, but eventually she had broken down and blurted it all out.

Victoria was pregnant. Tori, her perfect daughter, not yet even sixteen, was pregnant.

They hadn't had a clue, she and Geoffrey. They'd thought Simon was such a nice young man, from a good family. Polite, wholesome. And they were so young, Tori and Simon. Far too young to be having sex, or even thinking about it; when Madeline had been that age, such things couldn't have been further from her mind. She'd enjoyed the admiration of boys, and their company – no more than that.

But Tori and Simon had been having sex, and plenty of it: it wasn't just a one-off, her daughter had informed her bluntly, now that the truth was inescapable. All the while they'd been at it like rabbits. In the stables, in the fields, in the woods, even in Tori's room. Madeline's daughter, and that wretched, treacherous young man. Tori had seemed to take pleasure in telling her the details, as if she wanted to hurt her.

She'd trusted her daughter, trusted in her youth and her good up-bringing, as well as in her common sense. It hadn't even crossed her mind to talk to Tori about contraception or safe sex.

And when she'd started putting on a bit of weight, they'd thought nothing of it. Tori was, after all, spending more time with Simon and less time riding her horse; she wasn't getting as much exercise these days. The extra weight suited her, adding a flattering fullness to her face and a roundness to her young curves.

Now it was all horribly clear.

In her mother's absence, Tori had confided in her father, perhaps counting on him to be more understanding.

He had rung Madeline straight away. She had rushed home.

But what were they to do?

Tori was far too young to be having a baby, Madeline sobbed. She was only just coming up to her GCSEs. She would be sitting her mocks after Christmas, but by the time the exams rolled round in the spring, she would have a baby.

An abortion was out of the question: she was too far along, and Tori wouldn't consider such a thing anyway.

And at their ages, they could scarcely get married, even if they wanted to: Tori not yet sixteen, Simon barely seventeen. Even with their parents' consent, it would be a ludicrous travesty of a marriage.

Gone were the days when one could ship an embarrassment like a pregnant daughter off to a home somewhere, to return a few months later without the baby, and resume life as if nothing had happened. These days that just didn't happen.

But what were the alternatives? Tori was adamant that she wasn't going to give her baby away to some stranger. She would have the baby; she would keep it.

Tori's young life, as far as Madeline could see, was over. She had no future.

And Madeline would not be able to hold her head up.

That, thought Sophie as she hung up the phone, was the crux of the matter as far as Madeline was concerned.

She would be inconvenienced, and worse yet, the situation reflected badly on *her*.

It just wasn't fair, Sophie reflected, tears of longing stinging her throat like a draught of bitter medicine. The last thing a young girl like that needed was a baby, yet one was on the way.

While she, with her useless body . . .

Two doors down, as if on cue, the baby started screaming.

It was Monday morning before Jacquie could bring herself to ring Sergeant Merriday. She expected him to be angry with her, after what she'd said to the journalist, so the first thing she did was apologise, in as conciliatory way as she could manage.

'I hope I didn't get you into trouble with your boss,' she said.

'What do you think?' His voice was stony, taking her aback; she wasn't quite prepared for that.

'I didn't mean it personally. I know that you tried to help me. But I was angry. I felt that . . . well, I was feeling let down.'

Tim was not ready to accept her apology, nor to enter into any discussion of her state of mind. He'd had a tremendous dressing-down from the Superintendent first thing that morning; if there'd ever been any chance of changing his boss's mind about the scope of the investigation, or his possible involvement in it, it was now gone. He was still smarting, blaming her and her intemperate and ill-considered words to Barry Sills. 'What can I do for you?' he asked coldly.

'I just wanted to let you know that I've come back to

Westmead. I'm staying with the Precentor and his wife, in Quire Close.' Then, lest he think that she assumed he would have any personal interest in her whereabouts, she added, 'When you get the death certificate, perhaps you could let me know, and I could collect it from you. I'll give you the number.'

'Thank you.' Tim reached for his pencil and pressed hard into the paper as he took the number down. 'Is there anything else?'

Jacquie hesitated, in view of his hostility, but felt that she owed it to him to tell him of her change of heart. 'Yes, actually. I wanted to let you know that . . . well, I've changed my mind about what I said to that journalist.'

'In what way?'

'I said that there was nothing more I could do, that as far as I was concerned, the police had bungled it, and that was an end to it.'

'I remember,' he said. 'I remember the exact words, in fact. The Superintendent has tattooed them on my back-side.'

'Oh,' she said in a small, contrite voice.

He wasn't going to make it easy for her, Tim was determined; she certainly hadn't made it easy for *him*. He gripped the phone, waiting for her to go on.

'I've decided,' she said at last, 'that I'm *not* giving up. If the police won't investigate it properly, I owe it to my sister to try to find the person who killed her.'

'Don't be so bloody stupid,' he snapped. 'How do you think you'll manage that? If we haven't been able to? You have no resources, no means of carrying out any sort of investigation. All you'll do is muddy the waters.' His pencil was working furiously. 'And, as you keep reminding me, there's someone out there who's got away with murder for eleven years – it seems to me that if you start poking around in this, without knowing what you're doing, he might think it worthwhile to get rid of you as well. Do you think that would be doing your sister any favours?'

Jacquie caught her breath at the cold anger in his voice, his words like a shower of ice. He was right, of course: there wasn't really anything meaningful that she could do, and her interference could be dangerous. But she wasn't about to admit it, least of all to him; she wouldn't give him the satisfaction. 'That's my decision, I think,' she stated, her tone matching his.

'Very well, Mrs Darke. I'll let you know when I've heard from the coroner. Unless you happen to see him first.' Tim paused, and delivered his parting shot before slamming the phone down. 'Or vice versa.'

The sun on Sunday had been a temporary aberration in the weather; by Monday the rains had returned.

Sophie was alone in the house. Chris had agonised a bit, suggesting that perhaps he ought to make arrangements for a supply teacher for a few days, but she had assured him that she would be all right on her own, and he hadn't pressed the issue.

There were, however, a few items of shopping that she needed. 'I'll try to pop out between school and choir practice to get them,' Chris promised.

After the breakfast cereal, though, the shortage of milk had become critical; Sophie even considered ringing Jeremy or Trish Evans and asking for the loan of a pint. But before she could do that, the phone rang, and Leslie Clunch, as if reading her mind, offered to pick up anything she might need. 'I'm doing some shopping for Mrs Clunch,' he said, 'so it wouldn't be any trouble at all.'

She accepted his offer with mingled relief and reluctance; it would, after all, mean that he would have to deliver the things to her, and would reasonably expect to be entertained to a cup of coffee, at the very least.

For once, though, luck was with her. 'I can't stay,' he said, handing the bag of shopping in through the door, his face glowing with self-importance. 'I have quite a big afternoon ahead. A school party visiting the cathedral – I've been asked to lead the tour.'

So, that afternoon, when the doorbell rang, she had not even a momentary hesitation in going to the door: it couldn't possibly, she thought, be Leslie Clunch.

In her weakened condition, she moved slowly, and before she reached the door the bell rang again, twice in rapid succession, followed by a frantic hammering. 'I'm coming,' Sophie called.

To her utter astonishment, the person on the doorstep was Mrs Clunch.

Olive Clunch stood there in the streaming rain, an old coat thrown round her shoulders over her pink nightgown. Her massive tree-trunk legs were bare, and she wore slippers on her feet. She was clutching something to her chest; her teeth were chattering with a combination of cold, wet, and terror.

'Come in,' said Sophie quickly to the unexpected apparition, drawing her inside.

'I'm sorry. I'm sorry,' murmured Olive Clunch. She dripped water on the flagstones of the entrance hall as if rooted to the spot, seemingly unable to move any further.

Driven by practicalities, Sophie recovered from her

surprise sufficiently to strip off the wet coat from the woman's shoulders and find a blanket to wrap her in. 'Come in here,' she urged, leading her into the front room.

'I'm sorry, I'm sorry.' The words were repeated again, through chattering teeth, like a mantra. Water squished from her slippers on to the carpet. 'I'm sorry.' But she allowed herself to be seated next to the fireplace.

There wasn't a fire; Sophie hadn't had the energy to bother with one. But Chris had laid it, so a few minutes of effort with matches produced a nice cheery blaze, and provided Mrs Clunch with some time to collect herself. She edged nearer to the fire, still clasping whatever it was she was carrying to her damp chest.

'Would you like something hot to drink?' Sophie offered.

'No.' Olive Clunch shook her head; water dripped from her hair.

'Are you all right, Mrs Clunch?' What on earth had brought her out on a day like this? Sophie wondered, baffled. And to her house, of all places? For that matter, she had been under the impression that Olive Clunch was unable to walk at all.

'So sorry to bother you,' said the woman.

This wasn't getting anywhere. 'Tell me why you've come,' Sophie said bluntly. 'You're obviously distressed. I'd like to help you. But you'll have to tell me what's the matter.'

The teeth-chattering dissolved into sobs, tears mingling with rain on Olive Clunch's round, wobbly face. 'I didn't know where else to go,' she gasped. 'I didn't know who else to talk to. I thought of you.'

'Tell me,' Sophie repeated. She crouched on the floor

at the woman's feet, in spite of the discomfort to herself, as she felt her stitches pulling. 'Tell me what's happened.'

'Leslie,' choked Mrs Clunch. 'He's gone out.'

'Yes, I know.' Maybe, thought Sophie, Mrs Clunch was ill; maybe she needed something urgently – some medicine, perhaps – and had panicked without her husband there to look after her. But why, then, this mad dash through the pouring rain? Why not just pick up the phone and ring the doctor?

Gradually, with much prompting and through copious tears, the story came out.

For some time, Olive Clunch said, she'd thought that her husband was hiding something. The secret smiles to himself whenever he came down from the first floor, the general air of knowing more than she – more than anyone – had conveyed themselves to her. But her gentle probing had met with no success.

Everyone, her husband included, thought that she couldn't walk at all, explained Mrs Clunch. She had fooled them; she had fooled *him*. While he was away on his frequent shopping expeditions, his visits to Sophie, his trips to the cathedral, she had practised. One step at first, then two, and now, though it was painful and difficult, she could manage quite a bit more than that.

And today, just now, she had chosen her moment, knowing that he would be occupied for the better part of the afternoon at the cathedral.

She had, for the first time since they'd moved to Quire Close, ascended the stairs to the first floor of the house, dragging herself up with the aid of the bannister, one agonising step at a time.

There she had found the room where her husband slept:

the room with the window overlooking the length of Quire Close, the window where he spent so much time. It was a small room, meanly furnished with no more than a narrow bed, a chair and a chest of drawers.

And in the bottom drawer, she had found what she was looking for.

Magazines, she said with a face mirroring her distress. Nasty magazines, full of disgusting photos. Photos of young girls, mostly, with no clothes on, doing things that a decent person couldn't even mention. Couldn't even imagine, come to that.

'And this,' she said, unclasping her arms at last.

Sophie took the object from her: it was a small book, cheaply made, with a shiny purple cover bearing the words 'My diary'. It had a clasp and a lock, which was secure, but the flap which would have held the book shut had been cut.

Trembling, she opened it to the fly-leaf. 'The private journal of Alison Barnett,' Sophie read aloud in a whisper. 'April 1989.'

Jacquie had received word from Tim Merriday, in the form of a message phoned through to Miranda Swan, that he hoped to have the death certificate ready for her that afternoon; she was to come to his office at four to collect it.

She spent the first part of the afternoon alone in the cathedral, exploring its vast spaces and drinking in the atmosphere. There was a noisy school party having a tour, but this didn't spoil it for her; it only emphasised that it was a living place, with none of the sterile deadness of the Free Baptist Fellowship's ugly building. Here was beauty, here was life. 'I am so privileged to live here,' Miranda

Swan had told her, and Jacquie knew what she meant. After Sutton Fen, anything would seem pleasant by comparison, but this . . . this was bliss. 'I never take it for granted,' Miranda had added. 'Not for a single day. Not for a single moment. I'm so lucky.'

She *was* lucky. Jacquie was not normally an envious person, but she admitted to herself that she was envious of Miranda Swan. Not only had she managed to escape from Sutton Fen, but she had a husband who adored her, who was utterly devoted to her: you had only to see them together to realise that. They were absorbed in each other to a degree that she and Darren had never been, not even in the early days of their marriage. Generous as they were with their hospitality, gracious and attentive as they were to her as their guest, they had a way of looking at each other that made her feel like an intruder upon something sacred and private.

And she envied that, above all. It was something that she would never have, Jacquie told herself. Something that she would never experience.

She looked at her watch: it was time to be getting on to the police station.

Jacquie was not looking forward to the experience, after her last conversation with Sergeant Merriday.

The way was now familiar to her, and she recognised the girl at the desk, who nodded at her with a superior smile. 'Upstairs,' the girl said. 'You know where to go, I expect.'

She plodded up the stairs, dripping water from her umbrella, steeling herself for the sight of him. She hadn't seen Tim Merriday since that afternoon in Quire Close; she didn't want to see him now. He despised her, and who could blame him? She had undermined his career, had made things difficult for him when he was trying to help her. Yes, he'd let her down, but was that really his fault? He'd wanted to help her, and he'd tried his best; she had repaid him with ingratitude on a massive, public scale. She realised now how irresponsible she had been in speaking to the journalist as she had, but it was too late. Too late to apologise: he would never forgive her now.

The door was ajar; she knocked.

'Come in,' piped a voice which definitely did not belong to Tim Merriday.

There was a young girl sitting in the chair behind Sergeant Merriday's desk, swinging back and forth on its swivel seat. 'Hi,' she said. 'My dad's not here. I think he'll be back in a minute.'

Jacquie took in the girl's colouring, the features so like Tim's, and her heart did an unexpected flip-flop. 'You must be Frannie,' she said impulsively.

The girl smiled, and it transformed her face. 'How do you know that?'

Jacquie couldn't help smiling back. 'Your father mentioned you to me.'

Frannie gestured hospitably to the other chair. 'You know my dad, then.'

'Yes.' The smile left Jacquie's face as she sat. 'Yes, I know him.'

'He'll be back pretty soon. He's left me in charge of his office. At least that's what he said,' the girl grinned. 'I expect he just didn't want me tagging along after him, getting in his way.'

'But I thought . . .' Jacquie felt that she was at a disadvantage. 'I thought that you lived with your mother.'

'I do. But Mum's gone on holiday with Brad. He's her boyfriend.' The word was invested with suitable scorn. 'Her horrible boyfriend. So I'm staying with Dad for a fortnight. I expect he thinks I'm a nuisance.'

'I'm sure he doesn't,' Jacquie said. 'When he told me about you, I could tell that he thinks you're very special.'

Frannie narrowed her eyes and gave her a measured, appraising look. 'Do you like him?' she asked bluntly.

Startled, Jacquie surprised herself by saying, 'Why . . . why, yes, I do.'

'Do you think he's good-looking?'

This, Jacquie realised, was a dangerous question: the girl resembled him so much, a fact of which she was surely aware, so the answer would inevitably reflect upon Frannie as well. 'Well,' she said carefully, 'he has a very nice face. A very pleasant face.'

'That Liz person fancies him, you know,' Frannie stated.

'Liz?'

'That woman. The one downstairs. Who works here.' She pulled a face. 'She's all over him, like a bad rash.'

That one, thought Jacquie, remembering the young woman's proprietary tone of voice when referring to Tim. It caused an unwelcome twinge which she did her best to suppress: what did it have to do with her, after all? Tim Merriday was nothing to her.

Frannie lowered her voice without tempering its tone. 'I don't like her,' she said firmly. 'Do you?'

'I don't really know her,' Jacquie temporised, then caught a look of cynical amusement on Frannie's face so reminiscent of Tim that she couldn't help herself. 'But I'm sure if I did know her better, I'd probably dislike her as well.'

Frannie gave a hoot of delighted laughter, just as her father walked into the office.

It seemed to Tim, in that first instant, that the two of them – his daughter and Jacquie Darke – were fast friends, united in some way that he couldn't begin to understand. What could possibly have happened in the few minutes he'd been away? He was at a loss, all the more so because with Frannie there, he couldn't tell Jacquie Darke what he thought of her and her recent behaviour. 'Mrs Darke,' he said, as politely as he could manage, 'thank you for coming in.'

'Not at all,' she replied in kind.

Frannie looked back and forth between them, like a spectator at a tennis match, waiting for what would happen next.

'Frannie, would you mind giving me my chair back?' her father said. 'I'll let you have some money and you can go to the Coke machine and get something to drink.'

'I don't like Coke, Dad,' she reminded him. 'I don't like the way it fizzes up my nose.'

'Well, go and get a chocolate bar, then.'

She got up from his chair and took the money from his outstretched hand, but still she hesitated. 'How about if I just sit here in the corner?' she suggested. 'I promise I won't say anything.'

He hadn't been looking at her; his eyes had been fixed on the woman in the other chair. Now he turned to Frannie impatiently. 'No. I need to talk to Mrs Darke, and I don't need you here while I do it. You can occupy yourself for a few minutes, sweetie. Go downstairs and talk to Liz – I'm sure that she'd be happy to have a chat.'

'Yeah.' Frannie rolled her eyes at Jacquie; Jacquie

covered her mouth with her hand to smother a totally unexpected giggle.

Tim put his hands in his pockets and waited while Frannie took her departure. 'See ya,' she said to Jacquie, waggling her fingers.

'Yes. It was nice to meet you, Frannie.'

'You, too.'

By now Tim was even more baffled. He closed the door behind Frannie and went behind his desk to his chair, feeling that it gave him a bit more of an edge. Across from him, Jacquie was smiling. 'What,' he said to her, attempting to sound severe but managing only bafflement, 'was that all about, then?'

'You wouldn't understand.' On her part, she tried to look serious, and failed. 'Your daughter. She's a real character, isn't she?'

'Yes.'

He'd intended to give her a lecture, to dress her down as he'd been dressed down by the Superintendent. But facing her now, with that smile softening her face, he couldn't do it. His own heart lifted absurdly, and he found himself smiling back at her. Then he remembered the real reason for her visit; that sobered him, and his face sagged.

'I'm sorry,' he said, 'that I was delayed.' He took an envelope out of his jacket pocket and put it on the desk between them. 'But things turned out to be a bit more complicated than I'd anticipated.'

'How so?' She, too, was suddenly grave.

'I told you that the coroner promised me an amended copy of the death certificate. But when he finally got round to talking to the registrar, he found out that it wasn't as straightforward as he'd thought. It seems that once a death certificate has been filed, it can't legally be amended.'

'I don't understand.' Jacquie frowned.

'The name on the death certificate is "Unknown Female",' he said. 'And that can't be changed. The registrar was clear about that.'

'Then what am I to do?' She wouldn't be able to sell the house, she thought in a panic; she wouldn't be able to touch any of her father's money. She was trapped: she would have to live in that house for the rest of her life, get a job to support herself . . . Jacquie swallowed a lump in her throat, on the verge of tears.

'Oh, there's a way round it,' he assured her. 'And I've taken care of it. The coroner has sworn an affidavit, which he's attached to the death certificate. It says that he is satisfied that the person identified as 'Unknown Female' was in fact Alison Rebekah Barnett, and that he would be willing to attest to that in a court of law.' Tim slid the certificate out of the envelope and unfolded it. 'So that should be good enough for your solicitor. And you should be able to get your hands on your money.'

The gentleness, the concern in his voice nearly undid her. 'Thank you,' she said quietly. 'Thanks for all your trouble. You didn't need to . . .'

'Yes, I did. It's part of my job.' Tim forced himself to look out of the window, down at his desk – anywhere but at Jacquie Darke's face.

She reached out her hand and took the death certificate, her thoughts in turmoil. This piece of paper meant that she would now be able to claim her inheritance, but it also meant that she was holding the concrete proof that her sister was legally, irretrievably, dead.

* * *

'Who is she?' asked Frannie, elaborately casual. She had waited for her moment: in the car, on their way home.

Tim's mind was on the traffic. 'Who's who?'

'That woman. The one in your office this afternoon. You called her Mrs Darke.'

'Well, that's who she is. Mrs Darke.' He put on his left indicator and watched the line of oncoming cars for a break.

'Is there a *Mr* Darke, then?'

He gave her a distracted answer. 'Jacquie Darke is divorced. Not that it's any of your business. Or mine, for that matter.'

'Do you think she's pretty?'

Tim shot his daughter a quick look, eyebrows raised, before returning his attention to the other cars. 'Yes,' he said slowly, 'I do.' After a moment he amended it. 'Maybe not exactly pretty. But attractive, certainly.'

'How do you know her, then?'

Why, he wondered, was she giving him the third degree? 'I'm a policeman, sweetie. I know a lot of people.'

'Has she done something bad? Is that why you know her?'

He smiled, not looking at his daughter. 'That isn't why I know her, but as a matter of fact she *has* done something bad. Something very bad, that's got me in trouble.'

Frannie's face fell momentarily, but she persisted. 'Maybe she didn't mean it.'

'She probably didn't,' Tim admitted.

'So you like her anyway,' Frannie said, craftily casting it in the form of a statement rather than a question.

There was a break in traffic; Tim swung the car across

the road on to a less-populated side street. 'Yes,' he said at last. 'Yes, I suppose I do.'

Frannie turned her head away from him and smiled a secret smile out of the window.

For the first time since Dominic had begun visiting her in the afternoons, Sophie hoped that he wouldn't come. She had too much on her mind, too much to think about.

But come he did. He stirred the fire, he made the tea, he settled down for a chat. Somehow Sophie managed to attend to him, to carry on a normal conversation with him for a respectable amount of time.

He must have sensed, though, that something was not quite right. After the second pot of tea, he looked at her closely. 'You seem tired,' he said in a solicitous manner. 'Do you think you need a bit of rest? A nap?'

Sophie tried not to show her relief. 'Yes,' she admitted. 'I *am* tired. I think I could do with a rest.'

But when he'd gone, she didn't go upstairs to lie down. She curled up in the chair and gave herself over to her thoughts.

Olive Clunch's visit had shaken her deeply, raising so many questions in her mind that she couldn't deal with them all at once.

The diary. Mrs Clunch had allowed her to look through it, though she'd by no means had time to read it all. From what she'd seen, it was much of a muchness: page after page of large, loopy handwriting, agonising over the pains and joys of love. 'I know that Mike loves me. But why doesn't he ring? Why doesn't he write? Why doesn't he come?' That was the gist of most of it, interspersed with rapt descriptions of Mike's charms, heavily influenced by, it would seem, if not cribbed from, Mills and Boon romances: 'His eyes are like sapphires, and his teeth are like pearls. When he touched me, I thought that I would die of happiness.' Pretty turgid stuff, by any standards. Whatever else Alison Barnett might have been, she certainly hadn't been a poet.

Mike: obviously Michael Thornley, then. No wonder the police had been asking questions about him.

It wasn't really the content of the diary, though, or even its confirmation of the involvement of Michael Thornley, that interested Sophie: what captured her attention was its very existence, and the fact that it had been sitting in Leslie Clunch's chest of drawers for – how long? Eleven years?

Where had he obtained it? Why had he kept it?

Why, indeed, had he not turned it over to the police?

If the police had had that diary, they would have known, eleven years ago, the name of the dead girl. Alison Barnett, written on the fly-leaf. How different things might have been if they'd known that.

The probable answer to her first question occurred to her early on: he had had the girl's suitcase in his keeping; he had turned it over to the police after the body was found. But what if, before handing it over to them, he had opened it, and taken the diary? That's what must have happened, Sophie realised.

But why?

Two possibilities occurred to her.

The less unpleasant answer was in keeping with everything that Sophie had discovered, and intuited, about the man since she'd first known him: he was a voyeur, of the nastiest sort. He got his jollies from spying on other people, from looking at Sophie's legs, from reading (if that was the word) pornographic magazines. From poring over the love diary of a naïve young girl?

But the other possibility was too strong to be denied, and it gave Sophie the chills to think about it.

What if he had killed her? What if Leslie Clunch had murdered Alison Barnett, and had taken her diary – and perhaps other things as well – from her suitcase so that she would not be identified? What if he'd kept it as a trophy, as murderers from time immemorial had done?

Surely the suspicion must have crossed Olive Clunch's mind from the moment she'd stumbled across the diary. Why else would she have fled her house in the rain, running to show her find to a woman she scarcely knew? Why, if she hadn't suspected her husband of the most heinous of crimes?

But after she'd told Sophie her story, after she'd calmed down a bit, she had refused to entertain any such suggestion. She was sure, she said, that there must be a logical explanation for it. Leslie had found the diary somewhere; he hadn't realised its significance.

And she had made Sophie promise that she would tell no one about what she'd shown her, or what she'd said.

She had extracted a promise from her that she would not go to the police. 'They'd arrest him,' she'd said, with some truth. 'They'd take him off to gaol, and then where would I be?'

Sophie had tried to argue with her. 'The police need to know. It's important.'

'They're not interested,' Olive Clunch had pointed out. 'You must have read what that girl's sister said in the paper.

Why muddy the waters now? Leslie didn't do it. He couldn't have done it. I know him. So why cause such a fuss for nothing?'

Sophie didn't believe that it was nothing. Even if he hadn't killed the girl, he was guilty of obstruction of justice; Alison Barnett would have been identified eleven years ago, and her murderer might have been found, if he hadn't taken and concealed her diary.

In spite of it all, though, and against her better judgement, she had been forced to go along with Olive Clunch, however reluctantly.

'If you tell anyone, I'll deny it,' Mrs Clunch had said at last. 'I'll deny that I was ever here. I'll deny that there was a diary. I'll destroy it, if I have to. But I'm not letting them take Leslie away.'

The more she thought about it, the more Sophie could see where Olive Clunch was coming from. Her momentary panic, which had brought her so extraordinarily to Sophie's doorstep, had given way to self-interest as she realised how very vulnerable and alone she would be if anything happened to her husband.

Sophie had promised, and knew that she had to abide by that promise.

The room was getting chilly; the fire had died down to grey embers and was in need of attention, but Sophie didn't have the energy to get up. Shivering, she reached for the blanket in which she'd wrapped Olive Clunch. It was still damp, but she didn't care as she huddled into it.

Alison Barnett's face, long-imagined from the descriptions she'd read of the dead girl, floated into her mind. Blonde, pretty, plump.

Dead.

Had the last sight she'd seen, as the life was choked out of her, been the face of Leslie Clunch?

And then she remembered another dead girl. Another dead girl who had also been blonde, pretty, and plump.

A finger of cold fear crept up Sophie's spine.

It wasn't the first time the question had occurred to her, but now it had an added urgency, an additional frisson. What, she wondered, had happened to Charmian Clunch?

Chapter 21

Given the stresses of the day before, Jacquie had slept far better than she would have expected, and woke refreshed, unable to remember whether she'd had any dreams, good or bad. She found that she was thinking about Frannie Merriday: cheeky little monkey, she reflected, smiling involuntarily. That girl must make her father's life very interesting.

Snuggled under the duvet, Jacquie was beginning to contemplate getting up, when there was a gentle tap on the door.

'Come in,' she invited sleepily.

Miranda Swan pushed the door open and peeked in. 'I wondered whether you might like a cup of tea.'

'Lovely.' Jacquie sighed. 'I'm getting spoiled, you know. I won't want to go home.'

'You don't *have* to go home just yet. You can stay as long as you like.' Miranda put the steaming cup on the bedside table. In her pink quilted dressing gown, her curly hair tousled, she looked almost girlish.

Struggling into a sitting position, Jacquie reached for

the cup. 'I have to take the death certificate to Mr Mockler.'

'Mr Mockler.' Miranda pulled a face. 'That toad.' He had, she'd told Jacquie, acted for Kenneth Forrest in their divorce. Solicitor of choice for the True Men, it would seem. One of their number.

Jacquie giggled at the aptness of the description. 'I hate Sutton Fen,' she said passionately. 'And everyone in it. Especially Mr Mockler.'

'Don't stop there,' urged Miranda. 'Don't forget the Reverend Mr Prew.'

'Him most of all. And Darren,' Jacquie added.

Miranda sat down on the edge of the bed. 'You won't have to live in Sutton Fen any longer, you know. As soon as you've sorted out the money, you'll be free to go anywhere that you like.'

'I can't *wait* to get away from there,' Jacquie said passionately. 'Anywhere would be better than Sutton Fen.' But where? Once, she remembered, she'd thought that she might settle in Westmead. With Ally. But Ally was dead, and she had nothing to tie her to this place. Nothing . . .

As if reading her thoughts, Miranda went on in a thoughtful voice, 'I've told you that I love living in Westmead. I love Peter. I love the cathedral. I love *not* living in Sutton Fen.' She smiled wryly. 'This is where I want to be. But to be perfectly honest, Jacquie, I've had my problems here as well. You can't always escape from your problems, just by moving away from them.'

'Problems? You've had problems?'

Not looking at Jacquie, she traced the pattern of the duvet cover with one finger. 'Sutton Fen doesn't have the exclusive rights to being judgemental, in spite of what you might think,' she said reflectively. 'At first, it was fine here. People were welcoming and kind. It seemed like heaven. But when they found out about my divorce . . . Well, you would have thought I was a convicted murderer, or something equally terrible. I've been rather an outcast since then. Shunned. Uninvited to parties, stared at in the street.'

'I don't believe it,' Jacquie said. 'Who would care about something like that?'

'It's true.' Miranda raised her head and looked at her. 'It's partly the circumstances, I think – the fact that Peter and I . . . knew each other . . . before my divorce. Most people don't care, I'm sure. But a cathedral is a funny sort of place, with its own rules.'

'Like the Free Baptist Fellowship.'

'Rather like that,' Miranda agreed. 'And the thing about Westmead is that Elspeth Verey, the widow of the previous dean, seems to set all of the rules. She's decided that I'm unacceptable, and everyone else follows along.'

'But that's horrible!' Jacquie said warmly. 'Who does she think she is?'

'She's the *grande dame*. She's the arbiter.' Miranda sounded philosophical rather than bitter.

'No better than Reverend Prew!'

Miranda nodded. 'She has a bit more polish, a bit more subtlety, but the effect is the same.'

'How can you bear it? If no one talks to you . . .'

'I have Peter,' Miranda said simply, her face shining with transparent love. 'He makes up for everything.'

Jacquie fiddled with her teacup, embarrassed.

'And I have that building,' Miranda added. 'That sublimely beautiful building. The cathedral. I look out of my window and see it, and know that nothing on earth could be more wonderful than living in its shadow.'

She got up from the bed and went to the window, drawing back the curtains. The houses of Quire Close stretched out on either side, and at the end of the close, beyond the arch and towering over it, the cathedral shimmered in the morning mist, golden and grey and almost alive.

Sophie had been abstracted and terse with Chris in the evening, but if he had noticed it, he wouldn't have found it particularly out of keeping with her recent behaviour. These days they tended to stick to safe subjects: what to eat, whether to turn the television on, the continuing dreariness of the weather. Sophie hadn't even told him of her conversation with Madeline; the injustice of the situation – of Tori's pregnancy – was still too painful to discuss, and in any case it had been eclipsed in her own mind by more recent events.

In the morning, though, before he left for school, she asked him a question. 'Do you know anything about Leslie Clunch's daughter? How long ago she died, perhaps?'

He looked at her, surprised. 'I didn't even know that old Clunch had a daughter. Let alone that she was dead.'

Sophie sighed. 'Typical.'

'He's your friend, not mine.'

'He is *not* my friend,' protested Sophie.

Chris shook his head. 'I never have understood why you're so hard on him. He seems like a perfectly nice old man to me. And he's obviously very keen on *you*.'

He didn't understand – that was the problem. Chris didn't understand anything, including the fact that the only reason she put up with Clunch's visits was because of Chris.

But she didn't say it: it would only lead to another row, and that was the last thing she wanted.

Peter Swan had taken the early communion service in the cathedral, and was expected home for breakfast at any moment. The Precentor had a good appetite most of the time, but always seemed to be particularly hungry after the eight o'clock communion service; Miranda liked to indulge him with a cooked breakfast on those occasions when he was on duty.

'I don't go overboard, though,' she told Jacquie just before he arrived. 'I give him a poached egg on whole-meal toast, or a boiled egg. No fry-ups, though he'd dearly love to have one.' She smiled. 'It's taken me long enough to find him, and I don't want to lose him just yet because of one too many cholesterol binges.'

'What can I do to help?'

'Just sit down and have some coffee,' said Miranda. 'But don't, whatever you do, touch Peter's newspaper.'

Jacquie looked curiously at the copy of *The Times*, folded neatly by the Precentor's place at table. 'Why not?'

'Because,' said Miranda indulgently, 'he likes to read it over breakfast, and it has to be untouched by human hands. That's one of the little antisocial habits left over from his many years as a bachelor that I've had to learn to live with.'

Ah, thought Jacquie: then all is not quite perfection. The realisation gave her an obscure sort of satisfaction, mingled with disappointment.

Having divested himself of his damp clerical cloak, Peter Swan came into the kitchen in his cassock, greeted the two women, accepted a cup of coffee from his wife, then settled down at the table with his newspaper while he waited for his egg to poach. He scanned the headlines on the front page, making little tutting noises which were not meant to elicit any response, then opened it to the next page.

The quality of his tuts changed; he broke into a low whistle. 'Look at this,' he said. 'Here's something you'll both be interested in.'

He spread the paper out on the table so the women could see it. At the top of page three, spread across the width of the page, was a headline: 'Evangelical Pastor Caught in Love Nest with Secretary'. Below the headline were two large colour photos, unmistakable and familiar: one of the outside of the Free Baptist Fellowship, and the other of the black-bearded visage of Reverend Prew.

'Oh, God,' gasped Jacquie. 'What does it say?'

Peter Swan leaned over and read aloud: '"The Reverend Raymond Prew, pastor of the Free Baptist Fellowship in the Cambridgeshire fenland town of Sutton Fen, and more widely known for his role as the founder of the True Men movement, is in hiding at an undisclosed location, following revelations that he has been carrying on an illicit relationship with his secretary for several years, setting her up in what church officials describe as a 'love nest'.

'"Mr Prew, who is forty-seven, is married, and the father of eight children ranging in age from two to fifteen. He has been the pastor of the Free Baptist Fellowship, a nonconformist congregation with no formal ties to any denomination, for nineteen years.

'"In recent years he has been prominent on a wider stage, founding and heading the True Men organisation. This movement promulgates the strict Biblical view of the headship of men and the subservience of women, encouraging men to find their 'true selves' by exercising 'headship' over their wives, thus 'allowing' their wives to become 'true wives'. The organisation has, since its beginnings, been a target of feminist groups, who charge that it subjugates and degrades women.

'"The secretary, who cannot be named for legal reasons, is thought to be a twenty-one-year-old woman from Sutton Fen. Police are currently investigating allegations from an unnamed source that Mr Prew's affair with the woman began some years ago, when she was under the age of consent. It is possible, pending the results of the investigation, that charges could be filed against Mr Prew.

'"Sutton Fen is now a town in shock, finding it difficult to come to terms with the gap between the public face of Raymond Prew, and what he did in private. 'Everybody always thought Reverend Prew was so holy,' said one woman, who asked that her name not be used. 'Holier-than-thou, really. Just goes to show you.'

'"The Free Baptist Fellowship is, in the light of the revelations, in disarray; no one there was available for comment. And at the Manse, Mrs Esther Prew refused to speak to reporters.

'"But the True Men movement appears to be on a firmer footing. Mr Prew's chief deputy, Darren Darke, has taken over the running of the organisation. 'We are naturally very distressed,' Mr Darke commented. 'Everyone in our movement looked up to Reverend Prew. We realise that he's only human, of course, and subject to the same temptations as everyone else. But that is no excuse. As our leader, he had a responsibility to us, as well as to God's laws. We cannot condone in any way what he has done, though of course we will be praying for him as our Christian brother.'

'"Mr Darke went on to say, 'We cannot allow this set-back to destroy the True Men movement. Reverend Prew was our founder, but the True Men are bigger than just one man. We shall be carrying on, in the spirit of hope, doing God's will in this place.'

'"At this moment, it is not known how Mr Prew's affair came to light. It is rumoured that someone in the church received a 'tip-off' from an anonymous source.

'"Background checks on Raymond Prew have revealed that, though he styles himself 'Reverend', he does not in fact have any formal qualifications, and does not seem to have been ordained by any recognised body."'

Peter Swan leaned back in his chair. 'Well,' he said. 'Well, well, well.'

Frannie Merriday crunched her way through a bowl of Frosties, taking her time, chewing each bite thoroughly.

Her father looked at his watch. 'You don't want to be late for school,' he said. 'We ought to be going in a few minutes.'

'But Mum never leaves this early. I have at least ten minutes.'

'Your mother lives closer to your school than I do,' Tim pointed out.

'Oh, yeah.' She put her spoon down. 'Can I ask you a question, Dad?'

'If you make it quick.' He was dressed, ready to go, and Frannie's dawdling was beginning to get to him.

'That Jacquie Darke. What exactly did she do that was

so bad? She didn't kill anybody or anything like that, did she?'

Tim shook his head, bemused. 'Whatever would give you an idea like that, sweetie?'

'I just wondered.' She bent over to retie her shoelace so he couldn't see her face. 'So what *did* she do, then?'

'If you must know, she talked to a man at the newspaper, and said some pretty unflattering things about the police. My name was mentioned. My boss wasn't very happy about it.'

'No. I don't suppose he would have been.' Frannie put her cereal bowl down on the floor for Watson, who had been waiting patiently to finish off the milk at the bottom of the bowl.

'But she *did* apologise,' Tim volunteered, not at all sure either why Frannie was so interested, or why he was telling her this.

'Well, that's all right, then.' She began gathering up her books, which were strewn about the table, and stuffing them in her rucksack. 'Okay, Dad. I'm ready to go.'

'You haven't done your teeth,' Tim pointed out. 'You haven't combed your hair. And don't forget your oboe.'

'Yeah, yeah,' said Frannie, rolling her eyes.

Sophie couldn't get Charmian Clunch out of her mind. What *had* happened to her? When and how and why had she died? No one had ever said.

Jeremy would probably know, she decided, if anyone did. She picked up the phone and rang his number, hoping to catch him in, and was in luck.

'Sophie, my dear,' he said. 'Chris tells me that your delightful sister has gone home. What a shame.'

'Yes,' said Sophie.

'She made quite a hit with our Elspeth.'

Sophie sighed. 'I'm sure.'

'I've been meaning to call in and see you again. But it won't be today, I fear. I have a huge amount on. Advent is just around the corner, you know.'

'I won't keep you, then,' Sophie said. 'But I just wanted to ask you a quick question.'

'Fire away.'

'What do you know about Charmian Clunch?'

'The dead daughter,' he supplied. 'Late lamented, and all that.'

'Yes. Do you know when she died? Or how?'

Jeremy's voice was regretful. 'Before my time, I'm afraid. Well before. It's probably been fifteen years, or thereabouts.'

'But you usually know about these things,' Sophie said ingratiatingly. 'Hasn't there been any gossip about it? Hasn't Elspeth said anything? She would have been here at the time.'

'Elspeth's *always* been here, darling,' he pointed out. 'But she's not much of a one for gossip.'

'That's not what I hear.' The tart words were out before she had time to think.

'Oh, don't get me wrong. She laps it up – absolutely laps it up. But she's very stingy about supplying it herself. I mean,' Jeremy added, 'look at this juicy murder which is back in the news. Alison Barnett. Happened practically under Elspeth's nose, right here in Quire Close, and she claims she doesn't remember a thing about it. And I was counting on her for all of the inside information.'

Sophie frowned and tried to bring him back to the subject. 'But what about Charmian Clunch?'

'I'm afraid I can't really help.' He sounded regretful. 'Why don't you ask old Clunch himself? I know that you and he are quite pally. I'm sure he'd tell you.'

'We are *not* pally,' Sophie insisted through clenched teeth. 'He's loathsome.'

Jeremy laughed. 'I don't know what you have against him, Sophie dear. He's a harmless old man.'

Harmless? thought Sophie, when she'd apologised to Jeremy for bothering him, and put the phone down. Not harmless. Not at all. She remembered the magazines. She remembered the diary, kept in a bottom drawer for eleven years.

Not harmless.

The doorbell rang.

Sophie froze, her heart hammering.

Perhaps, she thought, if she stayed very still, he would go away.

He knew she was there; he knew she wasn't going anywhere. But perhaps he would think she was napping, or unable to come to the door.

After a moment the bell rang again. Then, a short time later, Sophie heard the faint sound of retreating footsteps.

Within a few minutes the phone rang. Sophie still hadn't moved. Curled up in her chair, she stared at the phone and let it ring on.

In all of her unhappy months in Quire Close, Sophie had never felt so trapped. A cornered animal: that's what she was. Like a fox at the end of a hunt, with nowhere to go, nowhere to hide. Like a rabbit, frozen in the glare of the headlamps of an oncoming car. He knew she was there; she couldn't escape.

There was no question of escape. She was weak; she could barely make it from one room to another without assistance, let alone leave her house. And he knew that, as well as she knew it herself.

Sophie squeezed her eyes shut and fantasised about going to the police, imagining the whole scene. She would ring that pleasant Sergeant Merriday; he would come round to see her. She would tell him about Leslie Clunch. About the diary. Everything. He would thank her for her valuable information and assistance; he would promise her that she need never be afraid of Clunch again. Then the police would march Clunch off in handcuffs, lock him up, and throw away the key.

A comforting fantasy.

But she had promised Olive Clunch that she wouldn't go to the police.

Sophie tried to remember just exactly what she *had* promised Olive Clunch. She'd promised that she wouldn't tell them anything about the diary, or how it had been discovered, or how she had learned of it.

She hadn't promised that she wouldn't talk to them *at all*, she told herself, and her eyes flew open.

Without giving herself time to think, almost without volition, Sophie reached for the phone.

'I never liked Raymond Prew,' said Peter Swan reflectively. 'Even before Miranda came into the picture. He and I were meant to be colleagues in ministry in Sutton Fen. But he always went his own way, and looked down his nose at the Established Church. You would have thought we were heretics, the way he treated us.'

'From his point of view, you *were* heretics,' said Jacquie. 'Believe me.'

'Do you know what I find interesting?' Miranda pored over the article, the poached egg forgotten as it hardened in its water. 'It's all these unattributed sources. "Allegations from unnamed sources", "tip-off from an anonymous source". Someone had it in for him. Do you suppose it was the feminists?'

'Why would you think that?' her husband asked.

'Well, it *does* say that the True Men have been a target of feminist groups.'

'No.' Jacquie straightened up, stunned, as the realisation – the certainty – struck her. 'No, it wasn't the feminists. It was Darren.'

'Darren?'

'Reverend Prew's faithful deputy.' She gave an ironic laugh. 'Don't you see? He put the knife in so that he could take over the True Men.'

'I know that you hate him,' said Miranda. 'And believe me, I don't blame you. But that seems a bit far-fetched to me.'

Jacquie shook her head. 'He knew,' she stated, remembering her last meeting with her ex-husband. He had asked her about Alison, about whether Ally and Reverend Prew had been lovers. The question which had baffled her so much at that time now made sense: already, clearly, he'd known about the affair with the current secretary – the woman who had, in time, succeeded Ally. Darren had been building up his case, hoping to uncover something else unsavoury about the man whom he was supposed to be helping. That particular ploy hadn't worked, but he'd been in possession of more than enough damaging information to destroy Reverend Prew and his ministry.

For just an instant, Jacquie almost felt sorry for Reverend Prew.

Almost.

Frannie Merriday sat at her desk as her teacher wittered on about China. At least Frannie thought it was China; it had been China the last time she'd tuned in. But she hadn't been listening for some time now.

Her mind was otherwise occupied.

It was a long time since Frannie had entertained any hopes, or even any fantasies, of her parents getting back together: at first she might have dreamed of it, but she'd recognised ages ago that it was a lost cause. With a wisdom beyond her years, she realised that they were fundamentally unsuited for each other, that they could never make each other happy. She loved both her parents, while understanding that they would never again love each other.

And besides, the status quo suited her very well.

She had the best of both worlds.

Her mother was flighty, inconsistent, indulgent. Frannie could get away with just about anything where her mum was concerned: she could eat what she liked, stay up as late as she wanted, watch anything she fancied on the telly.

Her father was much more strict, but she could always manipulate him with guilt. He'd never forgiven himself for the break-up of the marriage, for losing his wife and daughter, and Frannie knew how to use that guilt to her own advantage. It was usually a bit more difficult, and required more cleverness, but she could get just about anything she wanted from him in the long run as well.

And there was Watson. Frannie was passionate about cats; she adored Watson. With her mother's allergy to cats, she would never be able to have one at the cottage. But at Dad's, there was Watson.

If her parents got back together, Watson would have to go.

No, Frannie knew better than to wish her parents back together again.

But the status quo was under threat; already things were beginning to change.

There was Brad, for one thing. Brad and Mum, sleeping together, going off on holiday together.

Frannie didn't like Brad, but it wasn't an active dislike. He pretty much ignored her, which suited her fine. And she recognised that he was, on the whole, good for her mother. Mum was a happier, more cheerful person since Brad had come into her life, and when Mum was happy, Frannie was happy as well.

And Brad, Frannie sensed, was a passing thing. He had no intention of settling down with Mum, of moving into the cottage, of becoming a permanent fixture in their lives. Mum might not know that yet, but Frannie did.

Dad, though, was a different story.

Frannie had always known that her father's emotions ran deep.

He'd been hurt by the marriage break-up, and since then he'd kept himself apart from women.

For too long.

He was ripe for the picking, and when he fell, he would fall hard.

With Dad it wouldn't be just a flirtation, just something to pass the time. He would be head-over-heels. Before anyone knew what hit them, it would be wedding rings and a honeymoon and a love nest for two.

And then where would Frannie be?

It *would* happen, she was sure. Sooner rather than later.

It was up to her to ensure that it happened with the right woman.

Liz Hollis, Frannie was certain, was *not* the right woman.

Yes, Frannie allowed dispassionately, she was pretty enough. If you liked the type – too many teeth when she smiled, and the smile never made it to her eyes.

But that was just about all you could say for her. Her cooking left much to be desired, her taste in music was pretty appalling, and her decorating abilities were enough to make anyone throw up.

And she tried too hard.

Frannie knew without being told that Liz Hollis had her heart set on getting her claws into Tim Merriday, and not letting go. That was to be avoided at all costs.

Frannie reckoned that she was more than a match for Liz Hollis. As long as she moved quickly, and employed diversionary tactics.

That was where Jacquie Darke came into her plans.

Frannie's liking for Jacquie Darke had been as immediate and as instinctive as her dislike and disapproval of Liz Hollis. A woman like that, she judged, was just what her father needed: nice-looking without being flashy, a good sense of humour. Not pushy. Not out to snag him.

But Jacquie Darke had admitted that she liked Tim Merriday, that she found him attractive. And he, when pressed, had admitted the same thing about her. Even though she'd done something bad, had got him in trouble, he liked her.

Frannie knew a good match when she saw one. Jacquie Darke, whether she realised it or not, was just right for Tim Merriday. It might take a bit of work on her part, but Frannie was confident that she would be able to bring them together. She had another ten days or so with her father before her mum returned; that ought to be time enough to manage it.

Tim had covered a whole sheet of paper in mindless doodles. There were two words at the top of the page: Charmian Clunch. Below and around the name, he'd drawn a veritable *Cluedo* game, multiplied several times: knives, ropes, and lead pipes proliferated, as his thoughts pursued their own path.

He had been surprised to hear from Mrs Lilburn, and all the more so when her call had nothing, seemingly, to do with the Quire Close murder.

Charmian Clunch, she had asked about. The daughter of Leslie Clunch, retired Head Verger of Westmead Cathedral. The girl had died some years ago, in her teens. Could he possibly, enquired Mrs Lilburn, discover how the girl had died?

The question he posed to himself, now, was a simple one: why did Sophie Lilburn want to know? When he had – quite reasonably, he thought – asked her that, she had been evasive. Suspiciously so.

Mere curiosity was not a good enough answer. People didn't ring the police to ask questions like that out of curiosity. No, there was a hidden agenda behind her enquiry, and it was up to him to discover what it might be.

His contact with Sophie Lilburn, the previous week, had been brief, but she had impressed him as a sensible woman, intelligent enough to grasp his intentions, not given to hysteria nor jumping to unwarranted conclusions. Was she, in asking him this question, trying to impart some information to him that she was unable to do in a more straightforward manner?

The first step to discovering what she was up to, he decided, was to find the information she was seeking, and take it from there. That might give him some clue as to her motives for asking.

And besides, the question itself had captured his interest. What *had* happened to Charmian Clunch? Drugs? A virulent disease? An accident of some sort?

Still doodling, he picked up the phone with his free hand and rang the Registrar of Deaths. This would be the first port of call, then if necessary – if the information warranted it – he could talk to the coroner, or check the police files. 'I don't have the date,' he apologised. 'Maybe fourteen or fifteen years ago? Thereabouts. What I'm looking for is the cause of death.'

Sophie had been determined to stay awake that afternoon, but drifted off to sleep on the sofa. She awoke to the sound of a key in the lock, and a moment later Chris was standing beside her.

'What time is it?' she asked, groggy and disorientated.

'School has finished for the day.' Chris was smiling, as she hadn't seen him smile for weeks, almost like his old, ebullient self. 'And I just had to come home and talk to you. Before choir practice.'

Sophie found herself smiling back at him. 'What's happened?'

'Madeline,' he said. 'She rang me at school.'

'She rang *you*?' Abruptly Sophie snapped out of her somnolent good will. 'Why did she do that?'

'She wanted me to know about what's been going on. With Tori and the baby. You didn't tell me. But that doesn't matter now.' Chris swooped down and brought his face level with hers. 'Oh, Soph. This changes everything. You must see that.'

'I don't know what you mean,' she said coldly. 'My niece has been stupid and irresponsible. What does that have to do with me?'

It was as if he hadn't heard her. 'We can adopt Tori's baby,' Chris stated. 'It's the perfect solution. Perfect for her, and perfect for us. Madeline agrees with me. She was over the moon when I suggested it.'

'I told you.' Sophie's voice was calm, measured. 'You *know* that I told you. I don't want someone else's baby.'

'You said that you didn't want some *stranger's* baby,' Chris pointed out. 'Tori isn't a stranger. She's your niece. She's family. Your own flesh and blood. That's different. Surely it's different.'

Sophie shook her head. 'Not different at all.'

His face fell; his eyes filled with tears. Sophie looked away. 'Think about it,' Chris pleaded. 'Promise me that you'll think about it.'

'There's nothing to think about.'

'Then . . . then I'll be going.' Chris straightened up. 'I don't want to be late for practice.' His voice was forlorn.

Sophie shrugged. 'See you later.'

*   *   *

Tim looked at his watch: time to collect Frannie from school.

He would have to bring her back here to his office again; there didn't seem to be much of an alternative. She was too young to leave her at home on her own, and he wasn't sufficiently clued up about baby-sitters and such things to make any other arrangements.

It wasn't very satisfactory, and he knew it. There wasn't much here to keep her occupied and stave off boredom, and at the end of the day it wasn't very professional on his part to have a ten-year-old in tow. What if he were to be called out of the office to a crime scene?

If the Superintendent knew about it, he would blow a gasket. But fortunately the Superintendent didn't know. Yet. It was perhaps, though, only a matter of time before he found out.

Today was only Frannie's second day; she would be with him till the end of next week.

He would have to come up with a better arrangement, Tim realised.

Puzzling over the dilemma, he stopped at the desk to tell Liz that he'd be back in a few minutes.

'Frannie?' she asked with a sympathetic smile.

'Yes,' he admitted, then encouraged by the smile, went on. 'It's a bit of a nuisance, really. And I know I shouldn't bring her here. You don't have any better ideas, do you? For something I could do with her for a couple of hours after school?'

Liz nodded thoughtfully. 'There *is* my little sister,' she said. 'She left school in the spring, and has been looking for a proper job ever since. She does a bit of that sort of thing – child-minding, baby-sitting. Whatever you want to call it.'

'And you think she might be able to look after Frannie?'

'Quite possibly. I could ask her. Would you like me to do that?'

Tim grinned at her. 'That would be fantastic. I'll pay whatever the going rate is, of course.'

'No problem. I'm glad to be of help.'

Conscious of the time, he was already on his way out of the door, and spoke his last words to her over his shoulder. 'Liz, you're an angel,' he said. 'I could kiss you.'

'You will,' Liz said under her breath. 'Believe me, I'll hold you to that.'

Dominic was in Sophie's kitchen, making the tea, when the phone rang. She reached for it.

'Mrs Lilburn?' said a voice on the other end. 'It's Sergeant Merriday here.'

'Yes, Sergeant?'

'About Charmian Clunch.'

He paused, and Sophie waited impatiently. 'You've found something out?'

'I've just been on the phone with the Registrar of Deaths. He's managed to locate the death certificate.'

'And?'

'And I think that you and I need to have a little talk, Mrs Lilburn. Tomorrow. As soon as I've had a chance to see the coroner's files on the case. And the report of the inquest.'

Sophie gulped. 'The inquest?'

'Charmian Clunch didn't die a natural death, Mrs Lilburn.' He paused again. 'She committed suicide.'

Chapter 22

Jacquie had allowed herself to be talked by Miranda Swan into staying in Westmead for one more night. Yes, she needed to take the death certificate to Mr Mockler, and get on with sorting out the house, but one more day couldn't make that much difference.

So Miranda said, and so Jacquie agreed. It would mean that she could go once more to Evensong at the cathedral with Miranda. She could enjoy one last evening with the Swans, who now seemed like old friends.

And, she admitted to herself, it would give her the opportunity to say goodbye to Tim Merriday, and explain her reasons for going. She owed him that much. He might even accept her apology, now that, thanks to Frannie, they seemed to have got past the open hostility stage to some sort of an armed truce.

Without giving herself too much time to think about it, she went to the police station, determined to do the deed in person. Spotting Liz at the desk, she almost lost her nerve and retreated, but realised that Liz was busy gossiping to a WPC and didn't even see her.

The place was familiar to Jacquie now; the routine of going up the stairs was familiar as well. And knocking on the door of Tim's office resulted in a jolt of *déjà vu* as the events of the day before replayed themselves.

'Come in,' said Frannie, and once again Frannie sat in Tim's chair, swinging her legs.

This time, though, a delighted smile of recognition lit Frannie's thin face. 'It's you!' she said. 'Come in!'

Jacquie looked over her shoulder to make sure that she was indeed the source of Frannie's delight, rather than someone behind her.

'Dad's not here,' Frannie announced. 'Again. But he'll be back soon, I expect. You can talk to *me* while you're waiting.'

Jacquie perched on the edge of the other chair. 'It must be pretty boring for you, sitting round in his office like this.'

'Yeah.' The girl shrugged. 'But I have a book to read for school. About China.' She raised the book to show Jacquie, then shut it and prepared for conversation. 'It's pretty boring, too,' she admitted.

'I don't want to keep you from your schoolwork,' Jacquie said. 'Your father might not be very happy with me.'

Frannie leaned forward, put her elbows on the desk, and spoke earnestly. 'He's been mad at you, hasn't he? But I shouldn't worry about that too much. He likes you, really.'

'He does?' Jacquie asked, startled by the girl's frankness and intensity.

'Oh, yes. He told me so.'

Tim had been discussing her with his daughter; in spite of herself, Jacquie felt a warm glow.

'Do you like cats?' Frannie asked suddenly. 'You're not allergic to them, are you?'

Jacquie coped with the change of subject. 'Cats? No, I'm not allergic to them.' She smiled. 'I love them, in fact. My sister and I always wanted a kitten when we were little, but our mother *was* allergic. Or at least that was her excuse. I think maybe she just didn't want the bother.'

'My mum is allergic,' Frannie stated. 'She breaks out in pink splotches and starts sneezing.'

'How unpleasant.'

'But Dad has a cat. He's called Watson. You know, like Sherlock Holmes.'

That seemed just the sort of thing that she would expect from Tim, thought Jacquie, smiling. 'Yes, I get it. That's clever.'

'You have a sister?' queried Frannie, in another abrupt change of subject. 'I wish I had a sister.'

Jacquie's smile vanished. 'I . . . did. But she . . . died.'

'Oh, how awful,' Frannie exclaimed with ready sympathy. 'I'm really sorry.'

'So am I.'

'I've always been sorry that I didn't have a sister. But it would be much worse to have one, and then for her to die.'

'I'm not sorry that I had Ally,' said Jacquie in a reflective voice, speaking aloud thoughts that had never before been verbalised. 'She was *good*. Much better than me, always. But knowing her made me a better person than I would have been without her.'

'Yes,' nodded Frannie gravely. 'Yes, I understand that.'

'Fran—' said Tim, coming through the door with some files in his arms, breaking off as he saw that his daughter was not alone. 'Oh. Mrs Darke. You're here.'

'I'm sorry.' Jacquie rose from her chair, suddenly awkward. 'I should have rung and made an appointment.'

'That's all right.'

'I just wanted to tell you that I'm going back home tomorrow. Back to Sutton Fen.'

'You're going?' Frannie interposed in dismay.

Tim ignored the interruption. 'But I thought that you were going to stay on here, and try to do the police's job for us.'

'I've changed my mind about that.' Jacquie regarded him with dignity, her head held high. 'I was wrong to think that I should, and arrogant to think that I could. I wanted to apologise to you before I went.'

He didn't know what to say. Her words were bitter-sweet: the apology and the admission were welcome, but the thought that she was going away from him was something that he suddenly knew he didn't want to contemplate.

'But you're coming back, aren't you?' Frannie demanded. 'You're not going away *for ever*?'

Jacquie turned to the girl; it was easier to talk to her. 'I don't know,' she said honestly. 'I don't know what I'm going to do.'

'But we're just starting to be friends! And you haven't met Watson yet,' Frannie added, her lip trembling.

Tim still hadn't spoken. Jacquie looked at him sideways. 'Am I forgiven, then?'

'Yes.'

She smiled, inspired with a sudden impulse. 'Then can I kidnap your daughter for a bit, Sergeant Merriday? I'll take her out for tea. Frannie and I still have a few things to talk about, and you might welcome the chance to have your office to yourself for the rest of the afternoon.'

'Oh, yes,' said Frannie, scrambling from the chair. 'Let's have a proper tea. Dad, you'll come with us, won't you?'

'I can't do that, sweetie. You know that I have work to do.'

'But I can go, can't I?'

Tim looked from one to the other of them, again with the baffled feeling of being on the outside. He was powerless to protest. 'All right,' he said, shrugging.

A moment later the two of them had gone. Slowly Tim went to his chair and sat down behind his desk, pushing Frannie's abandoned school book out of the way and putting down the files he'd been holding throughout the surreal scene which had just taken place.

They were the files on Charmian Clunch's death, brought up from the depths of the police station.

He opened the top folder and stared at the dead girl's photo. She was only a teenager, several years younger than Alison Barnett. But in other ways, she was remarkably like her: blonde, rather pretty, well filled out.

Was there some connection between the two deaths?

He couldn't imagine how there could be: Alison Barnett had been murdered, and Charmian Clunch had committed suicide.

Yet there was that resemblance. And the fact that they had both died in Westmead, within a few years of each other. And above all, Mrs Lilburn's puzzling phone call, hinting at some secret knowledge.

Tim was no longer on the Alison Barnett murder case, but it was a measure of the lack of priority given to it that the Superintendent hadn't yet got round to telling him to pass the files on to someone else. Now he reached for the files, and, extracting a photo, put the two side by side.

The resemblance was remarkable. They might have been sisters, so alike were they. Come to that, they were both rather like Mrs Lilburn herself, though Sophie Lilburn was some years older and several stones thinner than either of them.

Sisters. He picked up Alison Barnett's photo yet again, this time searching for a different resemblance. Even allowing for the passage of eleven years, she was nothing at all like the woman with the short dark hair. The woman who was even now with his daughter, and who, this time tomorrow, would have walked out of his life.

Tim closed his eyes.

Frannie woke up on Wednesday morning without any prodding from her father, a warm furry ball of cat snuggled next to her, and a warm fuzzy feeling in her chest.

It had been a brilliant afternoon, a brilliant evening. She smiled to herself, stroking Watson.

'Just like I planned it,' she whispered to the cat. 'Even better, really.'

She and Jacquie Darke had had tea in the cathedral refectory; she'd been allowed by Jacquie – who told her to call her that – to eat whatever she fancied. She'd fancied some flapjack and some shortbread with chocolate on it, and a cream bun. She'd eaten them all, every bite, as well.

And they'd talked. Frannie had done most of the talking, she admitted to herself, but they'd become fast friends.

Then Jacquie had mentioned her intention to go to Choral Evensong in the cathedral. She couldn't believe that Frannie had never been, and of course Frannie had wanted to go with her.

They'd had to consult her dad, of course, when the

time came for Frannie to be returned to his office at the police station, and – miraculously – he had said he would come with them.

She'd loved it – loved seeing the boys all dressed up in their choirboy gear, and hearing the amazing sounds that they produced. Proper music. Beautiful music. Music that made you want to go down on your knees and pray to God, whether you believed in Him or not.

Frannie hadn't been so certain, before now, that she *did* believe in God. Her mum didn't, and it wasn't something she'd ever talked about with her dad. Now, though, His existence seemed pretty much a sure thing.

There was the music, for starters. And then there was the miracle of what had happened afterwards.

They'd sat with Jacquie's friend Mrs Swan at the service, and after it was over, she'd invited them all to come to her house for supper.

Dad had hesitated at first. 'Frannie's a fussy eater,' he'd said.

She had protested at that description, had promised to eat whatever was put in front of her, without complaint.

What was put in front of her was Chinese food. When Mrs Swan found out that she was studying China at school, she'd had the brilliant idea of getting a Chinese takeaway.

Frannie had never tasted Chinese food before. In spite of that fact, she would have said, if asked, that she hated it, that it was gross and disgusting. But mindful of her promise, she had eaten it, and found it to be delicious.

There had been all sorts of strange things, chopped up and mixed together. Bits of meat, bits of veg. Noodles and rice and spices. It was wonderful, and she'd said so, enjoying the look of amazement on her father's face. She'd eaten lots, in spite of the fact that she'd stuffed herself at tea.

The Swans were really nice people, even though they were old and didn't have any children, not even grown-up ones. Mr Swan – Canon Swan, he was – was funny and jolly, in a dry sort of way, and told her lots of hilarious stories about the choirboys and the sorts of things they got up to. Mrs Swan, she'd discovered, loved cats, and was planning to get a new kitten, now that they'd moved into that big house. She'd asked Frannie's advice about it, and had promised to seek Frannie's help when the time came.

And Jacquie was brilliant.

To Frannie's immense satisfaction, at some point during the evening, Jacquie and her dad had ceased to be 'Mrs Darke' and 'Sergeant Merriday' to each other, and had become 'Jacquie' and 'Tim'. Perhaps no one else had noticed, but Frannie certainly had.

They liked each other, it was more than evident. All that they needed was some time together, and maybe a little more help from Frannie.

But time, it seemed, was something they'd run out of.

Frannie frowned as she remembered that one little snag. Jacquie was leaving today, and she wasn't coming back. There wasn't much that Frannie could do about it.

Except for one thing. She slipped out of the warm bed, shivering as she went down on her knees beside it. Clasping her hands together, she arranged her face into as pious an expression as she could manage and raised it to the ceiling. 'Dear God and Jesus,' she whispered, 'please don't let her go. And if she does, then make her come back.'

It was in this unlikely pose that her father found her when he came into the bedroom a few minutes later to wake her for school. 'Frannie, are you all right?' he asked in concern.

'Yeah, Dad. I'm fine.' She scrambled back into bed, not wanting to tell him what she'd been doing.

'Time to get up.'

'Yeah, all right.' She stroked Watson, then got out of bed more willingly and cheerfully than she'd done since she'd arrived to stay.

Her school uniform was on the floor, where she'd dropped it the night before. Her father gave her a baleful look as she retrieved it, but before he had a chance to say anything about her slovenly habits, the phone rang and he went off to answer it.

Jacquie, thought Frannie, smiling to herself. She's not going, after all. Thank you, God.

But when, as she sat down to her bowl of Frosties a few minutes later, she contrived to ask him about the phone call, he gave her an unexpected answer.

'It's all fixed,' he said. 'A new arrangement for you after school, starting today.'

Even better. 'Is Jacquie going to look after me, then?' she guessed confidently.

Her father gave her a baffled look. 'Why would you think that? She's leaving today – you know that.'

'Then what?'

'You remember Liz?'

'Of course,' said Frannie, with a sudden foreboding that she wasn't going to like what was coming next.

'Liz has a younger sister. She's called Leoni, and she's going to come here to keep an eye on you until I'm home from work.'

Frannie's eyes widened in dismay. 'Liz's sister? Is this

the one who's the fussy eater? Who only ate pizza and oven chips for a year?'

'I expect so.'

Frannie could think of at least a thousand reasons why this arrangement was a bad idea. All she said, though, was, 'But I don't need a baby-sitter. I'm not a baby.'

'You can't stay here on your own,' her father said reasonably. 'It's only for a few days. And anyway, it's all fixed. Liz has very kindly arranged it.'

This time Frannie's words to God were not spoken aloud, but she understood that He would hear them anyway. She cast her eyes to the ceiling and said silently and accusingly, 'How *could* You?'

Tim hadn't made any promises, but he had hopes of seeing Jacquie Darke again before she left Westmead. After all, he told himself, he needed to visit Mrs Lilburn for a chat, so he'd be in Quire Close anyway. It wasn't as if he'd be making a special trip or anything.

He'd told himself that, and he'd mentioned it to Jacquie the night before. 'I won't say goodbye just now,' he'd said. 'I'll be in Quire Close first thing in the morning. If it's all right with you, I'll try to call by and see you before you go.'

Her smile indicated that it was all right with her. Emboldened by the smile, he had even taken her hand and pressed it, and she had not snatched it away.

But it was not to be. After taking Frannie to school, he'd stopped at the office to collect some papers, and there he had been waylaid. A car had been reported stolen from the estate on the outskirts of Westmead; there was no one else available to deal with it.

So by the time he made it to Quire Close, it was well after ten o'clock; he had arranged to see Mrs Lilburn at half-past nine.

Hoping against hope, he went to the Precentor's House first, telling himself that Mrs Lilburn could wait for a few more minutes.

Miranda Swan came to the door. 'I'm sorry,' she said, sounding as if she meant it. 'You've just missed her. She left about a quarter of an hour ago.'

This was becoming a habit, thought Tim, surprised at the depth of his disappointment. He managed to offer her his thanks for the night before. 'And it was so kind of you to include Frannie,' he said.

'Not at all. You have a delightful daughter.' She smiled. 'And I hope we'll be seeing more of you both.'

Apologising that he was late for an appointment, he took his leave of her and walked back up Quire Close. He rang the bell of number 22 and waited for what seemed a very long time before trying again. Still no one came to the door.

He was late, he knew, but she should have been expecting him. Tim retreated on to the cobblestones, got out his mobile phone, located the number, and rang the Lilburn house.

'Yes?' came a tentative voice after several rings.

'Mrs Lilburn? It's Sergeant Merriday. I'm sorry that I'm late, but I'm waiting outside.'

'All right.' A moment later she opened the door, just enough so that he could squeeze through, then shut it behind him and pulled a bolt across.

She was, he could see straight away, as tense as a tightly wound spring, even more nervous than she had been on his previous visit.

'I'm sorry,' she said. 'I have to be careful.'

Tim wasn't sure what she meant by that. He knew that she'd recently had an operation, and was still very much an invalid; she might have been referring to her physical condition. Or she might have meant something else entirely.

She led him into the sitting room and gestured him to a chair, then took up a position on the sofa, where she seemed to be keeping half an eye on the front window into Quire Close. 'Tell me,' said Sophie Lilburn. 'Tell me about Charmian Clunch.'

'I'll tell you,' Tim agreed. 'But then you'll have to answer some questions for *me*, Mrs Lilburn.'

She didn't make any promises, but she nodded.

'As I told you on the phone, Charmian Clunch committed suicide. She swallowed a bottle of paracetamol tablets, and by the time her parents found her, it was too late to save her. She was,' he added, 'sixteen years old.'

Sophie swallowed. 'Her parents found her?'

'Her father, actually. In her bedroom.'

Her glance darted to the window, then back to his face. 'And you're *sure* that it was suicide. It couldn't have been murder? A murder disguised as suicide?'

That, thought Tim, was an interesting question for her to have asked. More revealing, perhaps, than she knew. 'Not unless,' he said bluntly, 'someone did a clever forgery job as well. There was a note found with the body.'

'A note?'

'A suicide note. It was addressed to her father, and it said the usual sort of thing: "Daddy, I'm so sorry. I just couldn't take it any more." And there was a bit more in that vein. Her father testified at the inquest that it was her handwriting.'

'But what if he was lying?' she blurted.

Tim raised his eyebrows and gave her a sharp look. 'Why should he do that?'

'I . . . don't know.'

'You'd be surprised,' Tim said, 'how many sixteen-year-old girls kill themselves, or try to. For all sorts of reasons, but most of it goes under the heading of teenage angst. Boyfriend troubles, peer bullying, pressures of school and exams, parental pressure. Even something like difficulties with body image and weight loss. Charmian Clunch was . . . rather a big girl,' he added delicately. 'She might have been trying to lose weight, and become frustrated and discouraged when it turned out to be more difficult than she'd expected.'

Sophie looked down at her hands and spoke quietly. 'I know.'

That was a puzzling response, but he let it pass.

'So I don't think you need to put a more sinister interpretation on her death. Unless,' he went on in a different tone of voice, 'you have some particular reason to do so. Do you know anything, Mrs Lilburn, that you're not telling me?'

'Why would you think that?'

'Because,' he said, 'ringing the police to ask a question like you did is not a normal course of action. Not just to satisfy some sort of ordinary curiosity. There are other ways of doing that – asking round for local gossip, going to the library and checking old newspaper files, and that sort of thing. But to ring the police . . .'

'I . . . couldn't get out,' she said, not very convincingly.

'I've had an operation. I was just curious. I wanted to know what had happened to her, and you were the first person I thought of who might be able to tell me.'

Tim didn't believe her. 'Mrs Lilburn,' he tried again. 'I have a very strong feeling that you're asking for my help. But I can't help you unless you tell me what's really going on here.'

She seemed to shrink into herself, and once again her eyes moved involuntarily to the window. Sophie Lilburn was evidently in the throes of some great internal struggle; Tim said nothing, allowing her to think it through, to weigh up the options.

'No,' she said at last in a very small voice. 'No. There's nothing.'

Jacquie was once again back in her cold house in Sutton Fen. With a sense of *déjà vu*, she switched the heating back on and put on the electric fire in the front parlour. This time she'd stopped at a supermarket on her way back and bought some fresh milk and enough food to get her by for a day or two. She'd also bought a bottle of cheap red wine.

Drinking was bad enough; drinking alone was even worse. But Jacquie no longer cared. Her parents were not there to disapprove. And her fear of Reverend Prew, her respect for his teachings, had departed long before the rest of the world discovered what she had known for herself: that he was a fraud and a hypocrite.

She opened the screw top and poured a glassful into a tumbler, then carried the tumbler and bottle through into the parlour and sat by the electric fire.

He hadn't come. Tim Merriday hadn't come to say goodbye.

Jacquie tried to be philosophical about it. He hadn't promised, after all. He'd probably never intended to come, but had just said that he would to make things easier.

They'd had such a wonderful time the evening before. With the Swans and Frannie there to ease things, they'd managed to relax with each other, to enjoy each other's company in a non-stressful way. She had almost thought he meant it when he said that he would come in the morning.

But he hadn't, and that was that.

She'd read too much into his kindness of the night before, she told herself now. Wishful thinking. At the end of the day, he was a nice man and he felt sorry for her.

She sipped the wine reflectively and thought about how she was going to pass the rest of the day. The evening. The rest of her life.

On her way into Sutton Fen, she had stopped at Mr Mockler's office and delivered the precious document into his hands. That was done; her mission was accomplished.

'She's horrible,' stated Frannie. 'She has spots. She has bulgy eyes.'

'You mustn't judge people by what they look like,' her father said, thinking what a self-righteous prig he sounded. Frannie was right: Leoni Hollis was not the most prepossessing of young women. But he couldn't very well admit that.

'It's no wonder she has so many spots,' added Frannie malevolently. 'All those oven chips.'

Tim suppressed a smile.

'And anyway,' she went on, 'I'm not just judging her by what she looks like. She has a horrible mimsey way with her. She talks down to me and treats me like a little kid. Like a baby! She asked me which was my favourite Teletubby, for God's sake!'

'Frannie!' He was finding it increasingly difficult not to laugh out loud, and masked this with a show of disapproval.

'Sorry.' Disconsolately Frannie swung her legs, then allowed herself to be comforted by Watson, who rubbed against her and jumped up on her lap. She stroked him and laid her cheek against his warm fur, refusing to make eye contact with her father.

Tim attempted to deflect her. He could have asked her to pick up all of her things which she'd strewn all over the table, but that would start a new battle; he'd try a neutral subject instead. 'What would you like for supper tonight, sweetie?'

'I don't know.'

'How about a pizza? That pepperoni one that we bought at the supermarket?'

'No.' Frannie's jaw was set. 'I don't want pizza. I don't like pepperoni.'

'But you picked it out!' he protested.

'I've changed my mind, all right?' Her voice was belligerent, her lower lip was thrust out, her eyes were narrowed.

Tim sighed. The rest of the fortnight stretched out before him into eternity.

When the phone rang, Jacquie allowed herself to believe, for just an instant, that it might be Tim, saying he was sorry to have missed her, hoping that she'd had a good journey.

But the voice on the phone, though male, was not Tim's. 'You're home, then,' said Darren, not bothering to identify himself.

Jacquie ignored the hostility in his voice. 'Yes. I've been away for a few days.'

'I know. I've been trying to reach you.'

She would *not* apologise, nor explain; she didn't owe him any explanations. 'About Reverend Prew, I suppose. I saw it in the paper yesterday. In *The Times*.'

'Nothing to do with Reverend Prew,' Darren said. 'Can I come round to see you? Now?'

'Suit yourself.' She didn't really want to see Darren, particularly if he was in a mood, but she had no good reason to deny him, either.

He was there within ten minutes, and he didn't bother with any pleasantries. 'I want an explanation,' he said, following her into the front parlour.

Jacquie sat down and picked up her tumbler of wine; that stopped him in his tracks. 'Wine!' he shouted, pointing at the bottle. 'You're drinking wine!'

'I can't get anything past you,' she said ironically.

'Reverend Prew always said that you were beyond redemption. I wonder if he knew how wicked you really were.' His voice was venomous.

'I thought you weren't here to talk about Reverend Prew,' she pointed out.

'I'm not. I'm here to talk about *you*.'

She took a gulp of wine. 'I'm not sure I want to hear what you have to say, Darren.'

'You'll hear me, all right.' He reached into the pocket of his anorak and pulled out a small, boxy camera. 'Can you tell me what this is?'

Jacquie maintained her ironic tone. 'It's a camera. Next question?'

'Oh, very funny.' Darren came a step closer and held it towards her. 'Have you ever seen this camera before? And don't try to lie to me.'

She looked at it more closely; the hairs on the back of her neck stirred with a vestige of apprehensive recognition.

Darren didn't wait for her to reply. 'My wife found this camera,' he told her. 'On the top shelf, at the very back of the wardrobe. When she was having a clear-out.'

The wardrobe. Jacquie swallowed and remained silent.

'It had film in it, and there were a few exposures left. She used them up, taking pictures of the children. Then she sent the film away to be developed.'

'Oh,' said Jacquie softly. Now she remembered, very well.

Darren reached back into his anorak pocket with his free hand and flourished a wad of photos. 'Imagine her surprise,' he said. 'Imagine *mine*.' He flung the photos towards the coffee table; they scattered in all directions, some of them landing on the floor at Jacquie's feet. She didn't move; she didn't even glance at the photos.

'Your holiday, I presume,' he sneered. 'Your precious holiday with your precious sister. And I *encouraged* you to go, if I recall. You must have thought me a real mug. You must have laughed at me behind my back the whole time.'

'No, Darren,' she said, wanting to be truthful. 'It wasn't like that.'

'Then what *was* it like? A little pre-wedding getaway, you said. A pre-wedding *orgy*, more like. How did you have the nerve to come back to me, to walk down the aisle and make those vows, just a few weeks later? How could you look me in the face?' His outrage, inspired by hurt pride, took his voice up a few notches.

'It was just a bit of fun,' she said with more assurance than she felt. 'Nothing to do with you.'

'Nothing to do with me? But you were going to marry me. You *did* marry me!'

'And you left me, Darren. Don't forget that.' Galvanised by that fact, Jacquie got up and walked towards the door, pushing him in front of her and speaking deliberately. 'Thank you for bringing the photos. It was very kind of you. And thank your wife for me, as well.'

'You think you're so superior,' he snapped, then his vocabulary, never his greatest strength, failed him. 'But you're nothing but a . . . a slapper. A common tart.'

'And you,' she said as they reached the door, 'are a Judas. The lowest of the low. Don't think I haven't guessed that you were behind what's happened to Reverend Prew.'

'That's pretty rich, coming from you. I thought you hated him, and everything he stood for.'

Jacquie put her hands on her hips. 'I'm not defending Reverend Prew. Far from it. But if you can sleep at night after what you've done to him, then you're an even bigger bastard than I thought.'

She closed the door in his face as he stared at her, slack-jawed; it wasn't until she was back in the parlour that she discovered she was shaking with delayed shock.

After a moment she took a bracing gulp of wine, then gathered up the photos and forced herself to look at them. They were dark and of poor quality after eleven years in the camera; her first thought was how unexceptional they were. Darren's reaction had led her to expect that they would be disgusting – nothing short of a naked romp, if not worse. But they only seemed to show a few young people having a good time. Yes, in one of them she – or the impossibly carefree creature she had once been – was kissing a young man, and she was wearing a rather skimpy dress – not the sort of thing one would wear at the Free Baptist Fellowship, to be sure; nonetheless there was nothing in them to suggest that it had been much more than a bit of innocent fun.

It *had*, of course, been more than that. But the photos didn't reveal it.

Who, she tried to recall, was the young man? What was his name? There had been so many of them. And it had all been so long ago.

As she looked at the photos, it all flooded back, and for a moment she was transported in time and space. She remembered, as if all of the years in between had never happened, what it had felt like: the reckless abandon, the sense of time slipping away from her, the walls closing in on her, as her wedding day approached.

Understandable, she told herself, given the way that her marriage had turned out.

But what a silly young fool she'd been.

To believe – and she *had* believed it – that life could be compartmentalised like that: it was madness. She'd thought that what happened on holiday, away from home and the watchful eyes of her parents and Reverend Prew, somehow didn't count, that it could be put behind her and forgotten. History. Nothing to do with real life.

It hadn't been put behind her, though. It had been the unseen baggage, carried with her through her marriage and beyond. It had shaped her, had subtly influenced her relationship with Darren.

And on every occasion that Reverend Prew had taxed her with being a disobedient wife, not right with God, she had pushed the memories farther down, while all the time she was haunted by the niggling fear that he might be nearer the truth than he imagined.

How responsible, she asked herself now, was she for the break-up of her marriage? How different might things have been, if she'd never gone on that holiday?

If *they'd* never gone on that holiday. Alison had been a part of it, as well. The dutiful sister, not wanting to take the photos but going along with what Jacquie demanded. Just as she always had.

Alison.

Jacquie continued to flip through the photos, scarcely seeing them in her agitation. But towards the bottom of the pile, she stopped short. That day on the beach with the two English boys. Steve, one was called: he and a bikini-clad Jacquie were splashing water at each other.

But in the next one, Jacquie had turned the tables, and the camera, on Alison. There was her sister, in her decorous bathing costume, squinting into the sun and smiling. Next to Ally, sitting close and gazing at her rather than the camera, was yet another young man. Bespectacled, serious-looking.

Mike.

'Oh, God,' whispered Jacquie to herself.

Chapter 23

Frannie wasn't the only one who had been plotting. Liz was careful to get to work early on Thursday morning, so she would have no chance of missing Tim's arrival, positioning herself so that she could see him coming through the door and intercept him.

It all worked according to plan. Tim even made the first approach, smiling at her. 'I must thank you for fixing things up with your sister,' he said. 'That was a great help to me.'

'I hope it went well from your point of view.'

'Oh, it was great. Frannie seems to have got on quite well with Leoni,' he lied.

Liz followed up his lie with one of her own. 'Leoni said so, too, when I spoke to her last night.' Leoni's exact words had been that Frannie was 'a spoiled little madam who wants her bottom smacking', but Liz didn't think that anything would be served by telling Tim that. 'I'm so pleased that it's worked out,' she added.

'Well, thanks,' he concluded, and made as if to move away.

Liz stretched out a hand to detain him. 'Tim. There's something else I wanted to ask you about.'

'Yes?'

She fixed on her most brilliant smile. 'Saturday,' she said. 'You're off duty that day. I checked.'

'That's right. I've arranged it that way because of Frannie. So if Leoni was wondering . . .'

'No, that's not it at all.' Liz took a deep breath and rushed into what she had to say before she lost her nerve. 'I want to take you out for the day. You *and* Frannie. I've planned it all. A surprise.'

'Oh.' Tim was a bit taken aback. 'I wouldn't want to inflict Frannie on you all day,' he protested.

'Not at all.' She smiled even more falsely. 'Frannie and I get on like a house afire. She's adorable.'

There were a lot of words he might use to describe his daughter, Tim reflected, but 'adorable' was not one of them.

His immediate impulse was to turn Liz's offer down flat, for various reasons. Yet he hesitated. Frannie would hate it, but so what? She was being a distinct pain in the posterior at the moment, obstructive and difficult. He would have to do *something* to entertain her on Saturday; why not let someone else share the burden?

And at the back of his mind was the thought of Jacquie, as it had been so often over the past days.

If things had been different . . . he might have been spending the day with Jacquie. That was a prospect he would have welcomed with an emotion that was a great deal warmer than indifference.

But, he told himself sternly, Jacquie was gone. She had left; she wouldn't be coming back. If the other evening had meant half as much to her as it had to him, she would have stayed, would have sent that damned piece of paper by registered post to her solicitor and remained in Westmead for a good long while. She wouldn't have left before he'd even had a chance to say goodbye.

She was gone.

He could either spend the rest of his life regretting that fact, and wishing that things had worked out otherwise, or he could get on with it.

Not for the first time, he reflected that Liz was, after all, very presentable; he could do a lot worse. She was kind and generous. She'd done him a big favour in securing her sister for after-school duty, and he owed her one.

Perhaps, in the long run, it would be for the best.

'Yes. All right,' he said. 'That would be lovely, Liz.'

But Frannie was going to loathe it, he warned himself as he climbed the stairs to his office. She would have a fit. She would make his life even more of a misery between now and Saturday.

So the thing to do, the way to handle it, he decided, was just not to tell her. Not until it was too late.

After a sleepless night, as early in the morning as she dared, Jacquie made two phone calls. The first was to Westmead, to Miranda Swan.

She told Miranda that she needed her advice, and explained that something had come up. Something significant, possibly crucial, in finding the person who had killed Alison. She was fully aware, she said, that the police were not inclined to give much more than lip-service to the investigation, and that she had promised not to interfere. 'But this is important,' she said. 'It might just change their minds.'

'Then you must show it to Tim,' Miranda said promptly; after their jolly evening together, she, too, was now on a first-name basis with the policeman.

It was exactly what she'd hoped Miranda would say. 'If you think so . . .'

'I *know* so.' There was no hesitation. 'I know you've just gone home, but if you can bear it, why don't you come back? Right now, today?'

'Yes,' said Jacquie. Having delivered the death certificate, she'd done what she had to do in Sutton Fen; she hadn't even unpacked. The anticipation of that horrendous drive, for the second time in as many days, didn't thrill her, but her heart lifted at the thought of Westmead. 'I'll leave soon,' she said. 'I'll be with you this afternoon.'

After that she rang Nicola. She'd last talked to her the previous weekend, when she'd been back in Sutton Fen for the first time, and had filled her in on her discovery of Alison's fate. So much had happened since then, not least that she had made contact with Miranda Swan – and so much more than contact. She'd expected to have plenty of time to bring Nicola up to date on the latest; now it seemed that her time was limited.

Nicola hadn't yet left for work, but she was getting ready to go.

'I won't keep you,' Jacquie assured her. 'But I just wanted to let you know how things have been going. You won't believe it, but I've been staying with Miranda Swan in Westmead.'

Nicola evinced suitable surprise and delight. 'I *thought* it was Westmead where she'd settled with her new husband. But I didn't dream you'd really find her.'

'She's been so kind. They *both* have been. They've made

me feel like a member of the family. I hated to leave.' Jacquie went on to tell her that she was, in fact, returning there that day. 'I've come across something important. Something that could lead to the identification of Ally's killer,' she said.

'Go for it,' urged Nicola. 'And let me know what happens.'

Sophie, too, had a phone call that morning: one that was both unexpected and worrying.

'Elspeth Verey here,' the woman identified herself. 'I hope that you're improving.'

Sophie's initial guilty thought was that she had neglected to write to Elspeth and thank her for the flowers which Dominic had delivered on his mother's behalf. 'I'm a bit better every day. And I must thank you for the lovely flowers you sent, Mrs Verey. It was very kind of you.'

'Not at all.' There was a pause, then Elspeth continued. 'Mrs Lilburn, I think that it's time for us to meet and have a talk. There are a few matters I'd like to discuss with you.'

'I'm not at all ready to go out,' Sophie demurred.

'I wasn't expecting that you would be. If it's convenient, I'd like to call on you. Would tomorrow afternoon be suitable?'

'I'm not going anywhere,' Sophie assured her ironically.

'What time shall we say, then?'

Dominic would probably be coming at teatime. Before that, then. 'Three o'clock?'

'I'll see you then, Mrs Lilburn.'

As Sophie put the phone down, she remembered

Jeremy's warning. This must be about Dominic; the tittle-tattle in the close must have reached Elspeth's ears. She wasn't looking forward to what Elspeth had to say.

This time the lesson was maths, rather than anything to do with China, but it made no odds to Frannie: she had other things on her mind.

Dad and God, she thought bitterly. She had trusted them both. She'd been sure that they would come through for her. And they had both let her down.

She wasn't sure which of the two was worse: God, for allowing Jacquie to go, or Dad for foisting that dreadful Leoni on her, and then being such a pompous prat about it. Dad had let Jacquie go, too; she mustn't forget that. If he'd wanted her to stay badly enough, he could have stopped her going.

One thing she did know. She wasn't giving up yet. If God and Dad couldn't – or wouldn't – help, she'd have to take matters into her own hands somehow.

The fantasy was even more vivid, now that she'd had time to work out the details. Dad and Jacquie, married. She would stay with them at weekends; she wouldn't even mind sleeping on the sofa and letting them have the bedroom. Maybe they would even buy a bigger house, one with more bedrooms. Then she could move in with them. Mum might not like that much, but she wouldn't stop her going, and she'd soon get over it, with Brad to keep her occupied. Dad and Jacquie would certainly appreciate having her with them, especially when they had a baby. She could be such a help to Jacquie, looking after a baby.

A little sister. That's what Jacquie would give her. They'd be a real family.

It wasn't impossible; it wasn't beyond her grasp.

Dad and Jacquie liked each other; they'd both admitted it. More than that – they fancied one another. She could tell from the way they'd looked at each other on Tuesday evening, the way they'd talked, almost as if there was no one else in the room. It was just like Mum with Brad. Like the Swans, even though they were so old.

All she had to do now, thought Frannie, was to think of a way to get Jacquie back to Westmead. After that it would be a piece of cake.

Miranda hugged Jacquie with as much enthusiasm and warmth as if she'd been gone for months rather than just over a day. 'I'm glad you've come back,' she said, and Jacquie, gratified, knew that she meant it. 'I'll put the kettle on, and you can tell me all about what you've discovered.'

'That sounds wonderful.' Jacquie removed her coat, hung it in the cloakroom, and followed Miranda into the kitchen, where she basked in the welcome heat of the Aga. 'I've driven straight through. I haven't even stopped for a cuppa, let alone lunch.'

'No lunch? Then I'll make you a sandwich.' Miranda didn't waste any time in producing what she'd promised, and Jacquie wolfed it down gratefully.

'I didn't realise how hungry I was,' she said. 'I was just so anxious to get here.'

'Now, then. Tell me what this is all about.' Miranda poured out a cup of tea and set it on the table in front of Jacquie.

'Darren came by the house last night.' She grimaced.

'Don't tell me *he's* confessed to murdering your sister,' Miranda said facetiously. 'From what you've told me of the dreadful Darren, I wouldn't put anything past him.'

Jacquie's laugh was without mirth. 'No. But wait till I show you what he gave me.' She retrieved the photo from where she'd carefully tucked it in her handbag. 'This is my sister. Alison,' she said, handing it to Miranda. 'I'm afraid the photo is a bit dark, but you can get the general idea.'

Miranda studied it carefully. 'She's a pretty girl. The chap with her seems to think so, as well.'

'Yes.' Now that she was on the verge of sharing her discovery, Jacquie found that she was tense with excitement.

Still looking at the photo, Miranda waited expectantly. 'Well?'

'It's Mike,' Jacquie said. 'The father of her baby. The man she came to Westmead to find.'

Miranda raised her eyes to Jacquie's, already grasping the implications. 'And you think he was the one who killed her.'

'There is certainly a good possibility of that. Don't you agree? Tim told me once,' she added, 'that most murder victims are killed by people they know. And Mike was the only person she knew in Westmead.'

'Yes.' Miranda gave a thoughtful nod. 'You must show this to Tim.'

Faced with the prospect of seeing him again, and the likelihood that the encounter would lead them once again into an area of conflict, destroying their hard-won truce, Jacquie was on the verge of losing her nerve. 'But the photo is so dark,' she pointed out. 'Not really much good for identification. 'And he's not looking straight at the camera.' She took a gulp of tea. '*You* don't recognise him, do you?'

'I've only been in Westmead for a few months,' Miranda reminded her. She tilted the photo to catch the light and squinted at it for a moment. 'But I do have to say that he seems a bit familiar,' she said at last. 'I might have seen him. Or maybe he has a look of someone else.'

Jacquie was already talking herself out of it. 'Tim would say I was wasting his time if I went to him with this.'

'He'd say nothing of the sort.' Again Miranda bent her head over the snapshot. 'If only this were a bit lighter. Or a bit larger.' Then she slapped it down on the table with a shout of triumph. 'I've got it!'

'You know who it is?'

'No. But I have a wonderful idea.' Miranda grinned at Jacquie. 'There's a woman right here in Quire Close who is a photographer. A rather well-known one, from what I hear, but that's beside the point. The point is that she has her own darkroom, right there in her house.'

'And?' Jacquie didn't see where this was leading.

'And we could take this to her. She could blow it up, do something with the contrast. With a skilled enlargement of this photo, there's a very good chance that this Mike might be identified.'

Her enthusiasm was infectious. 'Maybe,' said Jacquie, almost daring to believe it. 'Would she mind if we asked her?'

'I'm sure she wouldn't. She's a nice woman – at least she seemed to be the one time I met her. And,' Miranda added, 'she's bound to be at home. Peter told me that she's recently had an operation. I've been meaning to call on her, and this would give me a good excuse to do it.'

'Let's do it, then,' said Jacquie. 'Now.'

* * *

The dreadful Leoni was even worse than she'd been on the first day. Then, perhaps hoping to create a good impression, she had made some effort to be nice to Frannie, had tried talking to her. Now, though, it was clear that she'd decided not to bother. She and Frannie regarded each other with open hostility.

'Do you want to watch the telly?' she asked Frannie. 'Children's BBC?'

'No.'

'Well, then. *I'll* watch it. You do what you like.' The girl switched on the set and used the remote control to flip rapidly amongst the channels till she found something that interested her: Ricki Lake, who was interviewing a woman who was in love with her ex-husband's wife's son. Spurred on by Ricki, the studio audience engaged in a spirited debate about whether such a relationship could be construed as incestuous by any recognised definition of the word.

Frannie got out her oboe, assembled it, put up her music stand, and sat down. She began playing scales.

'Can't you keep it down?' Leoni demanded in irritation.

'No. I have to practise.'

Leoni put her thumb on the volume control and held it down; Ricki's audience were now shouting at one another.

Frannie played louder.

'Oh, forget it,' muttered Leoni, pushing the 'off' button. 'I'll ring my boyfriend instead.'

'Not on our phone, you won't,' said Frannie. 'I'll tell my dad.'

'I have a mobile.' Leoni got it out of her handbag.

Frannie couldn't believe that Leoni – with her spots and bulgy eyes – could possibly possess a boyfriend, but refrained from saying so. If it were true, she reflected philosophically, there might be hope for *her* when the time came.

After a moment she became engrossed in her music, almost able to forget the odious Leoni. But when she'd finished her favourite piece, and closed the music, she realised that Leoni was no longer in the room. She had, it would seem, gone into the bedroom with her mobile phone and shut the door behind her, seeking either quiet or privacy, or both.

Frannie smiled. Now was her chance. 'Thank you, God,' she whispered.

Just to make sure that Leoni wouldn't come racing out as soon as she'd twigged the fact that Frannie was no longer playing, she sat for a minute, shaking the spit out of her oboe into Leoni's gaping handbag. Then she laid the instrument down on the table, opened the door of the flat, and slipped out silently, pulling the door shut behind her.

It was nearly a quarter of an hour before Leoni discovered that Frannie was not there. Absorbed in her conversation with her boyfriend, she didn't notice that the music had stopped, and even then she had no reason for alarm.

She needed a smoke, Leoni decided. Mr Merriday had made it clear that he wouldn't welcome smoking in his flat, but she thought that she could manage to get away with it by hanging out of the bedroom window. Trouble was, her fags were in her handbag, and it was in the other room.

Intent on seeming nonchalant in front of Frannie, she sauntered out and went to her bag, reaching into it for the packet of cigarettes.

The fags were damp, and Frannie was nowhere to be seen.

So that was the girl's latest game: hiding from her, trying to scare her. She was probably planning to jump out from behind the sofa and give her a fright. 'Where are you hiding, you little so-and-so?' she demanded. 'It's not funny.'

No reply.

'All right, then. See if I care.' Leoni took the fags into the bedroom; now she felt that she really deserved one. Just as long as the little horror didn't come sneaking in and surprise her in the act.

Most of them were quite damp – how could that have happened? But one, lurking in the corner of the packet, was dry enough to light. She slid the sash window up and leaned out, sucking on the cigarette and inhaling deeply. It was dark; it was spitting rain.

The little monster was sure to get tired of her game sooner rather than later, Leoni decided, contemplating the glowing tip of her cigarette reflectively. Worse luck.

Miranda rang Sophie and explained briefly: she had Alison Barnett's sister with her, and she needed to have a photo enlarged. It might provide a vital clue to the girl's murder.

'Alison Barnett's sister?' Sophie echoed. 'Of course I'll help. Bring her round.'

She hadn't been in her darkroom for weeks – scarcely at all, in fact, since Dominic had helped her to set it up. But the few tantalising words of Miranda Swan had excited her interest.

They arrived within a few minutes, and introductions were made. Sophie didn't say that she'd seen Jacquie Darke before: out of the window, that day the previous week when the bereaved sister had been in Quire Close with the policeman, Sergeant Merriday. It *was* the same woman, definitely.

'I'm really sorry to disturb you, Mrs Lilburn,' Jacquie said. 'Miranda tells me that you've had an operation recently.'

'Please, call me Sophie.' She didn't want to talk about her operation; she didn't want to tell these two sympathetic women that her useless womb had been cut out, that she would never have a baby. 'Tell me,' she went on quickly, 'how I can help you.'

Jacquie produced the photo. 'I'm sure that if this were a bit bigger, and a bit less murky, it might help to identify this man. He might have been the person who murdered my sister.'

Michael Thornley, thought Sophie, peering at the indistinct image. There would surely be someone in the choir who could identify him, if it were indeed he. 'Do you have the negative?' she asked.

Jacquie groaned. 'No. Is it necessary?' Darren, she was sure, had kept the negatives from the roll of film. Just in case he ever needed some leverage against her, something to blackmail her with.

'Not absolutely. It would just have made things a bit easier, that's all.' Sophie led them upstairs to her darkroom; her mind on the problem at hand rather than on herself, she moved more quickly than she had done since the operation.

* * *

It was cold, with rain falling like icy needles, and it was dark. Frannie was so jubilant at her escape, though, so full of self-congratulation, that she didn't even notice the rain or the cold. The dark was a bit more off-putting; she'd never been out after dark by herself before.

But she knew where she was going. And though she'd not been there on her own, the cathedral was like a beacon: enormous, floodlit, visible from anywhere in town. Frannie knew that as long as she headed towards the cathedral, she would be going in the right direction.

People in a hurry pushed past her, not noticing the coatless girl walking along so determinedly on her own. That was just as well: what, she wondered, would she have said if someone had stopped her?

Once she'd reached the cathedral, she sheltered for a moment beneath the overhang of the great west door, trying to get her bearings. This was the way she'd come with Jacquie. Which way had they walked after that, after Evensong? Where, exactly, was Quire Close in relation to the west door?

After a few minutes of trial and error, she found the arch leading into Quire Close. Now she had it made; she was in sight of her goal. The Precentor's House, down at the very end: Mrs Swan would take her inside, would let her sit by the fire and warm up. Mrs Swan would be able to tell her how to find Jacquie.

Frannie sped the last few yards down Quire Close. She couldn't reach the high, old-fashioned bell, but the brass knocker was easily accessible. She gave it a few good bangs and waited. A moment later she tried again; still no one came.

*   *   *

'She's done *what*?' Tim felt himself go cold; with some detached part of his brain he registered the sensation. He'd read about it before, heard people he was interviewing describe the feeling – 'my blood ran cold,' they'd say – but had never experienced it himself till now.

'I'm sorry,' babbled the wretched girl. 'She's gone missing. I just can't find her. I thought maybe she was hiding somewhere in the flat. Behind the sofa, like, or in one of the cupboards. But I've looked everywhere. She's not in the flat, Mr Merriday. She's not here.'

'But how could she have got out? And why would she do such a thing?' he argued, not ready to believe that Leoni Hollis could be right and that Frannie had indeed disappeared.

'I'd just popped . . . to the loo,' Leoni explained unconvincingly. 'Just for a minute. When I came out, she was gone. She'd been playing that squeaky old thing, and then she wasn't playing it any more, and she wasn't here. I swear, Mr Merriday. She's skived off.'

'Dear God,' breathed Tim. What did people do when their children went missing? They called the police. But he *was* the police.

Sophie explained the complicated apparatus. Without a negative, she said, she would have to photograph the snapshot itself, then develop the new photograph. The newly created negative could then be enlarged, and she might be able to do something about lightening it as well.

It would all take time. But they wanted to wait – to watch, insofar as they could see in the dark – while she carried out the procedure.

Jacquie wrinkled her nose at the unexpected smell of the darkroom. 'A bit . . . pungent, isn't it?'

Sophie laughed. 'I suppose it is. I'm so used to it that I never notice it any longer. It's a pretty potent mix of chemicals.'

'Can't you do it all on a computer?' Miranda asked. 'I thought I saw something on television about that.'

'Oh, that's the way it's all going these days,' Sophie agreed. 'Digital enhancement, and all that. But I suppose I'm a purist, old-fashioned enough to prefer the traditional way of doing things. Hands-on. And there's still something magical,' she added, 'about putting a piece of photographic paper into the developing fluid and watching the image appear from nowhere.'

Jacquie didn't think that she would ever get used to the smell, no matter how long she tried. But she was fascinated by the procedure. It seemed very complicated to her, as the piece of paper was transferred from one tray of odorous fluid to another, all in the dark. Sophie tried to explain to them what she was doing each step of the way; it was so difficult to see.

'Now,' said Sophie, taking the finished product from its final fixing bath, and clipping it to the drying line, 'This is a bit wet to handle just yet. I suggest that we go downstairs and have a cup of tea. By the time we've done that, it will be ready, and we'll be able to take a proper look at it.'

Frannie huddled into a sheltered corner of the stone porch, shivering. She didn't know where else to go, what else to do. Perhaps she could go to the cathedral and look for Canon Swan there, but it had started raining much harder and she was loath to leave her bit of shelter.

Surely someone would come soon.

She lost track of how long she'd been there. The cathedral bells continued to chime the quarter hours.

Then, just about the time she'd stopped being able to feel her fingers, she saw a pair of highly polished black shoes approaching. 'Frannie?' said the incredulous voice of Canon Swan. 'What on earth are you doing here, my dear?'

'I'm . . . cold,' she said, teeth chattering.

'I should think so, too. Come in. Come in, and we'll soon have you warmed up.'

He led her into the kitchen, close to the Aga, and fetched a blanket to wrap her in. 'Now,' he said. 'How about some tea? To warm your insides.'

'I don't like tea,' she managed through chattering teeth.

'That's not the point, my dear.' Expertly he made a pot of tea, lacing her mug with plenty of sugar and milk. 'Drink this,' he ordered, and she obeyed, warming her hands on the mug as she did so.

'Now,' said Canon Swan, when he was satisfied that she was beginning to thaw out. 'You can tell me what this is all about. What is your father thinking of, letting you out on your own after dark?'

'He doesn't know,' she confessed sheepishly. 'I ran away. Sort of. Not from *him*. From horrid Leoni, my baby-sitter.' She invested the last word with suitable scorn.

'Hold on. Your father doesn't know you're here?'

'No.'

He shook his head, frowning, and made a sort of tutting noise. 'He must be sick with worry, then. Don't you think so?'

That hadn't occurred to her. Insofar as she'd thought

about her father at all in relation to her plans, she was hoping that he would be enraged with the negligent Leoni, and sack her on the spot. 'I expect so,' she said meekly.

'Then I'd better ring him, hadn't I?'

Frannie nodded.

Canon Swan rang the police station, and on being told that Sergeant Merriday was no longer there, he tried the mobile phone number supplied by Frannie.

Tim answered on the first ring. 'Yes?'

'Sergeant, this is Peter Swan. I have your daughter here with me. At my house in Quire Close.'

'I'll be there straight away,' said Tim. 'Five minutes. Ten, if the traffic's bad.'

'He'll be here in a few minutes,' the Canon reported to Frannie. 'That gives you just about enough time to tell me what's going on.'

She hung her head. 'I'll tell you, if you'll promise not to tell Dad.'

'I promise.'

'I wanted to see Mrs Swan. I wanted her to tell me Jacquie Darke's phone number. And,' she added truthfully, 'I wanted to get Leoni in trouble.'

'Ah, Frannie.' He smiled at her, his stern, ugly face becoming once again that of the jolly man she remembered from the other night. 'If anyone is in trouble over this, I don't think it's going to be Leoni.'

'I expect you're right,' she agreed with regret.

'I've never met Michael Thornley,' said Sophie, taking her turn to pore over the photo. 'At least not as far as I know. But I have to say that he looks quite familiar to me, in an odd sort of way.'

'I thought the same thing,' confirmed Miranda. 'Is this a good likeness of Mike, Jacquie? As you remember him?'

'I wish I could remember better,' she said ruefully. 'But to tell you the truth, I never paid that much attention to him at the time. And it was years ago, now. I *think* it's a good likeness.'

The doorbell rang. Sophie froze, then told herself that it wasn't very likely to be Leslie Clunch at this time in the afternoon. And even if it were, she wasn't alone; there was safety in numbers.

It was Dominic, apologising that he was so late. 'I was held up at school,' he explained cheerfully. 'We had extra games today. Is there any tea left in the pot?'

'Come in. There's always tea for you.'

He stopped just inside the door, sniffing. 'You've been in the darkroom,' he said with a grin. 'I can smell it on your clothes. What have you been up to, then?'

She didn't want to tell him; it still didn't seem suitable to her to be discussing such a sordid business with him. 'It's a long story,' she evaded, taking him through to the sitting room.

'Oh, I'm sorry. I didn't know you had company.'

Sophie made the introductions. 'Jacquie, Miranda, my friend Dominic Verey. Dominic, I think you may have met Mrs Swan. And this is Mrs Darke.'

Dominic acknowledged Miranda and Jacquie with the good manners that his mother had drummed into him over the years.

Jacquie, Sophie saw, was looking at him in a very peculiar way, her brows drawn together. 'I'm sure we've met,' she said.

'Perhaps,' Dominic replied courteously; his mother had told him never to contradict a lady.

Jacquie looked down at the photo in her hand, then back up at Dominic. Wordlessly, in an almost involuntary gesture, she held it out to him. 'This,' she said, 'is very like you.'

Dominic took the photo and studied it, puzzled. 'Where did you get this, then?' he asked.

Of course, thought Sophie, going numb. That was why the man in the photo looked so familiar. 'But it can't be Dominic,' she heard her voice saying.

'No, it's not me. But people have always said we're alike.' He glanced, baffled, from Jacquie to Sophie and back at the photo. 'Where did you get this?' he repeated.

'I don't understand,' said Miranda.

'It's my brother,' Dominic explained. 'Worthington. What are you doing with a photo of my brother?'

Chapter 24

Frannie received a telling-off such as she had never before experienced in her life. Her father was livid with anger – anger which she instinctively realised was bound up with his love for her and his worry about her.

She was sorry for the distress she'd caused him, and she told him as much with downcast eyes.

'I just don't know what you were thinking of, Frannie,' he said in a deadly quiet, reasonable voice which affected her more than screaming or shouting would have done. 'Anything could have happened to you, out on your own like that. You might have been run down by a bus, or snatched by someone. You might have frozen to death, without a coat. I thought you had some sense, Frannie. I can't tell you how disappointed I am in you.'

'I won't do it again,' she promised.

'You're damned right you won't. And you will apologise, as well, to Leoni, and to Canon Swan.'

If he made her apologise to Leoni, she would do it with her fingers crossed behind her back, she decided. She was sorry that she'd distressed her father, and inconvenienced

Canon Swan, but she was not at all sorry that she'd upset Leoni; it was no more than the useless girl deserved. She would do it again, in a different way, if she got a chance.

It was a bit later, though, after her father had left her alone to reflect on her sins, that she got the idea to make a bargain with God.

'How about this, God?' she whispered. 'I'll promise to be nice to Leoni. I won't give her any more grief, and I won't complain about having her look after me. If you'll bring Jacquie back, that is. That's all you have to do. You don't even have to help them get together – Jacquie and Dad. You can leave that to me. And if you do, I'll be very good. For the rest of my life. I promise.'

Now there was absolutely no question about whether or not to go to the police: Jacquie knew that she had to do it, and Miranda backed her up.

'This is really important,' Miranda said. 'It's a real breakthrough. You must tell them, tell *Tim*. He'll know how to handle it.'

'But he isn't on the case any longer,' Jacquie pointed out.

Miranda smiled. 'Never mind about that. He'll know what to do.'

In the end, Miranda suggested that she should ask Tim to come to the Precentor's House, rather than sending Jacquie off to the police station. That way she could be there, discreetly in the background, in case her support were needed.

Miranda made the phone call, on Friday morning. She didn't explain to Tim what it was about, only that it was important.

Tim came promptly, and was stunned to find Jacquie in Miranda's drawing room. He blinked to make sure that he hadn't imagined her, conjured her up out of his own longing. 'I thought you'd gone,' he said, wanting to give Miranda an accusing look but unable to take his eyes from Jacquie's face. 'She told me you'd gone.'

Jacquie smiled involuntarily as her eyes met his. 'I *did* go. But I've come back. I have something to show you. Something important.'

A fair amount of explanation was necessary, though Jacquie wasn't keen to go into great detail about the circumstances of how she had come into possession of the photo after so many years. 'It had been in the camera for all that time,' she concluded, when she'd related everything else. 'My ex-husband found it and gave it to me.'

'And you're telling me,' he echoed, bewildered, 'that *this*, this Mike, the man in the photo, is not Michael Thornley after all, but Worthington Verey.'

'That's right.'

Tim studied the enlargement. 'You're certain?'

'There doesn't seem to be much doubt. I took this photo, eleven years ago, of a man I knew as Mike. And Dominic Verey says that it is definitely his brother. Worthington Verey.'

'But why "Mike"?' Tim shook his head.

Miranda answered. 'Michael is his middle name, his brother said. He was called after his godfather, the Archbishop of Canterbury: Worthington Michael Ramsey Verey.'

'The Archbishop of Canterbury.' Tim closed his eyes and groaned as he visualised his career disappearing down the plug-hole. 'Do you have any idea what a nightmare you've got me into?'

'Michael Ramsey is dead,' Miranda pointed out, smiling in spite of herself. 'He can't do anything to hurt you.'

'But Worthington Verey is very much alive, and so is his mother. And the Dean. And the Bishop. And the whole ruddy Church of England.'

'I'm sorry,' said Jacquie. 'I had to tell you.'

Tim leaned forward in his chair, his hands clasped between his knees. 'Of course you did. But do you understand the problem here?' he asked her.

'I can see that it's difficult.'

'Difficult? It's . . . impossible.' Now he addressed Miranda. 'Your husband is a canon. You must understand what we're up against.'

'The Established Church, in all its power and panoply.'

'Exactly.' He shook his head. 'Worthington Verey is an important man, by anyone's reckoning. A Clerk in Holy Orders – isn't that the phrase? I'm not sure what his exact title is right now, or his position, but he's very likely the next Dean of Westmead, if his mother is to be believed.'

'I looked him up in Peter's *Crockford*,' Miranda said. 'He's the Rector of St Mary's, Tidmouth, and Rural Dean of the Tidmouth Deanery.'

At that, another worrying thought struck Tim. 'You haven't discussed this with your husband, have you?'

'No,' she assured him. 'Though it was difficult not to – I'm not used to keeping things from Peter. But I didn't want to say anything to him until Jacquie had talked to you. The only other person who knows anything about this,' Miranda added, 'is Sophie Lilburn.'

'What about Dominic Verey?'

Miranda shook her head. 'We didn't tell him anything.'

'Only,' Jacquie amplified, 'that we happened to have a photo of his brother because he'd once known my sister. And I don't think he had any idea of who I was – or Alison, either.'

Well, thought Tim ruefully, that was something, anyway. The more people who knew about this, the more limited his own options were.

It *was* a significant discovery, he was convinced – the best and most promising lead they'd had in eleven years: an identifiable photo of the man who was Alison Barnett's link to Westmead.

But that identification suddenly opened up a whole new can of worms, a huge number of difficulties that hadn't existed before.

What was he to do with this new information?

If he started asking questions without clearing it with the Superintendent, especially now that he'd so definitively been taken off the case, he risked a repeat of the disastrous scenario he'd been through once before.

And if he *did* go to the Superintendent, he would be in trouble as well. The Superintendent was a friend of the Dean; the Dean was indebted to Elspeth Verey for his job. For all he knew, the Superintendent was a friend of Elspeth Verey's as well. If he wasn't careful, Tim knew that he could find himself back in uniform, issuing speeding tickets.

Tim wanted to catch Alison Barnett's killer: he had wanted that passionately from the day he'd seen her limp body on the ground, in front of this very house. For eleven years he'd wanted it. It had always been personal for him. Not just another case.

And now it was personal in a very different way.

If he could pull this off, he would have proven himself in Jacquie's eyes. No longer would she despise him for being a useless bungler. With her sister's murder solved, she might look on him with favour, and be ready for a fresh start. They could forget about the way their relationship had begun, and how quickly it had gone wrong. All that would be behind them. They could begin again, from scratch.

If only.

When he spoke, it was to Jacquie, almost as if Miranda had vanished from the room. 'I know I've told you this before,' he said quietly. 'And I know I wasn't able to deliver. But I *do* want to catch Alison's killer. If Worthington Verey murdered her, I promise you that I'll do my very best to bring him to justice. He shouldn't be above the law, just because he's a clergyman and his mother has so much influence.'

Jacquie regarded him with a level gaze, and her tone matched his in gravity. 'I believe you,' she said. 'And I believe that if anyone can do it, Tim, *you* can.'

Sophie was on edge, distracted, unable to concentrate on anything. That morning she'd given Chris short shrift, refusing to confide in him, though he could tell that something was very wrong. He'd retreated, hurt, to school, and left her to her broodings.

The events of the day before had unsettled her profoundly, shaking her confidence in her own judgement and the assumptions on which she'd built her world.

Dominic's brother, a murderer: it seemed a fairly good bet, in view of that damning photo. And what, then, of

Leslie Clunch? Where did that leave him? The purloined and long-concealed diary, the suspicious circumstances of Charmian's death – were all those things, then, no longer germane? Was he just a sick-minded, pathetic old man whom her overactive imagination had inflated to create a monster and a murderer?

If Worthington Verey had killed Alison Barnett, then Sophie was in no danger from Leslie Clunch.

That, though, was little consolation. If she had misjudged Clunch, she still had no pity to spare for him; nothing could change her visceral reaction to him, and the fact that she despised him.

And when, that morning, the doorbell rang, she was no less disinclined to answer it.

'Mrs Lilburn?' said a voice on the other side of the door. 'It's Sergeant Merriday.'

'Oh! Just a minute.' Could it be to do with Worthington Verey, then?

She let him in; she offered him a cup of coffee, which he declined.

'Sorry I didn't ring to let you know that I was coming,' he said. 'But I was in the close, and thought that it was time we had another word.'

Another word. Sophie led him through to the sitting room and took a seat facing him, apprehensive. 'What can I do for you, Sergeant?'

'It's about Leslie Clunch,' Tim stated, not beating about the bush. 'The last time we talked, Mrs Lilburn, you didn't want to tell me why you were afraid of him, why you distrusted him. I was wondering whether you might have changed your mind.'

Sophie clasped her hands together in her lap and stared

down at them, not wanting to meet the policeman's pale blue eyes.

Everything had changed. Why shouldn't she tell him? Yes, she had promised Olive Clunch. But now that there seemed to be little danger of him being arrested for Alison Barnett's murder . . .

With sudden resolution, Sophie looked up. 'Yes,' she said. 'Yes, I've changed my mind.'

Tim walked towards the arch at the end of Quire Close, hands in his pockets, shaking his head. He'd called in to see Sophie Lilburn on impulse, as much as anything to buy himself some time before he had to think about what to do with the explosive information about Worthington Verey. And Sophie Lilburn had given him more than he'd bargained for.

Once she'd started talking, it seemed she couldn't stop. Leslie Clunch: voyeur, dirty old man, at the very least. And at the most? Perhaps not a murderer, though the matter of Charmian's death seemed to bear further looking into, but he was certainly guilty of obstruction of justice. Would Alison Barnett's killer have been found eleven years ago if they'd had her diary, if they'd known her name? Quite probably. That put Clunch's crime in a different light, and it was very serious indeed.

There was no time like the present to deal with it, Tim decided. Clunch lived by the arch at the end of the close; this might be a good opportunity to have a word.

He was in luck. Clunch came to the door with an enquiring look.

Tim identified himself. 'I wondered whether you had a few moments for a little chat, Mr Clunch.'

Clunch looked over his shoulder towards the interior of his house and spoke quietly. 'My wife is asleep, Sergeant. She's an invalid.'

'If you prefer,' Tim said in a firm but unthreatening voice, 'we could go down to the station, where we wouldn't disturb her. If there isn't anywhere here for a private word. I wouldn't bother you if it weren't important,' he added.

The man hesitated for a moment, seeming to weigh up his options as curiosity and self-importance warred to overcome the natural aversion to the police which is shared by most of the population. Tim had seen that expression before, on the faces of innocent and guilty alike. 'All right, then,' Clunch said at last, stepping aside. 'We could go upstairs, I suppose.'

The house reeked of long-term illness, a fuggy closed-in smell. Tim, trying to ignore it, followed the old man up a narrow staircase to a tiny room with a window overlooking Quire Close. He crossed to the window and looked out while Clunch folded himself into the single shabby armchair. 'Nice view,' Tim said.

'Yes.'

'You can see all the way down to the end. To where Alison Barnett's body was found,' he added deliberately.

'We didn't live here then,' Clunch stated.

Tim was well aware of that, but he kept his face and his voice bland, noncommittal. 'Did you not?'

'No. We've only been in this house since I retired.'

There was a long silence which Tim did nothing to break. Declining to perch on the bed, he leaned against the window, hands in pockets, relaxed, and waited.

'Is that what this is about, then?' Clunch asked at last. 'About Alison Barnett?'

'Why would you think so, Mr Clunch?'

'Because she's been identified. It's been in the papers. People are talking about it.' His hands moved from his lap to the arms of the chair.

'And what are people saying?'

'That she was murdered by someone in Quire Close. Michael Thornley, I heard – one of the lay clerks. I remember him.' Clunch seemed to gain in confidence as he talked. 'I always did think there was something shifty about that bloke. His eyes were a bit too close together, if you know what I mean. I might have even said so at the time. In fact, I'm pretty sure that I did. To that inspector who was in charge of the case. "Keep your eye on that Michael Thornley," I said. But he didn't listen to me.'

It was such patent nonsense that Tim had to restrain himself from saying so. 'You do remember the original investigation, then, Mr Clunch.'

'Remember it?' Clunch's chest expanded as he relived his past glories. 'I was instrumental in that investigation, Sergeant. You may be too young to recall,' he added pompously. 'But I was probably the last person to see her – apart from the murderer, of course. I co-operated fully with the police. I gave them a full description. And I produced her suitcase. She'd given it to me for safekeeping, you see.'

Tim folded his arms across his chest. 'You had her suit-case.'

'Yes, that's right. As soon as I realised that it had to do with the murder, I handed it over.'

'Without opening it?'

Clunch bristled slightly, his honour impugned. 'Well, of course.'

'What about the diary?' Tim asked, in the same laid-back tone of voice.

'Diary?' The word ended on a squeak, and Clunch's eyes slewed from Tim to the chest of drawers.

'Why, Mr Clunch, did you not hand over Alison Barnett's diary along with her suitcase?'

'I don't know what you're talking about. There was no diary.' He spoke confidently, almost belligerently.

'If you didn't open the suitcase, Mr Clunch, how do you know there was no diary?' Tim returned his hands to his pockets and began to jingle his change.

There was a brief pause, and when Clunch spoke, it was with less confidence. 'There was nothing in the paper about a diary. I would have remembered if there had been.'

'How could it have been in the paper, when you were the only one who knew about it? You kept it, Mr Clunch. The police had no idea of its existence.'

Clunch swallowed and picked at the frayed threads of the chair arm. 'I suppose her sister told you she had a diary,' he stated. 'Well, I don't know anything about that. I told you, I didn't open the suitcase.'

Tim continued to jingle the coins, allowing the other man to stew in his juices for a moment. 'Would you object to a search of your house, Mr Clunch?' he asked at last.

Startled, Clunch looked up at him. 'A search? But my wife is an invalid. I told you. She can't be doing with that. And you wouldn't find anything. Alison Barnett's diary? Why would I have Alison Barnett's diary?'

Tim's mouth curved in a mirthless smile. 'You tell me.'

'You may not search my house,' Clunch said, a truculent set to his jaw. 'I won't allow it. And I shall complain to the Superintendent. Harassment, that's what this is. I'm a law-abiding citizen. I co-operated with the police from the beginning. What you suggest is outrageous.'

'Oh, I think that the Superintendent might see it a bit differently,' suggested Tim. 'When I tell him that I can produce a witness who has seen the diary, who can place it in your possession. I don't think I would have any trouble obtaining a search warrant, based on this information I have. And if you were to try to hide the diary, or get rid of it, before a search could be carried out . . .' He left his words hanging, and watched as Clunch disintegrated before his eyes.

In an instant the bravado was gone, and the pugnaciousness, leaving behind a trembling old man. Tears oozed from the corners of Clunch's eyes; he didn't even ask who or how. 'I didn't mean any harm,' he whispered in a paper-thin voice. 'I didn't kill her, you know. I just . . . wanted to keep it. To . . . read it.'

'If you'd like to give it to me now, Mr Clunch, perhaps we won't have to disturb your wife.'

'Yes. Of course.' Clunch sounded positively eager to co-operate now; he didn't even have to get up from the chair, but reached down to open the bottom drawer of the chest of drawers and pulled out a little purple book. 'Here it is. Better late than never, eh, Sergeant?' He handed it to Tim with a grotesque attempt at a wink, man to man. 'Here it is, and we won't need to say anything more about it.'

'Thank you.' Tim resisted the temptation to open the diary. He put it in his pocket as Clunch rose from his chair.

'If that's all, Sergeant, I'll need to start the lunch soon. Olive – Mrs Clunch – will be expecting—'

'Oh, I don't think that's quite all.'

Clunch subsided back into the chair. 'I didn't take anything else, Sergeant. I can assure you of that. Just the diary. Nothing else.'

'That may be so.' Tim looked at him levelly. 'But there is the little matter of obstruction of justice. You withheld material evidence that had a great bearing on this case, Mr Clunch. If we'd had the diary, if we'd known her name, the case might have been solved eleven years ago.'

'But I didn't mean any harm,' insisted Clunch. 'And now that I've given it to you . . .'

'I don't think it's quite as simple as that.'

Clunch swallowed, his Adam's apple bobbing on his scrawny throat. 'You're not going to arrest me, are you?'

'I'm keeping my options open.'

'But my wife,' Clunch pleaded. 'She needs me. You can't—'

As if to reinforce his words, at that moment a querulous voice called from below. 'Leslie! My tablets!'

'My wife. Can I go to her?'

Tim nodded. 'I'll wait.'

After Clunch had gone, he sank into the tatty armchair and thought about what to do next. It had been absurdly easy to get the diary; Clunch had caved in without much of a fight. Now he was almost beginning to feel sorry for the pathetic old man. And Mrs Clunch – what *would* become of her if her husband was taken from her?

Then he reminded himself about Alison Barnett, nameless for eleven years because of the old man's interference, about the countless hours of police time wasted. About Jacquie Darke, denied justice for her sister's death.

And Charmian. What about Charmian Clunch?

When, after a few minutes, he heard Clunch climbing the stairs again, Tim returned to his station by the window.

'You see?' said Clunch, a bit breathless. 'She needs me. All of the time. There's no one else.'

'Tell me about Charmian,' Tim said. 'Tell me about your daughter's death.'

Clunch gasped as if he'd been struck, sinking back into the chair. 'Charmian?' he quavered.

'How did she die?' Tim demanded bluntly. 'Did you kill her?'

The colour drained from the old man's face. 'Kill her? How could you even suggest such a thing? I loved my daughter. There isn't a day I don't think of her, miss her . . .'

'Then how did she die?'

Clunch turned his head away, as if ashamed of his tears. 'She killed herself,' he whispered.

Tim put his hands in his pockets and traced the edges of the diary. 'You drove her to it, then,' he suggested. 'You molested her, didn't you? Your own daughter.'

At that, Clunch turned to him with a look of outraged horror. 'Never,' he gasped. 'I never laid a finger on the girl. I never touched her.'

No, thought Tim, suddenly understanding. Touching wasn't Clunch's style. He was a voyeur; it all went on in his mind. 'But you looked, didn't you?' he said softly. 'You watched her.' He could imagine it all: peeping at keyholes, lurking round corners, always there. Panting, salivating. Enough to drive a sensitive young girl to take her own life. 'Daddy, I'm so sorry. I just couldn't take it any more.'

'She was . . . beautiful,' Clunch choked. 'I couldn't help it. I knew it was wrong, but I couldn't help it.' He raised a tear-stained face towards the policeman. 'And now I miss her every day of my life. My lovely Charmian. She's dead. Haven't I been punished enough?'

Sickened, Tim felt all at once that he had to escape – escape from the stifling atmosphere of that house with its pervasive smell of illness, escape from the self-pitying snivelling of the old man who had driven his daughter to suicide. He needed fresh air; he needed to wash his hands.

'I'm going now,' he said abruptly, moving towards the door.

An expression of relief crossed Clunch's face. 'You're not arresting me, then?'

'Oh, I'll be back,' said Tim. 'You can count on that, Mr Clunch. I'll be back.'

Sophie was not looking forward to Elspeth Verey's visit. She tried not to think about what was behind that visit, and why Elspeth had chosen this moment to confront her.

The time set for the visit was an awkward one, after lunch and before tea. Should she offer some sort of refreshment? Would Elspeth expect it?

Elspeth was aware that she was an invalid; surely she wouldn't expect much. But a cup of tea would be common courtesy, and Sophie knew from experience that it often oiled the wheels of conversation and eased potentially uncomfortable situations. So she laid a tray and awaited Elspeth's arrival. As the clock crawled towards three she looked round the room, trying to imagine how it would appear to Elspeth. Meanly proportioned, in comparison to her own gracious drawing room. Untidy, certainly, since Madeline had departed. Too late to do much about that, Sophie told herself with a philosophic shrug. The freesias which Elspeth had sent had begun to wilt, their delicate fragrance now overpowered by the smell of the stale water in the vase. And, Sophie saw at the last minute, the photo of Alison Barnett and the man called Mike had been left behind on one of the side tables; Jacquie had taken the enlargement, and forgotten the original. That could have been fatal. She shoved it into a drawer.

The doorbell rang dead on time, seconds after the cathedral's bells chimed the hour. Sophie answered it as quickly as she could manage. 'Come in,' she said. 'Can I take your coat?'

Elspeth Verey's coat was in fact a cape, which she unfastened and removed in one quick movement, revealing an outfit which reflected her customary distinctive style: a rich velvet tunic in a shade of silver which complemented her hair, worn over loose black trousers. She certainly knew what colours suited her, reflected Sophie, and how to dress for maximum impact. It was a style both timelessly elegant and nonconformist, setting fashion rather than following it. Sophie was glad that she'd taken some care with her own appearance, having changed from her comfortable invalid garb into a favourite dress and silk scarf, and even having applied some make-up.

They passed through into the front room, and though it was the first time Elspeth had been in Sophie's house, she wasted no time in perusing the room, but went straight for a high-backed chair near the fire.

'Would you like a cup of tea?' Sophie offered.

'No, thank you, Mrs Lilburn. This isn't a social call.'

Sophie, taken aback by the brusqueness of the other woman's words, nodded and took a seat on the sofa.

From the beginning she wished she hadn't. Elspeth's

chair was higher, which meant that she could look down on Sophie. It gave her an advantage, a position of superiority, which Sophie found almost threatening, given Elspeth's opening words. Her only defence at this point was silence; she waited for her guest to make the next move.

'I suppose you're wondering why I've called on you.'

Sophie dipped her head in acknowledgement, still saying nothing.

'It has to do with my son.'

Just as she'd feared, then.

'Dominic,' Elspeth added.

'Yes. Dominic.' She smiled as she said his name.

Elspeth did not return the smile. 'You may or may not be aware, Mrs Lilburn, that people in Westmead are talking about you and my son.'

Sophie felt herself flush. 'People in Westmead talk about a lot of silly things,' she said tartly. 'It shows that they have nothing better to do.'

'That's as may be. But I don't like it when my son is the subject of idle gossip.'

'Surely,' said Sophie, 'that isn't my problem. I have no control over what people talk about.'

Elspeth lowered her eyelids. 'The question I ask myself, Mrs Lilburn, is exactly what *is* your problem? Why do you feel it necessary to spend time with my son?'

Sophie wanted to tell her that it was none of her business. Instead she tried to be temperate. 'We're friends,' she said. 'I don't know why people find that so difficult to understand.'

'Let me be blunt, if I must.' Elspeth wasn't looking at Sophie. 'My son is sixteen years old. Sixteen,' she repeated for emphasis. 'It is not normal for a boy of sixteen to seek out as a friend, as you describe it, a woman of – I suppose you must be thirty?'

'Thirty-one.'

'A woman of thirty-one,' Elspeth continued. 'Nor is it normal for a woman of thirty-one to depend for friend-ship on a boy of sixteen.'

Sophie's calm voice, in reply, revealed nothing of her feelings: a complex mixture of amazement, irritation, embarrassment, and anger. 'What are you implying?'

Elspeth took her time in responding, choosing her words with care. 'There are some who might say – indeed, there are some who *have* suggested – that yours is an ... improper ... relationship. It is not unknown for women of a certain age to prey sexually upon young men. And Dominic is, I recognise, a very attractive young man.'

Feeling her flush deepen, Sophie interrupted. 'That is ridiculous. There's nothing like that between me and Dominic.'

Elspeth held up her hand. 'Please, Mrs Lilburn. Let me finish.' She leaned forward in her chair and looked at Sophie. 'I believe you. I don't think for one moment that you have seduced my son, or are using him as a sexual plaything. I'm only telling you what other people are saying.'

'Well, if that's what they're saying, they're wrong. And I feel sorry for them, if that's the best they can come up with.'

Elspeth continued, as if Sophie hadn't spoken. 'So I have to ask myself, Mrs Lilburn, if that isn't the motive for this ... unusual ... relationship, then what *is*?'

'I've told you. We're friends.'

Again Elspeth ignored the interruption. 'Shall I tell you what I think?'

'Please do.'

'I am aware,' said Elspeth, 'that you have been unable to have children. That you have, in fact, recently had an operation which will make it impossible for you ever to do so.'

Stung by the painful reminder, Sophie nodded; she was unsure, now, where this was leading.

'And I suggest to you that in your thwarted desire for motherhood, you have fastened upon my son and tried to make him into some sort of substitute for the children you can't have.'

The words hit Sophie as a blow to the stomach. Her stitches contracted painfully; in an involuntary gesture her hands went to them. For a moment she couldn't speak, then became aware that Elspeth was waiting for her response. 'It's not true,' she gasped.

'I would expect you to deny it. But it's quite clear to me.'

'No.'

Elspeth's voice went on with relentless calm. 'And what's more, Mrs Lilburn, you have attempted to set yourself up against me. You not only monopolise my son's time, you also try to usurp my role in his life.'

The accusation astonished her. 'How could I do that?'

'You encourage him,' said Elspeth, 'in his defiance of me. All of this ridiculous nonsense about a career in photography. He's *my* son,' she added, with a bit more warmth. 'I know him. I know what's best for him. He's too young and inexperienced to make his own decisions about the direction of his life. And we don't need your interference.'

'It's *his* life,' Sophie stated, defiant. '*His* future, not yours. And if my telling him that fact constitutes interference, then I suppose I'm guilty.'

'As I thought.' Elspeth clasped her hands elegantly in her lap and looked down at them. 'I won't have it, Mrs Lilburn,' she said.

'What do you mean, you won't have it?'

'I want you,' said Elspeth in a considered yet firm tone, 'to stay away from my son.'

Sophie gasped, but collected herself enough to point out, 'I don't seek your son out, Mrs Verey. He comes here. If you're going to tell anyone to stay away, why don't you tell him to stay away from me?'

Elspeth unclasped her hands and made an impatient, dismissive gesture, as though flicking away a troublesome insect. 'Don't split hairs with me, Mrs Lilburn. You know very well what I mean.'

It was monstrous, outrageous. Sophie was furious, but she tried not to show it. 'And if I don't . . . obey your command?'

Elspeth pressed her lips together, looking beyond Sophie to the window, in the direction of the unseen cathedral. 'I could ruin your husband's career here. Very easily indeed.'

She *could*, Sophie realised. Elspeth Verey's power and influence were undisputed. A word from her in the Dean's ear and Chris would be effectively finished.

It was blackmail, pure and simple.

Impotence, pain, and anger surged through Sophie; she was incapable of speech.

'You'll find a way, I'm sure, to tell Dominic that his visits are no longer welcome,' Elspeth said tranquilly. 'I'll leave that to you.' Her manner implied that there could be no doubt but that Sophie would obey. 'Perhaps you could tell him that he has no talent at all as a photographer, that he's wasting your time.'

Stung on Dominic's behalf, Sophie found her voice. 'He has a great deal of talent,' she asserted. 'And I've told him so.'

'That's not the point. And it's irrelevant, in any case. Dominic *is* going to be a priest, Mrs Lilburn. Whether you like it or not.' At that, Elspeth rose from her chair, making ready to leave, her mission accomplished.

Your son is gay: the words pounded in Sophie's brain, demanding to be spoken aloud. She wanted to shout them, to repeat them over and over, to watch the horror and disbelief on Elspeth's face, gradually turning to a realisation of the truth.

Your son is gay.

She clamped her teeth together, biting back the words. She couldn't do it to Dominic. Badly as she wanted to lash out, to hurt Elspeth Verey, she couldn't use the most powerful weapon she had at her disposal. It *would* hurt Elspeth; but it would hurt Dominic, and their friendship, in equal measure.

Was it, though, the most powerful weapon?

'A priest,' Sophie heard herself saying in a deceptively toneless voice. 'Like your other son.'

'Like Worthington, yes.' Elspeth's expression grew fond as she spoke her son's name.

Sophie took a deep breath and went for it. 'And how would you feel if I told you that your precious son Worthington was a murderer?'

'A murderer? Don't be ridiculous.' She didn't seem

alarmed at the suggestion, nor even contemptuous, but merely dismissive.

'I think he murdered that girl in the close.'

Elspeth stopped. 'The girl?'

'Alison Barnett. Eleven years ago.' She said it in such a matter-of-fact way, without a hint of hysteria, that she amazed herself.

'What on earth would lead you to make such an utterly preposterous suggestion?' Elspeth was still scornful, but she sank back into her chair. 'He didn't know Alison Barnett. He'd never met the girl. Why would he kill her?'

'He *did* know her,' Sophie stated relentlessly. 'Didn't he tell you, then?' How much, she wondered, watching Elspeth's face, *did* Worthington's mother know? Then, and now? Had she known of the affair? Was she perhaps even aware, in an acknowledged or unacknowledged way, of his complicity in the girl's death? Had he confessed to her? Had she suspected?

'What are you talking about?' Elspeth's voice was wooden.

Sophie spoke deliberately, her eyes still on the other woman's face. 'He knew her. They met on holiday. They had an affair, or at any rate they slept together. She was pregnant with his child when she was murdered.'

Elspeth's skin was always white; now it was paler than pale, and the pupils of her eyes were enlarged so that they almost crowded out the blue of the iris altogether. She opened her mouth, then shut it again; she moistened her lips with her tongue. 'That's absurd,' she said at last. 'A monstrous lie.'

'Is it?'

She seemed to rally a bit; her pupils shrank.

'Worthington is a priest. He is a married man. You are clearly confusing him with someone else.'

'Married men can have affairs. Even priests can have affairs. And Worthington Verey was the man who made Alison Barnett pregnant.'

'You can't know that. You're just saying it to upset me. Because of Dominic.' Elspeth's hands were clasped together again, but now it was not a tranquil clasp; there was tension in her hands, as though she had to hold them together to keep from striking out.

Elspeth *did* know, Sophie realised. Elspeth knew about it; her surprise was not at the facts themselves, but that anyone else should have discovered them. 'I would scarcely invent something like that,' she said. 'I wouldn't have said it if I didn't know it was true. I can't prove that he murdered her, but I *can* prove that he knew her.'

'Impossible.'

In a fluid movement, Sophie reached out to the drawer where she'd stashed the incriminating photo, slid the drawer out, and closed her fingers over the photo. 'Here,' she said, holding it out to Elspeth. 'The woman in the picture is Alison Barnett. Can you deny that the man is your son?'

Elspeth's glance flicked over the photo. 'That is Worthington,' she acknowledged. 'And perhaps it does prove that he'd met her. But the rest of it is no more than wicked speculation.'

'Her sister was there. On the holiday in Greece. She knows what happened.'

For just an instant, Elspeth seemed to shrink into herself. Then she rallied, reached for the photo, and before Sophie could stop her, she tore it to bits.

'Why did you do that?'

'He didn't kill her,' Elspeth stated. 'I know my son. I know what he's capable of, and what he's not capable of. Worthington doesn't have it in him to kill anyone. I can't allow you to go about casting such wicked slander on him, on the basis of such flimsy evidence. I'm just protecting my son. I'd do anything to protect him.'

A mother's wishful thinking, Sophie told herself. She would probably be the same. If she had a son. 'I'm sure you wouldn't stop at lying to protect him. And if Worthington didn't kill her, then who did?'

Elspeth's pupils had contracted to black pinpoints. 'If you're so clever, Mrs Lilburn, why are you asking *me*?'

It was as if the world had turned upside down. Sophie looked at her, and in that instant she knew the truth: Elspeth Verey had just as much as told her. She would, she'd said, do anything to protect him. 'Worthington didn't kill her,' she said softly. '*You* did.'

The fine-boned patrician face looked as though it were carved from stone, but her voice, when she spoke, was no less civilised than it had been earlier. 'I would do anything to protect him,' she repeated.

'So that's why you killed her. To protect him.'

Elspeth nodded, with no more visible emotion than if she were accepting the offer of a cup of tea. 'He's always been too soft-hearted for his own good. He came back from holiday and told me about that girl. Told me he'd fallen in love with her, that he wanted to marry her.' She made a dismissive gesture. 'It was ridiculous, of course, and I told him so. Out of the question.'

Sophie couldn't believe what she was hearing; she was loath to interrupt, but couldn't help herself. 'But if he loved her . . .'

'Love!' Elspeth's face twisted with scorn. 'What does a young man like that know about love? What Worthington needed wasn't love, but a good wife. The *right* wife, who would be a help-meet for him, like my mother was for my father. Like I was for Richard.'

'And Alison Barnett wasn't good enough for him.'

'She most certainly was not. I hadn't met the girl, of course, but I could tell enough about her from his love-sick ramblings to know that. She was a nobody. She came from nowhere. She was even a nonconformist.' Startlingly, Elspeth pulled the corners of her mouth back in what could almost have been a smile, if it hadn't been so chillingly humourless. 'And he was on the verge of being engaged to Heather. I'd known her parents for years – her father is an archdeacon, you know.'

'And you chose Heather for him,' Sophie guessed.

'Of course. But he could see that she was right for him. And she *has* been right for him. She's given him three lovely children, she's supported his career and helped him along. Just as I did for Richard.' Elspeth half-closed her eyes. 'Richard had just died. His father. Worthington was upset, of course. Emotional. He was going to throw Heather over for that girl. "Life's too short," he said. But I convinced him how foolish it would be. In the end he knew I was right. Just before his ordination he asked Heather to marry him, and she accepted.'

And then, thought Sophie, Alison Barnett had come to Westmead, pregnant with his child. What malign coincidence had brought her to Elspeth's attention? 'How did you meet Alison?' she asked frankly. 'How did you know that she was the one?'

Elspeth turned her gaze towards the window, towards

Quire Close. 'Pure chance,' she said. 'It was practically outside this house that I came across her. The night before Worthington's ordination, it was. Priory House was being renovated. We hadn't moved in yet. I'd had so much on my mind, with Richard's death, and the new house, and the ordination, and the engagement, that I'd forgotten to check on something that I'd promised the builders I would make a decision about. So I was on my way down to the house. I saw her here in the close. She was looking lost, so I asked her if I could help her. Then I saw what she was wearing. My father's cross.'

On and on her voice went, emotionless. 'I'd given the cross to Worthington – it was right that he should have it, and he always wore it. When he came back from that holiday without it, he was evasive – said he must have misplaced it somewhere. So I knew who she was, of course, as soon as I saw it. And I knew why she'd come to Westmead – to find Worthington. I invited her into Priory House. It didn't take much encouragement to get her talking – all I had to do was listen. Every word she spoke confirmed my conviction of how very unsuitable she would have been as a wife for my son.' Elspeth paused.

'And then she told me about the baby.' Her face, carefully controlled till then, twitched. 'She wanted him to marry her, of course. And he would have done it. The sentimental fool – he would have done it. She would have found him, and he would have married her. Thrown everything away – his career, his future, Heather – for the sake of *love*. Don't you see? I couldn't allow him to do that. I had to stop her, before she made him waste his life.'

Made him waste his life, thought Sophie, chilled to the bone. As she herself was helping Dominic to waste his life?

'It was so easy,' Elspeth mused. 'All I had to do was grab the cross and twist the chain. It happened so quickly – she hardly knew what had happened. I don't suppose she felt much pain.'

No. Just the struggling of her lungs for breath, the blackness descending . . .

'Then I went back to the Deanery, where we were having a little family celebration for the ordination and the engagement. Nothing ostentatious, of course. We were a household in mourning.'

In mourning, but not for the poor girl whose dead body was, at the moment of their celebration, slumped in Priory House. Not for the grandchild who would never be born . . .

'And later on, much later, when everyone was asleep, I came back to Quire Close. I got rid of her handbag, I reclaimed my father's cross. Then I carried her out to the close, and left her in front of the Precentor's House.'

It all made so much sense to Sophie now, viewed from the point of view of Elspeth's twisted logic. Everything had been done to protect her precious son. But had Worthington ever known, or suspected, what Elspeth had done on his behalf? Was he complicit in her monstrous crime by sharing knowledge of it?

Elspeth turned her fine eyes back to Sophie; it was as if she read her mind. 'My son never knew,' she said. 'I couldn't have burdened him with that. He had no reason to connect the description of the unidentified dead girl in the press with the girl he'd met in Greece. We never spoke of it. And immediately after the ordination he went off to his new parish, his first curacy.'

'And you thought you'd got away with it,' Sophie said.

'No one came forward to identify her or give her a name. There was no evidence to link you or your son to her. Eventually the police gave up.'

Elspeth nodded, a small smile of satisfaction at the corners of her mouth.

Sickened by the smile, Sophie spoke passionately. 'You killed someone,' she said. 'A girl who had her whole life ahead of her. And her baby. You killed an innocent baby before it was born. Your grandchild. Aren't you even sorry about that?'

'I did what I had to do to protect my son's future. I would,' said Elspeth deliberately, 'do it again.'

Suddenly Sophie was afraid. In fear for her own life. Up till now it had not occurred to her to be so; they were two civilised women sitting together in an ancient house in the shadow of the cathedral, not thugs engaged in a fight to the death on the mean streets of some urban slum. But Elspeth was mad – clearly so – and Sophie was a double threat to her. She was a threat because of her friendship with Dominic, and her knowledge of Elspeth's crime had now made her far more dangerous. Elspeth had murdered once to protect one son; what would another murder be to her, to protect them both and maintain the status quo?

She wasn't, Sophie knew at that moment, ready to die. She would never have a chance to make things up with Chris, to put things right between them. He would never know how much she loved him, and how sorry she was that she'd let him down.

Elspeth, her face determined yet impassive, and somehow more frightening than anything Sophie had ever seen, stood and took a step towards her.

'It wouldn't do you any good to kill me,' Sophie said, trying to sound calm. 'You'd only get caught.'

'I don't think so, Mrs Lilburn. Who would ever suspect me of murdering you? I would say that I'd come here to call on you, and had found you dead. I know that that tedious little man, Clunch, calls on you. He fancies you, of course. I would suggest to the police that he might have done it. You rejected his advances, and he strangled you with your own scarf.'

Sophie's hands went to her throat, trying to untie the scarf and remove it. But her fingers felt paralysed; the silk slipped through them, the knot held. 'No,' she whispered. 'It wouldn't do you any good. I'm not the only one who knows about the photo.'

Elspeth paused. 'Who else knows?'

'Jacquie Darke. The sister. She has another copy, an enlargement. Miranda Swan knows, as well. They've been to the police with it.'

Elspeth took another step. 'And whom,' she said scornfully, 'do you think that the police are going to believe? Those women, or me? I can explain it to them, just as I did to you: my son knew the girl, and that's the end of it. He had nothing to do with her death.'

'They won't believe you,' Sophie said desperately. Elspeth was now only a few steps away; her hands were coming forward.

'I think they will. My husband knew the Chief Constable. He was a close personal friend of the Superintendent. I still see them both socially, and their wives. They would have no reason not to believe me.'

Sophie shrank back against the sofa as the beautifully

manicured hands seized the ends of her scarf. 'No,' she gasped. 'Don't.'

'You've interfered in my life, Mrs Lilburn. In the lives of my sons.' Elspeth's hands were strong; she twisted the scarf.

There was pain, and a wave of blackness. Was this, then, the end? Was Elspeth's face the last thing she would see, as it was the last thing that Alison Barnett had seen? Sophie struggled, clawing at the scarf, at Elspeth's hands. But it was no good; she was far too weak to fight, and Elspeth was determined to kill her.

With all the strength that she could summon, Sophie screamed. It wasn't much of a scream, but it was the best she could manage, and it took the form of her husband's name.

And then, miraculously, the pressure on her windpipe slackened; she gasped convulsively for breath, gulping at the air. As the blackness lifted, she saw that Elspeth had released the scarf, that she stood rigid, her arms now pinned to her sides.

Behind her, restraining her, was Chris.

Sophie looked at him and burst into tears.

Chapter 25

Saturday morning. Tim buried his face in the pillow, not ready to leave his resting place on the sofa. He was exhausted, bone tired. The day before had been one of the most momentous of his career, and now all he wanted to do was sleep.

Thank goodness that Chris Lilburn had had the presence of mind to phone him directly, instead of just ringing 999. It had saved valuable time; it had saved the necessity for a lot of explanation.

Even so, he still found it almost impossible to believe: Elspeth Verey, the uncrowned Queen of Westmead, a murderer. That very status had protected her from suspicion for all of these years; that, and the fact that she was a woman. Why, Tim asked himself, had everyone always assumed that Alison Barnett's killer was a man?

Part of it, he thought, was due to pure logistics: there had been no marks to indicate that the girl's body had been dragged to its resting place in the close, and it must have taken a great deal of strength to carry her. But that sort of strength was often evidenced in people in crisis;

they did what they had to do, women as well as men.

Elspeth Verey was not a slight woman, and she *had* done it.

Tim's first impulse, when Sophie Lilburn recounted to him the story that Elspeth had told her, was to believe that Elspeth was lying, was shielding her son. She had said that she would to anything to protect him: did that include assuming a burden of guilt that she knew was his? It would, in many ways, be the ultimate sacrifice, and Tim was more willing to believe her capable of that than of murder. It was true that Elspeth knew about the chain with which Alison had been killed – that one piece of evidence that only the murderer should have known, though it was possible that she might have learned that from Worthington, after the fact.

But at last Elspeth had persuaded him, with her unshakeable insistence that Worthington knew nothing at all of the murder, that when it had occurred, he was safely ensconced in the Deanery with his young brother Dominic and his fiancée Heather.

And then there was the undeniable evidence of the fact that Elspeth *had* tried to kill Sophie Lilburn. That, as much as anything, had convinced him.

This morning Elspeth Verey would be waking up in the less-than-comfortable surroundings of Westmead police station's lock-up cells. And this morning everyone in Westmead would know about it. Barry Sills, with his uncanny radar and contacts in the close, had been on to the story almost immediately; it would be featured in today's *Westmead Herald*, at least in some sketchy form, and by tomorrow it would have hit the national newspapers.

'Dad, are you still sleeping?' Frannie, in her nightgown, trailed out of the bedroom with Watson in her arms.

'Mmm.' He didn't move; maybe if he pretended to be asleep, she would go back to bed.

'Because I just wondered what we were going to do today. It's Saturday,' she reminded him. 'And it looks like a nice day.'

Saturday. This, he remembered with a sinking feeling, was the day he had promised to spend with Liz. And he hadn't yet had the courage to tell Frannie.

It had been his intention on Friday – knowing that Jacquie was back in Westmead, feeling that that fact somehow changed everything – to tell Liz that he would have to cancel their arrangement. But events had overtaken him, and he'd had other things on his mind. Now it was too late. He'd have to go through with it. There would, he tried to convince himself, be plenty of other opportunities to see Jacquie. This one day wouldn't make any difference.

He turned over and squinted at his watch. Liz would be arriving to collect them within the hour. But he still wasn't ready to tell Frannie.

When Sophie woke that morning, it was with the most extraordinary feeling of well-being. Extraordinary, because the day before had been traumatic in the extreme, overturning so many of her assumptions and presuppositions, putting her in a position where she'd almost lost her life, very nearly been murdered.

But she *hadn't* been murdered. She was alive, and glad to be so; with that realisation so many other things had fallen into place.

The main source of her well-being slept beside her: Chris. For the first time in weeks he had returned to their bed, and they had talked long into the night. He had held her comfortingly, her back against his chest, nestled like spoons. Now, in sleep, he maintained that position from which she had always derived so much comfort.

She loved him: she knew that now. She had always loved him, had never stopped loving him. But the baby problem had got in the way, overshadowing everything else. It was precisely *because* she loved him that it had become such a problem. She knew that he wanted a baby, and she knew as well that it was her fault that she couldn't give him one. The guilt was enormous: she had postponed child-bearing because of her career, and for so many other unspoken reasons, until it was too late, and because of that guilt she had driven him away from her. When they should have been facing it together, they had pulled apart. That, too, was her fault.

He had saved her life, literally. In spite of the fact that she'd treated him so badly, been so horrible to him. Some impulse had driven him to come home that afternoon, to try to make up the argument they'd had that morning, to put things right between them. And he'd saved her life. He had been there when she needed him the most.

'But why?' she'd asked him later. 'Why did you come home just then?' It was a miracle, it was too good to be true.

'I'm not sure,' he'd admitted. 'It was just, suddenly, that I felt it had gone on long enough. All of this silliness. I needed to talk to you, to make you understand that at the end of the day it didn't *matter* about the baby. That it was our marriage that was the important thing. *Is* the important thing. I married you because I love you, not because I saw you as some sort of baby-factory. I wanted to tell you that, to try to make you understand.'

And in the depths of the night, snuggled together in bed, Chris had made the most astonishing confession: he had been jealous of Dominic Verey. Dominic was always there in the afternoons; that, Chris said, was why he didn't usually bother coming home between school and choir practice. He felt like an intruder in his own home, breaking into the cosy twosome.

'But that's daft,' Sophie protested, caught between indignation and laughter at the absurdity of it. 'There's been nothing for you to be jealous of. I've been so lonely here, and Dominic has been a good friend.'

Chris acknowledged, then, his sense of guilt for her loneliness. He had taken her away from London because it was what *he* wanted, and he had compounded that by immersing himself in a world in which she had no interest and no part to play, the male-dominated universe of the Westmead Cathedral Choir. He had sensed her isolation, but, not knowing how to deal with it or his own feeling of guilt that he was the cause of it, he had ignored it, thus compounding the problem.

Things would change, he promised her.

'I'm glad,' he said, 'that you've had Dominic to keep you sane.'

They spoke quietly, aware that they were not alone in the house: Dominic was now, in fact, sleeping upstairs, in the spare room. It had seemed the logical thing for him to come to them after his mother had been taken away; they had agreed on that.

As for Dominic's future, it was too early to say. His brother Worthington would have something to say about that. He might well want Dominic to come to Tidmouth and live with him, but now did not seem like the time to take him away from his school, in his first term in the Upper Sixth. 'He can stay here as long as he likes,' Chris had said in the night, smiling at her in the dark. 'I won't be needing the spare room any longer.'

But Sophie had another idea about the future of the spare room. It had come to her in the early hours of the morning, invading her sleep, and now she couldn't wait for Chris to wake up so she could tell him.

'Chris?' she whispered, turning over to face him.

'Mmm?'

He always, she thought fondly, looked like such a young boy when he slept, his dark hair tousled and his face so smooth and peaceful. 'Chris,' she said, 'I've been thinking. About Tori's baby.'

His eyes flew open. 'What?'

'You were right,' she murmured. 'What you said. Adopting Tori's baby would be the perfect solution. Perfect for her, perfect for us. There might be some problems, but I think we could all handle it.'

Chris didn't need to say a word; his sleepy grin said it all.

Jacquie hadn't slept well. She wasn't, to be honest with herself, quite sure how she felt. She had been living for so many days with the knowledge of her sister's death, with Alison's restless ghost. With the need, formulated or unformulated, for justice to be done. Now she knew the facts about her sister's last moments on earth. That should have provided some sort of closure, allowed her to put it all behind her and get on with things.

But it didn't seem to her to be as simple as all that.

Where, she asked herself, in all this, *was* the justice? An unbalanced woman had snuffed out Ally's young life, and the life of her baby, and had managed to get away with it for eleven years. Now she had been caught.

But Ally was still dead. Nothing would bring her back to life, and restore her to what she should have been by now: a happy young mother. No magic could erase what had happened.

And Jacquie would still have to live with that, every day of her own life.

How was she going to manage it?

She was musing on that when there was a tap at her door. 'Tea?' said Miranda.

'Yes, please.'

Miranda pushed the door open and deposited the steaming mug on the bedside table. 'And you've had a phone call.'

Tim, thought Jacquie, smiling to herself.

'I told her that you were still in bed, that you'd ring her later.'

Her. Trying to hide her disappointment, she asked, 'Who was it, then?'

'Nicola Jeffries, ringing from Sutton Fen. We had a lovely chat – I haven't talked to her for ages.'

'Did she say what she wanted?'

Miranda shook her head. 'But she said it was important – that she needed to speak to you this morning.' She excused herself to make Peter's breakfast, and left Jacquie alone with her tea and her thoughts.

Why, after all, Jacquie asked herself, *should* Tim ring her? The case was over, the murder solved. There was no further need for contact between them.

Except that she hoped there would be, she admitted. Maybe, now that there was no longer an official connection, things might be different.

She sat up in bed and sipped her tea, allowing herself to imagine it. If she were to stay in Westmead for a few more days, as Miranda and Peter had urged her to do, if she were to see him again, perhaps they could put their unfortunate history firmly into the past and make a new start. They'd got on so well that evening with the Swans; maybe Miranda could be persuaded to invite Tim and Frannie back again.

Frannie. Jacquie couldn't help smiling at the thought of her: strong-willed, irrepressible, and utterly engaging. If she'd been blessed with the child she'd so desperately longed for, she would have wanted one like Frannie.

Tim was not feeling nearly so benignly towards Frannie. She dawdled over her breakfast, then announced that she was going to have a shower and wash her hair.

'I think that we should do something fun today,' she stated. 'Maybe we could go to the cinema.'

He wasn't going to be able to put it off much longer, but the shower offered a brief reprieve. 'Let's talk about it after your shower,' he suggested, hating himself for his cowardice.

It was during the prolonged shower that Liz arrived.

She was dressed casually but carefully, and she smiled her approval at Tim's off-duty wardrobe. 'Just right,' she said about his jeans and polo neck. 'What is Frannie wearing?'

'Frannie's still in the shower,' he confessed. 'So I'm afraid it will be a while before we're ready to go.'

Liz's smile didn't falter. 'Oh, that's all right,' she said brightly.

'Would you like coffee while we wait?' Tim offered, feeling awkward in the face of her unrelenting chirpiness.

'Yes, please.'

She followed him into the kitchen while he made the coffee, then they went into the sitting room to drink it. Liz sat on the sofa, leaving plenty of room for Tim to sit next to her, but he went, instead, to one of the chairs and perched uneasily on it, facing her.

'I like your flat,' Liz said, looking round.

'You haven't seen it before, then.'

'No.' Her gaze took on a more speculative quality. 'You could do quite a lot with this place, Tim. A bit of paint, some MDF, a few interesting lighting effects.'

He remembered, with a private shudder, her aspirations as a decorator, and vowed to himself that she would not get her hands on his flat, in that or any other capacity. 'I like it the way it is,' he said firmly.

'Oh, but you *would* say that.' Liz gave a coy laugh. 'You're a *man*.'

'You've noticed.' His voice was wry rather than flirtatious.

Liz lowered her head, tilted it slightly to one side, and looked at him through her lashes. 'Oh, I've noticed.'

It was such a deliberate pose that Tim wondered, dispassionately, whether someone had once told her that she looked like Princess Diana when she did that. He was not moved.

He also didn't quite know what to say after that gambit, so it was almost a relief when a dressing-gown-clad Frannie burst into the room, her face glowing after her shower, her hair wrapped in a towel. 'All the hot water's used up,' she announced, then she spotted Liz.

'Hello, Frannie,' Liz chirped.

Frannie didn't answer her, but turned instead to her father. 'What is *she* doing here?' she demanded.

Tim frowned. 'Frannie, don't be rude. Say hello to Liz.'

'Hello, Miss Hollis,' she said deliberately, still not looking at her.

'Didn't your father tell you? We're having a day out.'

Frannie's eyes narrowed in her father's direction. 'He didn't mention it.'

'I wanted it to be a surprise,' Tim explained feebly and unconvincingly.

'Well,' stated Frannie, 'I hope you enjoy it. I'm not going.' Her head held high, she walked in a stately manner to the bedroom and shut the door behind her.

'I'll talk to her.' Embarrassed and furious, Tim followed Frannie.

Fortunately for him, there was no lock on the door; if there had been, he was sure, it would have been locked in his face.

Frannie was sitting on the bed, her arms crossed across her chest. 'I'm not going,' she repeated.

'Frannie . . .'

'You can't make me.'

She was right, of course: he couldn't make her. But he was all the more determined to bend her to his will, especially since he didn't want to go himself. 'I'm asking you,' he said, in what he thought was a reasonable voice.

She gave him a baleful stare. 'You didn't tell me. You knew about it, and you didn't tell me.'

'I knew you wouldn't like it.'

'And you were right.' She set her jaw in a way that Tim recognised with dread. 'I'm not going.'

If reason didn't work, he thought, exasperated, perhaps threats would. 'I'll cut off your pocket money, then. For the next six months.'

'I don't care. Mum will make it up. Or I might even ask Brad,' she stated, with calculated malice.

Tim winced.

Frannie smiled.

He decided to have a go at severity. 'I'm not leaving this room until you promise to do as I ask, and behave yourself like a civilised human being, young lady.'

'And *I'm* not leaving this room until you go out there and tell that awful person to leave.' Frannie flopped back on to the bed. 'So I suppose we're going to be in here for a while.'

Jacquie hung up the phone, bemused. Nicola wanted her to come back to Sutton Fen, straight away. Today.

An emergency, Nicola had explained. Her husband Keith's boss was in town. He was going to take them out that night for a slap-up meal at a very posh country pub; he had already booked a table for four. And he had specifically asked that they provide him with a date to make up the foursome.

Keith's boss, Nicola said persuasively, was a widower. Very rich, extremely good-looking. And lonely. A great catch, in fact. 'I'd grab him myself, if I didn't have Keith,' Nicola laughed. 'It's your big chance, Jacquie.'

'Oh, I don't think so,' she demurred.

But Nicola was not prepared to take no for an answer. She was desperate, she confessed, and Jacquie would be a fool to pass up this opportunity.

Eventually she had caved in, reluctantly and with misgivings. But she'd felt unable to say no when Nicola was so adamant.

Before she went, though, she decided suddenly, she would ring Tim and tell him goodbye. She must give him a chance to talk her out of it, a voice at the back of her mind added; she wouldn't require very much persuasion if it came from that quarter, she admitted to herself.

He would probably be at home today, with Frannie, Jacquie reasoned. Early on in their acquaintance he'd given her his card, with his home number on it. She found it and rang the number.

'Hello?' said a female voice on the other end. A female, but not Frannie.

Startled and taken aback, Jacquie apologised, 'Oh . . . perhaps I have the wrong number. I was trying to reach Sergeant Tim Merriday.'

'I'm afraid he can't come to the phone just now,' said the female voice cosily. 'Can I give him a message?'

Jacquie recognised the voice now – it belonged to Liz, that superior-acting young woman at the police station. She hesitated. 'Well . . . perhaps you might tell him that Jacquie rang.'

'Jacquie. He'll know who you are, then? He has your number?'

'Yes.' Jacquie swallowed, then made her mind up swiftly.

'But tell him he doesn't have to ring me. I just wanted to say goodbye. If you could pass that on . . .'

'Yes. No problem. I'll tell him.'

Jacquie put the phone down, her eyes stinging with tears.

How stupid she'd been, she told herself bitterly. How blind.

It all made sense now. Tim . . . and that girl Liz. It explained so much: the girl's proprietary attitude at the police station, Tim's rejection of her own advances, Frannie's hatred of Liz. Frannie had hinted at it; why hadn't she realised? He was involved with that girl. She was at his flat on Saturday morning; did that mean that she'd been there all night?

And she, Jacquie, had allowed herself to believe, just for a while, that he might be interested in *her*. That was ridiculous, she saw now. He'd been kind, because that was his nature, and he'd appreciated the way she got on with Frannie, but that was all there ever was to it.

He might have told her, another part of her brain argued: he should have said that he and Liz were an item.

But why should he? She had no right to assume that he was available, just because he was nice to her and she fancied him.

Yes, Jacquie admitted to herself at last, now that it was too late and all hope was gone: she fancied him. Perhaps even more than that.

Maybe Keith's boss was everything that Nicola had promised. Maybe he had bluer eyes than Tim Merriday's, and a sweeter smile. Jacquie doubted it, but she told herself that she would soon find out.

* * *

Where anger, reason, threats and severity had failed, bribery won out in the end. Tim promised Frannie that in the Christmas holidays he would take her to London to the panto of her choice, and that he would buy her anything she wanted – within reason – for a Christmas present. In return, she agreed to go out for the day with Liz. She couldn't promise to enjoy herself, she pointed out, but she would try not to complain, nor be rude.

Tim had to settle for that; it was better than nothing.

He and Liz waited for Frannie to dry her hair and get dressed. 'I'm sorry about Frannie,' he apologised, chagrined by her behaviour. 'But she'll be fine. You'll see.'

'Oh, Frannie and I are going to get on famously,' Liz predicted sweetly. 'She just needs to get used to me.'

A few minutes later Frannie emerged from the bedroom. 'I'm ready,' she announced in a sepulchral tone. 'Where are we going, then?'

'It's a surprise.'

'Do we need to take anything?' Tim asked, getting his coat.

Liz smiled and jingled her car keys. 'Nothing. Everything is under control.'

'Let me switch on the answerphone,' Tim said.

'Oh, that reminds me. While you were . . . in the other room,' Liz recalled, 'you had a phone call. From someone called Jacquie.'

'Jacquie!' Frannie shed her air of ennui and looked suddenly like a different girl, alert and interested. 'What did she say?'

Liz addressed Tim. 'She said that you didn't need to ring her back, but she just wanted to say goodbye.'

'Goodbye?' he echoed, dismayed.

'Goodbye?' Frannie demanded. 'But how can she say goodbye? She's not even here!'

'She is,' Tim told her. 'She came back to Westmead a day or two ago.'

'Jacquie is here and you didn't tell me?' Frannie accused him with shocked incredulity. 'Dad! I can't believe you didn't tell me!'

Liz looked from one to the other of them impatiently. 'Well, it doesn't matter now,' she pointed out. 'She's gone.'

'How long ago did she ring?' Tim asked, looking at the clock.

'Half an hour, I suppose. Maybe a bit longer.'

'Dad,' said Frannie, tugging on his arm urgently. 'I need to talk to you. In private.'

With a brief apology to Liz, Tim followed Frannie meekly into the bedroom.

She came straight to the point. 'We've got to stop her, Dad.'

'But she's gone. If she cared about us . . .'

Frannie put her hands on her hips, just as Gilly used to do when she was telling him off. 'Dad,' she said severely, 'sometimes you're awfully thick. Jacquie is mad about you, and you're mad about her. *I* can see it, if *you* can't. And it's *not* too late. We can catch her before she leaves.'

He wanted to believe it; he didn't waste any time in arguing. Now it was up to him to break it to Liz.

'Liz wasn't very happy, Dad.' Frannie couldn't keep the satisfaction out of her voice as they negotiated the congestion of Saturday-morning traffic towards Quire Close. 'Longleat! As if I'd never been there before. As if I was interested in seeing those mangy old lions again.'

'No, I don't think she was too happy.' Tim discovered that he didn't care; all he cared about at this moment was making it to the Precentor's House before Jacquie left. Surely, he told himself, he wouldn't be unlucky for a third time. The third time was supposed to be the charm. This time he wouldn't be too late to stop her going.

But the traffic was dire, crawling through the shopping precinct and round the cathedral. And in Quire Close, a whole coachload of tourists blocked the middle of the road. Tim leaned on the horn, scattering startled gawpers to either side, and drove down to the end.

He pulled the car up before the Precentor's House and had barely killed the engine before Frannie was unbuckling her seat-belt and running to bang the door knocker. He was right behind her.

Miranda came to the door, her eyes going from Frannie's face to Tim's. She shook her head. 'I'm really sorry,' she said. 'So sorry. You've missed her. I couldn't talk her out of going. She was determined to leave.'

'Sutton Fen?' Tim asked.

Miranda nodded.

'That's it, then.' Defeated, he returned to the car.

Frannie slid in the other side and rebuckled her seat-belt. 'You can't give up now, Dad,' she said in her most determined voice.

'You heard what Mrs Swan said, Frannie. Jacquie's gone.'

'But you know where she's gone, Dad. You have her address, don't you?'

He turned and looked at his daughter's purposeful face. 'Yes,' he said slowly, pulling out his wallet and extracting the scrap of paper on which Jacquie had written her address and phone number for him.

'Then what are we waiting for?'

Tim hesitated for just an instant, then nodded. 'Right,' he said, making his mind up. 'Let's go.'

Hours later, with barely a stop along the way, and with Frannie proving to be an unexpectedly competent navigator, they arrived in Sutton Fen. Tim pulled the car into the first filling station he saw and asked the attendant for directions to the address on the scrap of paper.

It was dark by now, but the directions were concise and they found it without too much trouble. A nondescript house on a nondescript street, with nothing to recommend it – except that Jacquie lived there. Tim parked the car at the kerb, then turned and looked at his daughter. 'I suppose this is it.'

'You go, Dad,' said Frannie.

'Don't you want to come?'

She shook her head. 'I'll wait here for now. Take your time,' she added. 'I'll be okay.'

'If you're sure.'

'Just go, Dad. And don't blow it.'

Jacquie had just made herself a cup of tea when the doorbell rang. Darren, she thought wearily, wondering what mischief he was up to this time. She wasn't in the mood for it; she would tell him to go away and find someone else's life to make miserable.

She opened the door and caught her breath in disbelief. 'Tim,' she said wonderingly. 'What on earth . . .?'

'Can I come in, then?'

Jacquie looked over his shoulder and saw that he had

not come on his own; Frannie grinned and waggled her fingers at her. 'What about Frannie?'

'Frannie's all right there for a bit. She told me to take my time.' Tim smiled. 'It seems I have a rather wise daughter. She knows that we have some unfinished business to talk about. And she knows that she'd be in the way.' He held out his hand to her.

Without another word, Jacquie took his hand and led him into the house.

STRANGE CHILDREN

Kate Charles

Friendless, and virtually an orphan, Tessa craves a
husband, a home and a baby, but above all she wants to be
loved. Attending the wedding of her on-and-off lover Ian,
Tessa finds that the bride thinks it amusing to sit her next
to her own ex-amour, Rob Nicholls. But in a manner
which takes them both by surprise, they embark on a
heady, wholly satisfying romance.

Despite her new found material and emotional security,
Rob's reluctance to allow Tessa to meet his mother
becomes increasingly vexing. Puzzled and hurt by his
attitude Tessa vows to discover the cause of the coolness
between mother and son.

Then Linda Nicholls is murdered . . .

'A bloodstained version of the world of Barbara Pym'
The Guardian

UNRULY PASSIONS

Kate Charles

Margaret Phillips, Archdeacon of Saxwell, is in the prime
of her life. She effortlessly combines her clerical duties in
the church with a rock-solid marriage to the charming
and devoted Hal.

Gervase Finch moves with his fiercely protective wife into
the parsonage in the nearby village of Branlingham, before
assuming the post as vicar. Although they love their
spouses, Rosemary Finch and Hal Phillips are drawn
together, both disturbed by ideals of womanhood:
Rosemary competing with the ghost of Gervase's first wife,
Hal married to a paragon.

Valerie Marler, a bestselling novelist, has also identified
Hal as the object of her unruly passion, and strives to
rewrite her past failures by pursuing her fictional ideal. But
when Hal refuses to play his part in her love story, her
revenge threatens to descend into tragedy.

'Thoroughly entertaining'
The Times

Other best selling Time Warner titles available by mail:

☐ Unruly Passions	Kate Charles	£5.99
☐ Strange Children	Kate Charles	£6.99
☐ Postmortem	Patricia Cornwell	£6.99
☐ Body of Evidence	Patricia Cornwell	£6.99
☐ The Body Farm	Patricia Cornwell	£6.99

The prices shown above are correct at time of going to press. However, the publishers reserve the right to increase prices on covers from those previously advertised, without further notice.

TIME WARNER PAPERBACKS
P.O. Box 121, Kettering, Northants NN14 4ZQ
Tel: 01832 737525, Fax: 01832 733075
Email: aspenhouse@PSBDial.co.uk

POST and PACKAGING:
Payments can be made as follows: cheque, postal order (payable to Time Warner Books) or by credit cards. Do not send cash or currency.

All U.K. Orders	**FREE OF CHARGE**
E.E.C. & Overseas	25% of order value

Name (Block Letters)_____

Address_____

_____

Post/zip code:_____

☐ Please keep me in touch with future Time Warner publications

☐ I enclose my remittance £_____

☐ I wish to pay by Visa/Access/Mastercard/Eurocard

Card Expiry Date

_____